Praise for Lexi Blake and M

"I can always trust Lexi Blake'_ ____
breathless...and in love. If you want sensual, exciting BDSM
wrapped in an awesome love story, then look for a Lexi Blake
book."

~Cherise Sinclair USA Today Bestselling author

"Lexi Blake's MASTERS AND MERCENARIES series is
beautifully written and deliciously hot. She's got a real way with
both action and sex. I also love the way Blake writes her gorgeous
Dom heroes--they make me want to do bad, bad things. Her
heroines are intelligent and gutsy ladies whose taste for submission
definitely does not make them dish rags. Can't wait for the next
book!"

~Angela Knight, New York Times bestselling author

"A Dom is Forever is action packed, both in the bedroom and
out. Expect agents, spies, guns, killing and lots of kink as Liam
goes after the mysterious Mr. Black and finds his past and his
future... The action and espionage keep this story moving along
quickly while the sex and kink provides a totally different type of
interest. Everything is very well balanced and flows together
wonderfully."

~A Night Owl "Top Pick", Terri, Night Owl Erotica

"A Dom Is Forever is everything that is good in erotic
romance. The story was fast-paced and suspenseful, the characters
were flawed but made me root for them every step of the way, and
the hotness factor was off the charts mostly due to a bad boy Dom
with a penchant for dirty talk."

~Rho, The Romance Reviews

"A good read that kept me on my toes, guessing until the big
reveal, and thinking survival skills should be a must for all men."

~Chris, Night Owl Reviews

You Only Love Twice

OTHER BOOKS BY LEXI BLAKE

EROTIC ROMANCE
Masters And Mercenaries
The Dom Who Loved Me
The Men With The Golden Cuffs
A Dom Is Forever
On Her Master's Secret Service
Sanctum: A Masters and Mercenaries Novella
Love and Let Die
Unconditional: A Masters and Mercenaries Novella
Dungeon Royale
Dungeon Games: A Masters and Mercenaries Novella
A View to a Thrill
Cherished: A Masters and Mercenaries Novella
You Only Love Twice
Adored: A Masters and Mercenaries Novella, Coming May 12, 2015
Master No, Coming August 4, 2015

Masters Of Ménage (by Shayla Black and Lexi Blake)
Their Virgin Captive
Their Virgin's Secret
Their Virgin Concubine
Their Virgin Princess
Their Virgin Hostage
Their Virgin Secretary
Their Virgin Mistress, Coming April 14, 2015

The Perfect Gentlemen (by Shayla Black and Lexi Blake)
Scandal Never Sleeps, Coming July 7, 2015

URBAN FANTASY
Thieves
Steal the Light
Steal the Day
Steal the Moon
Steal the Sun
Steal the Night
Ripper
Addict, Coming Soon!

You Only Love Twice

Masters and Mercenaries

Book 8

Lexi Blake

You Only Love Twice
Masters and Mercenaries, Book 8
Lexi Blake

Published by DLZ Entertainment LLC

Copyright 2015 DLZ Entertainment LLC
Edited by Chloe Vale
ISBN: 978-1-937608-37-8

McKay-Taggart logo design by Charity Hendry

Sign up for Lexi Blake's newsletter
and be entered to win a $25 gift certificate
to the bookseller of your choice.

Join us for news, fun, and exclusive content
including free short stories.

There's a new contest every month!

Go to www.LexiBlake.net to subscribe.

Acknowledgements

Thanks to my team of editors, beta and proofreaders, and designers. Chloe, Stormy, Riane, Rich, Liz, and Charity, I couldn't do it without you. Thanks to Top Griz who left the marines only to find himself surrounded by romance authors with a million questions. Thank you for the knowledge and patience. And thanks to his wife Kennedy Layne for sharing his wisdom with the rest of us.

Special thanks to my street team for always supporting me and helping me find the encouragement I need. Love you ladies!

This book is dedicated to anyone who has loved and lost and found the strength to love again.

PROLOGUE

Fairfax County, VA

Phoebe looked up at the house with no designs on actually living there. Yeah, she wasn't an idiot. This place was way too nice for a group home. It was a two story with big columns. Colonial. She'd read that in some book. She liked books. Books didn't lie to her for the most part. They didn't say one thing when the social worker was around and then smack her face the minute they were alone, so all in all she preferred books to the real world.

Also libraries were pretty fucking awesome because they didn't give a shit that you didn't have the money as long as you managed to turn the books back in on time. Phoebe always turned her books in on time.

A book from a library was the one thing she wouldn't steal.

Everything else was fair game and once she was inside, she would look around to see what her sticky fingers might be able to grab. After all, her eighteenth birthday was only three years away. A girl had to plan for that grand moment when she went from foster care to homelessness.

"Could you try to smile?" Alicia wasn't bad as social workers went. She was a lovely woman with caramel-colored skin who seemed to actually get that it sucked to be Phoebe.

"Could you try to not sell me to some weirdo pervert who'll make me do sex tapes and lick his big toes?" Yeah, just because Alicia wasn't so bad didn't mean Phoebe wouldn't give her shit.

Perfectly brown eyes rolled and Alicia frowned as she parked the very boring sedan she'd probably paid a whole two years worth of shitastic salary for. "I'm serious, Phoebe. Franklin Grant isn't the usual foster dad. He's very wealthy and very private, and over the years he's taken in exactly two kids and he adopted them both. You're the third he's shown an interest in."

"Why?" That information sent every spidey sense she had tingling because she knew damn well that too good to be true usually meant she got her ass kicked in some way.

Alicia's jaw firmed. "He has to talk to you about it. I'll be honest, I'm not sure exactly what he does for a living but I know he works for the government and he has a security level that means I can't even read his records. Usually this is a very long process, but if he decides to take you, you'll be adopted within the next six weeks and you'll have a family, Phoebe. He's promised to pay for your education and set up a trust fund for you if you agree to his terms."

Her gut dropped. What the hell were his terms? Who used a word like "terms" when it came to adopting a kid? Alicia talked like she had a choice, but Phoebe knew better. She hadn't had a single choice since the day her mom had overdosed on heroin and her dad had chosen to not take her in. Her father. He'd had a new family and the new wife didn't want Phoebe around her kids. It hadn't been a big shock. She hadn't seen her father in years but she'd still stood in his doorway praying he would let her in. She'd been seven years old and she'd seen her half siblings from the doorway before their mom had scooted them away like Phoebe was something dangerous.

It had been Alicia who held her hand and walked her away. Alicia had driven her to the first of a seemingly endless line of foster homes. She couldn't even remember some of their faces and others she would never forget. But Alicia had been the constant. She knew other kids got shuffled through social workers as fast as they did homes, but Alicia had always been there. She counted on Alicia.

Though she tried not to cry ever, the hated tears were suddenly in her eyes. "Are you selling me?"

She'd heard it could happen. Especially when no one in the world cared about what happened to a girl. Foster care kids ran all the time. No one gave a damn to find them.

Alicia turned to her, her jaw dropping open. "What? Phoebe, no. Honey, this man is interested in you because of your IQ scores. I have some suspicion he works for the NSA or the CIA. Do you understand? I think you're being recruited. If that scares you we can turn the car around and nothing and no one will make me bring you here again."

Phoebe looked out the window. It was a sunny day and the big colonial house stood out against the brilliant blue sky. In the distance, she could see a pasture with a couple of horses. The whole setting was peaceful and so foreign to a girl who'd grown up in some of DC's worst slums. What would it be like to wake up to green grass and trees?

She was scheduled to enter a group home in six weeks and after she aged out she would be on her own. There would be no education for her. There would be a fast food restaurant job if she was lucky enough to find a place to live. There would be years and years of trying to get by. There would likely come a time when she was desperate enough to try a little of what her mother had in order to get a moment's respite from how shitty life was. She would be in and out of prison until she finally took too much and found the place where all junkies went.

Wasn't anything worth trying if it meant a shot at getting out of this life?

"You said his name was Franklin?" Like the turtle. When she'd been younger, she'd read the Franklin books. Even when her mother had been alive, she'd hidden in books. She'd taught herself to read at the age of four, and one of the moms in the tenement they'd lived in had been a kindergarten teacher and lent Phoebe books. Franklin. Arthur. The Berenstain Bears. It was stupid, but the fact that this man's name was comforting helped to calm her.

"Yes. Franklin Grant. His family has been in Virginia for two hundred years, but he's the last of his line. I don't know why, but he never married." She looked at Phoebe. "Do you want to stay or go?"

Phoebe got out of the car and slammed the door behind her. Everything she owned in the world was in her satchel. Three T-shirts, four pairs of socks, a complete days of the week underwear set, though technically she was wearing Sunday on a Monday since she didn't get to do laundry very often, two pairs of threadbare jeans, a tube of lip balm she'd stolen from a pharmacy, and twelve dollars and fifty-two cents she kept in a plastic Hello Kitty wallet she'd gotten one year at Christmas. Everything else had been lost or stolen.

The door to the big house opened and two boys stepped out.

Alicia's door shut and she was suddenly beside Phoebe. "It's your call. If you want to leave, I'll take you back."

But she wouldn't take her in. She'd known that dream was done long ago. Alicia had three kids of her own. There was no room for Phoebe there. There seemed to be no place for her anywhere, but that house in front of her had a whole lot of rooms.

"I'll meet him. Who are they?" She was watching as the two young men walked toward her.

"That must be Grant's sons. He adopted them both. The word is they both tested incredibly high on their IQ tests and had some extra skills. I think one of them was a shooting champion. The other had a history as a hacker. I know everyone was surprised a boy with an arrest record managed to get adopted."

She'd avoided being arrested. Mostly. The one time she'd gotten caught, she helped the cops with a worse crime that had been committed in the same area. Detective Bates had happily expunged her record when she'd given him a serial rapist on a silver platter. Sometimes cops couldn't see patterns to save their lives. Phoebe saw them. She'd stood in his office and looked up at the wall of data he'd accumulated on the man and all the lines were there. He'd simply had them in the wrong places. She'd fixed it and now the man was serving seventy-five years and she had a friend to call when she got caught shoplifting.

Life was all about making use of the materials around. She'd learned that long ago, too.

"Hi." Both boys were dressed in slacks and button downs, but the one who greeted her had pitch-black hair and the prettiest eyes she'd ever seen. He was slightly taller than his brother, who she barely looked at because her eyes couldn't seem to move off him.

"Hi." Yeah, that sounded stupid and breathy and girlie.

"Are you Phoebe?" Dreamy Eyes asked.

She managed to nod. What the hell was wrong with her?

"Well, I'm James. It's nice to meet you. Dad's been talking about you a lot. Why don't you come up and meet him? He's in his office. If you decide to stay, I will warn you, he's made meatloaf for dinner. About once a week he gets it into his head that he can cook. He can't. It's awful, but we order pizza and then tomorrow Maria is back. Maria can actually cook."

James. Oh, James. He made her heart pound. He made her breath threaten to stop.

"I am here, too, you know." The second boy rolled his green eyes and chuckled.

She was being a bitch. She turned to the other boy. He was cute, too, but he didn't make her drool the way James did. "Hi." She thrust out her hand. *Dumbass.* Only adults did that. There was nothing to do but power through. "I'm Phoebe."

He gave her a grin and shook her hand. He really was cute, with golden brown hair and a ready smile. "I'm Tennessee, but you can call me Ten. Come on now. Stop making love eyes at Jamie here and let's get a move on."

"I'm not." She felt her whole body flush with embarrassment.

Ten shook his head. "God, I hope you are because he's staring at you, too."

James sent his brother a warning look. "Am not."

"Are too."

"I will end you, Ten," he said under his breath.

Ten laughed. "You'll try. Let's go, lovebirds. Don't keep Pops waiting. He's actually a really great man. I think you're going to like him."

Ten turned and started up the bricked walkway.

James was blushing as he looked back at her. "Don't pay him

any mind. He's kind of an asshole." James flushed further as he nodded to Alicia. "Sorry. He's my brother."

Alicia smiled. "So I've heard. I think I'll go in and say hello to Mr. Grant."

She started toward the door.

James suddenly seemed to find his feet endlessly interesting. "I could show you around if you like. Dad sent us out here to talk to you. I'm supposed to show you the house and then you can talk to him."

"Why?" She needed to know. "Why does he want to talk to me? I don't buy it. I've seen it all and this doesn't add up."

James's eyes met hers. "You're smart, Phoebe, and you could be something more. You could help your country. That's what we do. Dad finds kids who need homes and something to believe in and he gives us both. He took me in when I was eight and we found Ten when he was thirteen when he came to live with us. In a couple of years I'm going to college, but after that I'm joining my dad. You could be with us if you want to."

"In what?"

James's shoulders went back, his pride evident. "The Agency. I'm going to be a spy and you could be, too."

A spy. Yeah. That sounded cool.

Cooler than anything else she was going to do. When James turned and walked toward the house, she followed. It was all she could do to not take his hand.

* * * *

13 years later

"Hey, Phoebe." Ten walked into the room, his presence almost a nuisance.

God, she hated that, but she felt that way. She didn't want to see him, didn't want to see anyone. She wanted them all to go away so she could fade. She wanted to do nothing more than lie down and utterly fade away. Maybe if she didn't eat, didn't drink anything, she could see him again.

She didn't reply to Ten, simply stared at the wall.

"Everyone's leaving. I thought you might want to come out and say good-bye."

She hadn't wanted them to come over anyway, so she figured the hoard of visiting vultures could find their way out on their own. They had been Jamie's co-workers, people who knew their dad, but she hated them. She hated everyone.

"Don't do this to me."

She ignored him.

"Goddamn it, Phoebe. Don't you dare fucking do this to him."

Her eyes came open as if of their own accord. Ten had said "him" and her body responded. "I'm not doing anything."

The words came out on a growl. She was resentful. He shouldn't be here. He'd only been Jamie's brother. He hadn't been his wife, his lover. Ten hadn't been trying to have Jamie's baby.

"You're fucking giving up, Phoebe." She could practically feel Ten's will as he paced across the floor. Ten's cowboy boots thudded along the hand-scraped hardwoods as he continued to move. Ten always had trouble staying still. He paced when he was anxious. He'd been really anxious since that moment that they'd heard Jamie had been captured by jihadists. Ten had spent months trying to find him, months in the deserts of Iraq. And then more time trying to find his body because the fuckers had moved them, likely hoping their bodies would never be found, that the families would never be able to give them a proper burial.

The jihadists caught Jamie with an Army unit after their convoy had been hit by an IED. Jamie had been working on tracking a terrorist sect using a group of Army grunts as cover.

It hadn't been cover enough.

Her precious husband had been brutally killed along with every single one of his teammates.

All except for one. When Ten had finally found the place where Jamie had been held and murdered, there had only been one of the soldiers left. Jesse Murdoch. Why had he survived when her husband had been murdered?

Did it even matter since he was gone? It was so much easier to lie here. She didn't want to eat, didn't want to drink. She'd even stopped hurting. Her body was utterly numb.

She didn't move, didn't react because it didn't matter.

"Phoebe?"

She wanted him to go away. If she ignored him, maybe he would leave. It hadn't been real until she'd gotten Jamie's body back. For a year, she'd been able to pretend that he was simply on another job. The whole time they'd been married, they had both worked for the Agency. They often spent more time apart than together, so it was easy to fool herself. It had only been very recently that they had talked about getting out, settling down and starting a family. Even after they had the intelligence that stated he'd been captured, she'd been able to pretend that Jamie would be home as soon as the Agency could arrange it.

But the world was changing and the jihadists were more serious. It wasn't about ransom money now. It was about ideals, and they recruited more and more soldiers when they killed Westerners.

Ten had been the one to ID Jamie's body.

Why had Jesse Murdoch survived? Some people thought he sold the rest of them out. Had he sold Jamie out?

She hoped Jesse Murdoch died a rough death.

"Goddamn it, look at me. You are not this sad sack bitch who simply fades away because something bad happens."

That got her sitting up. "Something bad?"

Ten was a son of bitch who always played things down. Always. He'd done it since they were kids. He'd done it when their father had a heart attack and died. She wasn't about to let him do it now.

He leaned in. "Yeah. Do you think this is what Jamie would want for you? Do you think he would want you to lay here and die because you wouldn't get up and fucking fight?"

"Fight? Who do you want me to fight, Ten? Are you ready to send me to Iraq? Because I'm ready to go." It was everything she wanted. She could find the group that killed her husband and rain hellfire on all of them.

But it was harder than that. She was a woman. She'd worked in intelligence for years but she'd been in Asia and Europe. Her father had kept her out of the real war zones. She'd lived on and off for years in China, working on the political situation there and in Japan and Korea.

For the spy it had been a cushy assignment. Despite tensions with China, they always played the game. She'd been caught once and spent a few nights in a Shandong prison. Her interrogation had included a nasty bit of torture, but it hadn't been long before they'd traded her for a Chinese spy. She'd been back at work two weeks later. The Middle East was different. There were no rules to the spy game there, and she'd always known that Jamie was in danger.

Jamie had gone with Ten. Their father had sent the boys into danger time and time again even as they'd protected her. When Ten took over their father's job, Jamie had insisted on keeping his assignment despite the fact Ten had given him an out. She'd married Jamie five years before and every moment they'd had together had been precious. Every private day had been a blessing.

Now she knew that Jamie had the easier road. He didn't have to live knowing he wouldn't see her again. He didn't have to move forward knowing he wouldn't love again. God, he'd likely died thinking that he was leaving a son behind. The last time she'd talked to him she'd thought she was pregnant. By the time she realized her mistake, he'd been taken.

Stupid girl. She was still the same stupid girl who screwed up everything good in her life.

Ten got to one knee, his deep green eyes seeking out hers. Her young adulthood rushed back in and she couldn't help but remember all the days she and Jamie and Ten had spent together. Every good day of her life had been spent with them. Ten was her family.

"I can't possibly feel what you feel, sister." He put a hand on her knee. "I know you miss him. I do, too. God, I miss him. My whole damn life I've had you and Jamie. I can't lose you, too."

His words started to play at her conscience. Jamie had adored Ten. It had been the three of them for so long.

What would Ten do if they were both gone? He'd been alone for years—just like she had, and then he'd had a family. She still had a brother. She still had Ten.

"I don't want to go on." It felt good to admit it.

Ten lost his perpetual cool. His handsome face screwed up and tears flushed from those gorgeous eyes. "Please don't leave me. I can't be alone again, Phoebe. I love you. I know I'm not Jamie and

19

it's not the same, but I do love you. You're the only person I love in the whole damn world now that Jamie and Dad are gone."

It had been the three of them burying their adopted father when his fierce heart had betrayed them all. God, she missed Franklin Grant.

Did she owe it to them all to go on? Because it would be so much easier to take a few too many sleeping pills and float away. It was so easy to get them. Everyone wanted her to sleep and rest and not feel. Everyone except Ten.

Days she'd spent in this purgatory, but Ten was getting to her.

"What would I do?" She didn't know a life outside of the Agency.

"Work for me. I have a place for you to go. It's a long-term undercover op. It's cushy, sweetie, but it's so necessary. It could be years you spend there."

She didn't want to do it.

"Please, Phoebe. I don't trust anyone else to take on Taggart."

She couldn't help but sit up a little straighter at the very name. "Ian Taggart?"

He was a legend. He was a problem. He was a fine balance that she would have to walk. Intriguing. Even in her grief, she found the idea of playing the game with Taggart deeply intriguing.

"Yes. He's got connections that go around the world and while I like the man, I have to keep an eye on him. There's something else. There's a situation that's starting up in Florida."

She felt her jaw firm, her blood chilling. There was only one situation either of them cared about right now. "Murdoch?"

Ten nodded. "I've been tracking him and he's working with some FBI agent out of DC, though he recently took a job in St. Augustine at one of those fet clubs."

"You think he has something to do with Taggart?" Taggart was knee-deep in the BDSM lifestyle. She'd read all about it in his files. It didn't appeal to her at all. Jamie had been tender, so tender with her. He would never have hit her, never have tied her up so she couldn't fight back. Ten always said Taggart was a good man, but he liked to hit the women he had sex with so that made Phoebe doubt it. Some people in the Agency still believed that Taggart had murdered his wife.

20

It shouldn't surprise her Murdoch was into the same shit.

Ten ran a hand over his hair, a sure sign that he was frustrated. "It's a complex situation and I still don't understand the whole of it. You're better at patterns than I am."

"I can look at the file for you."

"It's still early, but someone is playing a game and I think I might have figured out who it is. I think Taggart's wife is still alive and somehow she's gotten tangled up with my investigation into Murdoch."

So maybe Taggart wasn't a killer. He also wasn't Agency. "You put too much faith in him. He left you a long time ago, Ten. He's on his own and he couldn't care less about you or the job we do."

She'd never been in a room with the man, but she'd always resented him because no matter what Ten said, she knew Taggart's leaving the Agency had hurt Ten. Ten had recruited the man, trained him and he'd walked away.

"You're wrong, Phoebe, but I'll let you form your own opinions of the man. I feel like shit not telling him about Charlotte, though. As far as I can tell, she's working on something to do with McKay and his ex-wife. It's a big old clusterfuck and Taggart won't see it coming. They're on a collision course."

"You can't tell Taggart a damn thing." He owed his loyalty to Jamie not Ian Taggart. For the first time in hours, she stood and felt her blood starting to thrum through her system. Jamie might still need her. "If this gets us close to Jesse Murdoch, then you keep Taggart in the dark. No one outside the Agency knows Jamie died in Iraq."

"I've kept his cover. As far as Tag knows, Jamie was just a friend of mine and he died in a Humvee accident while training rebels along the Pakistan/Afghanistan border. No one wants it to get out that some of our operatives are posing as soldiers."

Her mind started working again, a tiny bit of the fog of grief clearing out. "You work it from Murdoch's end and I'll keep an eye on Taggart and his group."

McKay-Taggart Security was rapidly becoming one of the country's premiere security providers. They were made up of ex-Special Forces and ex-FBI.

For the first time in days, Ten smiled. "I am so glad to hear you say that."

She had to make one thing clear. "You won't tell Taggart."

His smile died, but he nodded. "No. I'll keep quiet. He's my friend, but Jamie was my brother. We have to figure out if Murdoch turned on him."

"If he did, he's mine, Ten." She would seek retribution on the man who betrayed her husband. It didn't matter why he'd done it—whether out of greed or cowardice. Somehow Murdoch had been left untouched while everyone else died. It wasn't fair.

Sometimes life wasn't fair. Sometimes karma didn't work.

But Phoebe did.

She sat back down and Ten's hand found hers. They stayed that way for the longest time, until the light died and night fell.

When she stood back up, she knew it was time to go to work.

CHAPTER ONE

One Year Later
Dallas, TX

Jesse Murdoch sat back in his chair and thought about looking around for the cameras because sometimes the boys liked to play pranks on each other. Like the time Big Tag had filled Adam's office with balloons. It had seemed like such a lighthearted little trick until Adam had popped the first sucker and discovered they had all been painstakingly filled with lemon pudding. It had been retribution for Adam eating the last of Ian's beloved lemon-filled donuts, and it was a video they still played at office parties from time to time, along with the video of Eve finding the psychotic clown Halloween decoration in her closet and losing her shit and Grace trying to track down a mouse only to discover it was being radio controlled by her husband who—according to that tape—was never sleeping in their bed again.

So when Simon sat him down in the conference room and started his speech about Phoebe Graham being a spy, he'd looked for the candid camera.

He knew he had a reputation for not being the brightest bulb in the bunch, but damn, did they really think he was that stupid?

"Sure, Phoebe's a spy. I always knew it." Sometimes it was best to go along with these things. It helped him to fit in. Of course once the gig was up, he was going to find a way to get Si back. His brain was already working on how he could replace every single one of Simon's slick suits with unitards. Bright-pink ones.

Ian leaned forward. "Jesse, I need you to take this seriously."

Big Tag was good at never cracking up during a prank. "Absolutely."

Alex McKay sighed. "He's going to need proof. God knows I did."

"Yes, I need proof." He couldn't wait to see what they'd done. Phoebe would think it was a hoot.

And maybe it would make her laugh. Maybe if he could find a way to make her laugh, she might want to move past the "friends" stage they'd been stuck in forever. If he could find a way to get through the veil of sorrow he so often felt from her, maybe she would see how much he cared, how much he wanted to make her happy.

Simon took off his suit coat and hung it over his chair as he started to pace. They were really playing this for all it was worth. He looked every bit the concerned friend. "I didn't want to do this today, not with the baby shower and all."

Alex held up a hand. "It's fine, Simon. Chelsea thinks something's going down today and we're going to trust your wife. Besides, other than Chelsea, we're trying to keep the women out of this. If we can handle it quietly, it's all for the better. The baby shower is keeping them occupied. Phoebe, too."

"Adam and Jake are keeping an eye on her. They've been tailing her for days," Ian said, his voice grim. He turned to Jesse. "I hate to do this to you, and you have to know if I thought I could get rid of her without you knowing about it, I would do it. I know what it feels like, man."

Jesse sat up because not even for a prank would Ian Taggart talk about his feelings. "You're joking, right?"

His gut was suddenly in a knot.

"I wish I was," Big Tag replied. "I have to apologize because I'm the one who approved her hire."

"Could we save the recriminations until after Jesse knows the truth?" Simon asked.

It was stupid. This whole thing was some sort of misunderstanding because there was zero chance that Phoebe Graham was anything but a sweet, sexy, caring woman with an unfortunate addiction to Harry Potter.

Except the one time he'd offered to take her to Harry Potter World, she'd cried and hadn't talked to him for a day. He'd thought it would be a way to please her, but she'd shut him out and wouldn't tell him why.

He'd actually started to wonder if she went out with him because she was a woman who struggled to say no. She wasn't ever going to return his affection, but she certainly wasn't some spy.

"It was the way she moved," Simon said. "I never paid much attention to her. I think she was too relaxed that night when we had to flee from The Collective."

It had been months before. Simon had called and given him the code words that basically told Jesse to get his ass in gear because shit was going down. He'd been on a date with Phoebe. Well, he called them dates. Once, he'd heard her tell Charlotte Taggart that they weren't dating. It felt like dating to him. He'd bundled her up and picked up Simon and Chelsea in time to avoid what would have been Simon's arrest on trumped up murder charges. He'd dropped Phoebe off at her place and then they'd been on the run.

"What are you talking about? How does she move? Half the time I'm trying to make sure she doesn't break her leg or something." She was charmingly klutzy. He hated to admit it, but he kind of liked it when she stumbled because he always managed to catch her. She was smarter than him, but he could protect her. It was probably the only thing in the world he had to give her.

He'd been a grunt during his service days, and even here at McKay-Taggart he knew his real value was the fact that he was willing to step in front of a bullet for his brothers or their wives. He didn't mind being the one to protect Phoebe.

"It's all an act. Jake took some video of her when she didn't think anyone was watching. She's well trained. I would suspect she's taken more than one form of martial arts. Did you know she takes a Krav Maga class on Saturdays?" Simon asked.

"So she wants to be able to defend herself." He thought that was a good idea.

"Jake couldn't roll tape there, but he caught a glimpse and said she could practically teach the class herself," Simon replied.

"In long-term cover these are the things that ruin an operative," Ian mused. "She's trying to hold on to one thing that makes her who she was before she took the assignment. She's trying desperately to stay strong while she looks weak. She should never have taken that class. She only signed up for it three months ago. I would be very interested to know what pushed her to do it. It's reckless for a woman who's made all the right moves so far."

"Or she's a woman who wants to defend herself. That's not a crime. It's smart." They were being paranoid.

"Chelsea hasn't been able to break her cover yet. Adam gave it a shot, too. Do you know what kind of backing it takes to imbed a false identity so well those two can't break it?" Simon asked.

"So we have to assume she's an operative either for a foreign entity or something more nefarious," McKay added. "Did you run her past Damon?"

Tag nodded. "None of his MI6 contacts were willing to say they know her, but that doesn't mean shit. None of Damon's new guys could ID her. I think we have to look at worst-case scenarios here."

"Since when do you not go there?" McKay asked with a shake of his head. "You always go to the worst-case scenario first. So she's either a foreign operative or a Collective plant."

They were leaving out a scenario. "Or you're wrong about her."

McKay looked at him with sympathy. Fuck, but he hated being pitied. "We're not wrong."

He was starting to get a little mad. It was obvious to him that they'd been investigating his girl behind his back. She might not have slept with him, but he still cared about her, protected her. She would never wear his collar, but he had some claim on her. They should have told him the minute they had suspicions, but no, he was poor Jesse who got himself fucked up in the war. They were never going to take him seriously.

Well, buddy, why would they? You're the one who goes crazy from time to time and kills a bad guy with your bare teeth. Chelsea is likely still having nightmares about that. Do you really think they trust you?

Phoebe was the only one who took him seriously. She was always asking about his job and what his thought processes were. Hell, he would bet she was the only one in the world who actually imagined he *had* a thought process.

"Jesse, I get it, man. You care about her." Tag was staring at him. "She's got you by the balls, but I need you to think clearly and I need you to hear Simon out. He didn't do this because he wanted to hurt you. He did this because you're his partner. We're doing this because we're your brothers, and you know how I feel about that."

"Fine." They were putting him in a corner. He wasn't ready to walk away. He needed this job. Shit. He needed them. McKay-Taggart was the first family he'd ever really had. His father had died before he'd been born and his mother had dumped him on his granddad's porch not long after. His grandfather had been a mean son of a bitch who cared way more for his cattle than his only grandson. He'd fit into his Army unit, but they were all gone now. He wasn't ready to lose this. "What makes you think she isn't exactly who she says she is?"

"How did they know, Jesse? How did The Collective and Ten know where we were that night?" Simon asked.

He could come up with a couple of scenarios. "They could track us on traffic cams."

"Possibly, but we were careful to get into a neighborhood that was unlikely to have cameras," Simon reminded him. "Now it is possible that one of the groups after us that particular night searched until they found us the next morning, but then I need an explanation on why your vehicle was tagged."

"What?" He'd gotten his Jeep back about a week after they'd returned from Italy. "My Jeep didn't have a tag on it. If it does now, it was probably put there after the motel fight."

They'd been forced to leave it in the motel parking lot. It would have been easy for someone to place a tracking device on it then.

"You also have bugs all over your apartment." Simon's voice

was tight. "How many people have you let in? Alex installed your security system himself. Chelsea and I spend a bit of time there. Who else?"

He couldn't quite meet Simon's eyes because there was only one answer to that question. Jesse didn't have parties. He didn't have friends outside of work. His whole life was spent at that sad little apartment or at work or on the occasional date with Phoebe that sometimes ended with them watching TV at his place.

He remembered the first night they'd gone back to his apartment. He'd been surprised because she didn't seem to want to be alone with him. He'd gotten a little excited, his cock hardening at the thought of getting her into bed. He'd planned the whole seduction out in his head as they'd driven to his building. Thankfully his years in the military had forced a routine cleanliness into his life so he hadn't had to worry about his place being a mess. Not that there was much to mess up. He had a TV and a sofa and Grace and Avery had taken him out to buy him all the things he needed for a rudimentary kitchen. Serena had given him a couple of sets of sheets. She'd been excited about the thread count or something, but he could have told her that anything felt like paradise after sleeping in a rat-infested hellhole for months.

He'd been happy about that damn thread count though when he'd thought Phoebe would be sleeping on it. But the minute they'd gotten to his place, she'd pulled out the Harry Potter DVDs.

I want to share this with you. Please, Jesse.

Yep, he'd fallen asleep halfway through the first one.

It would have been so easy for her to slip off the couch and plant her bugs. Easy for her to have gone through his pathetic things so she could get a better perspective on how to handle him.

Had she been listening to him for months? Did she hear the way he cried at night when the nightmares got to be too much? Did she hear the way he paced the floor and told himself over and over again that it was all a dream and he was here and he was Jesse Murdoch. He was Jesse. He wasn't the man they tried to turn him into.

"I told you we should have brought Kai into this," Alex whispered furiously Tag's way.

"Kai isn't a member of this team," Tag pointed out. "And he's also out of town. He's in DC for the week."

Kai Ferguson was his therapist. He was a psychiatrist specializing in extreme PTSD. Ian had said he'd brought Kai in to help with Sanctum because Eve didn't have time to go through all the applicants and keep up evaluations on members, but Jesse knew the truth. Tag had basically bought Kai in an attempt to see if he could fix Jesse.

"I don't need Kai." He spent hours and hours with Kai and he didn't seem any closer to being normal. He still had the dreams and he still felt the beast deep in his gut always, always waiting to come up.

He still heard that voice. Dark and rich. Foreign.

You are my creature. You belong to me and you do my bidding. You're my dog.

He slapped at the side of his head, trying to get that voice out.

"Damn it." Tag was on his feet. "Get Eve in here."

"Don't. He's fine." Simon sat down in the chair beside him. "You're hearing it again, but you're not there, Jesse. It's all right. I was thinking about seeing that new comic book movie this weekend. What was it? I think the lead is called Thorp or something."

"He's Thor." Jesse breathed a sigh of relief as the voice faded and he was solidly back in the now where Simon often purposefully screwed up the names of comic book characters so Jesse would correct him. Shortly after they'd been paired up, his very staid and British partner had professed a deep and utterly false love of all things comic book and they'd started going to the movies or to comic book stores. Simon looked so out of place, but it had gone a long way to build trust between them. Simon Weston had been the first person since Iraq to sacrifice for Jesse Murdoch.

"And it isn't a Thor movie this week. It's a new Avengers. Thor's just in it." Somehow talking about something normal always seemed to bring him back.

"Well, Chelsea's very excited," Simon allowed.

Chelsea was an out-and-out dweeb, and Jesse loved her like a sister. He turned to Simon. "Chelsea thinks Phoebe's bad?"

God, he sounded like a kid begging someone to tell him the world wasn't so evil.

29

"Chelsea thinks she's certainly not what she says she is," Simon explained. "But then she also made me promise to remind you that because something isn't what it seems, doesn't mean it's necessarily bad. Please tell her I followed instructions. She was very specific."

He couldn't believe it. It wasn't true. He took a deep breath. There came a time when a man had to choose. He chose her. He loved this group, but he was falling in love with her. Maybe Chelsea was trying to tell him something. Maybe she was trying to tell him that the time had come to trust his instincts and his instinct was to protect and love Phoebe Graham.

"She's not a spy."

Tag's head fell back and he groaned.

He was going to lose his job, but he had to do what was right. He knew how it felt to be falsely accused. He knew how it felt to have absolutely no one in the world who had his back. He'd gone back to his hometown and they'd turned on him.

He wasn't going to leave her alone.

His phone buzzed. Text. He thought about ignoring it since almost everyone who would text him was in this room, but as his friends started arguing, he decided it was a good way to not have to listen for a moment.

He didn't recognize the number.

If you want to know the truth, meet me in the walkway between Elm and Main Street. 10 minutes. If you aren't there, I won't bother you again.

The truth? The truth about what? He didn't have time to deal with any mystery text. He needed to deal with Phoebe.

The door to the conference room slammed open and Liam O'Donnell strode through followed by his new partner. Erin Argent was the newbie at McKay-Taggart, but Jesse was pretty sure she already fit in better than he did. Tag sent her out into the field without a qualm. She'd already run an op on her own, taking down a ring of corporate spies with the ease of a woman who had spent half her life in the military, and not at the grunt level Jesse had been at.

"She's on the move," Liam said, his voice tight. He was carrying a shoulder holster complete with a SIG Sauer that he handed over to Tag.

"She walked out of here about three minutes ago," Erin explained. There was no way to miss the anticipation in the woman's voice. Erin was a full-on adrenaline junkie. The minute an op was over, she requested another one. While the rest of McKay-Taggart seemed to be settling down and having babies and buying houses, Erin spent her off time base jumping.

He didn't like the thought of someone as competent as Erin going after Phoebe. Phoebe was an accountant. She had no idea how to handle seasoned operatives.

Jesse stood up. Something was going on. If his apartment was bugged, then someone was watching him, but he couldn't accept that it was Phoebe. Maybe it had something to do with that text. He knew he should say something about it, but the situation with Phoebe took precedence. "Fine, I'll follow her myself. This is stupid. She's probably going out to pick up something for the party."

"I don't think so," Li said. "She told Grace they had everything ready and then she slipped out."

"She was actively trying to not be seen." Erin grinned a little. She had a wealth of fiery red hair she kept in a neat ponytail and freckles across the bridge of her nose that proved all that red was natural.

He wasn't sure Erin didn't have an overactive imagination. She seemed to fit right in with Tag and O'Donnell. She went to the worst possible case scenario just like Tag and she could down beer like O'Donnell, though he'd slowed down since having a son.

"I'm going to follow her." Jesse was sick of this shit. He was sick of feeling like the only person left out of the joke.

"Adam and Jake are tailing her." Ian looked down at his phone. "They've got her. She walked into that fast food place up the street two minutes ago."

"See. She's guilty of being hungry and not wanting a salad." They were all paranoid.

Tag pocketed his phone and nodded to Li and Erin. "Li, would you please set up a nice place where we can spend some time talking to our accountant?"

"You're setting up a fucking interrogation room?" It wouldn't be comfortable. It would be a room where Tag would hold her until he got the answers he wanted. Tag would scare the shit out of her. Phoebe already got nervous around the man. This would send her over the edge.

Tag turned his way, and this wasn't his friend. This was his boss, his CO. "You will stand down, Murdoch, or I swear I will have you in lock-down until this is over. If you can't handle this, tell me now and I'll make sure you don't move an inch out of this room until this is all over."

He couldn't let that happen. "I'm cool."

"I seriously doubt that," Tag said. "You can observe, but nothing more. This is not your op. Simon, you keep a leash on him. He watches from a distance. Is that understood?"

"Yes, boss." Simon put his suit coat back on. "We need to hurry if we're going to catch her. Tell Adam to keep close watch. I used to use public loos to change clothes and lose a tail."

Tag slipped the shoulder holster over his massive form and checked the clip on the SIG before holstering the gun. "Alex, you don't have to go. Eve will likely kick your ass if you miss the shower, so please feel free to coo over baby gifts while the rest of us take care of business."

McKay sent his best friend a happy middle finger. "Fuck you, Ian. I'm not staying here and might I say, I can't fucking wait for Charlotte to have that baby so you can join the rest of us." He turned to Erin. "Let me borrow your piece."

"I swear I will beat the shit out of you if you hurt her, McKay." Erin seemed unnaturally affectionate toward her Berretta M9 which she'd named Bertha. Jesse really thought it looked more like an Agnes. She handed the gun over, handle first. "I don't see why I'm stuck here. She knows me the least. It would be very simple for me to take her out. I promise I won't even feel bad about it. All that weak shit gets to me. I believe in Darwin, so I could shoot her very easily."

And he was so done with her. "You shoot her and we'll have a fucking problem, Erin."

"Is that right, Murdoch?" She got right in his face. "You think you can take me?"

He felt his blood pressure rise, his hands turn to fists. He didn't fight with women, but then Erin liked to play with the boys. If she threatened Phoebe, she would find out that he could put her on her ass. "I know I can."

"Down, both of you." Tag turned to his latest hire. "Look, Xena, I know you want to prove you're some kind of female warrior or some shit but that dude right there occasionally loses his damn mind and rips people's throats out with his bare teeth, so back the fuck off him."

Erin looked him over. "Actually that kind of makes me like him more. Fine. I won't touch the klutz. To tell you the truth, I'm kind of on Murdoch's side here. If she's an operative, I'll eat some of Li's haggis."

Liam shook his head. "Damn me, girl, but we're going to have to give you a geography lesson. I'm bloody Irish, not Scots. Why da fuck would I eat haggis?"

She shrugged. "They all sound the same to me."

Ian pulled his phone out and whatever was there made his jaw tighten. "We need to move. She's on Main but she's walking. We can catch her."

Ten minutes later, Jesse found himself on Elm waiting for a signal. It didn't get past him that he was right where that text had wanted him to be. Someone wanted him in that walkway, but he couldn't figure out why. He had to wonder if that someone who wanted him to learn the truth would care that he'd brought company along. Simon stood beside him. Jesse inhaled deeply, the smells of Italian and Mexican food filling his nostrils and reminding him he hadn't eaten. Campisi's was to his back, but he knew if he walked down the little alley that connected Elm to Main he would find Sol Irlandes. He'd taken Phoebe there a few weeks back. They'd had a nice meal and questioned the artistic value of putting a giant eyeball in the middle of downtown Dallas. The massive "work of art" sat across the walkway from the restaurant and overlooked Main Street. It was surrounded by a little park of perfect green grass. It was weird and he kind of found it fascinating, but Phoebe said it creeped her out.

"What are we waiting for?" He was impatient. He wanted this all over with so he could shoot everyone the finger and get back to the baby shower. He wasn't so much interested in watching Eve open gifts, but he definitely had plans for the appetizers Sean had cooked. His stomach rumbled. He shouldn't have to go through all this stress on a freaking empty belly.

"The all clear signal. Be patient."

"She's in the hotel. Adam, can you get into the CCTV at The Joule?" McKay's voice came over the comm in his ear. They'd all put them in so they could talk to Jake and Adam.

"Already there," Adam replied. "She's at the front desk."

"I have eyes on her," Jake said. "I can't get too close, but I won't lose her."

What the hell was she doing at a hotel? Was she meeting someone? "Do you think she has a boyfriend?"

He asked the question of Simon, not bothering to click the button that would send his voice to the rest of the team.

"I don't think this is about a hidden lover, Jesse," Simon replied. "Wait for it to play out."

The Joule was right through that alley. All the answers were right there. It was one of those swanky places he always felt uncomfortable in. If she was meeting a lover there, he likely had money because a place like that didn't come cheap.

Why would she lie to him? Why would she go out with him if she had someone else?

It explained a lot when he thought about it. She wouldn't go to bed with him because she had someone else. The bigger question was why she wouldn't just tell him. Maybe her lover had been the one to send the text.

"She's moving to a room. I think it's on the fifth floor," Jake said. "Adam, get me a number. Tag, you can move in."

They were all moving in, all playing a part in catching his girlfriend cheating on him. The humiliation didn't seem to stop. The minute he thought he was fitting in and his life was moving in the right direction, he got this shit.

Jealousy burned in his gut, but more than that, he was mad. All she'd had to tell him was she wasn't interested. She could have been honest, and then they wouldn't have this god-awful scene that was playing out.

"I've got the room number. 512. Adam, can you get me in?" Jake asked. "I've got Tag and Alex with me. We're getting in the elevator now."

He was done. He touched his comm and started walking. He turned right down the alley as he spoke. "Don't you get it, guys? She's fucking someone in that room. Leave her be. I'll sit in the lobby until she comes down and we'll have a talk about what it means to string a guy along."

"Jesse!" Simon yelled, the sound coming from both his comm and behind him.

He was so fucking done with this. She was cheating on him. Not really since they'd never actually had sex, but he'd kind of thought they were involved. It went to show how stupid he was. He was going to look even stupider if Tag took down Phoebe and her boyfriend in the middle of their afternoon delight.

He made it halfway to Main Street when he knew someone was watching him. He stopped under the awning of the Mexican place and looked up at the hotel. What room had they said she was in?

And that was when he noticed the red dot on his chest.

She wasn't cheating on him. She was setting him up for a kill. She was in that hotel. Maybe she'd even sent the text. In those seconds he stood there, the truth hit him. She'd never wanted him and now she wanted him dead.

She was watching him. She was hiding in the recesses of that hotel room with a sniper rifle. She hadn't had the guts to take him out face to face. No. She'd put a scope between them like he was an animal she was hunting.

"What the fuck are you waiting for Phoebe?" he yelled at the top of his lungs. "You want me? You want to take me out? Do it!"

He put his arms out so she had the best target possible.

Everything he'd survived and it had come down to this. A weariness settled over him and Jesse accepted the truth. He'd fought and fought to live and now he was going to stand here and let her do her worst.

He didn't want to live in a world where she betrayed him. He simply didn't.

CHAPTER TWO

Phoebe's breath caught as Jesse stopped in the middle of the sidewalk. Her hands were shaking. They never shook. She was always cool as a cucumber when she was on assignment. She went into what she liked to call "work mode." The minute she'd gotten the signal that she had an assignment, her brain shifted to a place where all of the emotional shit fell away and a cool precision took over.

She wouldn't admit it to Ten, but the McKay-Taggart assignment had been difficult in a way they never could have expected. She'd walked into that office expecting to spend her time figuring out how Taggart worked and how he fit in with Jesse Murdoch. It should have been simple. The workplace was often where her ops took her. She really did have a degree in accounting. It gave her insight into money situations and that told her a lot about the people around her. In her dreams, she'd wanted to discover they were working for the enemy or at the very least worked against Agency and US interests. She could safely shut them down and get Murdoch sent to Guantanamo Bay where he belonged.

And then she'd started having lunch with Grace Taggart.

And then with Serena Dean-Miles and Eve McKay.

And she'd actually met Jesse Murdoch.

She'd gotten soft—even about Big Tag, who hid a massive heart under about fifty miles of sarcasm. She'd seen all the pro bono work he did. He charged the hell out of corporate clients and then turned around and found some ex-Marine's missing daughter for free.

She couldn't even think about Charlotte Taggart without smiling.

She'd gotten lost in the group, caring for their daily troubles and woes and smiling at the way they took care of each other. It reminded her so much of how she and Jamie and Ten had been all those years ago.

In the beginning, she'd counted the days like a prisoner waiting for a pardon, and now she worried about the call that would end Phoebe Graham. Phoebe Graham was klutzy but reliable. She babysat kids and held Jesse Murdoch's hand, and only the faintest memory of being Phoebe Grant made her hold off on pressing her body to his, on spreading her legs and taking Jesse deep inside so there was no space between them. Her dreams had turned from tender reunions with her husband to finding out what it meant to be Jesse's sub.

She'd lost herself so deeply that getting that text had jarred her.

She stared through the scope, wishing everything could fall away. This was the moment when her brain should go on autopilot. Her training would kick in and it would be like some other Phoebe did this job. No emotion. No fear. Just the moment and a bullet for the target on the other end of the scope.

Jesse's arms went wide and she heard herself gasp. The door to the balcony was open and she could hear him in the distance.

"What the fuck are you waiting for, Phoebe?" Through the scope she could see how his eyes flared. "You want me? You want to take me out? Do it!"

Panic threatened. He knew she was here. Jesse knew she was here. She stared through the scope. He was standing there with his arms spread wide, inviting her to do her job.

She couldn't. She couldn't shoot him. She looked through the scope at the face she'd come to care for and knew that no matter what that text had said, she couldn't hurt him.

She was thoroughly and utterly compromised.

And he was just standing there. He was standing there making himself a huge target. What if there was a backup? It happened sometimes. Sometimes the person who sent the kill order would watch from nearby to make sure his or her order was followed and to bear witness to the act.

Or to deal with failure.

Where would Ten be? What the hell had he found that would cause him to place a kill order on Jesse? The only reason Ten would ever place a kill order was because he feared a coming attack.

Jesse wouldn't attack anyone. Well, not anyone who didn't trigger his very righteous PTSD.

Ten was wrong. Wrong. Jesse had to get out of here. He had to hide.

Just as she was about to shove the rifle aside and run to the balcony, there was the terrible sound of her door cracking open and a whole bunch of yelling.

Taggart was here. Her heart started racing and she had two choices. She could try to get away or try to warn Jesse.

She didn't even think about it. She jumped from her sniper's perch and ran through the open doors, her bare feet hitting the concrete of the balcony. She ran until she hit the railing.

"Get down! Get down!"

But she could see that he was already down, his body covered by a man in a dark suit. Simon. His partner had done his job. Ten wouldn't take out Simon Weston. There would be too much fallout. She had some time to figure out what was going on. All she had to do was get away from Taggart and get to her brother.

"Give me one reason I don't kill you right now," a dark voice said.

Taggart was right behind her. From the sound of his voice he was still in the suite, but the door was open so it wouldn't take more than two or three steps for him to get to her. Once he put hands on her, it would all be over. Shit. She put her hands in the air because she had zero doubt he would take any reason she gave him.

So she needed to come up with something really fucking fast.

"It's not what you think," she said evenly. Calm. She needed to stay calm.

"I think you're a liar, Phoebe, and I'm going to figure out what you're doing here. Si, do you have that fucking maniac under control?" Tag asked.

"He's not a maniac." Sometimes she didn't like the way Taggart talked to Jesse. Oh, she understood it on an intellectual level. It was a guy thing, but it bugged her because Jesse wasn't crazy and he wasn't stupid.

"Your opinion is not needed," Taggart said.

She could see Simon touch his ear. He was likely telling Taggart that he would take care of things.

"You have to get them off the streets. There could be a backup." She wasn't going to prevaricate or play coy. Now that she was staring this thing in the face, she knew she'd been lying to herself for a long time. She didn't know what had happened in Iraq, but she couldn't be Jesse's executioner and she couldn't stand here and watch it happen either. "They're in danger until you get them out of here."

She knew her career was over with that one little piece of advice, but there was nothing else she could do.

"If you think I believe a word you say, you haven't studied me hard enough. Turn around very slowly. I would deeply enjoy putting a couple of holes in you. I don't like being played."

Oh, but she'd enjoyed playing him. At least at first she had. He'd been a challenge and she'd needed it at the time. She'd enjoyed knowing things Taggart hadn't known. She'd waited and watched for the moment his supposedly dead wife would return and get her revenge on him.

And she'd watched as they'd fallen in love again, her heart aching because she'd finally figured out that he hadn't been the one to push Charlotte Taggart away. He'd been mourning her for years.

The way she mourned Jamie.

She stared out as Simon rolled off Jesse and started hauling him up. Jesse looked up, his eyes meeting hers.

She wanted to reach out to him, to talk to him, to beg his forgiveness.

39

He turned away as Simon hauled him into the restaurant. It didn't escape her attention that they'd sat in that Mexican place for hours not weeks before, and for a little while she'd forgotten why she was there. She'd been Phoebe Graham, not Phoebe Grant, and she remembered the moment she'd leaned over and brushed her lips against his and it had been on the tip of her tongue to invite him to stay the night. She'd been ready to sleep with him. God, she'd been ready to cheat on her husband.

Tears filled her eyes. She'd gotten soft here. She'd gotten soft around their damn kids and their lives and how they took care of each other.

"I said turn the fuck around," Taggart barked.

It was all over now. Her life at McKay-Taggart was done. She wouldn't be Phoebe Graham again. They wouldn't ask her how she was or invite her to lunch. They wouldn't joke around her. She would have to leave her little apartment.

She would have to start over and all alone this time because she wouldn't have Ten with her anymore. She'd been so compromised he couldn't trust her again.

When she managed to turn, she saw Taggart hadn't come alone. Her big probably-was-a-Viking-warrior-in-a-different-life boss had a SIG trained on her, but Alex McKay had a Beretta and Jake Dean was standing behind them. She couldn't see what he was holding, but she was sure he was armed to the teeth.

Not that he needed it. Any one of the three men in front of her could kill her without a weapon.

Unfortunately for them, she was pretty good herself, and she only had one person in the world left who gave a damn about her. She had to protect Ten at any cost.

She glanced to her left. The balconies were staggered. If they were uniform, then there wasn't a balcony under her, but there should be a balcony one floor down and to her right. If she was wrong, she would be seeing Main Street up close and personal, but maybe that wouldn't be so bad either. Maybe that would be a good way to go.

"We can do this the easy way, Phoebe," Taggart said. "You come back to the office with us and we'll have a chat."

She could guess what that chat would be about and how

friendly it would be. It would likely involve a bit of torture. She'd been in this position before. She still had a few scars from her brief time with China's MSS.

Somehow she thought Taggart would be kinder. Yes, he was a badass, but she was also female and she could play on that with him.

Or she could get the hell out while the getting was good. She should remember how to do this. The whole first fifteen years of her life were about survival and then she'd had respites of time. The year with McKay-Taggart hadn't been reality. This was reality.

She turned to her right and leapt over the balcony wall, adrenaline pumping through her system like a freight train. Immediately to her right was the fourth floor balcony suite. She threw her arms out, almost missing it.

"Goddamn it!" she heard Taggart yelling.

But she couldn't think about him right now. She barely caught the edge of the balcony, her knees smashing into the railing. No time to think about pain. She let it go, focusing on one thing only. She pulled herself up and threw one of her throbbing legs over the railing, making it to the floor. Without a second to breathe, she was on her feet again and happy that the hotel believed in French doors. She kicked with all her might right in the middle, where the laws of physics were on her side. The door slammed open and she ran through paying absolutely no attention to the man and woman who were probably really fucking shocked to have their midday tryst interrupted by an intruder.

She ignored them, the door to the hallway her only goal. There were three men who would be following her, but she had to think about Simon and Jesse, too. They wouldn't stay on the sidelines, and the McKay-Taggart group believed in communications. Taggart would have already told his whole team that she was on the move. She needed to go out the back or find a hidey-hole. She needed to get to the street. She could lose herself on the street, hop on the train, and disappear into the city.

Her mind moved a hundred miles an hour as she slammed out of the suite and into the hallway. She had no doubt one of them would be hard on her ass. She sprinted down the hall to her right because it made more sense to go to her left. The elevators were to her left, but she was looking for the stairs at the far end of the hotel.

She took a turn, but she could hear someone behind her. There was no way to mask the sound of feet beating against the floor at a dead run.

She had to be faster. She turned on the heat, forgetting about the ache, neglecting the pain. It was easy to forget the physical, but the sight of Jesse putting his arms wide and yelling for her to take him out wouldn't go away. She ran without thought to the way her lungs burned.

She could hear the man behind her getting closer. The door to the stairs was ahead. She saw it. She could make it. Distraction. It was what she needed. She hit the door and then stopped, swiveling on her bare feet. She held the door slightly open, waiting for the inevitable.

Human nature was her friend. When barreling through a door, almost no one used his or her bodies to slam a door open. It was normal and natural for a hand to press through first, and she used it to her advantage. The minute she saw that hand start to slip through the door in an attempt to push it open, she slammed her body weight against it and caught the arm with a hard crunch. She was rewarded with a shout and a moan, but she doubted she'd done more than bruise him.

"Goddamn it, Phoebe!"

She took off again. That hadn't been Taggart. She recognized Jake Dean's low growl and knew he wouldn't let a little pain stop him. She couldn't stay in the stairwell. She needed cover and she wasn't going to get it here.

She flew out the door that led to the fourth floor and immediately knew she'd gotten lucky. Phoebe had been in the business long enough to know skill wasn't enough. She needed luck and the ability to see the possibility of that big cleaning cart in front of her. Most people would see an obstacle to be avoided, but Phoebe saw something more. She saw sweet, sweet chaos.

As Dean bounded out of the stairwell, she tipped over the cart, spraying the entire hall with toilet paper rolls, fresh towels, and mini toiletries.

But what was a little chaos when she could make big chaos?

"Help! Help! Please don't let him kill me!" Phoebe screamed

as she ran past the shocked maid. "He's trying to kill me."

"Well, I wasn't before!" Dean yelled as he tried to maneuver through the ruin.

Phoebe ran even as doors opened and she could hear people calling for security and the police.

Yes, she might have to deal with them, but she suspected it would be far easier to get away from a couple of cops than it would be to slip past Taggart and his boys.

"We're about to have guests," she heard Dean say.

She could practically hear Taggart cursing her name.

An elevator opened in front of her.

"Hurry!" a masculine voice cried out.

Thank god for helpful bystanders. She took off and managed to make it into the elevator right before the doors closed.

She dragged air into her lungs, her body against the back of the elevator. She felt it start to move. "Thank you so much. My boyfriend went a little psychotic." She realized something was wrong. Why were they going up instead of down?

"Oh, sweetie, that's no way to talk about Jake. He's not psychotic. He's just grumpy most of the time," Adam Miles said with a grin on his face. He also had a needle in his hand. "Now, do you want to go the hard way or the easy way? Seriously, you should try the easy way. This is some good shit and that way you don't have to listen to Jake yelling about you breaking his arm or deal with Ian's really poor driving. The man has road rage. Now come to Papa and we'll have you out in no time at all."

Shit. She hadn't even thought about Adam.

She kicked out, trying to catch him in the gut, but he sidestepped her and before she could move, his arm wrapped around her and she felt the sting of the needle going in.

The world immediately started going hazy and soft. Adam was right. That was some good shit.

"Yeah, I got her. I know. You always underestimate me because I'm the pretty one. Meet me on six. I've got a way out." He easily picked her up, and she could see him looking down at her. "I hope you survive this, Phoebe. Serena really likes you."

She could feel tears slipping out of her eyes. So soft. She'd gotten so fucking soft. "Like her, too." Something. She had to say something before the very nice fog took her. "Save Jesse. Try again. They will try again."

And then everything was blissful darkness.

* * * *

Jesse looked up and down the street, but no one seemed to notice the big van stopped in front of the hotel. Traffic moved around them. Everything out here seemed perfectly normal, but Jesse was focused on what was happening in that hotel. Nothing was normal in there. Normal had just been blown out of the water.

"You know you're about to get the lecture of a lifetime," Simon said, opening the doors on the van. It was custom made, with bench seating in the back on either side and plenty of room for equipment. It reminded Jesse of a military vehicle. Tag was as well prepared as any unit Jesse had ever served in, but he supposed one could take the Green Beret out of the Army but you couldn't take the Army out of the Green Beret.

The side of the van was decorated with a magnetic sign that they could easily exchange before an op. For this particular mission, they'd chosen the sign that read *Clean Freaks Laundry Services.* Yep, they'd let Tag design the signs. There was also a *Master Painting Crew* sign, *Dig It Deep Plumbers*, *Little Bro Catering*, and *Adam's Dog Grooming Services.* But it looked like they were in the laundry business today.

Where was Phoebe? There was a knot in his gut that wouldn't go away. Simon had knocked his comm unit to the concrete when he'd tackled him and it wasn't working now. He couldn't hear anything. He could only watch Simon wince when someone screamed in his ear. It was the only indication he had that anything was happening at all.

"Damn it." Simon touched his earpiece. "Yes, I'm ready." He turned to Jesse. "I'm going to start the engine. You be ready to shut the doors and hop in. We're leaving ASAP."

Shit. There was only one real reason for that. Moving too fast could bring unwanted attention. "Who called the cops?"

Simon moved to the driver's side door. "Apparently your girl has everyone in the hotel thinking she and Jake are having a domestic dispute. Several of the guests have called the police and security is looking for them, but the security cameras are all down so they're having to do a floor by floor search."

"Do they have the package?" He couldn't believe he was calling Phoebe "the package," but he'd been emotional enough today. Now it was time to go cold.

She'd betrayed them all. He had to view her as the enemy. That was good. Enemy combatant. That's what she was and nothing more. She was just one more bad guy in a long line of them.

"Yes. They'll be here any second. Be ready." Simon slipped into the driver's seat and Jesse heard the engine come on. All around him people bustled, going about their lives and jobs. Dallas was a busy city and this was one of the busiest streets for pedestrian traffic, yet almost no one looked up at him. Even the valet stood at his station, staring down at his phone. The van was a defense in and of itself. It was nondescript and looked like a service vehicle, so no one tended to notice.

Rather like him. He was a grunt and no one noticed him except Phoebe.

Oh, he could find a woman for the evening. That wasn't a problem. There were plenty of pretty subs at Sanctum who would have sex with him, but he thought Phoebe had really seen him.

The doors to the hotel lobby opened and Big Tag strode out with Jake Dean at his side. Jake had his head down, his eyes covered in a pair of mirrored aviators and his right arm cradled against his chest. They walked past the valet, who looked up briefly and then got back to checking his e-mail or texting his girlfriend or whatever the hell he was doing.

"Your girl seriously fucked up my arm and I'm pissed. This is my fucking dominant hand," Jake complained under his breath.

Tag chuckled. "He's gotten soft in his old age."

"I still got this one, Tag." He used his left hand to shoot Tag the finger before climbing into the passenger seat.

"Where is she?" The question was out of his mouth before he could stop it.

"Adam and Alex are bringing her out," Tag said quietly as he looked up at the buildings around them. "Why don't you get into the van?"

He didn't want to get in the van. He wanted answers. "Who is she working for?"

"I don't know. I do know that if you don't get in the fucking van, you won't be working for me. There they are. Move it. She said there could be a secondary," Tag growled.

The service doors opened and Adam walked out followed by Alex, who was pushing a large laundry bin.

Phoebe was in that bin. God, if she was in that bin and it wasn't moving then they'd knocked her out or drugged her.

A secondary? Shit. She said there had been a secondary sniper and he might still be around. Someone was serious about wanting him gone.

He let that knowledge settle in his mind.

Jesse moved to the back of the van and got in. Alex pushed the bin to the van and tilted it forward.

There was Phoebe, her body completely slack. There was a black wig on her head. It was short and curled at her jawline. She'd put some makeup on, and for a second he thought maybe they'd gotten the wrong woman. She looked so different from the Phoebe whose hand he held. She had dark hair, but it was threaded through with reds and golds and there was so much of it. She usually put it in a ponytail or a bun, but when she let it loose it seemed to go everywhere. She certainly wasn't this polished, professional-looking woman.

"Jesse, we've got incoming," Tag reminded him.

The cops. He could hear the wail of sirens in the background now. He reached in and grabbed her, hauling her into the van. Tag reached down again and came up with what looked like a suitcase and Phoebe's purse. The gun was likely in that case. They wouldn't leave evidence behind.

Tag, Alex, and Adam were in the back of the van in a heartbeat, abandoning the bin to the street. The minute the doors were closed, Simon took off.

And he was left holding the woman who had tried to assassinate him.

"Adam?" Ian asked.

Adam needed no prompting. He opened his laptop and looked up with a smirk. "We're good. I took out all the hotel's CCTV cameras. Luckily Dallas is behind the times on security cams. No one is going to pick us up on a camera. They'll have to go off eyewitnesses and since no one was actually hurt, they'll dump it the minute something more exciting comes along. I've already texted Derek. He'll handle it."

There was a moment of silence before Ian turned to Jesse.

"Do I need to say it?" Tag asked, his jaw clenched so he spoke through his teeth.

"I'm fired." He was surprised he'd lasted so long anyway. He knew he should put her on the floorboard, but it probably wasn't clean down there and Phoebe was always very neat. He couldn't stand the thought of her body lying there. So he hauled her into his lap and tried to look like he didn't give a shit.

"No, you dumbass. I can't fire you because you would be dead in like fifteen fucking minutes. What the fuck was that? Which Army did you serve in, son, because it sure as fuck wasn't the one I did. My goddamn COs taught me not to walk into the freaking bullet."

And Tag was off. He was yelling and cussing and there was a certain comfort in it. Big Tag only got quiet when he didn't care anymore. Jesse had scared the hell out of him and this was his punishment. He would take it.

There was a lull in the yelling and he looked up. Everyone was staring at him so he supposed it was time to say something. "I'm really sorry."

"Sorry? You're fucking sorry? You would have been fucking dead." Tag was off again.

Jesse looked down at the woman in his lap. Her wig slipped and he could see that she'd put her hair in something that kept it close to her head. He didn't like it. She was prettier without the makeup and the shiny black hair. He wasn't sure why, but he needed to see her real hair. He slid his hands over her hairline, sliding the wig and the little cap off. Her hair immediately flowered out like it had been desperate to get away from the confines of the wig. Her hair tumbled over his arm. Her face turned up and he could see she wasn't completely out. Her eyes opened slightly and she looked like a sleepy kitten.

"Jesse. My Jesse. Good dream." She curved into him, rubbing

her cheek against his chest. She moaned. "He's so loud."

He couldn't help but chuckle because Tag really was loud.

Her eyes closed again and the van got quiet. Suddenly Jesse could feel three pairs of eyes on him.

"She's an operative, Jesse," Adam said quietly. "Very well trained."

"She nearly killed me," Jake complained.

Tag shook his head. "It's not even broken. Fatherhood made Dean grow a pussy."

Phoebe frowned, her eyes glassy. "Pussies aren't weak. I'd like to see Tag shove a baby out of his penis."

He'd never seen her drunk. She wouldn't ever have more than one margarita or glass of wine. She seemed like a fun drunk.

Adam laughed and shook his head when Tag sent him a forbidding look. "Sorry, Tag. She's got a point."

"She should be out," Tag complained. "You didn't dose her properly."

"I gave her enough to put down a freaking horse," Adam replied. "Which means she's likely been taught to counter the effects, and we all know that's what the pros do."

"She's involved in something we don't understand," Alex said, sympathy in his eyes. "You can't pretend she's Phoebe Graham anymore. You have to change your thinking about her. She isn't the woman you care about. That woman doesn't exist."

"And you're a goddamn idiot for thinking she did," Tag said.

Phoebe's legs started moving. Her head came up slightly and her eyes were about half open. "Fuck you, Tag. He's not dumb…not stupid. You stupid. Dumbass."

She sounded so drunk and yet the words were sweet to Jesse. Maybe he was stupid, but she was drugged. She didn't have any defenses but she was defending him. What was he supposed to do with that?

He'd heard her yelling at him. He'd heard her telling him to get down.

What the fuck was he supposed to believe?

He couldn't help himself. His arms tightened around her.

Tag's eyes closed and there was no way to miss how his fists clenched. "You know I don't think you're stupid, right?"

48

He knew it on an intellectual level. "Sure."

Taggart ran a frustrated hand through his head. "Damn it, Jesse. I think everyone's a dumbass. Ask Adam."

"He's an asshole," Adam agreed. "He's kind of a bully, but the dumb kind who pays really well and watches your back when you need it. I still fucking hate him. And love him. At the end of the day, he's my brother. My brother whose shampoo I will change for Nair when he expects it least."

Tag sighed and ignored Adam. "My point is, you don't get to do what you did. Goddamn it, Jesse, you practically begged her to shoot you."

"And she didn't." She'd yelled something at him. She'd run from her room and he hadn't noticed a gun in her hand. He'd glimpsed her before Simon had used his massive British body to tackle him down to the concrete.

"Well, we had broken into her room by then," Alex pointed out. "She used her placement on the balcony to get away from us."

Who did she work for? His brain worked overtime, but he could really only come up with one person. She would want to get away so she didn't have to admit why she was here. He couldn't imagine Phoebe working for The Collective. She wasn't the type to do something bad for a mere paycheck. He'd watched her babysit. When she picked up Carys or Tristan, she glowed in a way a woman who was doing it for underlying reasons never could. She kissed and loved those babies. She sang to them and held them close and when she thought no one could hear her, she prayed for one of her own. He'd caught her walking out of Aidan O'Donnell's room with tears in her eyes. It was always there, that deep well of pain he understood so well.

She didn't work for a paycheck. She worked for a cause.

"She works for Ten." He smoothed back her hair and noticed the blood on her shins. Her skirt had hiked up and he saw gashes on her knees and the lower part of her legs. "Think about it for a second and it makes sense. He's always hated me. She tried to run? Is that why her knees are banged up?"

Tag's eyes flared. "No. Ten wouldn't."

Alex sat back. "I don't know. It kind of makes sense."

"If Phoebe belongs to him, then he's hidden it from Chelsea,"

Simon pointed out. "Though honestly, the fact that we imbedded Chelsea with his group should lend a certain credence to him putting a spy in ours. Think about it. She's smart. She's American and educated and we can't break her cover. That means some serious backing."

Jesse knew truth when it struck him in the forehead. Phoebe moved again. This time she jerked like she was having a bad dream. He cuddled her close, trying to calm her. "She's Agency. You can't hurt her, Tag."

A certain peace fell over him. Tag couldn't shoot her and dump her body somewhere. Jesse didn't doubt for a second if he found out she was a Collective agent who could hurt them all that Tag would do exactly that. Tag could pull the trigger and not feel a moment's regret when it came to protecting his crew. But if Phoebe was Agency, she had a level of protection around her.

"Why the fuck would Ten imbed a long-term operative?" Tag let his head fall back, his eyes closing in obvious weariness.

"Me. He wanted to watch me." There was no real reason to watch Taggart, and Phoebe hadn't honed in on anyone except Jesse. "He wanted to see if they turned me. No one believes I made it out whole. I didn't."

"You're not a traitor," Simon said as he turned on to the freeway. He would drive for a while before heading to the office again. "The Army cleared you."

"The Army got rid of me. An honorable discharge on the basis of mental capacity doesn't mean they believed me. It means they didn't want to deal with me anymore."

"Jesse, no one here believes you had anything to do with the deaths of the members of your unit. No one," Alex said in a fervent voice.

He looked down at Phoebe. She sighed as she nuzzled his neck. Now she got affectionate. Story of his life. "She does and so does Tennessee Smith. Hell, so much of those months are a jumble in my head, I don't even know."

Part of his torture had been using hallucinogenic drugs that put him into a dreamlike state. When he would wake up, his chief tormentor would try to convince him he'd done all manner of hideous crimes. He'd woken up next to a girl one morning, her throat cut and her eyes open.

Only through working with Kai Ferguson had he come to accept that he hadn't killed her. Through hypnosis therapy he'd been able to remember the truth. She'd been dead when they'd placed her in the room. Somewhere in the daze of drugs they'd given him, he'd been able to remember the door opening.

This is a gift for you, my dog.

He felt the edges of his vision start to go dim, the way it always did when he had an episode.

"Jesse?"

Phoebe's voice brought him back from the edge. He took a deep breath and let go. He wasn't going to freak out. He didn't have to listen to that voice. He could listen to his own. Calm. Patient. He could be the man he wanted to be. "Yes, sweetheart?"

The man he wanted to be was good, even to his enemies. But damn, she didn't feel like an enemy cuddled so close to him.

Her eyes were dazed, and it was so obvious she was fighting the drug with everything she had. "You need to hide. Don't know who the order came from. Promise me you'll hide."

"Who are you working for?" Tag asked.

The interrogation wasn't starting now. No way. "Back off, Ian. I get why you drugged her, but you're not going to use it to manipulate her. I won't fucking have it. If this is how you do business, then you should let me out here and now and I'll take her with me. She's my problem. Mine."

Taggart sighed. "No one lets me torture anyone anymore. Fine. We'll wait until she's awake. And I can figure out if she's one of Ten's really fast." He slid his finger across the face of his cell and put it to his ear. "Hey, Ten. I have a serious problem. I need to borrow Chelsea. Yeah, Adam's getting his hair done. I need her to find out all she can about Phoebe Graham. Yes, my accountant. I've got her in custody. That's really not your business. It's got nothing to do with the Agency. This is personal and I'll handle it. She won't be a problem after today. Sure. Thanks." He hung up. "She's not Ten's. He would have fessed up because the last thing he's going to want is me looking into her background. Ten knows when to fold his cards and he didn't."

Jesse wasn't so sure.

"Am I going to Sanctum, boss?" Simon asked.

Tag let his head hit the side of the van a couple of times. "Damn it, no. We can't go to Sanctum. The cleaning crew is there and they would definitely have questions. Besides, Charlie texted me. She ate all the ice cream. We have to pick some up for the shower."

"Are you serious?" Jake asked. "We've kind of got a situation here."

"And my pregnant wife running out of ice cream is a situation, too. We can sneak her up the back and question her in my office. Once the women leave, we can move her until Chelsea comes up with something. The good news is now she can freely use Agency resources, and we should have a real name soon."

Would Ten leave his agent behind if she was compromised?

Phoebe's eyes fluttered open. "Jesse, I'm scared. Jamie died."

Who the hell was Jamie? "Hush, sweetheart. There's no reason to be scared. Sleep it off. I promise no one's going to hurt you."

"Jamie died. Can't lose you, too." She closed her eyes and went still.

Who was Jamie and did it even matter?

"I'm not going to hurt her," Tag said quietly. "But we need to find the truth. This is your op, Jesse. You call the shots. Don't fuck it up."

As the van moved down the freeway, Jesse prayed he wouldn't.

CHAPTER THREE

Phoebe came awake slowly to the sound of screaming. Someone wasn't happy. It sounded far away, like there was a door or two in between her and the source of the shouts. Female. The voice she heard was definitely female and definitely pissed.

She kept her eyes closed because she knew she'd been drugged. Likely with a sedative that also erased short-term memory because she couldn't remember what had happened.

Jesse. She'd gotten a kill order on Jesse. She remembered that. She knew she hadn't gone through with it. And then she'd run. It came back in bits and pieces and then she'd felt safe and secure.

That had to be a dream.

"Did you really think I wouldn't notice you bringing a prisoner up the service entrance? Who do you think I am? I might be pregnant, but my instincts are still good. You thought Eve's baby shower was the best time to interrogate a suspect? Are you kidding me?"

Ah, Charlotte Taggart, and she only ever screamed at one person that way. Ian. Shit. She was back at the office. They'd managed to get her from the hotel all the way back to the office.

Everyone knew she'd betrayed them.

Phoebe shoved that thought aside. Concentrate. There might still be time to get out of this, but not if they knew she was awake. Charlotte's anger at Ian was something she could use.

She quietly checked her hands. Tied behind her back. It felt tight and plastic. Zip tie. Her ankles seemed to be the same way. They were serious about her not going anywhere.

Now she had to figure out how to get out before she missed her check-in with Ten. She sent him a text every night to let him know she was safe. If she missed he would likely rain hellfire missiles on someone. She had to talk to her brother. She had to figure out why he would put a kill order on Jesse. Whatever evidence he had, it was wrong. It had to be.

But all hell would break loose if Ten thought she was compromised and captured. Luckily, she had some time. She could still get out of this without giving up Ten.

She heard something moving and shifting, like something was on the carpet, slithering her way. Her heart started to race and she couldn't keep her eyes closed. She would be giving up her best defense, but she couldn't help it. Something was coming at her.

Something pushed at her left arm, seeming to climb up her body. And then it bounced and she felt something wet hit her skin as a cooing cry of triumph could be heard.

She opened her eyes and looked right at a diaper.

"Tristan?"

The baby was bouncing, using her bound body to pull himself up and then to do that thing where he bounced and gurgled and looked so proud of himself.

"No, that's Aidan, love," an Irish accent said.

Liam? She couldn't move and now it wasn't because her hands and feet were tied. She was on her side and she could have rolled to get a better view, but then Aidan would fall and he'd probably cry, so she stayed perfectly still. "Do you want to explain why I'm a jungle gym?"

Li O'Donnell knelt down beside her. He was a gorgeous man with inky black hair and green eyes to die for. He actually looked a lot like her Jamie, but somehow she preferred Jesse's blond hair and blue eyes now. "Let's say I'm running a little experiment of me

54

own. Be careful. You've got incoming."

She felt something patting her cheek. A fat little baby hand came into view and then Tristan was staring down at her, his eyes wide and grinning like this was the funnest game ever.

"So you're some kind of super spy," Liam said.

She didn't feel like one now. "Would you believe this is all a misunderstanding?"

Tristan patted her hair while baby number three showed up, though Carys was more of a toddler. Sean and Grace Taggart's daughter plunked herself down beside Phoebe's head and started babbling to Tristan.

"Not for a minute, though I do suspect Ian's wrong about you. You see, I've been thinking about this for days. Ever since we discovered you aren't who you seem to be. Everyone else runs around protesting that they knew it all along. Bloody liars, they are. You fooled everyone, but I think somewhere along the way, you fooled yourself, too."

Tristan chose that moment to lean forward and give her a big gooey kiss. And then proceeded to gnaw on her ear. He was teething, but luckily the little sucker hadn't broken through yet. "Are you going to let the babies eat me? I read somewhere that if you lie still long enough pretty much any animal will try to eat you, even deer and bunnies. I'm a little worried babies are the same."

"Ah, the joys of Stockholm syndrome. You have a really bad case of it, love. Tell me something. Were you really going to pull the trigger?"

That was an easy question to answer, though it was made infinitely more difficult by the fact that now she was trying to balance three babies. "No. I wouldn't have killed Jesse, but you have to know someone else will. Please, Li. You might think I'm lying about everything else, but you have to believe me on this."

The door opened and she saw a nice pair of kitten heels striding her way. They stopped right next to Li and tapped impatiently. "I thought you were going to be the voice of reason here, Li." Avery O'Donnell. She knelt down beside her husband and her blue eyes were worried as she looked down. "Phoebe, are you all right?"

"I'm covered in babies." She would accentuate the positive

around Avery. This would be so much easier if she was dealing with Taggart. He wouldn't let babies kiss her, and he'd never sat up talking to her about life and love the way Avery had. Phoebe had kept quiet, but she'd learned so much about strength from the woman who had lost a husband and child and fought her way back. She wanted to be Avery, not be her enemy. "So I'm pretty good."

"Li, why don't you let her go?" Avery asked.

He put his hands up. "Not my op, love. But I will make her more comfortable. I've learned what I need to know. Come on, you little ankle biters." He stood and scooped up his son and Carys, hefting them easily and with obvious affection. "Auntie Phoebe's gotten herself into a mess, hasn't she? She thought she could be the big bad spy but she's a softie."

He couldn't know that. It might be true but she was going to defend herself. "I'm not a softie."

"Really?" Li stared down at her. Tristan was still mauling her ear in his sweet baby way. "You're the super-tough spy who can't even knock a damn baby over to make herself more comfortable. You've been perfectly still because you didn't want to hurt any one of them. Face it, Phoebe. You got in and we got to you. This is Jesse's op. Tell him you care. This will go so much easier for everyone if you drop any pretense of not caring. You love those kids and I bet you love a few of us, too."

Tears threatened again and she tried to blame the drugs still in her system. She kept her mouth shut.

Li sighed and Avery picked up Tristan. She was alone again and she felt it. Before she knew it, Li was gently hauling her up and she felt her hands come free, though he kept her legs tied. He settled her on one of the office chairs. Now she realized she was in the conference room with the big bay windows and the view of downtown.

He shouldn't have showed her such kindness, but then he went further. "Aidan needs a bottle. Do you want to feed him?"

Stupid, stupid tears. She nodded and found her arms full of baby boy. Avery passed her a bottle and Aidan cuddled right in her arms.

God, she'd wanted a baby with Jamie. She'd been ready to give up work and stay home and be the kind of mom she'd never had.

Lately when she dreamed, her baby had blond hair and blue eyes.

The door opened and she heard Charlotte yelling at her husband. "What? Are you going to execute her in front of the children?"

Charlotte did have a flair for overstating her case.

"No, baby. I was going to wait for their naps." And that was her boss.

Not her boss. God, it had gotten so jumbled in her head.

"Hey, are you all right?" Jesse walked through the open door and her heart almost stopped.

And it nearly broke because the way she felt about him was a betrayal. She was Jamie's wife. She could still feel him at night…except lately she thought about him less and less. It had been two years since he'd died and the world kept moving and she was the only one who could stop it. She had to do that for him.

She composed herself. "I'm fine. My legs hurt though. Could you get the zip ties off me?"

"Who do you work for?"

"I work for Ian Taggart, though I suspect he's going to fire me."

"Phoebe, I need to know who you work for." Jesse's voice was harder than she'd ever heard before. His jaw had tightened, and when he stood in front of her she could have sworn he grew a couple of inches.

"Phoebe Graham. Accountant. 1266745." She held the bottle, though Aidan's hands came up over hers. She wasn't sure how she could ever thank Li and Avery for these last few moments of sweetness. When this was done and she was back at whatever house she would live in from now on, she wouldn't be the same. If Ten allowed her, she would go back to China and bury herself there. She wouldn't make friends. She wouldn't watch babies. She would do her work and wait to join her husband again.

She wouldn't think about Jesse. She wouldn't remember what it felt like the first time his hand had found hers and for a minute she'd felt safe again.

"Do you work for Tennessee Smith?"

Damn, but she always knew he was smarter than anyone gave him credit for. She was fairly certain she didn't react to it at all. "Who is that? Are you talking about that guy who comes in from time to time? The one with the Southern accent? Why would I work for him?"

"Avery, would you please take the baby?" Jesse asked.

Avery stepped up, giving Phoebe a little smile. "Sorry. Li and I should probably move the kiddos. I think Grace is going forward with the party after Charlotte stops yelling at Ian. We're pretty sure the cake won't last so this shower is happening. If you think about it, it's really kind of fitting. Shower and an interrogation. It welcomes Cooper to the family properly."

Li had Carys and Tristan in either arm. He stopped in front of Jesse. "You need some backup?"

Jesse's face was perfectly stony as he shook his head. He didn't even look Li's way, his eyes steady on her.

Pissed. This was what Jesse Murdoch looked like when he was pissed. She'd never seen this side of him. He was usually so casual, so tender and polite with her. When she'd first met him she'd spent months studying him and trying to figure out who the hell he was. She'd envisioned him as hardened and cynical, as though she would be able to see his darkness immediately.

She saw a little of it now. She was shocked to find out it didn't have the effect on her she thought it would have.

Jesse was always sweet. When he looked at her with such softness on his face, she couldn't help but think about Jamie and the way he'd been.

She wasn't thinking about Jamie now. Her body tightened at the way Jesse leaned over, his eyes hard and that sensual mouth of his a flat line. He put both his hands on the table and squared his shoulders.

"What is your mission?"

A simple enough question and she wished she could answer him, but that answer led back to the one question she had to ignore. "To keep McKay-Taggart's books in tip-top shape."

"Do you think I can't handle you, sweetheart?" The words rolled from his mouth, dark and deep and rich.

Was this the man who spent his nights at Sanctum? She knew

what happened there. There was no question in her mind when she dismissed him for the night, he went to Sanctum, and she'd come to loathe the place though she'd never been inside. All she could see was Jesse finding the affection and comfort she couldn't provide. She'd closed her eyes more than once and been able to see him making love to another woman, but she'd never really seen him like this. She'd expected he was just as sweet when he made love as he was with her.

What if he was dirty?

"Do you think if you put me off enough I'll walk away and let you be? The time for that is over. It was over the minute you pointed that rifle at my chest. I know I've been following you around like a pathetic moron for months, but that's over, too. It's going to be my way all the way from here on out."

Her heart was thumping in her chest, her body warming. Arousal. At least she remembered what to call it. She'd felt it with him before, but Jamie always hovered between them. When Jesse would reach for her, she would see Jamie's sweet face and back away. Jesse wasn't reaching for her now. He was clearly drawing battle lines, and something about it called to her. A primal energy started to run through her system.

"Your way?" Her voice deepened, her body prepping for battle. This was what she needed. She needed him to see the real her. She needed to test herself against him and find out who was going to come out on top.

"Yes. Mine. I don't suspect you'll like my way so it would be easier to give me what I want and we can go our separate ways."

She didn't want to go her separate way. That was the whole problem. The idea of even spending a couple more hours with him tempted her beyond belief. Even if he spent the whole time interrogating her.

She let go of trying to play sweet Phoebe Graham and allowed Phoebe Grant to surface for the first time in a long time.

Phoebe Grant was what Jesse would very likely call a brat. She wondered how Jesse would handle Phoebe Grant. "Bite my ass, sweetheart."

A little thrill went through her spine as his eyes flared, emotion showing for the first time since he'd walked into the room. "Don't say I didn't warn you."

He strode to her, his boots sounding even on the carpet. He scooped her up and tossed her over his shoulder, her ass high in the air.

Phoebe worried she'd bitten off more than she could chew.

* * * *

Jesse pushed through the double doors, his whole being surprisingly calm. This was what he needed. He'd been sitting in his office waiting for her to wake up, thinking about how he would handle this interrogation with some modicum of civility.

It was so good to know civility wasn't going to be required.

It wasn't so good to realize that the minute she'd opened that bratty mouth, he'd gotten hard as hell and he wanted to fuck her more than he wanted to figure her out. There was a little voice playing in his head that told him to just get inside her and all those secrets would open for him. All he had to do was thrust inside her tight body and the mysteries of the universe would reveal themselves.

Yeah, he wasn't going to do that. He was going to do his job and find out who she worked for and then he would walk away from her. He wasn't going to hold her tenderly or hope she could love him. No. It was time to grow the fuck up. How was it being through what he'd been through in Iraq hadn't managed to teach him what this one woman had? He needed to shut down and do his job.

But that didn't mean parts of his job couldn't be very pleasurable.

"Uhm, Jesse, don't you think you should handle this in the conference room? It's where Ian planned on keeping her." Adam Miles's voice was an unwelcome intrusion.

"No." He knew the old Jesse would have stopped, but this was between him and Phoebe.

"Adam, I can really explain. This is all one huge misunderstanding." Phoebe tried to bring her head up.

That was an easy move to counter. He brought his hand down on that sweet, sweet ass. Phoebe had the damn prettiest ass he'd ever watched for hours and drooled over, and now he had zero reason to not spank that gorgeous flesh. He heard that sound, that smack as his hand hit her and he felt her shiver. She didn't scream. Nope. He'd thought if he smacked her good, she would call him a fucking pervert, but he'd been a dumbass idiot and this Phoebe just moaned a little as the slap went through her.

It wasn't the type of moan that would cause him to stop spanking a sub at Sanctum.

Motherfucker. He knew he hadn't been wrong about her. He'd thought there was a submissive streak buried under her "I'm a good girl so don't fuck my sweet asshole" exterior.

"The only explanation is I'm a dirty little spy and I need to tell my captor everything in order to keep him from slapping my ass silly." He couldn't be professional with her. It wouldn't work. It would only serve to put distance between them and now he could see that distance was what she'd worked for the whole time. She hadn't let him do more than hold her hand and give her an awkward peck. She'd had him convinced he just wasn't her type but he could smell her now. Yeah, that wasn't sweet or gentlemanly, but then that obviously didn't work for her. "She likes me slapping her ass. Take a deep whiff, Adam, and you'll be able to tell she's aroused."

She gasped and her whole torso came up off his. "Jesse!"

Yeah, she sounded like a pissed off girlfriend, but she wasn't his girlfriend. She was the woman who had played him and then nearly painted her initials on his chest. And he was the idiot who had stood there and almost begged her to do it.

He cringed at the thought of how stupid he'd been about her. He knew he was ping-ponging, caught between wanting to understand her and wanting to throttle her, but most of all, he wanted to get his hands on her.

He wanted to see just how much she'd lied about.

"You might want to think this thing through, Jesse," Adam began.

He was just about to tell Adam where he could shove his thought process when Big Tag strode out of his office. A thunderous look clouded his boss's face, but Jesse was ready to throw down with whoever he needed to. This was his op and his...fuck, he didn't even know what to call her, but Phoebe was his.

Ian stopped in front of them. "Take her to your office. Do what you need to do but keep it down. Apparently we're still having a baby shower and I have to attend or risk having my balls ripped off my body. I like my balls, Murdoch. Keep her quiet. Charlie's serious about this party thing. When did I fucking lose control? She's not even an employee here."

"No. I'm part owner," Charlotte said, her voice a sharp instrument. She was a beautiful woman with strawberry blonde hair. She rested her hand on the bump on her belly that seemed to get bigger every day. "Eve and I own half this company, you know. And we have all the boobs so try getting around us. Phoebe, I swear to god if I find out you've done one thing to put this company and our people in danger I will take you apart myself. Is that understood? You better hope you can prove you weren't going to hurt Jesse. He's one of my men and I will deal with you."

Phoebe's head came up again. "Your men? That's a little presumptuous, isn't it? You treat him like a puppy you can pat on his head and send away. He isn't yours and if you think you can take me, you're wrong."

Charlotte's lips curled up and Jesse realized Phoebe had just fallen into a trap. "She doesn't like the fact that I said you're mine, Jesse."

Big Tag was frowning at her. "I didn't either."

She waved him off. "I meant as a friend and employee, but Phoebe's brain goes straight for the sexual. I wonder why. Li's right. You're going to owe him a hundred bucks at the end of this thing. She's all Stockholmed out. Who wants cake?"

Ian's eyes narrowed as his wife strode off toward the break room. "Handle her, Murdoch. Any way you can and keep it the fuck down. I still haven't heard back from Ten."

He felt Phoebe's whole body go stiff at the mention of Ten's name. "I still think she works for him."

"Ten knows when a game is up. He would have told me."

"Or he would just burn her," Adam mused.

That was a more reasonable explanation, but Ian seemed unconcerned. He strode off after his wife and Adam sighed a little and then followed them.

No one was going to save Phoebe from him. No one would try to come between them. Satisfaction settled in his gut. At least his brothers recognized he had a claim on her.

"Jesse, you should let me go. I'm not a threat to you." She sounded so reasonable. "Honestly, I'm not a threat at all, but you are still in danger. If you let me go, I'll tell you what I can."

So she still thought he was an idiot. He walked down the hall and opened the door to his office. He slammed it behind and locked the door. The office was full of well-meaning busybodies, and he wasn't about to be interrupted.

He set her down and then took a deep breath.

She leaned against his desk, needing it to balance her. Her manicured fingers gripped the edge of the desk, tension throughout her body. "Can we talk?"

"Who do you work for?"

"I can't tell you that, but I can tell you that someone sent me that kill order and they won't just shrug and walk away. You're in danger, Jesse."

At least they'd gotten past one thing. "So you're dropping the whole 'I'm just an accountant' act?"

"I am an accountant," she replied beseechingly. "I have a degree from Georgetown. Not everything I said was a lie."

Just the little things. "Oh, I think it's safe to say you lied enough. What's your name? I think I should know the name of the woman who made me a fool."

She flushed. "I didn't, Jesse. Damn it. It wasn't like that. And my name is Phoebe. You know it's easier to work with something similar. A partial truth is easier to sell than a lie."

"Yeah, well, the partial part is the one that hurt. Did you have to pretend to like me?"

"I wasn't pretending. I do like you."

"That's something I can test, you know." He was feeling a little cruel. He didn't like it, but that didn't seem to matter.

"Jesse, I can't make you believe me. I can only tell you that I'm sorry you got hurt in all of this."

"You're sorry? I chase after you for months and you lead me on and you're sorry. That's good to know. Did you bug my house?"

She nodded slowly.

"So that's why you agreed to come over."

"The first time, yes."

Humiliation burned through him when he realized all the things she would have heard. "Audio or video?"

She bit her bottom lip before replying. "Both."

How she must have laughed at him. He did a lot of stupid things when he thought he was alone. One in particular made his blood pressure tick up. "Did you like the show? Did you like how I would grip my own dick and call out your name when I came?"

Her face went white as a sheet. "I didn't watch it. I didn't know. God, Jesse. I didn't get the feed. It went to my boss and he's never mentioned it. He never would. He's not like that, Jesse. He's a good man."

"Sure he is." Now he had to wonder just how close to this boss of hers she was. "I'm sure he's a great man."

She tried to stand, but stumbled, her bound feet a burden. He cursed under his breath and caught her so she didn't hit the floor.

The minute she was in his arms, his dick tightened again. He couldn't be around her and not want her. He'd wanted her when she was quiet and shy and he definitely wanted the Phoebe who told Ian he was stupid and told Charlotte off. Both times she'd been defending him. Had she figured him out so easily? Had she discovered that someone standing up for him made him soft? That a woman doing it flipped his switch hard?

She held on to his arms as he sat her on the desk. Her eyes stared up at him. Dark eyes that sometimes lit up when he walked in a room. She was that good at her job. She'd sometimes made him feel like the only man in the world. She'd managed to do it while she held him off sexually, so she was practically a spy goddess.

Maybe two could play at that game. He would love nothing more than to send her back to her mystery lover a little less pure. And if that man happened to be Tennessee Smith, that was all the better. He kind of hoped his office was bugged, too, and that old Ten was sitting somewhere dark with headphones on because Jesse meant to put on a show.

He got to his knees, his hands going to her ankles. He touched the skin there. "Does it hurt?"

"No, but it's not comfortable. Jesse, I'm not going anywhere. If nothing's happened yet, then maybe I have more time than I thought. I need to talk to Ian. I need to make him understand that you're in danger since you don't seem to get it."

He was in definite danger, but he was fairly certain no one was planning on blowing him away through his office window. It was made of bulletproof glass. He reached into his pocket and came back with his knife. He carried it with him as often as he carried his SIG. He flipped the blade open and then gently sawed through the tie, releasing her right foot. He let it go and immediately leaned back because he wasn't an idiot. She'd lied to him before. If she kicked out, he wasn't leaving his head there to get taken off. And if she did, then he would put her on her ass and she would quickly learn he wasn't playing things her way anymore.

She sat there, holding out her left foot. "Please? I told you, I'm not going anywhere for now. I will slip away eventually. I have to, but not until I'm certain you understand what kind of danger you're in."

He leaned in again and released her other leg. He closed the knife and slipped it back in his pocket before reaching for her ankle. There was a thin red line where the zip tie had chafed. "I got it too tight."

"It was fine." Her voice was quiet, her body utterly still as he moved his hand up to her calf.

"How much of it was a lie, Phoebe? If you already planted your bugs, why did you keep coming to my place? How many other team members have bugs? Did you babysit for Li and Avery so you could bug their place?" He ran his hand over her skin, tightening briefly and then moving on. He ran his thumbs along her muscles, up to her knees and then back to her feet.

She moaned a little before she replied. "I didn't do that. I was only watching you, Jesse."

Because he was the only one the US government thought might be working with jihadists. He was the only soldier they thought had been turned and twisted. There was even a part of him that understood, but it was buried under her betrayal. He could have handled it coming from anyone but her. There had been a time when he would have willingly opened himself up in an attempt to prove he was still faithful, but that time was past.

He wasn't a soldier anymore. He was Ian's man and Big Tag had asked him to find out who Phoebe was working for. He was going to do it.

"I get it. You wanted to watch me so you could find out if I had any contact with operatives in the Middle East." So smooth. So reasonable. He sounded like he really understood. He let his hand drift further up this time before coming back down to her feet. "Flex them for me. I want to make sure you didn't lose circulation."

"Jesse, I know you're not in touch with anyone from that time." She flexed her foot like a good girl, her voice tentative as though she wasn't sure what to make of him. "I've watched you very carefully. I know you're not involved in anything."

Good. He wanted to keep her off balance. "Did you have to play me the way you did? I would have just been your friend."

Honesty. She was right. A kernel of truth was always good when playing the spy game. It was something he'd had to learn the hard way. He'd always viewed himself as muscle, but maybe he could change. Maybe he could be more than the guy who took the first bullet.

She leaned over, her hands finding his hair as she forced him to look up at her. "It wasn't like that. Not in the end. Li and Charlotte are right. I came to care about all of you. I got a little lost here. I liked who I was when I was around you. I just liked being with you."

He stood and it wasn't lost on him how close they were or how she'd been forced to move her legs apart to accommodate him. He didn't give her any space. "I liked being with you, too, but you always put me off. I thought you wanted me to kiss you at first. The chemistry was there. It was there from the moment I saw you. Do you know what I wanted to do to you the first time I saw you?"

She shook her head.

"I wanted to eat you up. I saw you standing there that first day I came to McKay-Taggart and you were wearing a yellow dress and that little white sweater and I thought you looked like sunshine. I cornered McKay and asked if you had a boyfriend. That was the first day I brought you coffee, but what I really wanted to do was get my hands on you." Definitely no lies there. He'd thought he'd seen pure sweetness. He'd wanted to cuddle her and kiss her and take care of her. He thought he'd found someone who needed him.

He still wanted to eat her up.

"That's not a good idea." The words came out on a breathy sigh, and he couldn't miss how her nipples were hard against the filmy material of the dress she was wearing.

"No. It's not, but then I'm not known for being an idea man. I have to follow through on the ones I do have." He lowered his mouth to hers and hoped he could remember he was a man on a mission.

CHAPTER FOUR

Phoebe was pretty sure she couldn't breathe. He was so close, his lips hovering over hers. All it would take to push him away or draw him closer was a simple raising of her hands, but she was caught. She knew what was right. *Push him away. Don't let this happen. Don't let the last man to seriously kiss you not be James. Don't.*

But another voice seemed even louder in her head as he slowly moved toward her. *Bring him in. God, don't you want to know how it feels to have this man kiss you? Don't you want his hands on you? Don't you want to show him how worthy he is? Of love, of affection, of protection.*

One kiss. Just one. Soon she wouldn't see him. He would be as lost to her as Jamie was, and shouldn't she have this one kiss?

His lips touched hers and she was through with arguing.

He'd kissed her before but it had been an awkward thing. He'd been tentative and given her too much time to think. Jamie had inevitably come between them, but this was different. His hands came up and caught her face, holding her still for his long, slow discovery. The word stuck in her head as he moved his mouth across hers. Discovery. Something new and fresh. Something with potential.

She was discovering him.

Her hands came up as though drawn to his body. She found his lean waist and did what came naturally. She explored over the soft cotton of his T-shirt as he caught her bottom lip between his teeth and gave her the gentlest nip. She shivered, though it wasn't from the cold. Her body was hot, but then she was always warm around him.

His tongue demanded entry and she opened her mouth, feeling his triumph as he surged inside. He moved closer, placing himself firmly between her legs and letting her feel everything he had to offer.

His cock. Oh, god, that was his cock rubbing against her core. Her skirt had pushed up, and she could feel the denim of his jeans on her thighs. He moved in, spreading her legs further as his tongue glided along hers. Her body was melting. So long. It had been so damn long since she'd felt this electricity running in her veins.

"I told you I wanted to eat you up. Sweet. I knew you'd be so damn sweet." The words rumbled along her lips before he devoured her mouth again.

She let herself feel for the first time in forever. Feel the strength of his body under her hands, feel his heat, let her heart beat in time with his, let her mind sink into the experience.

The first time she'd seen him, she'd thought that the universe wasn't fair to hide such a coward under pretty skin and gorgeous eyes. When he'd shown up with that coffee, she'd poured it out. She'd gone home and cried and hated Ten for sending her. Why hadn't he let her go? She'd been happy fading away.

Slowly, she'd come to know the real Jesse Murdoch. She'd come to think of herself as protecting him, not spying.

His hand was on her waist, moving down, and she thought about all the times she'd put him off. She could have been doing this with him for months. She could have been in his arms, in his bed. In the moment, it seemed like a silly thing to have given up on.

So good. His mouth felt good and right on hers. And that big hand of his felt really good as it moved on her thigh.

Too good. "Jesse, we can't do this here."

He shook his head and his hand moved up again, fingers teasing at the edge of her panties. "Everyone else is busy. No one's going to bug us. Let me in. Just a little. I've wanted you for so long. Just a little, baby."

He kissed her again, stopping the weak protest she wasn't even sure she wanted to make. She gave over to him, his tongue plunging inside as she felt his fingers close to her core. She ran her hands up the strong muscles of his back and wanted to get rid of the material between them. Skin. She wanted to run her hands over his skin and really feel his heat.

"You want me." He whispered the words as his fingers found the folds of her pussy.

"I shouldn't." Doubt started to creep back in. She shouldn't want him because she'd promised to love one man for the rest of her life.

"Your pussy says differently, baby." He groaned a little as he slid a finger up through her soaked pussy.

Pure pleasure swamped her senses, consigning her every good intention straight to hell. This was why she'd stayed away from Jesse Murdoch, erecting wall after wall to keep them apart. She'd always known that this man could blow through her every defense if she let him.

But the thought of never seeing him again…she couldn't fight. She had to have this one beautiful moment with him. One physical memory to go with all the good days and nights she'd spent with him.

"You're so fucking wet for me." One finger slid through her labia and worked its way up to her clitoris. "Do you know how many nights I dreamed of this? How many nights I lay awake and thought about getting you underneath me? I wanted you to take my cock, Phoebe, but I thought I was too rough for you. I'm not too rough for you, am I?"

"God, no." Not even close. She needed more. He was playing with her, but it had been so damn long, she felt like she couldn't wait. She moved her hips, trying to get him to press down harder. She was close. She could feel the orgasm shimmering right on the edge of her consciousness. Just a few hard strokes and she would come.

It had been so long since she'd come.

She felt his free hand tug on her hair, lighting up her scalp and making her gasp. It didn't hurt exactly. It was just enough to get her attention.

His face was enough to let her know he meant business. Sweet Jesse's face had turned hard and demanding, his sensual lips curled in the sexiest little smirk. "No, sweetheart. Do you remember when I said this was going to be my way all the way? I've danced to your tune since the moment I met you, but this is where I rule. You want what I can give you, you better get used to following the rules, and rule number one is you obey me. Spread your legs wider."

This wasn't the Jesse she knew, but she'd sensed him under the surface. When she'd thought about him at Sanctum, she'd seen him like this. In control. Masterful.

She didn't have to think. She merely had to obey and pleasure would be given to her.

Shit. She'd been reading way too many of Serena Dean-Miles's books. She spread her knees wide, giving him access as he brought his fingers up. They glistened from the arousal coating her pussy. He stared at them for a minute before sucking them into his mouth, his blue eyes rolling back in what looked like pure pleasure as he sucked them clean.

"So goddamn sweet. Behave or we'll have trouble. I know you think I'm an idiot, but I can handle you. I can make you fucking beg for me."

"Please, Jesse." Her whole consciousness was focused on one thing. This moment. This man. Everything else fell away. It was so easy when he was in control.

"Yeah, baby," he growled against her ear. "This is going to please Jesse. This is going to make me feel so much better."

He pushed aside her panties and two fingers worked inside her pussy as his thumb found her clit.

Her vision went blissfully fuzzy as he fucked those big fingers inside and worked that sensitive pearl.

"You're so tight. You would feel so good wrapped around me." He worked her, taking her higher and higher.

Everything tightened as his thumb worked perfect circles around and over her clit. Closer and closer and closer until she snapped and pleasure swamped her system. A tidal wave crashed over her, and she panted as she tried to get her breath back. She let herself curl into his body. His free arm held her up or she would have been a puddle of goo on his desk.

Every muscle felt relaxed and loose. Warm. She was warm when she always felt so cold. She would be even warmer with Jesse on top of her. Now he would lay her down on the desk and bring them together finally. All that heat between them could be quenched.

God, she was going to miss him.

Jesse kissed her forehead sweetly as he drew his hand out of her pussy and straightened her soaked undies. "Baby, tell me who you work for. You can tell me."

The words didn't penetrate for a moment. He used a soft voice and she could almost fool herself that he was saying something sweet. "What?"

"Who do you work for, Phoebe? It's time for you to tell me the truth." A touch of hardness entered his tone.

Phoebe forced herself to push away. Between the orgasm and the drugs that had run through her system, she felt so weak. It didn't stop her though. She got to her feet, her knees shaking a little, and looked at him. His hair had gotten longer in the last few months. When he'd come to McKay-Taggart, he'd worn it in a purely military style, but now it curled over the tops of his ears and brushed over his brows. Blond and blue-eyed angel.

Who had just practically fucked her for information.

"Why?" Tears threatened. It had been a beautiful moment and he'd ruined it. Their last moment. The only one she could carry with her and he'd ground it into the dirt.

All of her life there had only been Jamie. She'd suffered through pawings when she was in foster care, but she'd managed to avoid what happened to a lot of girls in the system. She'd learned to defend herself. She'd only ever been intimate with two men, and one of them was dead and the other had just wanted information.

Jesse's eyes were colder than she'd ever seen them as he stared at her. He made no move to hide his erection. "I'm doing what you did. I'm working a relationship to make an operation go more smoothly. Wasn't that more pleasant than being deprived of food and water and human contact until you're willing to talk?"

"I didn't do this to you." Anger invaded her system. The

reasonable, rational side understood that she was at least partially angry with herself for being such a complete idiot. She'd ruined everything. She'd cheated on Jamie and it had felt so good.

Damn him, but two minutes on a desk with Jesse Murdoch had been better than all the sex she'd ever had with her husband. Her sweet, strong, brave husband. She should have been happy with what they had.

Stupid. She was so fucking stupid. She'd been Jamie's wife and now her body was a convenient tool for Jesse to play like a Master.

Jesse stared at her while he sucked his fingers into his mouth again.

And that infuriated her. She pointed a finger his way. "You don't get to do that."

His eyes were hot on her. "Yeah, I do. This right here, this is mine. I got you hot so this is mine and I'll do what I want with it."

"No, it's mine." She couldn't stand the way he was staring at her, sucking his fingers into his mouth. It had been hot before when she thought he'd meant it, but now she knew it was all an act and his fingers were nothing but ten little whores that went to do his bidding. Damn it. He didn't deserve to taste her. "You give it back."

It had been a long time since she'd felt this anger rising. She'd learned to channel it, learned to take that violent street-rat core of her being and suppress it. It was showing up again. Humiliation wasn't something she handled well.

Years had passed and she'd shoved down everything. She'd shoved down every time she'd had to play mousy and take Taggart's eye rolling. She'd buried her rage deep when they'd all laughed about how weak she was. She knew they weren't really being mean about it, but it didn't matter. She'd felt weak for years, and now she wanted every single one of them to know how strong she was—especially the man in front of her.

He stopped, his eyebrows rising. "Baby, I'm not sure what you want me to give back." A sexy smirk hit his face. "But I can get you to make more. It's obvious you're not ready to talk yet. Hop on the desk and I'll get my mouth on you. Then we'll see if you're ready to talk. You should know I can do this all day."

73

"I didn't do this to you." She had to stay calm. She couldn't lose her shit. Not now. Psycho Phoebe, as Jamie and Ten had called her, was gone and she was never coming back. Reason. That was what Franklin Grant had taught her to use. "I didn't treat you like this."

His hands came down and his shoulders squared as though he was ready for battle. "You damn straight did. You played me. You played me hard and well. You had me panting after you and then you pointed a bullet straight at my fucking heart. Do you see the irony, Phoebe? I was falling for you and you were here to kill me."

"I was here to watch you. I was here to figure out if you had turned." The one good thing that could come of this was she got to ask a couple of questions. "When you were discovered, you were hundreds of miles away from where they buried the bodies of your team. It took an Agency team another year to find the burial site. Why wouldn't you tell them where the bodies were buried?"

He flushed slightly and his hands clenched. "I didn't know. They didn't give me a map. They drugged me and shoved me on the back of a donkey or some shit and sent me on my way to the next torture hole. Is that what you wanted to know? Really, you should have just fucking asked or you could have read the Agency's reports, but you already did that, didn't you?"

She couldn't give him any more than he already knew. Her stomach was churning where just moments before she'd been happy and relaxed. God, she wished he'd never opened his mouth. "You were on the tapes."

His expression didn't change at all, but she could see the way his skin flushed. God, she hated doing this to him, but he was making it impossible for her to go back to being Phoebe Graham. Jesse would never have treated her the way he just had if she'd been able to stay Phoebe Graham. "You mean the ones where my unit...my friends were executed? Are you talking about those tapes? Yes. I was on the tapes and I looked perfectly fine with the experience, didn't I? I should be damn glad those tapes never made it out of the Agency's vault or I would have been on every news station as the grinning idiot who watched his friends die and he wasn't even tied up. Did you watch those tapes, Phoebe?"

Did she watch the tape where her husband had been executed?

"No."

Ten wouldn't allow it. He'd threatened anyone who might have shown it to her with a painful death, and Ten's people had believed him. She'd heard about the tapes. In every single one, Jesse Murdoch had been present with a smile on his peaceful face. At the time she'd been certain he'd done it to save himself, but she knew him now. She believed what he'd told the agent who had debriefed him in Germany. "How much heroin did they give you?"

It was the only explanation. Despite their "pure" Islamic beliefs, most jihadist groups made their money off heroin. Everyone with a brain knew terrorists had very little to do with real Muslims.

"Enough that I had to do some hard rehab afterward. Tell me who you're working for, Phoebe. I don't want to have to escalate this. I was tortured by the best. I don't want to do that to you."

The very fact that he would threaten it pissed her off. Especially when she knew damn well he wouldn't do it. Months and months with the man had proven that he had looked into that abyss and turned from it. Jesse Murdoch would protect and defend, but he would never torture.

Well, except in the sweetest way.

"Really?" She took a step forward. "You're going to torture me the way they tortured you? You're going to dope me up and kill a few of my friends and try to make me believe I did it?"

It was what they'd done to him. She'd read his file. It read like a damn horror novel, though at first she'd thought he was just really good at crafting fiction.

Jesse stopped, his arms falling to his sides and his eyes narrowing. "No. I won't do it and you know it. I don't need to. I know an Agency operative when I see one. Well, when I stop thinking with my dick, I do. You bastards. You're why we were taken. Do you think I don't know that?"

"What?"

He huffed a little, like he didn't believe her question. "Sure, you didn't know."

"What are you talking about?"

His lips curled just slightly. It was the cruelest look she'd ever seen on his sweet face, and her heart ached because she'd been the one to put it there. "They targeted my unit, Phoebe. It wasn't random. They were looking for an operative code named 'the spider.' The Agency was embedding operatives into troops."

Her stomach dropped. "No. That's not true."

No one could have known. No one would have told. Jamie had been caught in a random act of terrorism. It hadn't been their fault. No way.

Ten would have told her.

She'd been the one to come up with the concept. Ten had argued against it. Violently. He'd told her it would put the soldiers in the unit in danger, but Jamie had liked the idea. He'd been the one to talk Ten in to trying it, and it had failed spectacularly.

Was she the real reason Jesse Murdoch had spent all those months being tortured, his soul being ripped apart?

"Phoebe? Baby, are you going to pass out?" He immediately dropped the tough guy act and his arms went around her just as her knees went weak.

She hadn't eaten all day and the drugs were making her loopy. No. She was fooling herself. The guilt was making her sick. Had she done this to both Jamie and Jesse? She felt herself being hauled into strong arms.

"Do I need to get a doctor?" He pulled her close and it felt so good to be in his arms.

She wanted to pretend the last several hours hadn't happened. She let her head drift to his shoulder just as she heard the sound of a helicopter. Distant at first, and then she watched in utter horror as it dropped into view, blocking the sight of the Dallas skyline.

Her eyes widened as she saw a tall, lean man standing on the foot rail, a SIG in his free hand and a grim look on his face. He nodded and the chopper rose again, likely to set down on the roof.

"What the hell?" Jesse turned. He had caught a glimpse of the chopper before it rose. "Was that a traffic copter? I don' t think they're supposed to get that close to the building."

She shook her head. "No. You need to tell Taggart to let me go and lock the doors. If he lets me go, I think everyone will be safe."

She clung to Jesse for one second longer because her time was up.

Ten was here.

CHAPTER FIVE

Jesse kicked his office door open. He didn't even think about letting Phoebe down. He couldn't risk it. He believed her that something was about to happen and it was going to be bad, but the last thing he was going to do was put her out in the hallway and lock the doors behind her. He wasn't going to leave her out there like some sacrifice.

He wasn't ready to give her up. He was supposed to have more time. He knew it couldn't work, but he'd planned to get inside her and have that one memory. She would have let him do it, too. She'd been so hot when she'd spread her legs and let him bring her to orgasm. He'd felt her tighten around him and imagined it was his dick instead of his fingers, getting squeezed from all sides while she milked him dry.

Yeah, it had taken everything he had not to come then and there.

And then he'd been an asshole because he couldn't say what he'd wanted to say. So he'd struck out and he'd hated the hurt look that had come over her face.

"Jesse, the party's starting." Li walked out of his office,

holding Avery's hand. Her hair was mussed and she had a glow about her that told Jesse something had been going on in that office. He guessed a couple with a kid took whatever time they could get. "Grace just called and said all the rug rats are happy and fed and she wants pictures before we start."

Avery took a deep breath. "And I can smell the appetizers Sean cooked. I think he did that tenderloin bruschetta thing. I swear I gain a pound just walking into the man's house. I'm so glad you took Phoebe out of bondage for the party. You can do the questioning thing after Eve opens the presents. Oh, and I happen to know Li here plans on spiking the punch. A little whiskey might make the whole interrogation easier."

"Get the kids and take cover." He didn't have time for explanations.

Li went from relaxed to predatory in an instant. "Avery, get the women and the kids into the back room. Now, love."

She took off running.

"How long do we have?" Li asked.

"Three minutes at most. They're coming from the roof." Jesse hurried after Li.

"What the fuck is going on? Erin!" Li jogged down the hall.

Erin's office door opened. "What?" She frowned Phoebe's way. "What the hell is she still doing here? Don't we have a shallow grave for her or something? I thought she'd be fertilizing Big Tag's trees by now."

Phoebe ignored her. "You have to let me go. He won't play around."

"Who?" His arms tightened around her. "Tell me who the hell is about to burst in those doors, Phoebe."

"You have to let me go."

But he didn't. He had zero intention of allowing her to go anywhere until he had his answers. He sure as fuck wasn't giving her up to some Agency search and rescue that didn't even have the damn authority to work on US soil. No way, no how.

"Erin, can you lock her in?" Erin's office was the closest. He would prefer to tie her up, but it looked like their time was about to be up and he needed to be able to fight.

"Of course. Throw the princess in there. I promise she'll have

78

nowhere to go," Erin said, opening the door wide.

"Don't do this, Jesse. Please let me talk to him." Phoebe was starting to struggle. He hated leaving her. It was obvious she needed rest and food, and the desire to provide for her was riding him hard, but he couldn't do a damn thing if they took her away.

He set her down on the couch and walked away, locking the door behind him.

"What the fuck is going on?" Li asked.

"I think the Agency is about to attack the office," Jesse explained.

Li's jaw dropped. "The bloody Agency? Are you telling me that a Special Forces unit working for the CIA is about to walk into the office?"

"I'm afraid they aren't going to walk in. I think they're going to try to take Phoebe without giving themselves away, and I won't let it happen." He pulled his SIG from his holster.

Erin shook her head. "Dude, we can't attack an American military unit."

"I'm not attacking. I'm defending." They didn't get to walk into his home and take his shit. And yes, Phoebe would likely protest that she wasn't his shit, but she didn't get a say-so. Until he was satisfied and done with her, she belonged to him. Then the fucking Agency could do what they wanted to him.

"Get the doors locked," he yelled. It might buy them some time.

Li started to move for the office doors just as someone kicked them open.

Damn it. They hadn't even had time to lock the doors.

He caught a glimpse of a group of black clad men and then watched as a familiar looking cylinder rolled into the office.

"Bloody fucking hell!" Li yelled as the flashbang rolled in. He pivoted on his heels and leapt toward Erin.

Jesse turned as fast as he could as the world blasted with smoke. He protected his eyes before the flare flashed, but his ears rang.

In the distance, he could sense men moving in. He managed to stay on his feet, managed to keep moving. It wasn't the first time he'd been hit with one of those fuckers.

He turned briefly and there was already fighting. Li was on the ground, having taken the full brunt of the flashbang by covering Erin's body with his own. She was already on her feet, kicking out against a man who moved into the room.

He caught sight of eight men moving in, their guns at the ready. They moved in an easy formation that spoke of years and years of training. They were utterly silent, their faces covered by dark masks, but Jesse had learned to see through such trivial things. He remembered men by the way they walked, the way their shoulders set, and how their eyes moved.

He'd seen these men before. He'd watched them in battle. They might want to stay anonymous, but he wasn't about to let that happen.

"Tennessee Smith!" He couldn't really hear himself, but he was trying to shout.

One of the men stopped, but Jesse watched as his jaw squared. "Find her. We don't leave without her. Get it done."

Li tried to get up, but he had a gun pointed at his head.

Erin kicked out at her opponent and for a few seconds it didn't look like the man knew what to do. She caught him squarely in the midsection and Jesse knew his ears were clearing because he heard an audible huff as the operative briefly lost the ability to breathe. He had to give the kid credit as he came right back up. He caught Erin and hauled her back against his body. She immediately brought her elbow up and back, easily getting away.

She didn't get more than a few steps before the man tackled her. He tossed his full weight on top and wrestled her down to the floor.

Just like that Jesse knew Ten had given orders not to kill. There was no other explanation. No one was going to fire a shot. The guns were there to intimidate, but no one had told Big Tag that. Ten likely thought he could do a quick, get in, get out mission since it was the middle of the day. He possibly believed shock and awe would work, but what the stupid fucker hadn't counted on was Charlotte Taggart throwing a baby shower and the office being full of women and kids.

Tag was going to kill someone. Maybe a whole lot of someones.

A big guy with an M4A1 carbine pointed it his way. "Get on your knees."

No fucking way. He felt the pressure build. It always seemed to start low in his gut, though he knew it was all in his brain. Somehow the fear manifested itself in a physical way and it didn't matter that it was a lovely day in Dallas and the air conditioning was set low because Charlotte always seemed warm these days. None of that mattered because his vision blurred and he could feel the heat of the Iraqi sun on his face, feel his skin. It was too tight. He'd woken up after the IED had blasted his Humvee and he'd been shoved out of the vehicle, reaching back for the new guy.

"I said get on your knees. In a minute or two this is all going to be over and you can go about your day," the man said.

Jesse was caught between worlds. He was almost certain the man in front of him was Case Taggart, but about half the words that came from his mouth were said in Farsi.

He took a deep breath. He wasn't going to go there. He needed to stay in the here and now. Dallas. He was in Dallas and Ten had come to reclaim his lover.

Yeah, that wasn't going to happen.

He punched Case right in the face, secure in the fact that the soldier had likely been told not to fire a shot.

"Shit!" Case yelled before returning with a punch of his own.

Jesse took it right on the jaw. The pain flared, but it also kept him in the here and now. He looked to his left and the operatives had scattered, though their numbers had diminished since it was taking two of the eight to hold down Li and Erin.

"They won't shoot!" Jesse yelled.

"Like fuck we won't," the one pointing a gun at Li said.

Case pointed that gun at Jesse again. "Stand down. On your knees."

Jesse wasn't fooled again. Though the words the man used were a trigger for him, the actual trigger told the tale. "Your fucking safety's on, asshole."

He punched him again, hard across the bridge of his nose, and Case went down. Jesse looked up and Big Tag was moving into the room, his body protected by a large man in the same black uniform everyone else was wearing. He had his hands up and a tense look on his face as Tag forced him into the room, a SIG at the back of his head. There was no way Tag had the safety on that one.

"Let my people up or I will blow this motherfucker's head off his shoulders. And I don't want to do that. I don't even have plastic down. My wife has a strict edict that when I blow some dude's head off, I have the courtesy to put some plastic down. You're going to get my wife pissed at me."

"They have their safeties on," Jesse said. "I think that's Michael Malone you've got. Si would be sad if you offed him."

"I can live with disappointment," Simon said as he walked in from the break room. Unfortunately, he'd been caught. His hands were up, his eyes icy.

"Why don't you let my guy go and we'll talk about letting this one off the hook," a man with a slow Southern accent said.

"Or I could blow your head off." Charlotte Taggart placed a semiautomatic at the back of Simon's captor's head. "Ian, where is the plastic tarp? I told you, I don't want blood on the carpet."

Ian's whole body went tense. "Oh, there's going to be blood. I promise you that. You listen and you listen good whoever you are. That is my wife behind you. She's pregnant. If you try a goddamn thing, I swear to god I will spend the rest of my life hunting you down and when I catch you, I will ensure that you live a long time in as much pain as your body can take."

"Fuck." The guy immediately dropped his weapon. "Taggart, no one said anything about pregnant women. I promise. Check my weapon. There's no ordnance in it. None of us would ever hurt an innocent woman, much less a baby."

The door to the break room opened again. "What the fuck is going on? There are babies back there. And I'm pretty sure one of them pooped. Is Ten playing a joke on us? Is this some sort of practical joke?"

Jake Dean rushed into the room. "I got one down when he tried to leave the back room. He walked in and stared for a minute before practically running out."

"Shit. Did you kill Boomer?" Malone asked.

"He's napping. What the fuck is going on?" Dean asked.

"I want to know where Phoebe Graham is." Ten strode back into the room, but he wasn't alone. He had Sean Taggart in his grip, a gun placed against his head. Ten had pulled his mask off, obviously realizing the game was up.

"Fuck me, Ian. I'm sorry. I had headphones on. I didn't even know he was in the kitchen until he had me," Sean said.

"Because you're supposed to be safe here," Ian said to his brother before his eyes shifted to Ten. "I will kill this man if you don't let my brother go. Do you understand me? You have thirty seconds or I'll do it."

"And you have ten seconds to give me Phoebe," Ten shot back. "I didn't want to do it this way, but I'm not leaving here without her."

Something was wrong with this scenario. Ten was willing to burn down a whole lot of houses for a single operative. "She's alive."

"Then bring her out here. You give me Phoebe and I'll let Sean go, and then Tag and I never have to speak again," Ten practically snarled. "Don't you call me when you get in trouble, Ian. Do you understand me? I won't answer it. You're not the man I thought you were."

"She's safe, Ten. No one's hurt her." Jesse was watching Ten closely. Tennessee Smith was always in control. Always smooth and easygoing. Even when shit was going down, Ten was the kind of guy whose blood pressure never ticked up. He was a man who cultivated relationships and yet he was trashing an important one.

"Tag, I'm going to ask you not to kill my cousin," Simon said calmly. "Let's murder this one instead." He had his hands on the one who had captured him.

"Or we can kill them all," Tag promised. "I think that might be the best solution."

"Is she your lover?" Jesse wasn't so sure anyone had to die. Ten seemed more like a desperate man than a leader trying to get back a team member.

There was only the slightest movement of his eyes before he replied. "It's none of your business, Murdoch. Just produce her or I'll kill everyone you love."

That one expression made him wonder. His eyes had rolled back just slightly as though the question was too disgusting to answer. He would have expected his eyes to flare or soften at the thought of his lover.

Only one way to find out. "I think I'll keep her for myself. She likes to talk during sex. I think if I just fuck her a couple more times, I'll probably figure out everything I need to know."

"You raped her?" Ten's face had gone a mottled red.

Again, that response didn't feel like it was coming from a man who was pissed someone had taken what was his. More like a man who had something to protect, some responsibility he had to perform. And why would he go straight to rape? Jesse decided to push it a little further. He really wanted to see if the man would break. If he could get Ten to break, they would have the advantage again—and the danger would be off Sean, who had a kid and had left the business and should never have to deal with having a gun at his head again. "I didn't have to, man. She begged me for it."

"Are you kidding me?" Tag asked, looking at him like he was the dumbest of all asses.

But Ten dropped everything and charged.

Well, that answered one question. This was very personal for Tennessee Smith, and he was about to get his ass kicked. He prayed he could hold onto his sanity long enough to fight back.

* * * *

Phoebe heard the lock open with a satisfying snick. So her skills weren't as rusty as she'd thought. She'd made the torque wrench and pick out of office supplies from Erin's very sparse desk. The whole office looked like no one was home. There were no pictures, no little knickknacks. Erin Argent's desktop was empty with the exception of a computer monitor and a charging station for her cell phone. Inside the desk wasn't better. Phoebe had found gun oil and some cloths and a few office supplies, like the unopened box of paper clips that had become Phoebe's lock picking set. Other than that, it looked like Erin lived like a Spartan.

She got the door open just as a loud bang shook through the walls. She shrank back for a second before the acrid smell hit her nostrils.

Flashbang. Shit. She was going to kill her brother. That was so much damn overkill. She was just about to run toward the lobby when she heard a cry.

Oh, god. The babies. The babies were here and Phoebe had no idea what Ten had told his men to do. Fear gripped her. She knew her brother wouldn't ever take an innocent life but bad shit happened in the middle of battle. The idea that any of those precious babies could be lost made her sick, forced her feet to run toward that sound. She ran past the kitchen, catching the barest glimpse of Sean Taggart there. If he was worried, it didn't show. His head was down and he was cutting something in that quick manner chefs used.

Another cry pulled Phoebe away. It was a high-pitched little baby wail. She started to turn the corner when she heard a man talking. British accent. Simon Weston.

"I'm moving. You don't have to get rough. Just leave the children alone," Weston was saying in a perfectly reasonable voice.

Phoebe glanced around the corner just in time to see Charlotte Taggart start after the big guy who had Weston.

Phoebe slipped down the hall and into the room they had just come from. Avery, Grace, and Serena were huddled in the back corner with the children while Eve leveled a gun at Phoebe's head.

Phoebe could have had it out of her hands in about two point three seconds, but she wasn't here to fight. "Is everyone all right? Please tell me they didn't hurt the babies."

Eve stared for a moment and then lowered the gun. "We're fine. I don't know where the others are. Charlotte is following Simon. I couldn't stop her. If anything happens to her…"

"It's my fault. I know. Just barricade the door. They don't want to hurt anyone. They just want to get me and go."

"Then you should really go," Eve replied with icy eyes.

Tears formed as she realized this was her good-bye. Coldness from a woman she'd come to trust, but Phoebe was smart enough to know that a person rarely got a second chance. The old Phoebe—the one before Jamie and Ten, the one before Jesse—would have flipped her the bird and told her to fuck off. It was best to hide pain behind pure disrespect. But this Phoebe was still so raw.

She simply nodded and looked at the women she'd belonged with for such a brief time. She'd never had female friends before. They'd become quite precious to her. "Take care of those babies.

And Eve, I know you're scared, but you're going to be such a good mom. That baby boy...he's so lucky."

She started to leave but then felt a hand on her elbow. When she turned, Eve pulled her in for a hug.

"You stay safe, Phoebe. You know that woman you became while you were here, she was always inside you," Eve whispered. "You don't have to lose her. Well, maybe some of the klutziness, but you don't have to lose the core of her."

The core of Phoebe Graham had been a woman who helped the people around her, who gave and gave and rarely requested anything back. When she went back into her brother's world, it would be different. She would sink back into the personality she'd developed over years of service to the Agency. She would guard herself, her emotions.

It struck her that the year she'd spent at McKay-Taggart had been precious. It had been the first time in her life that she'd really made friends. Jamie and Ten didn't count. From the moment she'd met them, they'd felt like family, and a very exclusive one. Their father had taught them to trust no one outside the family, to let no one else in. They only had each other, but for a brief time, Phoebe had Eve and Serena and Grace and the others.

It had been nice to have a little community to help take care of.

Grace stepped up and there were tears in her eyes. "Go on, sweetie. I'm worried they'll kill each other."

She shook her head. "Te...the man who's coming to get me wouldn't really kill anyone. This is his version of shock and awe. He won't use deadly force."

"Yeah, well, no one told Ian, and whoever is out there is about to get Ian's version," Serena said. "And he will definitely be looking to kill someone."

Shit. Ten was going to get everyone killed. Without another word she turned and raced down the hall. She had to hurdle over a body encased in a familiar black uniform. The big man had been dumped in front of the break room. She didn't see blood, but that didn't mean one of her brother's men wasn't dead. The minute the McKay-Taggart men figured out they were in trouble, they would use any and all means to deal with the situation.

"Are you kidding me?"

Frustration dripped from Ian Taggart's tone as she approached the lobby.

And then she heard a hard thud and a sound that could only be fists hitting a body.

"Stop it!" She simply yelled the words as she entered the room. It didn't matter who was fighting. It had to stop. They were supposed to be allies and she'd ruined that, too.

It was worse than she'd imagined. Everywhere she looked someone was pointing a gun at someone else or had Phoebe's friends on their backs. And the worst was the ball of rage that seemed to be made up of her brother and Jesse.

So much for keeping his cover. His mask was off and she could see the rage on his face. "Tennessee! Stop it!"

He punched out, twisting and turning with Jesse as they both seemed intent on killing the other.

"Charlie, get the fuck out of here," Big Tag commanded. "Do you have any idea what kind of trouble you're in? Dean, could you secure the package better than Jesse did?"

Phoebe squared off against Jake Dean because she wasn't about to get locked in another office. "He could try, but I swear I'll take out his balls this time. Remember what I did to your hand, Dean? Back off. Come on, Taggart. You know who I work for. Now can we try to keep those two from killing each other?"

"You're not going to run?" Taggart still had a hold on Malone.

"There's no reason to anymore," she explained with a huff. "I was trying to protect that dumbass in there."

"Which one?"

She was just about done with Taggart. "My brother, you idiot. I'm serious. The best thing to come out of my cover being blown all to hell is the fact that I can have a serious talk with you about how you treat Jesse. He's not stupid. He's smart. He's way fucking smarter than you since he knew all along I was working for Ten."

"Your brother?" Tag's hand came down as he released Malone. "Ten is your brother?"

Yeah, she probably shouldn't have mentioned that. "Not by blood, but he's my brother all the same. And he's being a moron." She looked back over to where Ten and Jesse were. Jesse had caught sight of her and he turned her way. That gave Ten just the distraction he needed. He charged at Jesse. "Stop it! All of you."

Ten got Jesse on his back. "You think you can play around, you little shit? You think you can fuck around with her? You're going to learn how we do things in my house." He punched Jesse right in the face.

Jesse's eyes went slightly glassy.

Tag shoved Malone out of the way and holstered his weapon. "Ten, get the fuck off him. He doesn't like being on his back. It's a trigger."

"Yeah? Well, I don't like a lot of things." Ten reared back. "I'm taking this fucker with me. I'm renditioning him. I have some questions I can't ask on American soil. Malone, tell Ace to fire up the chopper. How about we head to the Middle East, Murdoch? I know you love it there."

"You leave him alone." She walked right up to her brother and started to push him off, but Taggart caught her around her waist and hauled her back.

"Don't. He's dangerous," Taggart said. "Do you see that light in his eyes? He's not with us anymore."

Sure enough, Jesse started to fight, but not in the controlled way soldiers did. He thrashed, bucking Ten off him and rolling to his knees. He looked up at Ten, snarling like an animal.

"Everyone move back," Taggart said in a calm voice. "Si, if you can work some magic here, I would appreciate it."

"You're being a little overdramatic," Case Taggart said with a roll of his eyes. "Step back, boss. I'll handle him."

Before anyone could say a thing, Case stepped close to Jesse and Jesse pounced. He was on the bigger man, wrapping his hands around Case's throat and saying something in a foreign language. Phoebe didn't speak any of the Middle Eastern languages. She'd concentrated on Chinese and Korean and all the subdialects.

"Jesse!" She called out for him when Ten jumped back in.

"You're making things worse," Weston growled.

"What's he saying?" Phoebe winced as Ten got Jesse in a chokehold. At least it would be over soon.

Or not. Jesse managed to move his head and catch Ten's arm, biting down enough to draw blood. Ten shouted and dropped back.

"He's saying he'd rather die," Taggart explained. "He'd rather die than go back to being a dog. Someone's dog. I don't know all the words. It's been a long time."

"Charlotte, will you talk to him? Chelsea was able to talk him down last time," Weston explained as Jesse turned on Ten.

Case started to walk up behind him, holding the butt of his rifle up.

"Stop!" Phoebe used her most authoritative voice and pointed a finger at Case. The man wouldn't know subtlety if it bit him in the ass. "If you hurt him, I will make sure your next assignment is in the ass end of Africa. You'll be pulling the leeches off your dick on a daily basis. Do you understand me? Charlotte, stand back. I'll do it. He's my responsibility."

It had been right there on the tip of her tongue to say "he's mine." Every time someone questioned her rights to him, her damn alpha girl seemed to come out. She had to watch it because he wasn't hers. However, she'd gotten him into this position and she would be the one to get him out.

Taggart released her. "Be careful. He really does go a little crazy when he's in this state."

Ten and Case stood ten feet from Jesse like he was a dangerous lion they didn't want to touch but couldn't let get away because he might eat all the villagers. The only good news was everyone seemed to have stopped fighting. They were too busy watching what was going on with Jesse.

"Phoebe, get back. That's an order," Ten commanded.

She'd never been really good at taking orders. It was easier to ignore Ten than to argue with him. "Jesse, it's me. It's Phoebe."

"Softly," Weston explained. "He'll respond to the feminine side, not to someone in charge. Make yourself vulnerable to him. It worked before with Chelsea and he has a deeper connection with you. Let him hear the Phoebe he cares about."

He didn't look anything like the Jesse she knew so well. His eyes were wild, sweat covering his brow though it was nice and cool in the office. It was the blood on his mouth that completed the transformation.

Still, she didn't hesitate.

"Hey, Jesse." She moved toward him and he backed up, looking between the men.

"Damn it, Phoebe. Get back," Ten ordered.

"You get back, Ten. You got us in this situation. I have to get us out," she argued Ten's way.

Jesse looked down and found the one thing he really didn't need. Ten's gun had dropped. Jesse got it in his hands and started pointing it around, speaking in rapid-fire Farsi.

"He's telling everyone to get back," Ten translated. Ten spoke a little in the same language, but that caused Jesse to start to stalk his way.

She couldn't let that happen. The way Ten stilled let her know that Ten hadn't come in with blanks. She lowered her voice, softening it. "Jesse, please. Please help me."

"You have to get closer to him," Simon advised.

"Shit. I'm going to get killed." Ian lowered his voice and said something Phoebe didn't understand.

Jesse's eyes flared and suddenly that gun was being pointed at Taggart and Jesse was dragging Phoebe behind him.

"He didn't mean it," Simon explained quietly. "Jesse, you're in Dallas. This is Simon and Ian. Ian would never hurt the girl. He just wanted to get your attention."

So Ian had threatened her in Farsi and that had brought out Jesse's protective instincts. Maybe it was time to bring out some other instincts. She wrapped her arms around his lean waist and brought her body against his. "Please, Jesse. I need you to come back to me."

She let her hands move up his chest and felt his breath hitch. Yes, she was getting to him.

"Please, Jesse. You promised. You promised you would take care of me." She went up on her toes and let her mouth rest against the outer edge of his ear. "I could take care of you, too."

"That's disgusting," Ten muttered under his breath.

But Jesse pulled her around so she was cradled against his chest. He stared down at her and she reached up to wipe the blood off his face. "Phoebe?"

God, she was going to miss him. "Yes."

It took him a moment, as though he needed time to move from one place to another, one time to another. "I'm sorry."

She nodded, enjoying the closeness. It felt good to be in his arms as herself, with no untruths between them. "I am, too."

"Are you all right?" Taggart asked.

Jesse's arm tightened around her. His eyes found the floor and she could practically feel the shame rolling off him. "I'm here. I'm sorry. I forgot for a minute."

"You're fine." She understood PTSD. Maybe not in the way Jesse experienced it, but she remembered how even after she moved into the big house in Virginia, she'd slept with a knife under her pillow, and she'd almost taken Jamie's head off one night. "Ten deserved it."

Her brother stepped forward, holding his left arm. "He bit me. The little fucker bit me. And he told me how much you liked him fucking you. He's a liar because I know damn well you wouldn't sleep with him."

She felt her whole body go hot and she tried to step away from Jesse. She didn't want Ten to know how close she'd come to betraying Jamie. He wouldn't understand. She didn't understand. She'd promised to be faithful to him and Jesse shook that vow.

"Did she call Ten her brother?" Charlotte asked. "I thought Ten was alone."

Taggart stepped up, handing Charlotte his SIG. "Are we done with the preliminaries? We can get to the explanations later."

Ten's body seemed to swell as he faced off. "Yeah, we're ready to get on to the main event, son."

"Oh, I am so not your son, but I'll show you that I'm definitely your better, you son of a bitch. You think you can walk into my house?"

"You threatened to kill my sister," Ten growled. "You think I didn't know what you meant with that phone call?"

"Does it matter that he didn't hurt me?" Phoebe tried.

Charlotte moved in. "Nope. I think we need to let those two hash this out like men, and by men I mean ridiculously immature boys. Come on. I think we could all use a drink after this. Well, I can't, but I can find the Scotch for the rest of you." She winced as Li started things off by getting to his feet and immediately punching Case Taggart.

"Get off me, you little pervert," Erin said, elbowing Theo. "Do you always get a hard-on when you attack a woman?"

"Only you," Theo admitted as he tried to offer Erin a hand.

She took the proffered hand and used it to toss Theo on his back and begin a fight of her own.

Jesse stepped back, shrinking away as if he was dirty or something. She couldn't handle that. She would have to leave him soon, but she wasn't going to leave him like that.

Ian threw the first punch, but Ten was way meaner than he looked. He ducked hard and kicked Taggart right in the balls.

Charlotte groaned and put a hand over her belly. "I am really glad I already got that man's sperm. It looks like this baby might be an only. Oh, jeez. I hope Ten froze his swimmers. Ian did not take that well. I think he just punched Ten's balls back inside his body. That was a good uppercut. You get him, baby." She sighed. "Who wants cake?"

Mike Malone looked away from the fights going on around him. "Cake?"

Charlotte's eyes narrowed. "Fine, but I'm going to poison yours. I'm joking. It looks like my party is fucked. We should eat what we can. Sean, are you all right?"

Sean had joined his brother, leaping into the fray.

"And there go the appetizers." Charlotte was surprisingly calm for a woman whose husband and employees were currently engaged in battle. "Jesse, come on. We need to get you cleaned up."

"I'll take care of it." She wanted to be the one who made sure he was all right. It was all she could give him at this point.

Jesse pulled away, stepping around her. "I have a clean shirt in my office. I'll be back."

She watched as he walked away, his every movement stiff.

Charlotte eyed her as the room got worse. Jake Dean was getting into it with Deke and Alex and Adam walked in, carrying bags of groceries. They both stared at the chaos around them. Alex looked around and the minute his eyes lit on Ten, he was working his way toward the middle of the massive fight.

Adam sighed and joined Charlotte. "I'll finish the bruschetta. It looks like Sean is having fun. Give me a couple of minutes. Simon, any way I can get you to help?"

"Well, I'm not getting involved in that. I just had this suit pressed," Simon said, taking the bag from Adam.

"That's my cousin," Malone interjected, following the men. "What are you making? Because I skipped lunch."

"At least we don't have to worry about you getting away now," Charlotte said and then winced again as her husband took a hard uppercut. "Or maybe you should run. I might go with you."

She followed Charlotte to the back room, her thoughts on how lost Jesse had looked. And on how he'd pulled away. No matter what, her time was almost up.

CHAPTER SIX

Jesse sat down at the conference table, a fresh shirt on his chest and all cleaned up. How many times was he going to have to clean up blood and pretend he hadn't gone fuck all insane because someone put him on his back or said the wrong words?

"Hey, I think your boss killed my boss," Michael Malone said as he sat down across from Jesse. He had a plate in one hand and settled a glass of punch on the table. "Are there any openings here? Because I had that bruschetta and it was amazing. No one cooks like that on our team. All we ever get are donuts and coffee."

Apparently, the shower had gone on, just with a wider guest list. While Ten and Ian had continued to beat on one another, the rest of the group had settled their differences over cake and punch.

Where had Phoebe gone? She'd disappeared with Charlotte and he hadn't seen her for thirty minutes. She swore she had no reason to run, but Jesse couldn't trust her.

"What's bruschetta?" A massive dude with a knot on his head the size of Cleveland walked in. Boomer. He was ex-Special Forces, now Ten's man. He wasn't the brightest bulb in the bunch, but Jesse sympathized. Apparently every team needed one.

"It's like toast except they put lots of good tasting crap on it." He hadn't known what it was either before he'd spent time with Sean.

Boomer nodded. "The thing with the steak on it. Yeah, that was really great. Does anyone have some aspirin?"

The dude had taken a chair to his skull according to Jake.

"Hey, I think this one pooped." Deke walked in carrying Tristan with the ease of a dude who didn't mind a little poop. He was grinning as he strode through the door with the baby in his arms. Li and Avery walked in behind him with Aidan in Avery's arms. "He smells like hell. This place is full of kids. I like it. Now I know why Ten invaded. The kids are so damn cute."

Serena stepped in, holding her hands out for Tristan. "I'll take him. Oh, gosh, baby boy. You do smell bad. I'm going to change him and then we're going to head home with Grace and Sean. Sean's got a bag of peas on his eye, so I'm going to drive his car while Grace takes Avery home. But I'm going to require an update ASAP. The last time I looked, Ian was dragging Ten back into his office. I want to make sure he doesn't cook and eat the bastard."

Jesse had caught a glimpse of that, too. Tag had dragged Ten back by his shirt, like a lion dragging a carcass back for a nice private meal, though this particular carcass had still been talking. He'd heard Ten talking about protecting the country and making sure valuable assets didn't get tainted by suspicious persons.

He might be dumb but he wasn't ignorant. Jesse could guess who was potentially tainting McKay-Taggart. Him.

For as long as he'd known about McKay-Taggart, Jesse had understood they worked with the government on some of the worst cases to threaten the homeland. They fought side by side with the Agency to put down double agents, arms dealers, and terrorists.

Had Big Tag given him a job so he could keep an eye on him? Had this all been about watching Jesse Murdoch to make sure he didn't carry out some nefarious plan? Was that why he was constantly monitored?

Simon sighed a little as he sat down beside him. He adjusted his suit and let his head rest against the chair. "Where's Tag? I got the message that we were having a briefing."

Simon was his best friend. He was well aware they made an

odd pair—an Oxford educated lawyer turned spy and an Army grunt. When he thought about it that way, it didn't make a lick of sense. It made a lot more sense that Simon hung out with him to make sure he didn't fuck up or suddenly turn terrorist.

That one moment. He still dreamed about it. When he closed his eyes he could feel the Humvee under him, moving across the desert. He could feel his comfort with the people around him, see their faces as they laughed and joked. He could see Alannah smile and give him a little wink as the Humvee bounced. She held her hands up like she was on a roller coaster. It was a private joke between them. In that moment, he'd been happy, content despite all the danger around him. He'd been safe.

And then he wasn't.

God, he'd give just about anything to get back to that moment before the IED had blown. To that moment before his innocence had been forever lost.

"Jesse?" Simon's head had come up.

Jesse turned slightly, keeping his voice calm. It was easy since he felt hollow. He wasn't sure how much emotion he had left inside him. Phoebe had done this to him, though at the end of the day she was just doing her job. But Phoebe had shown him that there was no going back. He would always be under suspicion because he'd survived and they had died. "I got the same text. I'm sure he'll be here soon."

Jesse was used to waiting. When he got an order to be somewhere, he got his ass there and then he waited. He didn't complain or get restless. He just waited.

How could he change his nature? Because he needed to. He needed to walk away from McKay-Taggart. He wasn't sure what he would do, but he had some land back in Wyoming and maybe it was time to shut himself off from everyone.

"It's all right, Jesse. No one blames you for biting that bastard. I just wish you'd taken a bigger chunk out of him."

He was such a joke. He really was a dog without a leash sometimes. "I think I should hand in my notice."

Simon's chair turned. "No."

Just a flat denial and no explanation. "You don't get a say in this. I'm going to tell Tag when he comes in. I can be on a plane to

Laramie by tonight."

He didn't have much to pack. Almost everything he owned had been picked out by Charlotte and the other women. He would grab his duffel and pack his clothes and make arrangements to ship his guns. He had a couple of pictures he wanted to take, but not a lot else.

Simon leaned forward, his eyes going to his cousin who suddenly seemed deeply interested in his punch glass. "We can talk about this later, but don't think for a second I'll let you leave."

Jesse really didn't care if Malone was listening in, or Deke for that matter. Hell, apparently everyone had been listening to his private humiliations for months. "You don't get a say."

"I bloody well do. I'm your partner. This affects me, too. You can't just quit."

"Watch me." He knew he was being stubborn, that he should have just slid his resignation onto Big Tag's desk and walked out, but somehow he couldn't leave without having it out with Simon. Everyone else, he could handle. Simon and Phoebe had been his people. God, he thought he'd had people again but he needed to always remember that moment in the Humvee. When he really thought about it, his life had ended there and he was just a walking shell now. It was just that for a moment, he'd felt alive again.

His mind suddenly went back to Jimmy, the new guy. He'd only been in the unit a few weeks when they'd been caught. He remembered how stoic the man had been. He'd just had one request—that whoever survived take his wife a message. Jimmy had been messed up when he'd given Jesse the message and it hadn't made a lick of sense to him, but he'd promised.

Jesse had failed in that, too. He hadn't been able to find the wife of the private. He'd fucked up and gotten the name wrong because no one in Army personnel could tell him anything. Hell, after all the crap he'd been fed, maybe the man had never existed at all.

He kind of deserved what he got.

"Jesse, I will not allow that woman to break you," Simon hissed his direction. "Do you understand me? She lied. She fooled us all."

"And what about you? Did you lie, too?" He had to know.

97

Even though he was still going to walk away, he needed to know if Simon had ever been his friend.

"About what?" Simon asked, his voice low.

"He wants to know if you were watching him, too," Malone said, his eyes grave. "He thinks because my team was monitoring him that maybe you guys were doing the same. You know you aren't the only one who spent time in a prison over there, Murdoch."

"I'm the only one with a set of videos devoted to how I watched my team being killed. I bet the Agency's played them over and over." Many soldiers had been guests of the jihadists but not many had gone through what he had. They hadn't been a guest of the Caliph, as he called himself.

"I got captured," Deke said, settling into a chair. "I still have the scars. I was tortured for almost nine weeks they tell me. I lost track of the days. My team found me, took out the little prison I was in. I still think about it a lot. Ace was taken for longer. I think that's why he keeps to himself a lot. Not me. I wasn't allowed to do that. I got home and my damn sisters wouldn't leave me be. They covered me in babies. Yeah, five sisters can make a lot of damn babies. I tried to tell them I wasn't safe, that I could hurt them, but they just kept handing them to me. One of them would go to sleep and I'd find myself rocking another. Somewhere along the way I figured if I was okay around those tiny things, I probably could control myself enough to work again. You're not the only one, man."

He'd had no one to come home to. "I'm the only one your unit is monitoring."

"That's not true," Malone said. "We monitor a lot of people. Hell, we monitor ourselves half the time."

"Yeah, well, your boss has a hard-on for me. He's a fuckwad with serious issues." He didn't get why Ten had it in for him. He'd never met the man before he'd come to McKay-Taggart. He could understand being monitored, but this felt personal, and Jesse couldn't grasp it.

Deke snorted. "Look, Ten might be a little paranoid, but you have to understand what's sitting on his shoulders. Your boss can focus on his team because most of the time the damn world won't explode if Big Tag makes a misstep. That's not true for Ten. Taggart made a choice. He chose to walk away and concentrate on his own shit. Ten can't. He was raised to do this job, and he was raised to believe that he's all that's standing between the US and all of our enemies."

"That's a bit arrogant," Simon interjected.

"Is it?" Malone asked. "I think a man like Ten has to be arrogant. Do you have any idea what he's sacrificed for this country? You ever seen the man with his shirt off? I caught him once coming out of the shower. There's a reason he doesn't work out with the rest of us. His back is a ruined mess. Looks like brands. Maybe iron pokers. It looked like one was sent straight through him. He's got matching marks on both sides. So don't think the man doesn't know what pain is."

"Yeah, well, we've all got issues." He really didn't care what Ten had been through. He couldn't right now. Maybe later he would find some well of sympathy, but he was tapped out for the moment. "So did you know Phoebe was his sister?"

Boomer sat up. "The hot chick is his sister? Shit. I was thinking about hitting on her."

"Think again because I'll make that massive knot on your head look like a tiny bump," Jesse threatened. Damn it. He had to start thinking before he spoke. "Or hey, give her a try. Maybe she won't be as cold for you."

"Really? You're going to play it that way, Murdoch?" Naturally Phoebe chose that moment to walk in. He watched as she moved to the conference table. They were right. She moved with ease and grace now. Had anything at all been real about her?

He just shrugged.

She sank into the chair beside him and sent him a stare that every man who had ever been involved with a woman knew meant trouble. "So now I'm the ice queen? Could you figure out which kind of evil I am, please? Because before I was a slut."

"I didn't say that." He'd never once used that word about a woman. It was ugly. No woman should be made to feel bad about her natural sexuality. He was an idiot, but at least he had a code. "I'm sorry if it came off that way. I was trying to figure out your relationship with Ten. I wasn't calling you names. I wasn't trying to embarrass you or anything. I was just trying to see how he reacted."

Her lips curled up. "Apology accepted. It was smart, you know. It was a good play. Ten certainly wasn't ready for it." She turned to the other men in the room and her face went icy cold. "Who decided it was a good idea to raid an American company on American soil?"

The three of them looked back and forth, obviously not quite sure how to handle the new girl in the room. Malone finally spoke up. "That was Ten's call. It's Phoebe, right?"

"It's ma'am to you. I might have spent the last year embedded but I'm still your superior, Malone, and don't think I didn't vet every single one of you. Just because you don't know who I am, doesn't mean I don't know who you are. I know your names, your histories, and why you were chosen for this team. I also know that I chose you because you're supposed to be smart enough to know when the time has come to tell the boss he's lost his damn mind."

She had a really sexy voice when she got all authoritative. He'd never minded a woman being in charge. He totally blamed his grade school teacher, Ms. Tucker. There had been so few children that she'd taught grades one through five, and she'd been the first female authority figure he'd ever had. She'd been sweet and kind, and she knew how to kick a little ass when she'd needed to.

Malone and the rest of the men sat up straighter. "Look, ma'am, all I know is the boss got on the phone earlier today and when he got off he went into psycho mode. We didn't even get a mission briefing. All we were told was we had to extract an operative without loss of life. He showed us your picture and gave Ace directions where to set the chopper down."

"I damn near shit myself when I realized where we were," Boomer admitted.

"Dude, too much information," Deke said with a shake of his head.

Boomer merely shrugged. "Big Tag scares me. I know what our Tags are capable of and I think that dude's meaner."

"No, he's just older," Case Taggart said as he walked in.

"I don't know. I saw what he did to Ten with that stapler." Theo was right on his brother's heels. They were twins, but Jesse could tell them apart. Theo had a lightness that escaped Case.

"Which is why you should probably stay away from him," Case said with a pointed stare his brother's way.

Theo sat down. "It's just dinner. Our sister-in-law is very persuasive."

"Grace is not our sister-in-law," Case argued. "Neither is Charlotte."

"She is and why are you so opposed to having more family?" Theo shook his head. "We don't have any as it is."

"We've got each other and the team. That's all we need." Case paced behind them as though he wasn't about to get comfortable. Stubborn. Yeah, he was a lot like Big Tag. "And while we're on the subject, you should stay away from that red-haired chick. Do you think I didn't see that? You let her get the jump on you."

Theo turned a nice shade of pink. "I'm not used to fighting girls."

From what Jesse had seen, he wasn't very good at it either. Erin had gotten him and good. If Theo was interested in Erin, he might have a touch of masochist inside. Of course, he wasn't one to talk because just being close to Phoebe was making his dick stir.

"Where is Tag?" He needed to get this thing moving. The faster Tag showed up, the sooner he could leave and avoid making an idiot of himself.

"He's having to haul Ten in. Apparently there's the issue of someone's balls swelling," Jake Dean said as he sat.

The rest of the team walked in after Jake, some with cake and punch, and some with ice packs on various parts of their bodies. Ten's team straggled in with them. Erin looked up, eyeing Theo Taggart like an annoying pest she couldn't get rid of. Yet she also couldn't quite keep from watching. Her eyes strayed to him constantly.

"Are you all right?" Phoebe turned in her chair.

He couldn't look at her. "I'm fine."

"You have a bruise on your jaw. Should you have some ice on it? I could get you some." She pushed her chair back. "I'll be right back."

"Don't." He practically growled the words her way. She was so much easier to deal with when all she did was stammer and blush and seem to follow orders.

"Jesse, you're hurt," she argued.

"And I'll survive. I don't want any help from you."

"Well, that's too bad because you're going to get it," Phoebe shot back. "Don't think for a second that just because I back off getting you an ice pack means we're not going to discuss the fact that someone is trying to kill you."

"That would be you."

She sighed, a frustrated sound. "I told you I had zero idea who that kill order was on before I got to the hotel."

"You lined up your shot fast enough," Simon pointed out.

"Look, just the fact that you casually say phrases like kill order tells me everything I need to know." He didn't want to find her attractive. He didn't want to look at her. Hell, he didn't want to think about her because the minute he did, his heart rate ticked up and he lost his damn mind.

"That's pretty hypocritical of you." She turned back in her chair, staring straight ahead. "I was doing my job just like everyone in this room has done their job. Actually, I didn't do my job or you would be a chalk outline in the middle of downtown Dallas."

"I should thank you for that?" There was still that little piece deep inside that wished she'd just done it. It would all be over and he could move on to whatever the hell happened to dead men.

She frowned suddenly, turning to Simon. "Why were you there? In the alley, I mean."

"I made you a couple of months back. We've been following you ever since," Simon explained.

She flushed slightly. "It was the night The Collective came after you, wasn't it?"

He'd been scared for Phoebe that night, but now he knew he should have just taken her with them. She'd likely have dropped a couple of Collective operatives. "Yeah, Simon figured it out and then we found the tracer on my Jeep."

"Might I point out that you guys were about to be horrifically murdered when we showed up?" Deke said.

Malone nodded. "Taggart was running late, cousin. If Phoebe hadn't set us on your trail, Chelsea would now be in Collective hands and you and Murdoch there would be six feet under."

"It doesn't matter." Phoebe held a hand up. "Yes, I did put the trace on your Jeep. I've been filing a report on what happens in this office once a week. I've kept in contact with Tennessee, but until today I had not received any kind of orders beyond watching and reporting. Hello, Mr. Taggart, Ten. You both look worse for the wear."

Jesse looked up as Big Tag and Ten walked into the room. Limped was more like it for Ten. The right side of his face was swollen and his lower lip had cracked a bit. Big Tag managed to almost look like a man who hadn't had his balls abused by a pair of cowboy boots. He winced just a little as he eased into his chair.

"Nothing's broken," he said. "Jesse, you okay?"

"I'm better than most." His ribs still ached and he had a spectacular headache, but he would live. "Can we get this over with? I'd like to get home."

"He's planning on quitting." Simon was like a little boy tattling on his brother.

"No," Phoebe protested.

"Who's quitting?" McKay asked.

"It better be Phoebe," Erin said under her breath. There was only one chair left and it was beside Theo Taggart. He tried to hold it out for her but she rolled her eyes. "I'll stand, buddy."

"I'm not your buddy," Theo warned, his jaw hardening.

"No, you're not, kid," Erin agreed.

Theo stood, matching Erin's aggressive stance. "I'm not a kid either."

"Oh, is the baby looking for a mommy?" Erin could be obnoxious to say the least.

"I'll show you what I'm looking for, sweetheart." Theo took a step her way.

"I'm too old for this shit," Tag groaned. "Theo, dude, she will tear your dick off."

"The heart wants what the heart wants, I guess," Theo tossed back with a smirk on his face.

Tag stared at his brother. "Then your heart really needs to have a long discussion with your dick because again—she will rip it off. It's why I hired her. Please, can we stuff the sexual tension down where it should be? Like deep down. I don't want to hear about anyone's fucking feelings or dark desires or childhood anxieties. Shove it down like a man and yes, I mean you, Erin."

She sat down with a sigh. "I'm not the one with a case of the feels, boss. Your little brother has obviously never been around a girl before."

"I take it back," Case said, smiling for the first time. "I like her."

Ten shoved a hand through his hair, a weary look in his eyes. "My men better stand the fuck down. I might have broken a couple of ribs, but I can still shoot you. Sit and behave. We have a problem."

"A major problem. Turns out the kill order didn't come from Ten," Taggart announced.

"What kill order?" Boomer asked. "Hot new boss lady said something about it and then Murdoch looked all sad and shit. I still don't get why we're here."

Ten looked at Taggart. "He's actually the single best sniper in the country. All right, let's go over some things. I sent Phoebe in when it became apparent that Taggart was going to get involved with Jesse Murdoch, a man who has been on several watchlists since he was rescued from a jihadist prison."

"Lots of people got taken," Li said, sitting forward. "Most of them are welcomed back. I know what happened with Murdoch was unusual, but why wasn't he given the benefit of the doubt?"

"Shortly before we found Murdoch we received intel that an Iraqi psychologist was working with a jihadist group to try to turn American soldiers and then release them back into the military," Ten explained.

"From there they were supposed to become sleeper agents, waiting for a time and place to strike," Taggart continued. "Given what Jesse said about his captivity, the government and the Agency came to believe Jesse had been in that particular program."

"Shit, that's very *Manchurian Candidate*," Simon said under his breath.

"But if he'd really been turned, he likely wouldn't have mentioned the psychological torture." Phoebe didn't look his way, but he could tell she was aggravated by the way her fingers drummed along her thigh. She kept her hand under the desk as though she didn't want anyone to know.

He wanted to reach out and still her hand, to give her some comfort.

"Or he could tell us exactly what he told us because it would throw us off the scent," Ten argued. "You know as well as I do that the best covers always contain a grain of truth."

"He's not a traitor. Do you even read the reports I submit?" Phoebe sent Ten a stare that would freeze lava.

"It doesn't matter now." He could easily put an end to this argument. "I quit. So you don't have to worry about me tainting McKay-Taggart anymore. I'm going back to Wyoming. I'll keep a low profile and I won't try to lose whatever tails you feel necessary to set on me."

"No." Taggart took a sip of the ridiculously strong coffee he liked.

"You can't stop me." He should have known his boss would make things difficult.

"Yes, I can. And so can Ten. We've agreed to a few things. Mostly we agreed to beat the shit out of each other again at the first convenient time, but we also agreed that something is wrong here. Phoebe, you're the first person in a very long time to fool me."

"I wasn't trying to fool you, sir. I was trying to do my job," Phoebe pointed out.

"Nonetheless, you have my respect. Unfortunately, you also have my distrust and bitterness, and don't discount those. I have to say the over-the-top scaredy cat shit threw me off. And the Harry Potter crap was a nice touch. I don't think there's been a spy in the history of time who hid behind Harry Potter bobble heads. Adam, call Guinness."

"On it," Adam replied with a grin.

Did anyone give a shit that he kind of had every right to quit? He was about to say something to that effect when he saw Ten's skin pale and he turned to Phoebe.

"You brought them here?" Ten asked. "You brought the bobble heads into this office?"

Phoebe looked down at the table. "I'll talk to you about it later."

Taggart's eyes went from one to the other, his brain obviously working overtime. "All right then. Who has the number to her Agency phone?"

"Just me. This wasn't exactly a normal assignment. I'm given a lot of leeway in how I run my department. Black ops within the Agency are taken pretty damn seriously. I answer only to the head of the CIA. I recruit my own men and I tend to run my own missions."

"Yeah, into my fucking office. You're paying for that carpet. And for the chair Dean broke on Boomer's head. That was a good chair."

"Well, I wasn't aware you'd turned the whole place into a nursery, Tag. I kind of thought you ran a security agency. Now I can see you're all far too busy talking baby talk and drinking fucking tea." Ten shook his head like that was the worse thing a person could do.

"It was punch, boss. And it was really good. You see they made it with sherbet..." Boomer stopped. "Is this one of those times when I shouldn't talk?"

"Yeah. Most of the time you shouldn't talk, buddy." Ten's eyes closed and he took a long breath. When he opened them again, he turned to Taggart. "I'm sorry, Ian. She's my sister. When you said she wouldn't be a problem anymore, I lost it."

"And are you sorry for putting a spy on me in the first place, asshole?" Tag asked.

"Nah, I had good reasons and I'm not apologizing until you apologize for Chelsea. I'm not stupid. I know why she took the job. Now let's get down to business. I did not send that message," Ten said.

Phoebe sat up straight. "Then who did? Is there any way it could have been a drill?"

"I don't know." Ten nodded. "I'm going to look into it. So everyone can stand down for now. This was all one huge mistake and I sincerely apologize for bringing you into it. I'm going to figure this out and someone is going to pay."

"Yes. You will. I'm billing your ass," Taggart said with a long eye roll. "And we're not friends anymore."

"Like I said, I'm sorry about a lot of things." Ten stood on shaky feet. "My team, let's get up to the chopper. Ace is waiting for us there. I've got one more thing to say to Taggart, but I'd like to say that in private. Go on. We'll talk more about it back at base. We head back to DC in two weeks and have an assignment the day after that. Get some rest and heal up. We're going to be on the move for a while."

Ten's men proved just how well trained they were by leaving without another question.

That wasn't the way McKay-Taggart worked.

"A drill? Are you fucking kidding me?" Dean glared at Ten.

"If you think you can cover this up, you're wrong." Adam Miles was already on his computer.

Taggart held a hand up. "Out. Everyone. Now."

"I'm not going anywhere until I get an explanation." Simon didn't move from his chair.

"You'll get explanations later. I promise," Ian said. "Just give us the room. I will handle the situation."

Slowly, they all got up. Jesse figured he was the only one who was happy this clusterfuck seemed to be over. He started to move, but Tag held a hand out.

"Not you, Jesse. You and Phoebe stay." Tag looked up at his partner. "Alex, could you make sure no one disturbs us?"

The door closed and he was left alone with Tag, Ten, and Phoebe.

Naturally he was the one who got to stay. "I told you there's no need. I'm leaving on the first plane out of here. I don't give a flying fuck what kind of mistakes were made. If Ten's worried I'll sue the Agency or something, he can bite my ass."

"I didn't send the kill order," Ten said.

"I get that it was a mistake." He was tired and just wanted to get out of here.

Phoebe turned her face up to him. "It wasn't a mistake. I know what I saw. Who has the phone?"

"Adam," Tag replied. "He's going to fill in the rest of the team. He's working with Chelsea—who was planted in your organization for just this reason."

Ten slammed a hand down and then winced. "Motherfucking shitty day."

Shit. There was something he hadn't mentioned, hadn't really even thought about. Damn it. He was the Boomer. He was the dumbass. "They sent me a text. I wasn't in that alley by coincidence. Simon and I were supposed to wait outside the hotel."

"Yeah, I was going to talk to you about that, dumb…" Tag began and then Phoebe leaned forward. "I mean we should have a discussion where I remind you that I am actually the boss and you should follow my orders."

Phoebe sat back.

"Dumbass."

When Phoebe started this time, Jesse held a hand out to stay whatever she was about to say. "It was a stupid move and Tag calling me a dumbass is the equivalent of him saying he gives a shit."

"About a dumbass." Tag pointed at him. "You could have been killed. She could have shot you right there. We would have watched you die."

"I'm sorry, boss." He knew what that felt like. He wouldn't wish it on his worst enemy, much less a man he respected and loved like a brother. "I lost my head."

"What did the text say?" Tag asked.

Jesse handed Ian his phone, letting him read it for himself.

"Who sent you the text?" Phoebe had turned again, concern on her pretty face.

"I suppose the person who wanted you to kill me." And that meant there was no question about it.

There was a traitor on Ten's team, and he was gunning for Jesse.

CHAPTER SEVEN

Phoebe couldn't help but stare as she sat in the bar of
Sanctum. Not that there was much to stare at. The club was closed
at this time of day, but she'd been told there were a couple of
employees working. It was a good time to take in the place she'd
wondered about for so long. Taggart sometimes had meetings here,
but only with the core team. She'd been invited to come to the club
once, but she'd passed on the invitation.

She'd been too scared to come. At first she'd been scared
because she didn't understand and then she'd understood far too
well and the idea of seeing Jesse in leathers was too tempting.

She didn't have a choice now. She was staying at Sanctum for
the next few days and she wasn't staying alone.

"Do you need a drink?" Ten asked as he eased down onto the
sofa. Only the tightening of his eyes betrayed the pain he must have
been feeling. Taggart had done a number on him, but then he'd
gotten some good licks in on Taggart.

"I think I need all my faculties around me. I wasn't expecting
to be turned into bait today." Hell, she hadn't been expecting any of
this. Her plans this morning had been to finish up the quarterly

taxes, wince when she showed Ian how much he owed on quarterly taxes, secretly giggle because it was fun to watch the big guy explode, go to the baby shower and watch as Eve opened the bouncy seat she'd bought at Target for little Cooper. She hadn't had any idea her whole world was going to blow up in her face, but then it wasn't the first time that had happened. She hadn't expected Jamie to die in a hellhole thousands of miles away from her.

"If you're nervous about the plan, we can come up with something else," Ten offered.

"It's a good plan." She'd come up with part of it herself.

"It's a desperate plan. I still can't believe one of them is a traitor. I chose every single one of those men."

She felt for her brother, but she couldn't fool herself. "Someone sent that message to Jesse and they knew the number to my private line. They knew what to say and they knew how to prep that room. What did you find out about whoever booked the room?"

"According to Chelsea, it was done on a stolen credit card over the Internet. The concierge took the case from a delivery service—also paid for by the stolen card—and he had instructions to set the case on the bed as a little gift for the man's wife."

The traitor never had to even enter the hotel, so they wouldn't have any CCTV footage. Thank you, Internet. "Any word on the phone used to text Jesse? Wait. Let me guess. It was a burner."

"Purchased with cash and no longer in use. You sure you don't need a drink?"

She shook her head. "Not now."

"Phoebe, that was my very special way of saying I need a drink and I don't think I'll make it to the bar."

"Stubborn." She got to her feet and quickly found where they hid the good stuff. Glenlivet, old enough to do anything it damn well pleased. She poured two fingers into a Scotch glass and then added another two because her brother wasn't going to the doctor anytime soon. "Are you sure we shouldn't call a medic in?"

"Nah. Bear was the medic on his SEAL team. He patched me up. I'm fine. Damn Taggart got the jump on me. I'm getting old."

And there was a reason he didn't go into the field anymore. His body had taken enough damage to kill most men. He never talked about it, but she and Jamie had been at his side after a mission in South America had gone south. They'd helped him recover from numerous surgeries, including the metal plate he now had in his head. She hated to think how close she'd come to losing him. Which was the only reason she was still talking to him now. "That was not the smartest move. Taggart wouldn't have killed me."

He took a long swig of Scotch. "When he said you wouldn't be a problem anymore, all I could think about was him tossing your body in a dumpster. I got a little upset."

"A little?" He'd risked everything he'd ever worked for. If Taggart wanted to he could cause Ten no end of grief. Luckily, he was more worried about Jesse than he was angry about what Ten had done, and if her brother had really thought about the situation for two seconds, he would have known it.

"Fine. A lot." He sat back, regarding her seriously. "Did you really take the bobble heads up to McKay-Taggart? I thought they were in storage. I packed them up when I packed up your house."

God, she'd hoped he'd forgotten that little tidbit of information. "I changed my mind the night before. I just needed them close."

Every time she looked at them she remembered how she'd laughed when Jamie had given her the first one for Christmas the year she turned seventeen. He'd bought them for her every birthday and Christmas until she had a complete set. They would laugh and have little races to see whose head bobbled the fastest, and then they would go back to reading because of all the books she'd read, Harry Potter had been her favorite. Jamie had read them after he realized how much she loved them. Those stories had become the first way they had really communicated.

"Are you sleeping with Jesse Murdoch?"

Her heart twisted at the hardness in Ten's voice. "No."

"But you want to."

"I'm not going to." She was tired and it was hours before she could do anything about it. She wondered if she could even sleep with Jesse in the same room. It was part of their "cover" that they stay together. "I understand why we're playing things the way we are, but nothing is going to change. We're pretending to be lovers. Nothing more. Did your men buy it?"

111

"It doesn't matter. I told them we're out of it, that you decided to stay on at McKay-Taggart with your boyfriend and Taggart is stashing you here until he can find the assassin. They now understand that it wasn't a drill and there was no misunderstanding. They definitely got the point that Taggart is going to find the assassin."

"So it's safe to say that if this person is really hell-bent on killing Jesse, they'll pick up the pace."

"And they'll know exactly where he is and who he's with. I suspect they'll underestimate you. All of my men now have tails. The minute one makes a move, we'll be on them." A long moment passed with Ten taking one drink and then another. "You know you can't stay alone forever, Phoebe."

"It's too soon." Her stomach knotted. She wasn't ready to talk about this.

"It's been two years." Ten wouldn't let it go. "Do you think Jamie would want you to be alone for the rest of your life?"

"I think it doesn't matter because I'm not sleeping with Jesse."

"But you want to." He said it more softly this time.

"Damn it, Tennessee. What do you want me to say? I like the man. I think we were wrong about him. In all the time I've watched him he hasn't done anything suspicious."

"He talks in his sleep. A whole lot of Farsi. He talks about the man he called the Caliph."

"And what does he say? Does he pledge his will to him?"

A sharp shake of Ten's head was answer enough.

"He's scared of the man." If there was one thing she knew it was that Jesse hated the man who had tortured him.

"He's angry, too," Ten conceded.

"Has he done or said one thing in all the time you've watched him that made you believe he's some kind of sleeper?"

"I think that sleepers are asleep until someone wants them to wake up. That's why they work so well. They can stay inactive for years," Ten said ominously. "I worry someone is going to wake that boy up and we won't know how to deal with him. You won't be able to handle him. You'll be right there in the line of fire."

She couldn't help but think about how Jesse had calmed down at the sound of her voice. He hadn't once threatened her even when he was in that state. He'd been protective. "He won't hurt me."

Ten stared ahead. "Nah, this is my fault. I made a mistake sending you in. It was a stupid idea. I should have given you a team and settled you in at Langley. You would have been safe there."

She couldn't let him go on feeling guilty about assigning her to McKay-Taggart. It was time to confess. "I wouldn't have been okay at Langley. I wouldn't have taken on a team. No matter how it turned out, this was the right assignment at the right time."

"You would have settled in."

"I thought about killing myself."

The room seemed to stop. She'd never said the words out loud, never told a single soul, but now it weighed on her.

"What? What are you talking about?"

"After you brought Jamie's body back, I couldn't breathe. I couldn't sleep. I didn't want to eat. I thought I had accepted that he was dead, but until you brought his body home, I think there was a part of me that was waiting for a miracle. It might have seemed like I threw myself into work, but my mind was always on him. When you came home with him, I couldn't even hope anymore. Right before the funeral the doctor gave me some sedatives and I counted them out. I sat there and I counted out all of them, trying to decide the right dosage. It's hard because if you take way too many, you can throw them back up, and then it's all for nothing. I needed just the right amount so I could be wherever Jamie was. That's the worst part you know. Not knowing where he is."

"You did not." Ten's jaw had tensed and she could see the sheen of tears in his eyes. "Tell me you didn't try that."

"I thought about it, and then I decided to honor you and wait until after the funeral."

"But that was when we decided to send you in."

She smiled just the tiniest bit. "Yes. You gave me something to do, something about Jamie. I wouldn't have taken on a team. I would have pled off and then I would have done what I needed to do. But you gave me a way to avenge my husband and that saved my life, Ten. And then I got to be Phoebe Graham. I liked being that Phoebe, and suddenly I realized that avenging Jamie wouldn't bring him back. Slowly I started to really like the people around me, and I knew that revenge on Jesse Murdoch was stupid because he was innocent. He needed protection, not surveillance."

Ten drained the Scotch. "I'm going to need another."

She reached out and covered her brother's hand with hers. "You saved me, Ten. I know it might have ended up costing you your relationship with Taggart, but you saved me."

"Tag and I have an understanding." His hand turned over and grasped hers. "I tell him everything and he only gets to punch the shit out of me ten more times. He's holding them in his back pocket for when he needs to let off some steam."

She didn't like the idea of Taggart jumping her brother. "No."

Ten shook his head. "It's fine. No broken bones. That's our only rule. You stay out of this. You let me handle Tag the way I need to. I made mistakes. Big mistakes."

"You made them for your family." She'd caused him to make some of those errors.

"And he's protecting his. Speaking of the devil." Ten nodded as Taggart stalked into the room. He was carrying a duffel bag of some kind and there was a grim look on his face. "Nice place you've got here, Tag."

"You motherfucker. You got into my Scotch."

Ten immediately shot him the finger. "I need more. My spleen hurts, damn it."

"Pussy." But it was said in that guy way that seemed almost affectionate. He took the empty glass from Ten and stepped over to the bar. "And that's not the good stuff. That's a twenty-five. I've got the fifty hidden. I think we could both use middle-aged Scotch. Phoebe, could you join me? I'd like to go over the rules of the club with you."

There were rules? She thought the only rule was to not let Jesse get horribly murdered. She glanced at Ten, who nodded and then joined Taggart at the bar.

"So I take it the crying every time I came close was a protective measure," he began.

No one said he was a dummy. "It was a way to make sure you didn't spend too much time with me. If you had spent any real time with me, you likely would have seen more than I wanted you to. I quickly figured out you're an intolerant bastard. A couple of hysterical fits of tears and a dash of drama and you didn't want to be in the same room with me."

"Nice play. It won't work on me again. So, what's your poison? Don't tell me you don't have one because all spies drink. It's a rule."

"Vodka tonic." If she was going to have some kind of discussion with Big Tag, maybe she did need something.

"I thought you were more a margarita girl."

So Jesse had talked about her. "Phoebe Graham drinks margaritas and piña coladas. Phoebe Grant drinks vodka."

A single brow arched over his stark blue eyes. The man could really convey serious judgment with that one brow. "Damn, you're going to hurt Jesse's feelings."

"I think I already did that."

Taggart huffed a little. "I was talking about the fact that Jesse finally had someone to drink those fruity things he likes so much with. That boy never met an umbrella drink he didn't like."

She could imagine how Tag teased him about his love of piña coladas and mai tais. "You have to stop making fun of him."

"Then how will he know I like him?" Taggart expertly sliced and twisted her lime. "I don't think you're going to have a lot of say in Jesse's life once you dump him."

Of course he could convey tons of judgment with words, too. "I'm not dumping him. We were never really together as anything more than friends, and now I have to leave. My job here is done."

"Oh, I think he feels like he's been dumped. Maybe not dumped so much as betrayed and gutted."

She hated the guilt that flooded her system. She'd fucked up so badly. The first rule of the game was to never make it personal, but she'd failed at that before she'd even begun to play. "I never meant to make him feel that way."

"You care about him?"

"Yes."

"Then spend the next few days proving it."

She just managed to not roll her eyes his way. "And how should I 'prove it,' as you say so eloquently?"

Taggart laughed. "Hey, women think sex is purely physical for a guy, but for most of us, it's really how we express shit."

"You mean like feelings?" She loved the way Taggart went

slightly green at the very word.

"Yeah, that's what I said. Look, Ten told me about your husband. I hope you don't hold it against him. He's really good at keeping secrets. I didn't even know he had a family." He slid the vodka tonic her way and then turned and opened a small door revealing his Scotch. "I'm not telling you to fuck Jesse, although you would probably both feel better, but I get that you're going to be a nun for the rest of your life. That's cool. It's a choice at least."

"Screw you, Taggart. My life, my choice. You just don't have any idea what it means to lose someone."

There was that judgmental brow again. "Really?"

She'd forgotten about his wife. It was easy since she was alive and such a part of his life now. "Fine. You do and you chose to deal with it differently. I don't judge you. You should understand how I feel. Do you honestly believe you could ever love another woman? If she hadn't come back, would you have found someone else?"

He poured out the Scotch, more liberally than she had. "No idea, but she did come back. According to Ten, your husband is never coming back. So I think I can tell your future."

"Nice. I didn't know you were clairvoyant."

"I have many hidden skills." He grabbed a second glass for himself. "You'll head back into the service, but you won't play things the way Ten does. You'll go back in as an operative, and you'll take all the risks you can because you'll have a death wish. The good news is in our business, people with a death wish usually find their desire granted and quickly. Does Jesse know he was in the same prison as your husband?"

She wished Ten hadn't mentioned that little truth. "No."

Taggart slipped the Scotch back in its hiding place. "Then I'll talk to him about it."

"No. He doesn't need to know." She couldn't see how having that information would do anything but hurt him. "Look, as soon as this mission is over and we figure out who's trying to kill Jesse, I'll be out of here and he can go on with his life."

"His life in Wyoming? Because he's planning on quitting and punching cows and stepping in their shit."

She shook her head. "He's not serious about that. Just tell him he can't quit and he'll settle back in."

"It's not about the job," Taggart replied. "It's about you. He's been fine on the job, but finding out his awkward little princess is really a warrior queen put him on his ass. Now he's questioning every single friend he's made. You did that to him. You broke him. You better fix him."

"How the hell am I supposed to do that?"

One big shoulder shrugged. "I don't know. It's not my problem. I gave you a very viable solution. Men are simple. Sleep with him for the rest of his life and he'll probably be fine. See, simple. You women are the ones who make things hard."

"I'm married." The words came out of her mouth before she could think to stop them.

"No. You're a widow. Your vows were until death parted you and it did. Your story is not going to end like mine. He is not going to walk through those doors. He's not going to sneak up and tell you it was all a trick. He's dead and unless he was a sorry son of a bitch, he likely wouldn't want you to be alone."

"He was the best man I ever knew," Ten said quietly. She hadn't heard him walking up behind her. He groaned a little as he leaned against the bar. "We were just kids when we met. Nothing fazed Jamie. I mean, it did, but it didn't. He came up through the same system Phoebe and I did, but it didn't wreck him the way it did us."

Phoebe shook her head. "He was lucky. He didn't have the same trouble we did, Ten."

Ten's lips firmed as though he was holding something in. He finally turned her way. "No. That's not the truth. He never told you about it. He went through every single thing we did. Some worse."

Her heart twisted. "No. He said he was all right. He lived with his aunt until she died."

"Who beat the shit out of him," Ten said. "He had those scars on his arm. You remember the one."

"He said he was playing with a nail gun."

"She burned him with cigarettes when he didn't behave," Ten stated flatly. "She was a monster and yet Jamie was still open, still willing to try in a way I wasn't when Franklin adopted me. He was a light and I miss him every fucking day, Phoebe. And I know one thing. He wouldn't want you to die with him. He would want you to be happy."

He would, but she wasn't sure she could be happy without him. How many shots did a person get? In her experience, it wasn't many. She'd had her real true love. There couldn't be two of them. She took a deep breath. Explaining that to these particular two men wouldn't do a damn thing. Ten had never been in love and Taggart wasn't exactly being logical. It was apparently okay for him to have shut himself off after he thought Charlotte died, but she was supposed to just jump right into bed with someone else.

Except it had been years and she missed the feel of arms around her. Jesse Murdoch made her miss the feeling.

"Look, I'm here for a few days. How about we just say that I'll keep an open mind." She couldn't say she wasn't intrigued by what happened here at Sanctum. And if spending time with Jesse helped him at all, she would happily do it. She just couldn't allow herself to feel too much for him.

Taggart handed Ten a glass. "I can't ask for more. Oh, wait. I own this place and I totally can. I can give you an entire contract to look over and sign, or I'll shove you out on your pretty ass and let Erin pretend to be you."

"Erin so can't pretend to be me. I don't think Erin has a sensitive bone in her body." Everyone kept trying to shove other women at Jesse and she really didn't like the idea. It was totally illogical and unreasonable, but the thought of Erin with her hands on Jesse made Phoebe want to rip all that red hair off her freaking head.

"Apparently she's sensitive enough to know my little brother gets a boner around her. I need to have a long conversation with that boy. Talk about a death wish. Hey, Ten, put the glass down." The minute Ten set the glass on the bar, Taggart casually popped him right in the nose, the sound crunching through the air.

Ten cursed and held his nose. "You asshole."

Taggart grinned. "Oh, I'm never going to be able to hoard them properly. It's too much fun. And I've got nine more of them. I should have gone for an even dozen. Imagine how much fun meetings will be. We'll be sitting at some briefing and I'll just punch you right in front of the Joint Chiefs of Staff. Good times are coming our way, buddy."

"I thought you were done with me," Ten managed to say.

"Yeah, well, I didn't know you had a family. We do strange things for a family, and sometimes we forget who our family is and we walk away without saying the things we should," Taggart allowed, and Phoebe got the feeling he wasn't just talking about today. "I'm still pissed about you keeping things from me."

"He was going to tell you about Case and Theo." She could clear one thing up very quickly. "He just needed time to get them on the team. If you had met them in the beginning, they would probably be working for you. Ian, we need men like them. I know you do good work, but this country still needs the Agency and the Agency needs men like your brothers. Like you."

"I walked away because of my family. I suppose I could walk back in for them, too. Don't think this means I answer to you, Ten. It just means I'm willing to work with you if it means getting to know my brothers. And you. I walked away when you needed me. I'm not without blame here. Now, Phoebe, go and read the contract and talk to Jesse because I'm sick of the drama. It's getting late. Ten and I need to drink some Scotch and discuss how we're going to torture and kill the asswipe traitor when we find him."

"Are you going to punch him again?" She wasn't sure she should go.

Ten waved her off. "Go. Let us talk about manly stuff. Call me if you need me, but I'll be back when the club opens for business. Maybe I can look at some pretty girls. I can't say I want to have anything to do with the whipping crap, but the costumes are nice."

"Your sister's going to be in one Friday. That is if she doesn't hide in her room," Taggart pointed out.

"Maybe I'll just stay outside then," Ten said, going a little green.

Taggart laughed and poured Ten another. Someone was going to have to drive him back to base. "Do you have any idea how happy I am that my asshole dad only knew how to make boys? I'm so glad that baby in Charlie's belly has a penis. I have no idea what to do with girls."

As she walked away, she kind of hoped whatever sonogram Charlotte Taggart had proved false. If any man deserved a daughter, it was Ian Taggart.

What did Jesse deserve? A woman with a whole heart. A woman who could love him without reservation or regret. Unfortunately, for the next few days, all he had was her. So why did a little piece of her thrill at the idea of walking the club with him? For the first time in forever, she had no idea what was going to happen that week.

It made her feel alive. Yeah, that was dangerous.

* * * *

Jesse stared at the bed. Damn Tag. What the hell was he thinking forcing him to share a bedroom with Phoebe for god only knew how long?

They should have let him go back to Wyoming. He had half a mind to bust out and leave anyway.

"Hey, we brought your things," a soft voice said behind him.

He turned and Chelsea Weston stood in the doorway, her husband behind her. Simon towered over his wife, but his eyes were soft as he looked down at her. "She packed for you. She claims I would pick the most uncomfortable things possible. I tried to tell her you don't own anything that qualifies. And you should really prepare yourself."

He was about to ask for what when Chelsea flew across the room and threw her arms around him.

Simon laughed indulgently, picking up the bag she'd dropped. "Sorry, she hugs now. I can't quite stop her."

Jesse sighed and hugged her back. How had he ever doubted Simon? Simon was his partner, and maybe it had started out with Simon being forced to watch him, but they were friends now and Jesse promised he wouldn't question that again. He would be grateful for the friends he'd made in this place. "I don't mind."

He'd spent so much time with no one to hold on to that he liked the fact that the women of McKay-Taggart hugged often and well.

Phoebe had started hugging him about three months after they'd met. She would wrap her arms around him and lay her head on his shoulder for a long while before breaking it off and saying good morning or good night.

Chelsea broke away, sniffling. "I can't believe she nearly killed you."

He hadn't thought about the fact that Chelsea could get a little protective. Chelsea likely wouldn't listen to logic, but he had to try. "In her defense, she didn't pull the trigger."

"There is no defense for what she did," Chelsea said with complete conviction. "I don't understand why Satan hasn't taken her out yet. She should be strung up. You know what, if Ian won't do what needs to be done, then I will. I will make her life a living hell. She will wish I'd just put her on the no-fly list. I'm going to put an APB out on her ass. I'll get her on the sex offender list. Hell, I'll put her number up at Craig's list with a long menu of sexual services she's willing to provide for very little money. See how she likes that."

Chelsea could be a little fierce when she cared about a person, but Jesse thought she was also being the slightest bit hypocritical in this case. "Uhm, aren't you kind of doing the same thing to Ten's unit? He knows about that now, by the way."

Chelsea waved him off. "I'm doing it for good. She's obviously evil. And Ten's giving me a ten percent raise if I don't leave. You can bet Ian won't be doing that with Miss Happy Trigger Finger."

"No, I think it's safe to say I'm going to be looking for another job."

Jesse turned and there was Phoebe. She'd let her hair down at some point and gotten rid of the sweater she always wore around the office, swearing Taggart kept it too cold for her. Jesse was pretty sure now she'd done it all to hide the fact that she had the most beautiful set of breasts he'd ever seen. They weren't huge, but they were so perfectly formed he couldn't take his eyes off them.

"And I prefer Ms. Grant," Phoebe said as she walked into the room. "My trigger finger is very precise, not happy, which is why our boy is standing here right now. I didn't follow direct orders. I didn't shoot him and I wouldn't have. And I hate flying, so you'll have to come up with something better than the no-fly list."

"How about the APB where I tell them to shoot on sight, bitch?"

"Chelsea, down," Simon growled.

Phoebe just sent him a sad smile. "Don't bother. I'm not going to win with her. We weren't friends before so there's no relationship to fall back on. Also, we're a little too much alike to ever really get along."

"As if." Chelsea didn't seem ready to give up the fight. "I want to know why my brother-in-law trusts you to be alone with Jesse."

"He trusts Ten so he trusts me. He also saw me not pulling the trigger. Ian and my brother are downstairs right now talking. You could ask him."

"Your brother," Jesse said, testing the words. He was still having a hard time believing it. "Ten is your brother."

"Adopted, but yes, we consider each other family. The only family we have left," Phoebe replied. "And that stunt he pulled today was stupid, but I have to admit that if I thought he was going to die, I might do the same thing."

"Well, I think this plan is stupid," Chelsea said, crossing her arms over her chest.

"This plan depends on you," Phoebe pointed out. "You and Adam are supposed to trace the assassin. We're stuck in here until you do. Are you telling me you can't do it?"

Jesse had never heard that challenging tone from her, and he realized what had been missing from his relationship with her before. Challenge. Oh, she'd held him off when he'd wanted her, but that desire seemed like a sad little thing compared to what he felt now. She'd seemed like she could use a lover and he knew he wanted one.

Had the old Phoebe just been sweet and convenient? Why did he want to get to know the new one so fucking bad? And yeah, he meant that in a strictly biblical sense because he wasn't a fucking idiot. He had to admit, the new Phoebe got his motor running. Hence the "sharing a bed, bad idea" problem.

Or was it?

"Oh, I'll do it," Chelsea said, getting in her space. "I'll find this guy and then you can leave, and nothing Ian says or does is going to change that. I'll get rid of you myself if I have to."

"Chelsea," Simon began, "don't forget where we are."

Chelsea turned to her husband. "You can spank my ass all day, babe, but I'm still saving Jesse from her. God only knows what Ian was thinking."

It was good to know someone wanted to save him. He just wasn't so sure he wanted to be saved. Now that she was standing here, he was wondering if it would really be so bad to have a few days with her. He would never have even thought about seducing Phoebe Graham because she'd seemed so very fragile, but Phoebe Grant could obviously hold her own.

Would it be so bad to fuck her out of his system? He was stuck here with her for days, weeks maybe, with very little to do. He could view it as a challenge. Get her into bed for the duration of their time together and then wave as she walked away and never think about her again.

"Ian was thinking that this is a fairly safe house. It's got security and Jesse and Phoebe are contained. While you conduct your investigation, they should be safe here." Simon neatly summed up Big Tag's plan.

"Then I should get to work because I don't want to leave him for long with that woman." Chelsea turned on her heels and strode out.

Simon sighed. "I'm sorry. My wife loves very few people, but when you're one of them, she loves quite fiercely, though she doesn't always see reason. I for one thank you for not pulling that trigger as I was very close to Jesse at the time and this is my favorite suit," Simon said with a wry twist of his lips.

Jesse had to smile. "Yeah, I would never have heard the end of that. Si, tell Chelsea thanks for picking up my stuff."

"I'll take care of your place, and I believe Mr. Smith is handling things on his sister's side." Simon nodded Phoebe's way. "Are you two going to be all right?"

"We'll be fine," Phoebe said. "I promise I won't let anyone kill him. I gave up my cover to save him."

"Your cover was already blown. See that you don't fuck up again. We'll see you in a few days, Jesse. Or are you planning on skipping downstairs while you're here?"

Friday. He was talking about Friday night. Sanctum would be open for business. He would be stuck here with Phoebe for days. There was no way he was going to miss playing. "I'll be there."

Simon turned to Phoebe. "If you intend to play, Ms. Grant, I suggest you spend the next few days learning how to behave in this club. Jesse is the Master here, and he'll decide if you play or not. You'll obey him in the dungeon or you can stay in your room. I assume Tag gave you a contract."

She suddenly didn't look so tough. "I'm supposed to read it, but I'll probably just stay here."

Oh, he had to fix that. If one good thing was going to come from this, he intended to play with her.

"That's probably for the best," Simon said. "I'm sure Kori would be jealous if you didn't. She sends her love, Jesse."

"Does she?" Jesse stared at Simon, wondering if he'd lost his damn mind. Kori was one of the club submissives. She and her friend Sarah were two of the funniest brats Jesse had ever met, but she certainly wouldn't be jealous. She was a friend. He scened with her from time to time, but it was in a buddy way.

"Yes, she's worried about you. Call me if you need anything. We're all taking shifts watching the club, so don't think you're alone." Simon closed the door behind him.

Jesse was fairly certain that Kori wasn't worried about him since no one would tell her a damn thing. She wasn't a member of the team, so no one would mention anything to her. She worked for Kai Ferguson, keeping his records and making his appointments, which was why she was allowed in the club. Why would Simon mention her?

"Kori? You have a girlfriend?" Phoebe was staring at him, her eyes narrowed.

Oh, now he got it. He shrugged. "She's a friend and a girl."

"And a play partner, I take it."

"Sometimes."

"Well, you never mentioned her before, so I'm a little surprised to find out that you have a regular woman you see."

Was she fucking kidding him? "I never mentioned her like you never mentioned that you weren't really the person you said you were. Like that never mentioning her?"

She frowned. "I was surprised because you talked about all the people in your life, but you never mentioned her. Even when we were dating, you didn't mention you had a lover."

She was so jealous. There was no way to mistake the hard set of her eyes. She was pissed about Simon mentioning Kori. "Why the hell do you care?"

"Because whatever I did, I really was your friend. I really did spend all that time with you. You never told me you were sleeping with another woman."

He couldn't lie to her. Lying would make it that much harder to get inside her Agency-issued panties. "I don't sleep with Kori. She's a friend. Simon was trying to push you into a corner to see how you would react. I did, however, sleep with a prostitute for a while. It seemed better than getting into a relationship with a woman I didn't really want when the woman I did want so obviously had no interest in me sexually."

She flushed, the pinkening of her skin evident even in the low light of the room. "It wasn't like that."

"Wasn't like what?"

"I didn't have no interest in you. It's just...I'm married."

"You're a widow." He'd been told that much. She hadn't seemed very willing to talk about her husband or how he died, but Jesse had been told he'd been Agency and dead for a few years. According to Ten, they'd all been trained by their adoptive father to enter the CIA.

He was utterly fascinated by her.

"It doesn't matter, Jesse. As soon as we find the traitor, I'm going back to Virginia. I'm going back to the Agency and I'll disappear. I'm an excellent long-term operative, despite the debacle of today. So no matter what I do or don't feel for you and all the others, I will leave and go back to my real life." She walked to the window and touched it, tapping gently. "Bulletproof glass?"

"Tag's a paranoid freak, but then everyone really is out to get him." Weariness bore down on him. It was getting dark. He didn't want dinner, didn't want a shower, didn't really want to talk. He wanted to sleep and forget the day had happened. "I'll sleep in Kai's room. It's across the hall. He's in DC at some conference. He's not due to be back for a few days, so I'll crash in there."

"No, you won't. We're staying right here, watching each others backs." She unzipped her bag and brought out a SIG, checking the clip. "I had the security feed sent through my computer so if anything happens, we'll get an alarm, but we need to stay together."

"There's only one bed." Shit. "I'll sleep in the chair."

"Jesse," she said softly. She laid the SIG down on the nightstand beside the bed. "It's a big bed. There's no reason we can't both be comfortable."

"I probably won't sleep," he confessed, but he was already thinking about how much better it would be to rest beside her. If he got into bed with her, he had a chance at getting physical. He really wanted that chance. If she was going to leave, he wanted to know what it felt like to be inside her, but he had to weigh that against what he knew tended to happen when he slept. "I have bad dreams sometimes. Really bad dreams. I don't want to hurt you."

"I know," she said softly. "Despite everything I've done to you, I know you won't hurt me."

He wasn't sure he could hurt her. She would have to really care about him to be vulnerable, and she'd made it plain that she couldn't really care about him.

She looked at him across the bed. "Jesse, I can handle your bad dreams. And I think we could both use some sleep. It's been a horrible day."

It had and yet he wanted to hold her. The day might not be so bad if he could hold her. He really was stupid. "All right."

"According to Chelsea, she's a genius, so she will find our bad guy with very little trouble. This shouldn't take too long."

It probably wouldn't. He kicked off his shoes and tossed his body on his side of the bed. He wasn't going to argue with her anymore. He would likely never have taken the chance with her before, but she'd proven herself to be far tougher than he could have imagined. Hell, if someone had told him Phoebe knew how to handle a gun, he would have laughed.

She'd really looked competent with that SIG. Kinda hot. Really hot.

Damn it. New super spy Phoebe was sexier than sweet, needed protecting Phoebe.

He closed his eyes, wondering how much time he had left with her and what the hell he was going to do when she was gone. She'd been his goal for months and months. He'd believed if he could get someone as gentle and sweet as Phoebe to love him, maybe he would be able to think of himself as worthy. Love had been his goal. He'd wanted what Li had with Avery. What Sean had with Grace. A soft, gentle woman to take care of and protect and prove that he wasn't some animal.

New Phoebe didn't need protection. New Phoebe likely didn't need him at all. So why did new Phoebe get his dick hard so damn fast? He turned to his side, away from her because he had a freaking hard-on. Yep, he was the fidiot who got an erection for the woman who'd lied to him.

He heard her moving around, heard her snap the blinds shut and close the bathroom door. The door to the bedroom snicked into place and then everything went dark as she turned off the light.

The bed shifted as she slid under the covers.

"Do you hate me?"

He rolled on his back again. Did he hate her? He should. He should despise her for what she'd done, but hate seemed to be one thing he wasn't capable of. "I'm mad at you, but I don't hate you."

A long moment passed between them, and he thought she might have dropped off to sleep.

"I'm glad because you're the best friend I've made in years." She sniffled and turned to her side. "I'm sorry I hurt you. I didn't mean to. I really do...I just hope after all this is over that you find someone. I can't think of anyone else in the world who deserves it more than you. You're going to make someone an amazing husband, Jesse Murdoch."

The room went quiet again. Jesse stared at the ceiling and hoped Chelsea and Adam did their jobs as slowly as possible because no matter what Phoebe said, he intended to get inside her soon. He would let her go on to her happy Agency job afterward, but he was going to have her.

CHAPTER EIGHT

"So you get to sit around and watch the telly, and Sean brings you food and Big Tag's still paying you?" Li asked with a shake of his head. "Damn me. I need to get a couple of assassins after me, too. Sounds like heaven."

"I'd switch places with you," Jesse admitted. He sighed and looked out over the club. It was still early in the evening. Not even ten o'clock, so the scenes hadn't really started, but most of the team had shown up. "Who's got the baby? Or are you here strictly to give me shit?"

Li's lips curled up in a grin. "Nah, although I do live fer dat. We turned the conference room into a nursery for the night. I know we won't be able to do it once the kiddos are older, but fer now, they're perfectly happy pooping in there for the evening. We're paying a couple of the subs to watch over them, but they're mostly asleep."

He wondered if Phoebe knew the babies were downstairs. It might get her to come down. "I'm glad you came up with a solution, and my house arrest hasn't been all fun. Tag won't even let me go out into the courtyard."

There was a small courtyard with a basketball goal and a couple of benches, but Tag had yelled at him for going out and shooting some hoops. Apparently snipers were fucking everywhere and they loved to murder dudes getting some exercise.

"Is she making you crazy then?"

That was part of the problem. He'd spent so much time with her over the last couple of days that he should be totally sick of her. He'd eaten every meal with her. Sean brought them dinner, but the morning after they'd been locked inside, Grace and Serena had shown up with groceries for breakfast and lunch. He'd expected to eat cereal and sandwiches, but he'd woken up the morning before and found her making pancakes and bacon. She'd smiled at him and handed him a cup of coffee. He'd cut up fruit at her direction and they'd had a good morning. Quiet. Peaceful.

It felt right to be with her.

"No. We're all right. She just didn't want to come downstairs."

"Is she worried we're going to attack her? Verbally, that is. Big Tag told us we couldn't attack her physically." His hands went up when Jesse growled his way. "I wasn't the one who suggested it. My very lovely lady pit bull partner did. I had a talk with Erin. She's going to play it cool, though I think we should just put them in a ring full of Jell-O and see how things go."

Actually, that wasn't an unpleasant idea. "Tell me what's happening in the outside world. Sean is the only one I see on a daily basis, and he talks about what wine we should drink with dinner. I don't drink wine."

Li chuckled a little. "That's Sean for you. Do you want a rundown of active cases or do you just want me to get to the good stuff?"

"Have they found anything out?" There was really only one case he desperately wanted an update on, and that was his. "All Big Tag will tell me is they're working on it."

"Whoever it is, he's good. He's careful. We think he's likely been in place for years and has only been called into service recently. There's a reason Chelsea and Adam can't find anything."

Because there wasn't anything to find. It was why sleepers were so very dangerous. They could use non-traceable forms of communication. The US Postal Service didn't keep records of the mail they delivered. All anyone needed was a stamp and if the person on the other end of the letter was smart enough to burn it, then there was no evidence the communication ever existed. It required patience, but it was possible to stay off the grid. "Is Chelsea okay?"

"She's impossible. Simon had to order her to sleep." Li leaned forward, the light from the bar illuminating his face. "I've been thinking about something."

Jesse leaned in. Li O'Donnell wasn't considered the brains of the operation, but Jesse had learned that when Li got serious, it was time to listen. He often saw things the others didn't, had insights that escaped everyone else. "What?"

"Why would a sleeper come after you? I can't get it out of me head. A sleeper like this is a valuable asset. Intelligence agencies will spend years developing an operative like this. Ten's team was only recently put together, and every single man on it came from Special Forces or something like it. These weren't new recruits. They're the best of the best."

"They should totally be killing someone more important than me." Jesse understood what he was saying. Put like that it really didn't make a lot of sense.

"Exactly. Ten's unit has access to any manner of top secret information. Hell, they provide security in foreign countries for some high-ranking diplomats and politicians. This sleeper could go after anyone. Why you?"

"I don't know."

"That's what we need to figure out. While Chelsea and Adam chase their tails, I'm going to study you. You're the answer. You're the one who leads us to the sleeper. This is about you. We have to figure out why they want you dead."

"Has anyone else like me died recently? You know, a soldier held prisoner?"

"No. I checked that first. I'm also looking at Ten's group for the likeliest suspects. Ten swears he's the only one who knew that number, but unlike our paranoid boss, Ten's lazy. He had the phone transferred in from the head office. There's a record of it in the system. Chelsea did find that."

"Then it could be anyone."

"No. Phoebe's name and location are only on a NOC list. If someone's got hold of that, we're in for a lot more trouble."

NOC stood for non-official cover. It was the way the Agency kept up with who was where and what name they were going under. It was highly classified. "So you think they found out through some other means?"

"Again, Ten's been a little comfy. He calls her once a week and they've met three times in the last year. He could have been followed any of those times. Someone put it together and decided that she was the easiest way to get rid of you." Li settled his beer on the counter. "The question becomes why not just take you out himself. The answer—because he's got eyes on him. Because he's got a team around him that might ask questions. That tells me whoever is pulling the strings doesn't want to lose his puppet, but he was willing to take the chance."

"And when he decides to sacrifice his pawn, he'll do something desperate. He'll come after me himself."

"I wouldn't worry too much about that. You're safe here. It's more secure than a prison, and someone is always watching. Also, I've been informed your girl doesn't intend to let you die. Kai will be back tomorrow, too. I think he looks like a hippie surfer, but Ian swears he's deadly."

Jesse had kind of hoped he could avoid Kai altogether. Kai had been his therapist for months and he liked the man, but Kai was not going to take his decision to leave at the end of this well. Jesse could practically hear the lecture. "Let's hope he doesn't have anything to worry about. I doubt the sleeper is going to invade Sanctum the way Ten did. I'm probably stuck here for a while. At least Big Tag springs for cable."

Li slapped him on the shoulder. "Don't worry. We'll figure this out. Now the question is what do we do about your problem?"

"I thought we just talked about that."

"I was referring to getting Phoebe to come out of her hidey-hole so you can play with her. Tell me you don't want to play with the girl. Or have you been playing privately?"

Jesse snorted and thought about having another piña colada. Two was the set limit at Sanctum if a Dom or sub wanted to play, but Jesse rarely had more than one. Maybe he should just be honest with himself and acknowledge the fact that he didn't want to play if he couldn't play with her. "No. The only games we've played are board games, and I'm pretty sure she cheats. Can you cheat at Jenga?"

Li grinned, the smile making him look younger than normal. "I bet she could find a way. The Agency likes their operatives to be wily ones." He sobered slightly. "So why isn't she really down here? Are you not getting on now that she doesn't cry at the drop of a hat?"

"She didn't cry that much and we're getting along all right." When he really thought about it, the last several days had been peaceful. He'd enjoyed her company, and she'd actually talked to him. The night before they'd had something called osso buco, and she'd drank some of the wine Sean had brought and Jesse had enjoyed a beer. They'd sat in front of the fire in Kai's living room and talked about where they grew up. Jesse had told her about Wyoming and she'd talked about horse country in Virginia. She'd even talked a bit about her husband and some of the trouble they'd gotten into as teens. "I like her."

"I could tell. You know, I'm glad my wife understood why I did what I did. We wouldn't be together if she'd taken a hard line against men who met her under false pretenses. Unlike Chelsea, who curses the poor woman's very name, I understand the position Phoebe was in. Yes, she lied, but it was her job. All I'm saying is if you want the girl, get her. Don't be afraid the rest of us are going to think poorly of you or that we won't accept her. I guarantee this will be nothing but a tale to tell your kiddos one day. Go upstairs and coax her down. She'll see it's not so bad."

He wanted her. His need to seduce and dump her had lasted an entire night. When he'd woken up next to her that first morning, she'd been curled up against him and all of his badassed revenge had gone up in smoke. That was who he was. He was surrounded by men who understood what vengeance meant, but he was a puppy begging for affection. He was exactly what the Caliph had called him. A dog. Dumb. Loyal when he shouldn't be. He shook his head. "No, she's fine where she is. She's nervous about the BDSM stuff. We went over the contract and I explained how things work in the dungeon, but she decided it wasn't for her. She's going to read or something."

"Little chicken," Li said, taking another beer from the bartender. "If there was ever a woman who needed some dominance, it's that one. Scared of her own shadow. She could use some discipline."

"She was only pretending to be skittish, Li."

"Perhaps, but I think it's interesting that she chose that persona to hide behind. You know as well as I do that it's best to stick close to your own self when going undercover. She decided to be the girl everyone worried about, the girl all the other women tried to protect. That says something about her."

He hadn't thought of it that way. "She was raised in foster care until she was a teen."

"There you go. That makes sense then. She spent her whole life taking care of herself. She chose to be a person who needed to be protected. Do you understand?"

Jesse shook his head. "I don't understand a damn thing about her."

"Well, that's because she's a woman. I love my Avery, but I rarely understand why she does the things she does. I only know that I'll do anything at all to make sure she keeps doing them. That woman's a mystery to me and I won't ever finish solving her."

Phoebe was completely a mystery. So was his reaction to her. Not one single dream. He'd slept better than he ever had. He didn't even wake up when she rolled out of bed. It was incomprehensible to him.

Li looked up, his eyes widening slightly. "Well, it looks like you were wrong about her."

Jesse followed his line of sight and his jaw damn near dropped.

Phoebe walked into the bar wearing the clothes he'd put out for her earlier that day. He'd laid them out with very little hope that he'd see her in them. A scarlet corset sat over a tiny spandex miniskirt that revealed far more than it covered. He'd left out the fishnet hose that had come with the outfit because he would rather see her legs. Her feet were bare, showing off the way her toes were painted a hot pink.

"Hi." She stepped up to the bar. "Can I have one or is that something just for the Doms?"

Li eased off his barstool. "I'll leave you two. Phoebe, you look lovely."

She frowned. "Really?"

"Really. Welcome to Sanctum. Jesse, don't let that one get too far away. Every unattached Dom in the place will be after her." Li nodded toward the dungeon. "Big Tag is here with Charlotte. He's doing some kind of exhibition where he spins around floggers like a bloody baton twirler. What's the world coming to?"

Jesse sort of, kind of realized Li was walking away. His whole focus was on the woman in front of him. "You can have a drink. I suggest one before and one after."

"After?" She tugged at her skirt as she tried to get on the barstool. "Does this have to be so short?"

"If you don't like it I could exchange it for a thong." He thought he'd been pretty damn kind to give her a sort of skirt.

"That's worse." She cursed under her breath.

He slid off his barstool, picked her up, and set her down. "There. Better?"

She wiggled a little, obviously trying to find some modesty. She finally settled on crossing her legs and looked as prim and proper as a woman in a corset could. "Not really. You couldn't have given me some undies?"

His cock jumped at the thought that she was sitting right beside him and her pretty pussy was just a twist of that skirt away. "Nope. But the fact that you didn't try to sneak any makes me think you're already better at this than most of the other subs when they started."

She straightened up. "I can follow orders when I think they're reasonable. Or when I think I can't possibly get around them. I thought about putting on some of my own underwear and then calculated the chances of getting away with it. They weren't good. Someone would have noticed and according to that contract, you would have the right to spank me."

"You liked it when I spanked you."

"I...I...well, I was caught off guard and I don't know how I felt about it. Seriously, can I get a drink?"

She could have stayed upstairs. There was still a bottle of wine left over. She wasn't down here to drink. She was down here because she was curious.

He caught Mike's attention. "Can I get the lady a piña colada?"

She shook her head. "I would prefer a vodka tonic."

He frowned. "Really?"

"Sweetie, you might be able to drink those three thousand calorie drinks all day long and still look like a Greek god, but I can't."

Mike started making her drink but it bugged Jesse. "You're beautiful, Phoebe. You don't have to change a thing."

Her hand slid over his. "I know you feel that way. It's one of the things I actually really like about the men at the office. Not a one of you has a thing for stick-thin women. But I have to stay in shape. However, if you want to tell me I'm pretty again, I won't hold it against you."

"You're gorgeous, baby." He took a long sip of his drink. "Why are you here?"

She accepted her drink with a polite "thank you" before turning back to Jesse. "I'm curious. I shouldn't be. If you asked a few months ago what I thought of this lifestyle, I would have said it was abusive."

"That's because you were ignorant about it."

"There is that," she conceded. "I was also afraid of it. I thought there was one way to love and be loved and I'd found it. My husband was very gentle with me, very protective. I couldn't quite get the two ideas to mesh in my head."

"What changed your mind?"

"I don't know that it has. Not the intolerance part. I get that it's not abusive. It's a form of communication in the end. It's a way for partners to state what they want in an environment that won't judge them. I don't hate that. I just don't understand why you can't just make love. Why does there have to be all the other stuff involved?"

At least they were talking about it now. Before, she would always change the subject, and he'd gotten the idea that she would never be interested and any sex life they had would be vanilla. He could have handled it, but they could be so much more. "I know what you're saying. I kind of thought the same things when I hired on and Big Tag insisted I come to Sanctum. I didn't get why I had to wear a set of leathers and spank some chick in order to be on his team."

"And I would be surprised if you handled it well. How could you accept some woman calling you Master after what you went through?"

It was a reasonable question, though he winced a little at her tone. Patience. He hadn't understood at first either. "It's just a word, Phoebe. It has the power we give it. That's what I learned from here. I learned that whatever happens between two consenting adults isn't wrong. I still won't do any blood play or knife play. That bothers me, but that's okay, too. Sanctum is a place where I can just be me and no one judges me. They accept me. Big Tag brings us all here because this place, this life, binds us together. It makes us a family."

He could have sworn he saw a sheen of tears in her eyes before she covered them with a shake of her head and a bright smile. "Okay. I can understand the beauty of that. So what do we do, Sir?"

That got his motor running triple time. "Phoebe, you understand there doesn't have to be anything sexual about play, right?"

"I understand the theory behind it. It can be about exploration and relaxation. Most club encounters don't end in sexual intercourse. Although Simon tried to make me think yours do."

"I have never had sex with a submissive at this club."

"Why?"

"Because they weren't mine. Because my heart was engaged somewhere else."

Her eyes closed briefly as if she was in pain. When she opened them again, she put a hand over his. "Jesse, I don't know what I can offer you. I know I would like to try this thing with you. I know I enjoyed that moment in your office before you were a complete douchebag and ruined everything."

Well, at least she called it like she saw it. "I'll try not to be a douchebag again."

"I'm still leaving at the end of this assignment. I have to get back to my real life."

He wasn't sure why her real life had to be thousands of miles away from him, but he didn't want to argue with her tonight. She was here. She was bending. He wasn't going to make her break. "Then we should set the parameters. You've given me yours; I'll give you mine. Just for the night. Anything else, we discuss as it comes up, but you have to talk to me, Phoebe. This doesn't work in any way if you think I can read your mind."

"It's hard to talk about," she admitted. "My husband and I were very young. We just kind of went with the flow, if you know what I mean."

"I take this seriously. I take you seriously, and that means I can't go with the flow. The flow often leads to misunderstandings, and I don't want that. Tonight, I'm in charge. You're going to obey me or we go upstairs and we play games for the rest of the night. I'm willing to be patient with you."

"I don't know that we have time for patience." She shook her head. "I've thought about this for days. I want to explore this with you. I read the contract. I'm actually quite good at following orders. I also understand that I should have a safe word."

He could make that easy on her. "Tonight your safe word is no. You tell me to stop and I do. You see something that flips a trigger and we sit down and talk about it. I'm in charge, but my main goal is to see that you're safe and happy. That's all I want for you. It's all I've ever wanted for you."

Her hand found his again. It seemed easier for her every time she took it. "You're a good man, Jesse Murdoch."

"I'm glad you think so. I know I'm not as strong as the other guys."

"What? That's ridiculous. You are the strongest man I've met and I won't hear anything else. And that's a…what do you call it…a hard limit for me. I think you're wonderful and I won't hear you say anything differently." She bit her bottom lip and her eyes narrowed. "Hey, do I get to spank you when you talk bad about yourself?"

"I am a really good man. Strong. I'm so strong." A light happiness filled him. Doms could learn things, too.

She finished her drink and slid off the barstool, holding out her hand. "Show me around?"

He pushed his glass away and entangled his hand in hers. "Sure."

He wanted to show her everything. If they had so little time, he was going to make the most of it.

* * * *

The only time her hands stopped shaking were when they were in Jesse's. Phoebe stood close to him and watched as Jacob Dean used a paddle on his wife's backside. She gasped with every smack, but there was no way to miss how Serena's skin flushed and her eyes dilated in what looked like pure pleasure.

Adam Miles stood to the side, watching indulgently. There was a plush robe in his hands, ready for Serena when she was through with her scene.

Jesse stepped aside, allowing a woman to move through the crowd. It put him behind her. She couldn't see him. Just as she was about to turn and move to be close to him again, his arm wrapped around her from behind, pulling her against his body.

Safe. She was safe again. She let her head rest back on his chest.

The last several days had been a mixture of heaven and hell. Heaven was waking up to find herself in his arms, snuggled close and warm. Hell was realizing that her brain hadn't even tried to fool her. She'd known it was Jesse who held her so close. Years of dreaming of Jamie, of holding on to that moment right as she woke up when she could fool herself that he was still with her, that her nightly visits with him were real, and a couple of days close to Jesse had erased them.

Guilt seemed to be her best friend. Grief had taken that role for so long that the guilt was almost a welcome change. Grief gave her no reprieve. Guilt would flee for a while. It gave her moments where she forgot to feel bad. She'd spent whole days with Jesse, cooking and talking and playing games, and it would only hit her at certain moments. She would be laughing and getting close to him because her body seemed magnetized when he was around. She would find herself reaching for him or turning her face up to his, their mouths so close together. That was when guilt came back with a vengeance.

"Do you see how careful he is with her?" Jesse whispered, his breath warm against her ear. "It sounds like he's really giving it to her hard, but he's actually going easy on her. He spreads out the smacks, giving her time to rest before he goes at it again. It's all about sensitizing her skin, flooding her system with arousal."

His voice was getting her aroused. He'd been explaining scenes to her, but not in an academic way. Jesse talked about feelings and what the Dom was trying to achieve. They'd watched several scenes and Jesse had explained how the implements of "torture" were really there for the submissive's pleasure.

The one time he'd spanked her, she'd had the orgasm of a lifetime shortly afterward. Could she shove her guilt aside long enough to try again? This time it wouldn't end in the building being invaded. This time she would make sure Jesse got something out of it, too.

She just wasn't sure what. She'd never taken the lead when it came to sex. She'd just been happy to please Jamie and get a little something in return. Jamie's arms around her had seemed like the best thing in the world, the only feeling she needed out of sex.

Damn but she wanted that fire Jesse had introduced her to. She craved it, and being close to the man who had given it to her had just made things worse. She might have been able to forget it if he wasn't always there, always tempting her by taking his shirt off and smiling that insanely gorgeous smile of his.

"Ah, I think they're done," Jesse whispered. "They'll be in a privacy room before you can blink."

Sure enough, Adam was right there, wrapping the robe around his wife's body and lifting her into his arms. Jake grabbed his kit, shoving the paddle inside, and then he was racing after them, the eager look on his face making Phoebe tear up.

They were alive. They were in love. God, she missed that.

"You had enough? We could go back to the bar," Jesse offered, moving to her side again now that the scene was over.

She wasn't ready to go back. If they went back to the bar, the evening would be over and they would eventually go upstairs and turn off the lights and she would lie there wishing for something she shouldn't, feeling alone and guilty.

"Can we watch Ian?" The big guy seemed to be getting something ready. He'd walked up on stage and started moving equipment around. Charlotte stepped up on stage with him. She looked surprisingly innocent in her modified fet wear. She wore a long skirt, but her breasts were covered with a leather bra. Her belly was on full display and her hand seemed drawn to it. She was always resting her hand there as though she found it soothing to make the connection. She smiled brightly at her husband, who frowned her way.

"Sure. He's doing a demo tonight," Jesse explained. "Though it looks like he won't be using his wife. This is what we like to call an extra scene. It's one the Dom didn't really see coming."

She loved how open and happy he looked. He was smiling and relaxed, like he'd been before her secret had come out, except there was really nothing between them, no wall of untruth to hold her back. Just that guilt creeping back in the happier she felt.

"What do you mean you're not using me?" Charlotte Taggart's words rang through the dungeon.

"I already told you I'm using another sub, one who isn't pregnant with my child."

"Don't be ridiculous. I'm fine, Ian. The baby is fine."

He turned back to his wife. "I told you I won't risk you going back into the hospital."

"The doctor said the possibility of that is very low."

"The doctor can bite my ass." He leaned over and Phoebe could only barely hear him. "The doctor has never had to mourn you, Charlie. So no. This is simply an exhibition. I took a class and I would like to practice and see if anyone else wants to learn how to do this. If they do, I'll bring in an instructor. There is nothing intimate or personal about this scene. However, if your jealousy is so great you can't allow me to even perform an exhibition on another person, I'll skip the scene."

She had to admit that Taggart had the intimidation thing down. She wasn't sure what she would do if she were in Charlotte Taggart's shoes. Charlotte merely rolled her eyes. "You are such a drama llama. Fine. But I get to pick your partner."

"Drama llama?" Taggart's jaw had dropped a little. "You do know I'm more like an elephant. I never fucking forget. The minute that boy is born, your ass is mine. I've got a list of punishments that will make your head spin."

"I'll look forward to it and she's a girl." She winked Taggart's way and turned to the crowd. Phoebe nearly shrank back when she realized where Charlotte's eyes had fixed. "Phoebe, I think my husband would feel infinitely better if he got to beat on you for a while."

She shook her head and started to turn to walk right back upstairs. "Nope."

"Chicken."

Phoebe stopped and turned, staring at Charlotte and trying to judge if she was serious. "That is the most immature thing I've ever heard come out of your mouth."

"Oh, then you haven't been listening to her very long. Give her time. It gets way worse." Taggart stood on the stage, his eyes lit with mirth. He did have the most bent sense of humor.

"Chicken shit," Charlotte continued. "That's actually what I meant to say. You're a little chicken shit, Phoebe Graham. Or is it Grant?"

Taggart nodded. "See, there it is."

"Do you really think calling me names is going to work on me?" Anger started to build in her system. She hated the bullying crap.

Charlotte stepped off the stage, moving carefully down the stairs. Phoebe was well aware that every eye in the dungeon was on them.

"Maybe we should go back to our room," Jesse offered, looking between Phoebe and Charlotte.

"Maybe we should have this out here and now." She wasn't backing down from some pregnant chick. "You know it's really unfair of you to pull this shit while you're pregnant and I can't show you just how chicken I'm not."

Charlotte grinned as she approached. "That's the best part of being pregnant. I can say anything I like and no one gets to punch me. As to why I'm being such a bitch, that's easy. I'm doing that for you."

"Well, don't let me forget to send you a fucking thank you note."

"If I don't push you, you're going to end up going back upstairs and you won't have tried a damn thing. Jesse won't push you. He's too sweet, but I think you need a little shove because I think you'll enjoy it."

"Shouldn't that be my call?"

141

Charlotte's head shook. "Absolutely not because you're a chicken."

This was the most immature argument she'd ever been in, and she couldn't seem to force her way out. "I am not. You know I spent time in a Chinese prison. It wasn't exactly the Ritz and I've got the scars to prove it. I'm not some wilting flower."

"Then you can handle one little flogging," Charlotte shot back. "They're not even stingy floggers. Are those deerskin, babe?"

Taggart held up a set of floggers. "Yes, two perfectly matching floggers. Same weight, same material. Deerskin. They're soft and produce a nice thud."

Floggers. Those were big old floggers and Ian Taggart would be wielding them. "I'll do it with Jesse."

"Uh, I'm not qualified to do Florentine," Jesse said. "It's two floggers working in time. If you do it right, you pretty much create a circle-eight pattern. It's really cool to watch, but you have to be careful to stay on the big muscles, the shoulders, butt. You don't want to hit the wrong place or you could damage the sub's kidneys. I would have to practice on Darla for a couple of weeks before I would be willing to do it."

"Who's Darla?" She'd figured out that Sanctum was full of gorgeous, submissive women and they all seemed to want her man…well, they all seemed to want Jesse.

It was annoying.

Jesse's hand found hers, squeezing gently. "She's a life-size doll. We use her to practice on."

She still didn't like Darla. And she definitely didn't like the idea of being at Taggart's mercy.

Jesse let go of her hand. "It's all right. We'll go to the bar and have another drink or we can just call it a night."

Damn Charlotte Taggart and her manipulations. "No. I'll do it. Does my safe word work on him?"

"In this setting it does." Sometimes when Taggart smiled he looked like a shark getting ready to go into feeding-frenzy mode. Unfortunately, this was one of those times.

"It's just no for tonight, Tag," Jesse explained.

"That's no fun. I thought she would pick expellifucktis or something," Tag replied.

"It's expelliarmus," she corrected. "And actually that's a good one. I really wouldn't be thinking that in the middle of this and it is a disarming spell that forces your opponent to drop whatever they're holding, so it works."

Now she sounded like a nerd.

"Is that Harry Potter stuff?" Jesse asked.

Yep, she was a super nerd. "Yes and I think Ian would make a good Voldemort."

"He was a pussy." Taggart gestured to the play area. "Now if Hermione here would please take the stage, we can get started. Jesse, tie her to the middle cross, please."

"Cross?" Phoebe hesitated.

Jesse pointed to the back of the stage where there was a wooden *X* on the wall. There were leather cuffs on the top and bottom of the *X*, obviously where her hands and feet would go.

It struck her suddenly that she would be all alone up there. She would be stripped down and vulnerable and at the mercy of a man who likely had none.

Was this their version of revenge? Was this how they got back at her for lying to them? She stared at that cross and hated Phoebe Graham in that moment. This vulnerability wasn't her. She was strong. She'd built up walls over her lifetime that were so strong almost no one could get through them.

Until Jamie died and she found out that all the shit that came before was nothing compared to how hollowed out grief could leave a person.

The old Phoebe would have shoved everyone the finger and then told them to go to hell because she wouldn't have cared about them. This stupid weak Phoebe didn't want to be laughed at, didn't want to find out what they really thought of her.

"I don't want to be tied up." She would be helpless. She couldn't be helpless.

Taggart looked down at her, his face as soft as it ever got. "I'm not going to hurt you. I promise you that. Like I told you, all my rage is far better expended on your brother."

She shook her head. "I can't stand the thought of being tied up. This isn't right for me."

"Phoebe, this is about learning to trust," Ian explained. "You wouldn't be the first sub who couldn't stand the thought of being tied down and vulnerable, but you'll also never know what it means to utterly trust a partner so much that he could do anything and you would know it would be all right."

"I can't."

"All right." Tag gave up. "I'll get someone else. I can't flog her with her just standing there. There's too much risk that she would move at the wrong time."

"Let me be her cross," Jesse said suddenly. He stepped forward. "She can hold on to me, lean on me. That way I can tell if she's handling it all right."

Taggart seemed to think about it for a moment. "She can use her safe word at any moment, but she's got to be still until I stop."

"I won't move."

Taggart nodded and gestured for Jesse to join him in setting up the scene. Phoebe was left watching them, wondering if she was making the right choice.

If Jesse was with her, she could try it. It would be better to know than not. If they made fun of her, or if Taggart decided to hurt her for kicks, then she would know that he was the same as all the other assholes she'd met. She didn't think so, but then she'd only seen how he treated the people he loved. How would he treat her?

People liked to hurt other people. That was what life had taught her. Her childhood had been one long succession of adults who failed her. She'd watched her foster brothers and sisters damn near kill each other over as little as an extra soda. Only Ten and Jamie and their dad had ever offered her refuge, and then they'd sent her off to fight a war no one even knew was raging.

"Just hold on to Jesse." Charlotte was suddenly at her side. "I promise it won't hurt. It's like a really nice massage. Try to let your mind drift. Hear the rhythm of the floggers moving and let go. Jesse will catch you. He won't let anything happen to you."

Phoebe turned to Charlotte. "I thought you were hoping to watch me squirm."

"Only in a good way. Phoebe, if I hadn't challenged you, you would have stayed out there in the audience all night. You needed a push and I gave it to you. Trust me, I know how to deal with stubborn women who need a swift kick in the ass from time to time. I'm Chelsea's sister after all." She got serious for a moment. "I think you need this every bit as much as she did. Women like you, like us, we need to be able to let go from time to time. We need to know we have a safe place."

"I had one once."

"I know and you can have another one." Charlotte reached up and smoothed back her hair, a gesture that made Phoebe wish she'd had an older sister.

"Why are you being nice to me?" It didn't really make sense when she thought about it.

"Because you're my friend."

"I lied to you."

"Oh, honey, we all do things we probably shouldn't. We do them for our jobs. We do them to survive. We do them because we love someone. When the chips were down, you picked him and that's all I need to know. I hope that you're smart enough to pick yourself when the chips are down the next time."

"What does that mean?"

"It means that I think walking away from Jesse would be an act of sacrifice you don't need to make. When you have to decide between him and your job, between him and your first husband— and somewhere in your slightly fucked-up head that's happening— choose what will make you happy. Choose a future, not the past. Choose us because guess what, we come with him in all our glory and that includes a head of the family who likes to flog people. I also chose you because you won't use this time to try to get my husband to cheat on me." She turned suddenly, pointing a finger at a blonde girl who shrank back. "That's right. I'm talking about you. I hear everything and I will murder you if you touch him." When she turned back to Phoebe, she had a hand on her belly, rubbing it thoughtfully. "After the baby. I'm not actually allowed to murder anyone while I'm pregnant." She leaned in. "And that girl back there didn't actually touch him. She just mentioned to someone that Ian was probably sexually frustrated because his wife is a whale and she offered to take care of him."

"I'm not pregnant. I could murder her." She hated mean girls. Loathed them. It was one of the great things about the McKay-

Taggart women. They supported each other. They were kind to each other even though they could be deeply sarcastic about it.

"See, you fit right in now." Charlotte nodded toward the stage. "They're ready. And don't worry about Ian. He'll take care of you. You don't know it yet, but you are one of us."

It was a sweet thought, but she certainly hadn't earned it. She stepped up to the stairs, deeply aware of the crowd around her. She turned to her right and there was a woman in a corset smiling at her with encouragement. She was a bigger girl, very likely considered overweight in the outside world, but here she was beautiful. Here, she was accepted.

It suddenly occurred to her that Ian Taggart hadn't liked the outside world very much. They were alike in that thinking. But while she'd simply put up walls to keep it out, Ian had done something about it. He'd created his own world and invited people in. He'd built a place where he felt comfortable and in doing so made others comfortable with themselves.

He'd built something lovely.

Jesse stood at the edge of the stage, his hand out to help her up. God, she loved how big his hands were, how callused they were. His hands were solid. They were hands that had worked, hands that protected. She slid hers into his and immediately felt stronger. "Think about this for a moment, Phoebe. You know he can't flog you in that corset."

Naked. She would have to be naked from the waist up, of course, though no one had to see her except Jesse. She turned and looked at the crowd. They weren't all gorgeous. Many were normal and yet there was such beauty in their acceptance of themselves and others. "Can you help me out of it? I had to find Avery to help cinch me in."

Now Avery was watching from the sidelines with Li. She gave Phoebe a thumbs-up.

Even with Ten and Jamie, she'd been a little apart because she was the only woman. They could love her, but they would never understand what it meant to be her. Charlotte and Avery understood, and that somehow made it easy to decide to shed her armor. And hey, the corset hadn't covered much anyway.

Jesse's lips quirked up in a crazy, sexy smile. "Really?"

A confidence like she'd never felt before poured through her. "Yeah, really."

He would like her. He would praise her and it would be okay.

"Come here." His voice went deep, his stance suddenly very straight and proud. It made his shoulders even wider, his chest and abs stand out. Not that they needed much help. He was wearing nothing over them but a leather vest that seemed to showcase just how often the boy worked out. His muscles were perfectly cut and she suddenly had the deepest desire to touch them. "You belong to me tonight. In this place and for this one night, you're mine."

Just one night. Just one place. It was unreal, like a few hours that would only really exist in a dream. She could be his for a little while. For a few moments, she could find that safe place Charlotte had talked about. It wouldn't be a betrayal of James. It was just a momentary vacation from reality. "Yes."

He pulled her close and his hands went to the back of her corset. "Ian, could you give me a knife?"

Before she knew what was happening, she felt pressure as the corset pulled tight and then blessed relief as it completely let go. She hadn't realized how tight it had been, how hard it was to breathe. Oh, and she definitely hadn't known how good the cool air would feel on her skin. Jesse pulled the corset apart and her spine tingled with the delicious chill.

But only for a moment because the chill was replaced with the heat of those big hands rubbing over her body. As soon as Jesse handed the corset and knife to Ian, he immediately ran his hands down the line of her spine. His head turned down, his eyes going right to her breasts.

Her nipples perked up and no matter what Charlotte had said about this scene being impersonal, she was wrong. Taggart might be wielding the flogger, but this scene was really about her and Jesse, and there was nothing impersonal about that. He'd never seen her breasts before, but she couldn't hide them again when he was so obviously enjoying the view. His eyes were hot on her skin and he pulled on her hips, bringing her into contact with his lower body.

Yes. He liked her breasts quite a bit. His erection pressed against her belly. The few times that had happened, he'd shied away, but not this time. This time he looked right at her, confidence evident in the way he held himself. "Yeah, that's for you. That's what you do to me."

Desire was a drug thrumming through her system, making the whole world seem softer than it had before, slightly unreal. She didn't argue when he gently turned her, his hands going to her hips as he displayed her to the crowd.

Crap. She was an exhibitionist. There was no way to fool herself. She was hot and bothered and it was mostly about the fact that Jesse's hands were on her, but she had to admit, she liked being half naked in front of the crowd. She should be shrinking back, covering up.

Why? Why should she? Because someone told her she should? Charlotte was right. This place was safe.

"I have a beautiful sub, Master Ian," Jesse said. "I like showing her off."

"She is lovely, Master Jesse." Ian Taggart was looking at her breasts, but with an almost clinical detachment. "You're a lucky man. Now let's see if we can get her to relax."

He turned and began showing off the floggers he held, explaining what they were made of and how important it was that they be properly matched and weighted for Florentine flogging. Jesse led her back to the cross as Taggart continued his lecture. She heard his voice but her focus was on Jesse's hands, his body, as he shrugged out of his vest and all she could see was his beautifully muscled chest. He placed his back toward the cross and spread his legs wide, boots solid against the floor.

"Stand on my feet. It will put you in the proper position."

"I'm heavy." It would seem odd to be so close to him, almost dependent on him.

"None of that. I don't want to have to stop the scene and spank you."

He would do just that. She could see that this was a different Jesse, and she found him fascinating. She stepped up, placing her bare feet on top of his boots. His hands found her waist, balancing her. It was easy to let her chest rest against his. Her breasts against his chest, her legs rubbing the leather pants that covered his body. Warmth immediately suffused her and her skin felt alive. She turned her face and allowed herself to really study him for the first time. She'd pushed him away too many times because she thought she should. Now she took in the planes of his face, the way his jaw squared. His lips were sensual, big and so kissable she wanted to run her tongue across them. His blond hair was too short. If he was hers, she'd get him to grow it out so it was thick and wavy and she could sink her fingers into it. Blue eyes stared down at her, so serious.

"Relax. I'll be able to feel your reactions. I'll be watching you."

He would take care of her. She wouldn't be alone for a moment.

She laid her head against his shoulder.

A sexy beat began, spilling from the speakers that dotted the club. She heard Ian explain that it was helpful to keep a beat.

"He's going to start now. He's going to be easy at first."

She couldn't help it. She tensed up, but Jesse was right there, whispering in her ear. "It's all right. It's going to be good. You can stop at any moment."

But it occurred to her that she'd been stopping far too often. She'd been screaming a safe word at the universe for years, and she wasn't safer or happier for it. She was just lonely and afraid.

She had a choice and she chose to lay her head back down, to trust Jesse and the very man who should hate her. She had to trust Taggart or go back to her room and cling to her side of the bed because she was too guilty and afraid to lie in Jesse's arms.

The first *thud* hit her shoulder, a little whisper across her skin. It was followed by a twin caress on her opposite side. It wasn't bad. It was nice, a brushing of soft falls over her flesh.

She opened her senses, allowing touch and sound to rule. So often she lived only in her head, ignoring her body like it was secondary and somewhat useless in comparison. She chose intellect over everything else, but now she allowed herself to simply feel, to hear without questioning.

Thud. Thud. Thud. Like a train running endlessly down the tracks. Not in a hurry. No particular destination, traveling to simply travel.

Thud. Thud. Thud. Like the horse she'd learn to ride on, big hooves eating the distance, joy in the freedom of riding.

Thud. Thud. Thud. Though she was still, she felt as if she was moving, the insistent *thud* of the flogger taking her someplace she'd never been before.

Taggart kept pace with the music, his flogger moving in time to the rhythm. Over and over he struck with loving precision, bringing her skin alive. He struck her shoulders, her butt, the tops of her thighs. She could feel the almost circular pattern he was making, but after a moment, she took a breath and stopped thinking about the academics of the situation. She let out the air and felt her muscles relaxing even as the strikes got harder.

No pain. There was no pain from his flogger, just a hard *thud*, striking her and forcing the tension to flee.

She felt loose, like her muscles were melting in the most pleasant way. There was heat and pleasure at her back, but Jesse was at her front. She was surrounded and she gave in, allowing herself to sink into the sensation of being wrapped in tactile pleasure.

"I can feel you," Jesse whispered against her ear. "I felt the moment you gave over. Do you know how beautiful you are?"

She didn't answer him. It wasn't really a question. He continued to murmur in her ear, his words somehow matching the floggers beat. They drugged her further, taking her to a place where there wasn't a lonely future, no tragic past. There was only the now, and it was full of possibility. She didn't have to be Phoebe Grant, grieving widow. She was just a woman, relaxed and submissive in the arms of her lover.

She wanted to be his lover. Even if it was only for a night.

The thought whispered along her brain. She could steal a few days. She didn't have to be alone. No one had to know.

"She subs out fast."

"I think she needed that."

They were talking, Taggart and Jesse, and she realized that the wonderful thudding had stopped. "It's already over?"

Taggart chuckled. "That was a good fifteen minutes. I think it's enough for your first time."

How had it been so long? If she'd been asked, she would have said she'd been held by Jesse for a fraction of the time.

"I think she needs some aftercare, my brother," Taggart said as Jesse lifted her up.

It was a good thing because her knees were distinctly weak. Her whole body felt loose and her head sweetly befuddled.

How had she gotten high off some dude flogging her?

"Because you're a sub." Jesse grinned down at her as he started to move off the stage.

Had she said that out loud? She felt small in his arms, small and protected. It was so easy to cuddle down and allow him to take over. She let her eyes drift closed, but she wasn't about to fall into sleep. She wanted something more. She wanted a memory of him.

"I think we can handle the aftercare upstairs." He reached the back stairs that led to the second floor and their private quarters. "Do you want me to draw you a bath or do you just want me to tuck you into bed?"

"I want you to make love to me."

He stopped in the middle of the stairs. "What?"

"Make love to me."

He stared for a moment and then he picked up the pace, practically running to get to their room.

No matter what happened, she would have her night with him. She would have one memory of the man she shouldn't love.

CHAPTER NINE

Jesse hurried down the hallway. From downstairs, music thudded up softly, but he was no longer tempted to go back to the club. He'd thought he would settle Phoebe in and then go back down for one last beer, but there was no way he wasn't honoring her request.

He'd had some hope that she would let him rub her feet and talk about how the scene had made her feel. He'd never imagined that her aftercare request would involve actual sex.

Should it?

He kicked open the door and made his way to the bed. She was a soft bundle in his arms. He would have been content to simply hold her. She was warm and half naked, and he would likely never forget that moment when he'd slid the corset off her and saw her breasts for the first time. They were perfect. Round and just enough to fill his hands. He'd loved the way her nipples had felt against his chest, the way she'd leaned into him when she gave over.

It had been the single most intimate moment of his life and he didn't want it to end. No matter what he told himself, he wanted more with her, and not in some dumbass, dump-her-afterward way so he could feel better about himself. That had been a momentary insanity. Now that he was alone in the room with her and her skin glowed like a pearl, he was willing to admit he would take any time he could get with this woman. He would take anything she offered him and be grateful for the time they had.

He would do just about anything to keep her.

He gently laid her down on the bed and then turned on the nightstand light. He couldn't do this in the dark. He needed to see her. When he dragged the skirt off her hips, she didn't fight him. She just looked up as he tossed it aside.

Her chest moved as she stretched out on the bed, a tired smile on her face. "I liked that, Jesse. I didn't think I would."

He'd known what she needed. He'd known it for months, but she'd seemed so standoffish. Would things be different if he'd taken charge? It didn't matter now. He was in charge of this. She'd told him to make love to her and she still had a safe word in place. "I'm going to kiss you now, Phoebe."

She nodded up at him, eyes suddenly going serious. "I want you to kiss me. I've thought about it for a very long time. Kissing you in your office wasn't enough."

He'd thought about it since the moment he'd laid eyes on her. Too much time had passed, and now he had to be careful he didn't simply devour her whole. He had to make this good for her. He had to make her crave this the way he craved her.

He sat down on the bed beside her, his hand covering her breast. When he ran his thumb over the hardened nipple, she gasped and her back bowed, pressing her breast up into his hand. "You're so fucking beautiful. They were all watching you. They were all thinking about how beautiful you were."

Yeah, he hadn't missed the way she'd responded to being shown off. He'd felt a shudder go through her when he'd turned her around. At first he'd been worried it had been from distaste, but then she'd leaned against him and her body had gone languid.

"I can't believe I did that."

"You liked it. Do you think you would like me to really show you off? That was just a little taste. I could properly show off my gorgeous sub."

"How would you do that?"

"I would show them your breasts." He cupped the other one, pressing them up so the nipples were aligned and just above his thumbs. "Look at how beautiful these breasts are. They belong to me. I'm the man who gets to play with them. See these pretty nipples? It's my tongue that drags across them, my teeth that nip at them, my mouth that sucks on them."

He moved his hand up to her chin. "Such a pretty face, and look at that mouth." He dragged his thumb across her plump bottom lip. "That mouth was made to kiss, and it was definitely made to fuck. I'm the Dom who gets to shove my cock into this lovely mouth. My cock gets loved on by these lips and that tongue."

She looked up at him, her eyes flaring just before she swiped her tongue along his thumb. The sensation seemed to go straight to his cock. It pulsed and threatened to break through his leathers in an attempt to get to her, but he was going to prove beyond a shadow of a doubt that he was in control.

"We'll get to that later. Don't you want to know what else I'll show off when I get you naked on a stage again? What else do you think I'll touch and show everyone? What else will they want to see?"

Her face flushed and she moved a little restlessly under his hands. His words were getting to her. She might have thought she was vanilla before, but he was going to show her just how much fun being dirty could be. "My pussy. You'll show off my pussy."

There was his eager puppy cock once more trying to have its way. He loved the breathless way she said pussy and yes, she had properly answered his question so she deserved a treat. He trailed his hand down her torso, past the valley of her breasts and over her softly curved belly. His eyes took in every inch of her gorgeous skin, illuminated by the low light. She practically glowed for him. Her breath hitched as his fingers brushed over the mound of her pussy.

"Spread your legs. They want to see you." He could role-play. He'd never actually done it before, but it was kind of fun to pretend. "They want to look at this pretty pussy and dream that they get to touch it. They don't. I'm the only one. Spread your legs wide so they get a good view of just how fucking creamy and wet you are."

It was true. He was going to lose his damn mind over her scent and the silky feel of her skin. He stared right at it and blessed the day he walked into Sanctum. Sex had been something to do under the covers, with the lights out and as unoffensively as possible before he'd gotten into the lifestyle. Some people could have active, fully satisfying sex lives without play, but he'd found he wasn't one of them. He needed this, and he loved the freedom of not hiding what he wanted to do. He wanted to stare at her pussy, to study it. So that was what he was going to do.

"So pretty." He slid a finger, parting her labia. "Do you always shave? Your skin is so damn soft. Like silk."

"I did it today. I took a shower before I decided to go down and look for Avery. I knew if I went downstairs you wouldn't let me wear panties, and I didn't want to look like Sasquatch if someone caught sight of my cootch," she said on a shaky laugh. "It was pretty much a seventies disco down there."

It didn't look like one now. She'd done an incredible job. She was bare and smooth and ripe. Pearly fluid coated her labia. Arousal pulsed from inside her. He slid his fingers all around, carefully exploring that soft, feminine part of her. He breathed in the scent of her.

She was ready. He could shove his cock inside right then and there would be no barrier. He could take her and she would welcome him, but he needed more. He had no idea how much time they had. There was a conference in the morning, and the outcome could be the two of them released back into their lives. She would go one way and he the other. He wasn't going to have his only memory of her being a quickie.

Long and slow. Thoughtful sex. That was what he owed her. He also owed her that kissing he'd promised. He leaned over and let his mouth hover above hers, suspended in the potential. "Do you know how long I've waited to kiss you like this? There's no one outside the door. There's no one who's going to interrupt us. I can just kiss you for as long as I want."

"Months," she whispered back, her hand going up to his hair. She smoothed her fingers over it. Her eyes were steady on his. "I don't count your office as our first kiss. You were being an asshole.

So make this one count. I've waited months. Months and months of waiting."

He was glad she was willing to forgive him for that debacle in his office, but she was wrong about that timing. "Forever. I've waited forever."

He let his lips touch hers and heat spiked through his system like a live wire sparking. He molded his mouth to hers, tasting her for the first time. She filled his senses, became the center of everything in that moment. She was the sun, warming him, making him feel alive and male and so good that he wondered why he'd waited.

Her fingers sank into his hair and he knew. He'd waited on this Phoebe. He'd waited because the real woman was so much more than the façade. This woman had all the passion, all the affection he'd sensed in the construct. She'd hidden behind a mask, but there was no hiding now.

When her mouth flowered open and her tongue glided against his, he nearly lost it. He wrapped his arms around her and pulled her to his chest, nestling their bodies together. His tongue surged inside, a marauder who wanted to take everything she had to give and then demand more because she was it for him.

He'd never wanted a woman the way he wanted this one. How could he even have fooled himself for a second that he would be satisfied with a night? He wanted a lifetime with her. She was the prize he got for surviving. All the horrible shit he'd been through fell away the minute she walked in a room.

"I want to touch you," she whispered against his lips. "I want to see you."

It would kill him, but he was determined to give her what she wanted.

He forced himself to stand up. He'd left his vest downstairs and he would very likely get an unholy lecture on cleaning up his shit from Ian, but he'd been too eager to be alone with her. He was still wearing his pants and boots. As quickly as he could, he toed out of his boots and worked the laces on his leathers. Phoebe sat up, pushing back her hair. Even though she was naked, she looked oddly innocent to him, sitting there and staring at him like a child about to receive a gift she hadn't thought she would get.

"I think you're beautiful, too."

He shoved his pants off, kicking them to the side. "I've got a lot of scars."

She ran her hands over the place where the IED had nearly opened his gut. The scar was jagged because he'd been stitched up by someone who'd only wanted him alive in order to torture him. They hadn't thought a lot about how pretty his abs would look.

He fought a shiver as she brushed her fingers there.

"We've all got scars. It proves we did our jobs. Did you like it? Showing me off? Did it do something for you?" She asked the question in a halting tone, her skin flushing like she was nervous to hear the answer.

Did she think he would judge her? "It got me so hot, baby. I loved it. I loved everyone seeing how beautiful my sub was. It made me feel good, worthy."

"You are so worthy, Jesse." Her hand went lower and her eyes drifted down. "Did I say you were beautiful? You're gorgeous."

He'd never had a woman praise his cock before. Yeah, that did something for him. "Touch me."

Her right hand came up and she grasped him. "Like that? How do you like it?"

He put his hand over hers and tightened. "Hard. Grip me hard. I want to feel it."

She nodded and then followed his lead, pumping him up and down. "Would you ever do more than show a sub off?"

So good. It felt so fucking good. He could already feel his balls tightening. It had been a long time. *Concentrate, Murdoch.* She'd asked a question that was really more like a land mine waiting to go off. He wasn't completely dumb. "I've never shown a sub off before. I've played, but I've never displayed my beautiful sub because I never had one until tonight. But if you're asking me what else I would like to do to you in public, that's easy to answer."

Her lips curled up in the sauciest grin. "Alright. I'll bite. What else would you do?"

Oh, so many things. He looked down and watched as she pumped his cock. "I didn't even get to show off your ass. You have a spectacular ass."

"I'm glad you like it." She leaned over and he had to stop

himself from shouting out when she licked the head of his dick.

Fuck. He wasn't going to last if she kept it up, but he couldn't seem to find the will to stop her either. "I would spread you out and show you off and then I would take you. I would let them watch as you take my cock. You'll take it because it belongs to you, because your pussy is where it needs to be. You'll wrap your legs around me and you'll shout out. You won't be quiet when I fuck you. You'll give them a show. You'll let them know just how good it feels to be fucked by me and I will make sure you scream. Don't even think you can hold out on me. I won't let it happen. I'll fuck you so long and so hard, you'll give me everything I want. Suck me, Phoebe. I want your mouth on me."

He watched as she leaned forward and her lips wrapped around his cock. He let his hands sink into the soft silk of her hair and stared as she sucked on his cockhead. He let his instincts drive him, allowed his hips to move, to force her to take more. Her tongue dragged over his skin, making his spine nearly curl in pleasure. So hot. Her mouth was hot and tight. Perfect.

He shoved another inch in and she took it, her tongue swirling around his stalk. Her hand worked the base. She gripped him hard and gave him the slightest edge of her teeth. He couldn't take another second or he would come right down her throat, and that wasn't how their first time was going to go.

He pulled away and she looked up at him, her mouth a gorgeous red. "What's wrong?"

"Nothing, but it's my turn. It's my turn to put my mouth on you. It's my turn to taste you. Lie back and spread your legs again." His cock was throbbing, but he was determined to make this night last.

* * * *

Phoebe didn't think. She simply reacted to the command in Jesse's voice. She let her body sag down, allowed herself to sink into the softness of the comforter at her back. Her brain was fuzzy with desire and she was riding the wave.

Strong hands gripped her ankles and pulled her to the edge of the bed. She looked down the length of her body at him. He was spectacular. Tall and lean, every inch of him perfectly muscled. She loved how strong he was. And she couldn't take her eyes off his cock. It stood out slightly from his body. She could still taste him on her tongue. Salty but clean. The feel of his skin was burned in her brain.

He pulled her legs apart, exposing her again. He'd stared at her before. It had been odd, but she'd loved how desire had lit his eyes as he looked at her pussy, how his hand had moved toward her as though magnetized to her.

Now it wasn't his hand that moved to her. He dropped to his knees in front of her and then his mouth hovered right over her pussy. His breath heated her, making her flush again with arousal. Every time she thought she couldn't get more turned on, he did something else that threatened to blow her mind.

She watched, unable to take her eyes off him. She watched as he lowered his head to her pussy, covering her with his mouth.

Pleasure coursed through her. She couldn't help but gasp and try to move. His tongue was soft against her flesh, sending tingly bliss all through her system.

"Don't move." Jesse's command rumbled along her flesh. "Stay still or I'll have to spank you and then we'll start again. This is my time and I will have it. And if you think I wouldn't do this in front of a crowd, you're wrong. I would eat this pussy in front of them and let them know you taste as sweet as honey."

She couldn't help it. Just thinking about it did something for her. She held herself still as he devoured her. His tongue traveled the length of her female flesh, delving inside and then licking its way back to torture her clit with slow caresses.

Over and over again he stroked her with his tongue, leaving no part of her unloved. His fingers parted her labia gently, giving himself access to her core. She felt one finger slip inside her, finding a rhythm and rotating while he tongued her clit.

It was torture to lie there. She wanted to move, to fight him for her pleasure. She wanted to force him to give her more. More of his talented tongue, more of his lips and teeth and fingers. More Jesse. She wanted all of him and she wasn't sure she could settle for less.

But he'd earned her submission. He'd been patient and kind and he'd taken her to places she'd never been before. So she fisted her hands in the silky comforter and let him pleasure her at his slow, decadent pace.

"I want you to come for me. I want you to come all over my tongue."

He gave her a second finger as he drew her clit into his mouth and sucked hard.

Phoebe couldn't hold out. Sensation swamped her, dimming her sight as he took her over the edge. She cried out his name as her body was suffused with pleasure.

Before she could come down from the crazy high he'd taken her to, he was up on his feet. In the hazy aftermath, she watched as he rolled a condom over that beautiful cock of his. Alarm bells went off in her head, but they were a distant thing. What was more relevant was the fact that she wanted to give this man everything he'd given to her.

She made no protests when he moved her up the bed and made a place for himself between her legs.

"You're so fucking gorgeous when you come. Let's see if I can make you do it again." He pressed his cock in.

She was sure if she hadn't been so well pleasured from before, it would have been difficult to take him. He was so big. He was bigger than...

He pressed in until there was no room, until there was nothing between them.

"Oh, Phoebe, you feel so good. Do you know what you do to me?" He gave her his weight and she was deliciously crushed. So unlike...

He kissed her, making all thoughts flee as he held himself hard inside her. His tongue glided against hers. She relaxed again and allowed her hands to find his back. Jesse pulled out slowly. Inch by inch she could feel him moving. He dragged his cock out almost to the end and then pushed back inside.

He picked up the pace and she matched him. This was what she'd been waiting for. She slammed her hips up. He stared down at her, his gorgeous face tight with desire.

"Give it to me," he growled. "I like the way it feels. I like your little claws in my back."

She hadn't even realized she was sinking her nails in, but it seemed right to do it. This was a struggle, a sweet struggle. She held on to him as he fucked her hard. He wasn't polite or gentle about it. He pounded into her and her whole body and soul responded. This fight was what had been missing before. She wasn't something sweet and gentle. She was his equal. She was his mate and she could prove it.

His hips twisted, grinding down on her clit just as he stroked deep inside. Phoebe went right over the edge again, crying out and calling his name this time.

Jesse's body tightened and he held himself still, his chest hitching as he dragged air in. He relaxed finally and rolled to his side. He reached out and put a hand on her belly. "I'm crazy about you, Phoebe. I could love you if you let me. This could be good between us. You don't have to go back to Virginia."

The words sank in. Virginia. Home. Where she and Jamie lived, except Jamie wasn't alive anymore.

She'd just slept with a man who wasn't her husband. Shame flashed through her system. She sat up. "I need a minute."

"Phoebe?"

She didn't look back. She ran to the bathroom and shut the door, her insides turning. She'd made love to someone who wasn't Jamie. They were supposed to be forever. She'd taken vows. She'd made promises.

She closed her eyes. She did it all the time. She closed her eyes and summoned up a picture of Jamie in her head, except she couldn't quite see him this time.

She'd given herself to another man and then thought about how much better the sex was. How could she do that? How could she even think it?

She looked at herself in the mirror and didn't recognize the woman staring back. She wasn't the controlled and contained woman she'd become under Franklin Grant's tutelage. She wasn't Jamie's wife. This was Jesse's lover, his sub.

She wasn't ready. She couldn't let go.

Tears rolled and she let herself slide to the floor, feeling further from both of them than she could have imagined.

161

CHAPTER TEN

Jesse couldn't even look at her. It hurt too much. He knew the minute she walked in the conference room. It was like his body had an active radar where she was concerned. How long would it take before he couldn't feel her under him? Before he couldn't taste her on his tongue? He feared he might die remembering what it felt like to make love to Phoebe Grant.

And he remembered what it felt like to hear her crying in the bathroom, a locked door between them.

Despite his promise to Ian, he'd slept in Kai's room the night before, ceding the guest room to Phoebe so she wouldn't spend all night in the bathroom.

He hadn't seen her all morning. She hadn't come to the kitchen for coffee or breakfast. He'd knocked on her door when Tag texted him to come to the conference room and he'd been told she'd meet him there.

It was like nothing had happened between them at all.

"Tell me you have something." He was careful not to look her way. If she was crying again, he wouldn't be able to take it. Listening to her cry the night before and not being able to do anything about it had made him feel like a criminal, like he'd stolen something from her when all he'd wanted to do was give.

She was still in love with her husband. Last night had proven there was no place in her heart for him.

Big Tag sat back, his eyes going between them like he was trying to figure something out. Ten watched him, too. He had the sudden urge to walk out before they both knew just how much he'd fucked up. "We don't have as much as we wish we did, but I think we're getting closer."

"We need to get this thing done. I can't keep the team here in Dallas for much longer," Ten admitted. "I don't want to take this team out into the field unless I'm sure we're solid. We're supposed to be in Dubai in a week for some energy conference. We're gathering intel on some of the new players."

Tag nodded. "Yeah, we're running security for one of the smaller countries attending. Jesse's supposed to go, but I think I'll have to send Alex instead."

They were working for the king of a small country named Loa Mali. Big Tag had met Kashmir Kamdar when he'd worked an op in India. The country was putting an enormous amount of their money and workforce into sustainable energy. Though they were small, the king still required a security detail, and he'd offered McKay-Taggart the job fully knowing they would also have their own mission while there.

"You can't do that," Jesse argued. "He just had a kid."

Tag's eyes flared. "Well, they've all just had kids. I swear this team breeds faster than horny rabbits. I promised Kash I would send at least four of us. Erin and Simon and Li are going. I need one more. I can't send Adam. I need him here solving this problem. So I'm down to Alex or Jake. Jake is a whiny bitch about out of country assignments since Princess Serena gifted the world with his son. Alex just met his little poop machine. How attached could he be?"

"God, I love you, Tag. You make me look sensitive," Ten shot back.

Tag and Ten started in on each other and Jesse wondered how much more he could seriously fuck up. He was supposed to be on that detail. He'd been prepping for the assignment for a month.

He'd been looking over the profiles Adam sent him and memorizing the power players. Though he was mainly there as muscle, Tag wanted the team to investigate some of the CEOs of the energy corporations for possible Collective ties. The shadowy group had been quiet since losing their head bad dude a couple of months back, but Jesse had no doubt they would come back with guns blazing at some point.

"So what exactly have you found out?" Phoebe asked and he finally looked at her. She was clean, neat as a pin. Her hair had been pulled back in a severe bun. She looked nothing like the woman who had screamed in his arms the night before. Contrary to his fears, she didn't look vulnerable at all. She looked hard, focused. This was the CIA operative.

"Chelsea found that someone used several of the Agency assigned cells to call a number in Turkey. It's never a long conversation. Not really a conversation at all. It's more like ten to twenty seconds and then the call is disconnected, but Chelsea assures me there was a connection," Ten explained.

"Why not use a burner?" Jesse couldn't understand why this person would risk getting caught when he could easily use a burner phone.

"When we're on assignment, they're not allowed to have anything non-Agency assigned with them. No ID, no equipment, and definitely no personal cell phones. Their packs are checked before they get on the plane. These calls occurred while they were on one particular mission."

"Whose phone was used? That's simple." Phoebe set down her coffee mug.

Ten shook his head. "No, it's not. It's four different phones. They belonged to Malone, Boomer, Deke, and Ace. None of them have relations in Turkey. The operation in question wasn't in Turkey and had no ties to Turkey. We were in Southeast Asia."

Turkey was considered to be the gateway to the Middle East and the jumping off point for radicalized Muslims joining the jihad from the west.

"The calls all happened in a two-day period. Nothing suspicious before or after," Ten explained.

"Someone's desperate," Tag said under his breath.

"Then we're looking for an inciting incident. This person has been careful up until now. Something spooked him," Phoebe pointed out.

"Or his employer." Ten sat back in his chair, his eyes serious.

Li's words played around in Jesse's head. He'd said he thought that this was about him.

You're the answer. You're the one who leads us to the sleeper. This is about you. We have to figure out why they want you dead.

He had to find the answer. He needed to stop thinking about his nonexistent love life and concentrate on getting them out of this situation. He had to think about what the real question was, and he had two men in front of him who might give him the answer.

"Why me? Like what are logical reasons someone would want to take me out?" Jesse mused out loud.

"It could be personal," Tag replied. "But it doesn't feel that way to me. Instinct tells me it's bigger than that. Besides, why would someone on Ten's team have something personal against you?"

He could only think of one incident. "I clocked Boomer after he and Malone shoved Si and me in that shed."

Ten shook his head. "Everyone's clocked Boomer at one point in time. That boy's had more concussions than a quarterback. He's not the type to get pissed about something like that. Now you take his Cheetos and he turns into the Hulk. That boy is all about his gut."

"I don't think this is personal," Phoebe said, sounding deeply professional. "If this guy really is a sleeper, then he wouldn't risk his position on a personal grudge. This was expertly set up. I was the one who screwed everything up. If I hadn't been made, no one would have been the wiser."

"So if this is a professional hit, it's got to be about stopping you from doing something." Tag tapped his pen against the desk. "The only op you're scheduled for right now is the one in Dubai, but you're one of four agents. So why you?"

"It could have been a message to you, Tag," Ten offered. "We just never got the message because he didn't actually die."

They started arguing, but Jesse tuned them out. This wasn't about Tag. It wasn't about the team. It was about him.

"What are you thinking?" Phoebe asked, leaning toward him.

"That this is about me. I just can't figure out why."

"Taggart's right. If this is about you then it's about stopping you from doing something." She frowned as Ten and Tag continued to argue. "Or it's about something you know that you shouldn't."

A bitter laugh came from his mouth. "Yeah, well, we all know I don't know much."

"Jesse…" She turned again, facing him, and her face had flushed. "You didn't do anything wrong last night. That was all about me."

God, he'd heard this speech before and he didn't want to hear it from her. He nodded when he thought he should, but he didn't really hear her as she started to explain how she wasn't ready and it wasn't a good time. Yadda, yadda, yadda.

It all came back to *I don't want you, Jesse.*

He knew that. He knew what it felt like to be rejected. If this was about what he knew, rejection was high on the list. Other things he knew—how to be tortured and nearly turned into a mindless slave. He knew the sound of pure evil. Yeah, that was a good one. He knew what the devil looked like.

In the end, there was really only one thing vitally important that he knew and no one else did. Him. The man in his nightmares.

"I know him." The truth hit him square in the chest. "I know *him.*"

Phoebe stopped her obviously prepared speech. "Who?"

Even Ten and Tag were now paying attention.

"The Caliph. That's what he called himself. I've seen him, heard him. I'm about to go back to the Middle East. One of the things you had to do for the conference was send in the names of all security personnel. We're required to go through checks, too. Kamdar had to submit our names in order to bring us as his security detail. What date would he have done that on?"

"Grace did it." Tag was suddenly on his laptop, his hands working the keys in a staccato rhythm. After a few seconds he reached for one of Ten's notes and groaned. "Shit. She did it the day before the phone calls. She submitted those names and that is what led to the phone calls. He couldn't be careful anymore. It was too important."

"He has to have taken or borrowed those phones. I can't believe I've got four traitors." Ten had gone a little pale.

"Why would this man care if you were at a conference?" Phoebe asked. "Obviously I understand that he wouldn't want to be recognized, but why would he be there in the first place? Shouldn't he be running his little army somewhere?"

"He was an educated man. Highly educated. In that part of the world, it means he's wealthy. He spoke English with a British accent." He wracked his brain for everything he could think of about the Caliph. It was hard because a lot of the time he'd spent with the man had been in a drug-induced haze. "He talked about Oxford."

"So he's very wealthy." Ten sighed and restacked his papers. "And that means oil in the Middle East."

"Shit. The last thing he wants is to be outed as a jihadist at this thing. This conference is for moderates only," Tag explained. "One of the things they're supposed to discuss is how to deal with resources falling into the hands of radicals and how to protect their companies from it happening. Jesse, I think you're on to something."

He shrugged. "It was really Li's idea. He thought it was about something I knew."

"Dude, take a compliment. You sound like a girl who doesn't want to be told she's pretty more than a thousand times. You were smart. Not going to say it again." Tag's words came out of his mouth with the efficiency of a machine gun.

"I didn't know you said it the first time," Jesse muttered under his breath. Somehow, in telling him he was smart, Jesse still managed to feel dumb. But Tag was right. He was on to something. And he had another theory. "What if I wasn't the Caliph's first? Deke told me you have a couple of people on your team who were captives at one time or another. Who was gone the longest?"

Ten opened his laptop. "Ace and Deke were both gone for a couple of months, Ace slightly longer. Boomer was held for a week before he managed to escape. He made a sling shot, if you can believe it. Fucker took down three men with rocks, escaped, and then almost got his ass caught again because he got lost in the center of Kabul. Some friendlies took him in and hid him until his unit managed to pick him up. I don't think this is Boomer."

"No," Jesse agreed. Boomer was too open, but the other two were candidates. "It makes sense if we run with the idea that the Caliph doesn't want me to potentially identify him, it would be his man who would make a move to take me out. What if I was a failed experiment? That doesn't mean others didn't succeed."

Ten ran a hand through his hair and his jaw tightened. "I can't believe it."

Jesse shouldn't have expected different. He wasn't intelligence. He was just a dude with a gun and protective instincts. "All right. What do you think?"

Ten glared his way. "I think you're right and I don't want to believe it. Are you always so literal?" He slammed the top of his laptop into place. "I'm sorry. I'm struggling with the fact that I have a traitor in my midst and I haven't seen it. He could have hurt my men. I take them seriously. That team is my responsibility and I fucked up because I'm missing something. I didn't see something."

"You see the mask he wants you to see." A chill went through Jesse's system. How did he make them understand? "I know what he was trying to do with me. He was trying to break me down. To utterly strip me of everything that made me Jesse Murdoch. He would tell me that what I thought was me was really just a mask. The real me was underneath and must be hidden to everyone but my brothers. He was our father, the one who made us see the truth."

"Who were your brothers?" Tag asked, his voice deep.

"I don't know. I didn't meet them. He promised me a family if I just gave over to him. If I could drop the false persona forced on me by the superficial Western devils, I could find my real family. It all sounded more reasonable when there was heroin in my system. Now it sounds like a load of bullshit, but with the heroin it really does make sense."

"Don't joke about it," Phoebe said, sounding emotional for the first time.

"Why not? When you think about it, it's kind of funny." They'd tried to train him like a dog. Called him a dog.

"Gallows humor," Tag said with a faint smile. "Chicks don't understand it. I could have told the fucker your skull's too thick to shove that shit through. He knew how to get to you, though. He knew what buttons to push."

"Yeah, like you did."

If Tag was offended, he didn't show it. "It was obvious you wanted a place to belong. I simply gave it to you."

And he would be forever grateful. "You gave me a family, Tag."

"Yeah, which is why no matter what happens, your ass is not going back to Wyoming. So what would we look for? You're the expert here, Murdoch. We're going to follow your lead."

Ten nodded in agreement. "I'll open my files. See what you think. There are psych assessments in there. I'm using my authority to give you eyes only clearance. Do you understand?"

"Don't talk about anything I read in those files. Got it." He was surprised that Ten would offer to let him look at the files. "The last thing I expected to get was top secret clearance."

Ten stared at him for a moment before speaking. "I was wrong about you. I was angry with you about…"

Phoebe slapped her hand against the desk. "Tennessee!"

"No. I'm telling him because you won't. Damn it, Phoebe. This is not some secret to hoard. You think you can bring him back if you don't tell anyone? You think you can make all this less real if we don't talk about it? I'm your brother and I was his brother, and I am not going to keep quiet anymore. I'm not going to hide and pretend like it didn't happen."

"I can't believe you would do this." She stood and after a second, stalked out of the room.

What the hell was that about? "Does this have something to do with her husband?"

"It has to do with Jamie and you deserve to know the truth. You deserve to know why I hated you for so long."

"Do you hate me now?" He hadn't liked the look on Phoebe's face as she'd left the room. It had been a punch in the gut. Whatever Ten was going to tell him meant the world to her.

Ten shook his head. "I was irrational. You're not the man I thought you were."

He wanted to know. It was an ache in his gut. The truth was right there. He would know why the Agency had it in for him. And knowing would hurt her. She didn't belong to him. She didn't want to. It was all right to choose himself over her. It was logical. He couldn't do it.

"Don't say another word, please. If me being in the dark brings her peace, then I don't need to know."

"You have the right."

"Does it affect this operation? Will me not knowing potentially hurt someone?"

Ten shook his head. "No."

"Then let it lie. It's enough to know this bad blood between us can be over." He looked at the door where Phoebe had disappeared. "You should go talk to her. Tell her I didn't want to know. I don't want her to feel bad."

"What happened between the two of you?" Ten asked, standing up. "I know it's none of my business, but it's obvious something went wrong. She wasn't comfortable with you and she always is."

"It just didn't work out." God he ached, but he'd learned not to let it show.

"She hurt you," Ten said.

"How do you know I didn't hurt her?"

"Because I've come to know you and you wouldn't hurt her to save yourself. Damn it. She might not understand it, but you're good for her. She needs you."

Jesse shook his head. "She doesn't. She needs him. She loves him. There's no place for me."

"I'm sorry, Jesse. She's going to regret it in the end. I'll go talk to her." He reached into a briefcase and pulled out the files. "I was going to have you look at them even before you figured it out. You're a good operative, Murdoch. I would be proud to have you on my team."

"You would be dead because you're not poaching anyone else," Tag swore.

Ten gave him a little salute. "I'll remember that. Go over those files with Murdoch for me."

"Does that mean I've got my clearance back?" Tag asked.

"You never lost it," Ten admitted. "I never took you off. I always hoped we could work something out. Now I hope I can make my sister see reason. I always was an optimist."

Ten closed the door behind him.

"You okay?" Tag asked as he divided up the files

He was hollowed out. He was empty. "I'm good."

"That's what I like about you, Murdoch." Tag handed him half the files and they got to work. "No matter what, you say you're good. Just know we're here for you. All of us. If you need to talk, I got Alex on speed dial."

That was his boss. The good thing was, he wasn't much of a talker so he and Big Tag could get along. "I'd rather you just got me a beer."

Tag slapped him on the shoulder. "You're my favorite. I'll be right back. We're getting this solved, Jesse. And if you want my two cents, she's an idiot. I'll get us both a beer and we can figure out which one of these boys is a crazy asshole who we're going to take out a little rage on."

He stepped out of the room and Jesse stared at the door. He was damn glad that he still had his family. He was glad he'd done his job and he didn't need to leave.

But the most important door had closed, too, and he was fairly certain Phoebe wouldn't open it again.

* * * *

Phoebe couldn't breathe. She tried to but then she would think about the fact that there was no way Jesse didn't hate her now. He would loathe her. The only man alive she'd made love with and he was going to hate her because Ten had decided he wasn't the enemy.

She knew he wasn't the enemy. She'd known it for a long time, but that didn't mean he had to know everything. God, she couldn't be with him. She knew that now. She'd wrecked him the night before and she hadn't meant to. The last thing she wanted to do was hurt Jesse more than she had. She'd made every mistake she could with him. She didn't even deserve a chance to apologize, though she'd hoped to try.

What would she apologize about? She would have to pick from a long list. *I'm sorry I lied about my identity. I'm sorry I planted bugs in your apartment and let my brother spy on you. I'm sorry I ruined last night.*

I'm sorry I'm the one who came up with the plan that ruined your life, killed my husband, and still tortures you to this day.

He would be right to hate her.

She felt like she was twelve again and being kicked out of yet another home. She could still hear the voices of the bad foster parents telling her there was something wrong with her, that she ruined everything. All these years later and she could still hear them when she couldn't even remember the names of the ones who had been kind to her. There had been several. Men and women who had helped but for one reason or another, she'd had to leave those homes, too.

"Phoebe!"

She picked up the pace, not wanting to deal with Ten. She flew up the stairs. He didn't understand. Ten didn't love anyone. Not really. Oh, she knew he loved her as much as Ten could possibly love someone. Ten was funny and fierce and so guarded. She knew he would kill or die for her, but why couldn't he keep one damn secret?

She managed to get to her bedroom. To the room where she'd made love with Jesse. She wasn't about to fool herself. It hadn't been sex, and that made it so much worse. It had been the best night of her life and just for a moment, she hadn't been able to remember what Jamie looked like. It had been just a second, but Jesse had clouded her vision, her heart, to the point that Jamie had been lost again, and she couldn't allow that to happen. If she lost Jamie, he would really be gone forever.

She started to shut the door but a cowboy boot got in the way.

"Hey, I need to talk to you."

"Go away." She pushed on the door.

Ten proved he was stronger. He simply pushed back and the door came open. "Are we pretending to be obnoxious teenagers again? What the hell was that scene downstairs?"

Nope. He wouldn't understand. She loved her brother but he had all the sensitivity of a rhinoceros. He was wrong about Tag making him look good. "I would like you to leave."

He closed the door behind him. "Phoebe, what the hell is going on with you?"

"I don't want to talk about it. I just want a new assignment."
She had to deal with the fact that not only was Ten her brother, he
was her boss. He controlled the only part of her life that held any
meaning now. "I would really like to go back to Virginia."

His face went stony. "No."

"No? What do you mean no?" He couldn't just say no.

"I mean I'm not sending you back to Virginia. You would be
right back where you started. You would sit in that house and you
would mourn him and let your life waste away. I will not be a party
to that."

She could concede on that point, but she had another plan
ready. "Fine. Send me back to Asia. I'm sure you need someone
over there with my skills."

"Where you can waste your life pretending to be someone
else?" Ten stepped into the room, his eyes going straight to the bed.
There was no way he could miss the rumpled sheets or the damn
condom wrapper on the nightstand. Why hadn't she gotten rid of
that? She'd been running late this morning and she hadn't cleaned
up anything but herself. Ten picked up the wrapper, holding it up.
"Goddamn it, Phoebe."

Shit. She didn't need his judgment. "That's none of your
business."

"Everything you do is my business."

Embarrassment flashed through her system. When had Ten
started acting more like her dad than her brother? "Ten, it didn't
mean anything. It was a mistake."

He shook his head and tossed the wrapper in the trash. "Yeah,
that's what I thought you'd say. And that's exactly why I won't put
you back into active duty."

"What do you mean? Are you that angry that I cheated on
Jamie."

"You can't cheat on Jamie." Ten's hands fisted at his sides.
"Jamie is dead. Jamie is buried and he ain't coming back. I'm
benching you because you want to join him, because you are
actively seeking to kill yourself and I won't be a part of it. I won't.
I will not bury another sibling."

She couldn't blame him for thinking that way, but he had to
see that she needed to work. "I'm not being reckless, Ten."

He started to pace, a sure sign that he was upset. "No? You're being stupid if you really think sleeping with a man who obviously adores you is a mistake. You should have been purring in his lap this morning, but you barely looked at him. I knew something was wrong with the two of you. I thought you'd had a fight, but that isn't what happened. You didn't fight. You fucked and then you felt guilty. What did you do? Throw him out?"

"No. I locked myself in the bathroom. When I came out, he'd moved into the other room." She could still hear him promising not to bother her, swearing he wouldn't touch her again if she would just stop crying. He'd said he couldn't stand to hear her cry.

"You are being a fool. That boy would do anything for you."

Tears clouded her eyes. "He's wonderful, but I can't. I'm not ready."

"And you'll never be ready because you refuse to let go." He took a deep breath and stepped toward her. "You have to know he wouldn't want this for you. Jamie wouldn't want you to go through this. He would want you to be happy."

"Then he shouldn't have died." The old bitterness welled up. Sometimes she just ached for him but she also had moments when she hated the universe and everything in it for being alive when he was dead.

She'd forgotten the ache and pain while she'd been in Jesse's arms. For just a second, she'd been alive again and the world held potential.

"If you had been the one to die, would you want him to go on without you? Would you want him to ache for the rest of his life?"

Why couldn't he understand? "I loved him. How can you want me to forget him?"

"Because you have a life to live. Because you'll have more years without him than you ever had with him and you have to move on. You can't live every one of those years in mourning. I miss him, too. I have to move on or I'll go crazy. Don't you remember all the things you wanted out of life? You wanted to be a mom."

"I wanted to have Jamie's baby."

Ten stopped in front of her. "That is no longer an option and it's such a fucking shame because I think you would have been a great mom. I know this sounds so stupid, but I wanted that family, too. I wanted you and Jamie to breed like rabbits and get out of the service. I wanted you two in that big house Dad left us, raising babies and horses and having a good life. When I used to think about why I do what I do, it was always so you and Jamie could be happy and safe and so that I could go to your place for Thanksgiving and be weird Uncle Ten who likes to hold babies and play catch with the kids."

The sweetness of the vision pierced her, making her ache all over again. "I wanted that, too. I never meant to be a lifer. Plans change."

"But they didn't and that's what's killing me now. Yes, Jamie died and we will mourn him forever, but we have to move on. I don't know what I believe in—God, the universe, whatever—but I do know that you are being given a second chance and you're too stubborn to take it. You will never find another man like the one you just walked out on."

She wasn't about to argue with him about Jesse. "He's so good. I care about Jesse, but you have to know that you just wrecked everything. Any chance we had of being friends is gone. He can't forgive me for what I did. I came up with the plan that sent him into hell. I did that. I've been lying to him. He didn't know Jamie was with him."

"He still doesn't know."

"What?"

"He wouldn't let me tell him. He said if it hurt you for him to know, then he didn't need to know." Ten sighed and sat on the edge of the bed, looking wearier than she'd ever seen him. "I've gone over every possible scenario in my head. He's too good to be true. I've even thought about the fact that if someone wanted to send in a sleeper, it would be interesting to send in one no one else trusts. Hide him in plain sight. Jesse would be perfect. You could train him to know what to say, how to act, how to look vulnerable enough that someone like Taggart would want to protect him, train him, give him access. Like I just gave him access to top secret files."

"I can't believe you gave him clearance." She knew he was trustworthy. It just wasn't like Ten to change his mind.

Ten nodded slowly. "There comes a time when you have to put the past aside, put paranoia and experience aside and go with your gut. Sometimes things aren't what they seem, but every now and then they're exactly what they look like. I viewed him through the eyes of an operative and a man who lost his brother and was looking for someone, anyone to blame for it. But it changed when I did one thing."

"What was that?"

"I decided to look at him through your eyes. And I made a decision. I will trust him. I would trust him with you and therefore I'll trust him with my life, too, and the lives of every person in this country. He won't let us down."

"He doesn't know?" A little hope lit inside her. Why, she wasn't sure. She just knew she didn't want him to hate her. Even if he never spoke to her again, she didn't want him to curse her name and wish he'd never met her.

"He wouldn't let me tell him."

"We can't let him die." She didn't want to even think about a world where he wasn't alive and vibrant and so sweet it hurt to look at him.

Sometimes he wasn't so sweet. Sometimes he was in control, demanding. Yes, she'd liked that Jesse, too.

She turned and looked out the window. In the distance, she could see the McKay-Taggart building. She probably wouldn't be going back there. She wouldn't see all those kids again.

"Why are you doing this? Why are you pushing him away?" Ten asked.

"Because I can still feel Jamie. It's like he's still here with me." She could feel his arms around her, sense him close. It had almost gone away, but if she concentrated hard enough, she just knew she could get it back.

"If he is, it's because you won't let him go. I don't know what happens when we die, but I know Jamie wouldn't want you to hold him here. And he probably couldn't leave until he knew you were safe. You're safe with Murdoch. Let him rest, Phoebe."

It wasn't the only reason she couldn't be with Jesse. "Do you think some people are just cursed? Like nothing can really go right for them."

She heard him moving and then his arms came around her. For so long the only people she had any kind of affectionate contact with had been Jamie and Ten.

"I think some people are too stubborn to see what's right in front of them. My mother dumped me in a trash bin. She meant for me to die. I should have died. From what I understand, I was dead when they did find me. It was just luck, you know. Some bum was poking around, looking for food. He found me and I was blue. Most bums would have run to get help or maybe just run. Not this one. No, he was a former Army medic down on his luck. He held me in his arms and did CPR. He brought me back and wrapped me in his coat and walked two miles to the police station. How random is it that a fucking former Army medic just happened to fall on hard times and just happened to pick that trash bin at exactly the right time? You know how Franklin found me?"

When she thought about how close Ten had come to not existing, to being nothing more than a baby no one wanted, her heart clenched. She covered his hands with hers. "I thought you won a sharp-shooting contest."

"Hell, I didn't have the money to enter a damn thing. I had a foster dad who taught me how to shoot. He was a good man. I was with him for a long time before he got cancer and had to let me go. I snuck in. I stole one of the entrant's badges. I don't even really know why I did except I wanted to remember what it felt like to be with him. They figured out I hadn't paid after I won and they were calling the cops on me."

"And that's when Franklin showed up, right?"

"Nah, that's when Jamie distracted them long enough for me to run." Ten laughed. "I ran right into Dad. I remember him looking down at me and saying a boy who could shoot like that didn't have to run from anything. Two days later, I was living with him, going to a prep school. It seemed random, coincidental. Maybe it was. Maybe it could have gone another way, but it didn't and that's how I found my family. I just can't accept after everything we went through that none of us gets to be happy. You have a shot with Murdoch. Jamie would want you to take it."

"I was happy. I was happy when it was you and me and Jamie, and accepting anything less seems wrong." But it wasn't less, she realized suddenly. What she had with Jesse wasn't less. It was different. It was special. "I could love him. I just can't let myself. I would be living a lie. How would Jesse feel if he woke up one day and realized I had lied to him about my part in his capture?"

"You made a command decision. I honestly think he'll understand. What he won't understand is why you didn't trust him enough to tell him." His arms tightened around her. "I'm leaving you here, sister, and that's an order. When Murdoch goes to Dubai, you're going with him."

"And after the op is over?"

"I'll tackle that problem when it comes, but you should know I won't be able to send you back to Virginia alone. If you make that choice, then I'll go, too."

"You're already based in Virginia."

"No, Phoebe. If you go back, I'll quit the Agency. I'll do it because my main job in life will be to watch over you, to protect you—even from yourself." She felt him lay a brotherly kiss on her cheek before letting go. "Hell, maybe we can open a brother/sister detective agency. That oughta be good for a laugh. You think about what I said. I'm going to help Tag and Murdoch, and by help I mean I'm going to help myself to their Scotch because it's already been an excruciatingly long day."

She heard him step away and the door closed. She looked out into the distance. After a long moment she closed her eyes and tried to bring up that picture of Jamie that was always right there.

All she could see was Jesse. She feared she'd traded one ghost for another because Jesse seemed as far from her as Jamie was.

CHAPTER ELEVEN

Jesse stared at the files in front of him. He'd been staring for so damn long the words were starting to blend together. It felt like he'd been looking at them for hours. He glanced up at the clock. Yeah. It had been hours. Hours and he still wasn't any closer.

Every man on Ten's team was remarkable in some way. Ace could fly anything with wings. Boomer was a sniper of extraordinary talent. Deke had forgotten more about explosives than most people knew. Hutch was a hacker to rival Adam and Chelsea, while Bear was a mechanical genius. Michael Malone had an IQ off the charts, and the two younger Taggarts were already taking after their older brothers and showing great leadership skills.

Unfortunately, not a single one of the files had a red flag on it that said "also turned into a traitor by crazy freak." He knew he should discount most of the team and simply look at the ones who had been taken for periods of time, but he had to consider everything.

He sat back, rubbing the space between his eyes.

"Can I get you anything?"

He turned and Phoebe stood in the doorway to the conference

room. She'd taken her hair back down and looked more like the Phoebe he knew. Maybe it had been easier when she looked cool and professional. His dick reacted to softer Phoebe. His dick was a perpetual optimist. It was also a moron that didn't know when to stop. "Nah, I'm fine."

"I can't believe he left you with those files." She was shaking her head as she walked into the room. "My brother is a freak about files, and especially about his team. I would have been surprised if he let Taggart look at them, much less anyone else."

It was nice to know he could still surprise her. Too bad she was surprised that someone would trust him. "He did let Tag look at them. He also didn't get far. He and Tag ran out to grab a late lunch. If it helps, he told me he would kill me if I used anything against him."

"You would never do that." She gave him a tentative smile. "He trusts you. It's a good thing. It means you don't have to worry about him watching you again, though he's really fast to ask you for a favor. You'll have to watch out for that. He'll have you picking up packages for him in the weirdest places, and sometimes the packages end up trying to kill you. I should know."

He knew what she was trying to do. She was trying to find their easy camaraderie again, but he just couldn't do it. Even being friends with her would be too hard. He just had to survive until she could go back to Virginia and the house she shared with her perfect husband. He nodded and stared back at his file. "I'll keep that in mind."

"I'm sorry." He heard her move toward him. "You know I was married. I haven't done that with anyone but him. Have sex, I mean. It hit me afterward. It really wasn't about you."

He looked up at her, surprised. "No one else?"

"No. I was a virgin when I married Jamie. Well, not when I married him, but I did end up marrying him, so I sort of lost my virginity to my husband. I certainly hadn't slept with anyone since I lost him."

"I didn't mean to hurt you." It had been the last thing on his mind. Pleasing her, making her want him—those had been the things going through his mind. He'd failed.

"It wasn't like that. You didn't do anything wrong. That's what

I'm trying to explain to you. I had an emotional reaction."

And he'd wanted to hold her. Even as he understood she was longing for another man, he'd wanted to comfort her. "It's all right. We made a mistake. We won't do it again."

She flushed, her face going pink, but she nodded. "Yes. We won't do it again. I just wanted you to know that I…I'm going to miss you when this is done."

"Sure." She would remember the dude she wished she hadn't slept with and he would remember that he'd failed utterly. It was a great trade-off.

"Do you want to talk?"

"No."

She frowned at him. "No?"

What did she want from him? "No. You said what you had to say, Phoebe. I get it. I won't bug you again."

"You don't get anything. You don't understand and that's why I want to talk. You're saying all the right things, but I can see you're still blaming yourself. It's not right. Let's talk about it and maybe you'll understand what's going on."

Tag was right. Chicks talked too much. Better to shove that shit deep and move on. He was going back to hookers. Hookers didn't need to talk. They got the job done and went their own way. "We're cool. I won't hit on you again and then you don't have to lock me out of the bathroom. It's as simple as that."

Her face flushed a nice shade of pink. "Is that all you're upset about? That I locked you out of the bathroom?"

Maybe it would be better if he played this cool. He spent all his damn life being an earnest idiot. He wasn't going to fall to her feet and beg her to let him in. It wouldn't work. He'd played her fool more than enough. "My toothbrush was in there. Oral hygiene is very important to me."

A long sigh came from her as she shook her head in obvious frustration. "Jesse, please talk to me. I know I hurt you and I want you to understand."

He held a hand up. "It's cool. Hey, it wasn't that great for me anyway. We definitely don't have to do it again. At least I don't have any desire to do it again. I don't think you do either."

Now she went a pasty white and there was no way to miss the

way tears clouded her eyes. "All right then. I'm going upstairs for a while. Let me know if you need something."

Shit. He started to get up to go after her, but forced himself to sit back down. He wasn't the bad guy here. He was trying to put some much-needed distance between them. Yeah, he'd been a douchebag, but that didn't mean he should run after her and fall at her feet.

"That was rough." Kai Ferguson leaned against the doorframe. He was dressed in khakis and a white button-down shirt with black loafers. It was what Jesse liked to think of as Kai's shrink uniform. He wore the same clothes, though in different colors, almost every day. At night he wore leathers, but even then there was something soothing about the psychologist. Despite his neat clothing, his hair was long, brushing his shoulders, though he usually had it back in a queue. He reminded Jesse of a brainy surfer half the time.

It struck him that Kai Ferguson likely had secrets of his own. There was probably something nasty bubbling under his calm surface.

Damn but he wished Kai hadn't been a witness to that scene. "Sorry. You didn't need to see that."

"To know you're in trouble? No. All I had to do was read the file on Phoebe Ian sent me to know that."

"Aren't you supposed to be at some conference?" He'd started working at Sanctum a few months before, setting up an office in the previously unused second floor of the building.

"Came back because Tag said he could use some help. Apparently Alex and Eve's baby arrived early. They weren't expecting him for another week, but the birth mother went into labor yesterday morning. The baby's perfectly healthy so they have leave to take him home. Cute little thing, but now Eve wants maternity leave, so I'm here to take her place. The downside is I was making time with a schizophrenia specialist. The upside, I got a private jet all to myself, complete with top secret files. Apparently you got the files, too. Any thoughts?"

He would do just about anything to not have to think about what had happened between him and Phoebe. "I think it's one of the soldiers who went missing. I've pulled their files in particular."

"I agree. I talked to Tag when I hit the ground and he told me

182

your theory. Very smart and I believe accurate. I've been going over the psych evaluations. Naturally there's nothing that would cause alarm or they wouldn't be on the team. I would really like to interview them. I think the real proof isn't going to be in words on a page. I need to meet the men. There were two things that concerned me."

Jesse sat up straighter. If Kai had something that bugged him, he wanted to hear it. "Yes?"

"First of all, Deke resisted when the team went in to save him. They actually had to knock him out to get him back to base. According to the reports from the squad leader, he even broke one of their noses and afterward he told them he didn't want to go home."

Odd, but it didn't mean he'd turned. Jesse remembered how it had felt. He hadn't actively fought the team who came for him, but he hadn't cared much either. He'd been afraid to go back, afraid he didn't belong there anymore. "You feel dirty. At least I did. I didn't have a family to go back to, but if I had, I would have felt weird about it. I didn't want to be around anyone I knew. I felt like the man I'd been was gone, and being around old friends would just remind me. Sometimes it got so bad, I wanted to die."

It hadn't helped that no one welcomed him back. He'd been met with suspicion and distrust, and people who wondered what he'd done to live when everyone else had died.

"I understand what you're saying and that's fairly normal, but I have to take into consideration that it could have been an emotional reaction to leaving a place he now thought of as home," Kai mused. "Ace, on the other hand, was very calm. There's nothing in his reports that even says he has nightmares. He could be stoic. He could be lying to preserve some sense of manliness, but I get suspicious when there's no emotion at all present."

"Maybe he's not an emotional guy." He'd met a lot of soldiers who knew how to hide what they were feeling. The battlefield wasn't the place for a bunch of feelings.

Kai adjusted his glasses as he spoke. "We're all emotional, Jesse. It comes out in different ways, but the smart person can read it for what it really means. Take the reaction you had to Ms. Grant. You intended to get her to believe that you are no longer interested in her and that she's bad in bed. Way to punch a chick in the gut by the way."

His stomach dropped. Did they have to go back there? "I didn't mean it like that."

"How did you mean it?"

Jesse looked down at the files again. "It doesn't matter now."

Naturally Kai wouldn't leave it be. The man never let up. "If I had to guess, you two finally had sex and then she realized she wasn't ready, but couldn't talk to you about it until this morning. You realized you love her and think you can never have her. It's one more thing you want in life that you don't get, one more thing you managed to taste before it was taken away from you. So you tried to throw up a wall between the two of you."

He was getting a little irritated. "Do you have a point, smarty pants?"

"I do and it's about the problem with Ace Monroe. Even when we know we should stay calm, we lash out. My point is one way or another, there should have been some kind of reaction, whether it's relief or anger or anxiety. The other two who were taken were treated for depression briefly. There was nothing in their records that drew my attention, but I would need access to them personally to really understand them. I can't do that right now so I've got time for a session with you. How about it, neighbor? I could go and get Phoebe and have a little couples counseling. After all, I kind of have to live with you two. It would be nice to not be in a war zone."

Jesse had zero illusions about why Kai had been brought in. Eve had felt Jesse needed more specialized treatment and Tag had found Kai, a former Army Ranger who now specialized in treating PTSD in returning soldiers. A whole crew of sad sacks now came in and out of Sanctum via stairs that led directly to Kai's office. Unfortunately, Kai's office was also his home. He'd set up a whole suite of rooms where he worked and lived. Jesse and Phoebe were staying in his guest suite. And Jesse had stayed in Kai's room the night before. Where the hell would he go now? "Sorry about this. I'll try to convince Tag to let us use a couple of the privacy rooms now that you're back."

Kai's lips ticked up. "I don't think you'll convince Tag of anything. That is one man who could use some time on my couch. I dream about it at night, you know. Ian Taggart is one large mass of previously undiagnosed personality disorders. He's like a walking, talking Nobel Prize. Well, if they gave them out to psychologists."

"You know what I'm saying." In his own way, Kai was as sarcastic as Ian.

"I'm happy to have some company, man. I've started to feel like the Phantom of the Club some days. No, really. It's lonely during the day. I found myself playing the keyboards and laughing maniacally. Scared the crap out of the cleaning staff." Kai settled himself in a chair across from Jesse. "I was mostly joking about the couples therapy, though from what I understand, you could probably use it. You've been through a lot in the last few days. You want to talk about it?"

"Nothing to talk about." The last thing he needed was a therapy session. He had to talk about the crap with the Caliph. It was kind of required so he didn't go nutso again, but he didn't need to drag his nonstarter of a relationship with Phoebe into it.

"Spoken like a true stoic. There is always something to talk about. Especially when your week started with an attempted assassination by the woman you love."

"I don't love her." He sure as hell wasn't going there.

"Okay. By the woman you've spent the last several months with. Every free second of the last several months with."

"Yeah, well, she followed me around a lot. It was all part of her plan."

Kai grinned and slapped his hands together. "Good, we've reached the 'rewriting history' phase of the breakup. It's my favorite part."

"Screw you, Kai." He needed a new therapist.

"Hey, I'm here to talk."

"I don't want to talk."

"Okay, how do you feel about listening?"

"I don't want to listen either." He wanted to forget he ever met her.

He actually didn't like that thought. The idea that he wouldn't think about her again, could really forget her, made him anxious. Why couldn't she be like the other girls who had rejected him? Or the ones it just hadn't worked out with? He could remember their names, but their faces were a little cloudy. Some were pleasant memories, others mild regrets, but not one of them had shaken him the way Phoebe did.

"Excellent. I knew you would make a spectacular houseguest."

Jesse groaned. Months on the man's couch had taught him that Kai wasn't like other shrinks. Kai was way more obnoxious, and he was like a dog with a bone when he got going. "Say what you're going to say, man."

"All right. I'll do just that because despite what you believe, you need to hear this." Kai placed his hands on the table and regarded Jesse seriously. "This is not about you. That's what I'm going to say. Phoebe's issues are not about you. I talked to Ian earlier and he told me a little bit about her past and her relationship with Ten Smith. And Chelsea might have sent me all the files the Agency has on her. I don't think Ten knows about that. Chelsea wanted me to see if I could commit her to an insane asylum. She sent me a list of the top three with the worst records in the US, though she said she'd found some nasty ones in South America, too. Chelsea is all Team Jesse if you didn't know."

He couldn't help but smile. And then frown because Chelsea could actually be a little vindictive. "Phoebe's not crazy. I wouldn't mind reading those files though."

"I don't think that's a great idea."

"Why not? She did it to me." He was feeling vengeful. It would go away. It always did and he would feel like crap about it. But he was curious about her husband. She wouldn't talk about him except to say he'd been Agency and he'd died. He was curious about the man she did love. What kind of man could hold on to his wife after all these years? Probably a saint.

Kai shook his head. "So you want some revenge on her? You want to react in a way that runs counter to who you are as a person? Because the Jesse Murdoch I know isn't interested in revenge. He's a protector."

That was a load of crap. "He's an idiot."

Kai's eyes widened behind his glasses. "Have you wondered about why Ian Taggart took you in? By all accounts, he really should have had you arrested. Or killed. He's that kind of guy. You shot his wife. Oh, from what I understand you were trying to get

Alex, but you got Charlotte. You put everything about that operation in jeopardy, including the lives of two of his best friends and his wife. And yet, Ian took you in and gave you a job."

He'd thought about it a lot lately. "I think maybe he was trying to make sure I didn't turn. Maybe he was working with the Agency."

Kai shook his head, his gold and brown hair moving against his shoulders. "That wasn't his reason. He needed a man like you."

"A grunt who would do anything he would say?"

"Dude, we need to work on your self-esteem. No. He was in a position where his men were getting married and having kids and he needed someone he trusted to watch their backs and to make the right decisions. Like backing up Simon even when you knew damn well it put Tag in a bad position. You could have lost your job over that, but you chose friendship and loyalty over yourself. You're a selfless man, Jesse. It's a unique trait, one that I believe you were born with. Oftentimes a certain goodness comes from nurture, from having a loving family around you. But I believe some people are simply born good, selfless. They're the universe's way of making sure there are always heroes among us."

He wasn't a hero. "Well, it sure wasn't taught to me. My granddad was a bastard. Never hit me or anything, but he never let me know I was anything but a burden. My mom said I reminded her too much of my dad, and she couldn't even look at me. She dumped me on the old man when I was just a kid. He made sure I went to school and had food, but that was about it. I was on my own for everything else."

"And what did you do when he got cancer?"

He'd taken a leave and gone to see him, but his granddad had told him not to come back. He'd been so bitter, he'd turned away everyone. And still Jesse had felt a responsibility to do something. "I sent back everything I had so he could be comfortable. Like I said, I was stupid. Always have been."

"No," Kai insisted. "You're the unique human being who can be kicked again and again and still maintain his peace, his love. It's why they couldn't break you in Iraq. He used advanced torture techniques meant to erase who you are so he could build a new you, one who he controlled. He apparently managed it with others, but not you. You are unbreakable because there is a core of deep strength inside you."

"I never thought about it like that." He'd kind of thought he was too stubborn for it to work.

"What happens to a dog who gets kicked too many times?"

That was easy. And it hurt a little because Kai knew what that meant to him. The Caliph had called him a dog over and over again. Jesse was the dog and the Caliph was the master. He told himself they were just words. "He gets mean."

Kai leaned forward, his voice passionate. "Yes. You are not a dog, Jesse Murdoch. You are a man, and a remarkable one at that. I've studied hundreds who went through something like you and only a few maintain your light. So I'm going to give you some advice. You thought she could save you."

He had. Deep down, he'd thought Phoebe was the woman who could heal him. He thought if he could get her to love him, he might feel worthy. He nodded, not wanting to speak.

"You were wrong."

"I know."

"No. You don't understand. You thought her love could save you, but I'm going to tell you a secret I've discovered. Your love is the only love that can save you. Your love is powerful and worthy and more important than being loved in return. You already saved yourself. You do it every day when you wake up and make the decision to be a partner and a friend and yes, you saved yourself when you decided to love her. Don't take that lightly and don't regret it. It's never, ever a mistake to love someone."

"It is when it hurts her." Kai's words meant something to him. They really did. When he thought about it, he couldn't control whether Phoebe loved him back. He could only love her or try to force himself not to love her.

The truth was, he liked loving her. It made him feel alive. He'd never felt anything like it before in his life, and he didn't want to kill it. Throwing up that wall between them had felt wrong. It had been mean and he'd done it because he was trying to protect himself, trying not to ache. It hadn't worked except to make him feel worse.

"It doesn't hurt her," a new voice said.

He looked up and wished the damn conference door had a lock
on it. Was everyone going to walk in on his personal conversations
today? Tennessee Smith strode in with a big bag from Sean's
restaurant. Big Tag followed behind him.

Ten set the bag down. "Someone needs to break through her
walls and I can't do it. I know what happened between the two of
you last night, and I'm going to do something I swore I'd never do.
I'm going to ask you for a favor, Murdoch."

"What's that?" Jesse asked, wary.

"Don't give up on her." Ten sounded more serious than Jesse
had ever heard him before. Ten was always laid back, easy going,
as if nothing really mattered. He was the quintessential good-time
guy, which was a mask, of course. A man couldn't do what Ten did
and be easy going. He played a role like many of them did, but now
he looked like a concerned brother. "She needs you. Phoebe had a
rough childhood, and she's got it in her head that her husband was
her only shot at being happy."

"She has abandonment issues," Kai explained.

"Jamie didn't abandon her. He died," Ten shot back.

"It's all the same in her head. She's not thinking straight. She's
falling back on old thought patterns because in some ways they're
familiar and comforting, even if they keep her from what she wants.
We tend to regress to our natural neuroses in times of crisis." Kai
pulled out a chair for Tag. "Like this one here has a god complex."

"It's not a complex if I really am the most powerful person in
the universe. Then it's simply a fact. And if you psychoanalyze me,
Ferguson, I will murder you in your sleep." Tag started unpacking
boxes.

"He's also got anger issues," Kai said with a sigh. "But I'm
right about the abandonment. It doesn't matter that Jamie didn't
want to die. It only matters that he's gone. She expects the people
she loves to leave her. It's easier to hold on to the past than to try
for an uncertain future."

"So what do I do?" If there was a shot with her, he would take
it. Maybe he was too stubborn to get the picture the world
constantly tried to paint for him. Maybe he should listen to the
voices that told him everything would go to shit. Or maybe he
should give in to his true nature and not give up. Maybe he was

alive today because he hadn't given up, and if he tried harder, he could have the future he wanted.

"Do you love her?" Tag asked.

He did, but really admitting it meant opening himself up. It would be so much easier to say no and move on, but Kai was right. If he was going to get past all this shit, he had to do the one thing he'd never done before—he had to give a shit about himself. He loved Phoebe Grant. It was meaningful. His love was worth something. "Yeah. I love her."

"Do you think you're good for her?" Tag asked.

"I think he's good for her," Ten replied. "She smiles around him. She's passionate about him. When she says his name, she lights up and god, she's been dim for so long. It's good to see her smile again."

Ten's words went straight to his gut. If he could make her smile, make her happy, then shouldn't he fight for the right to do so? Even if it meant fighting her? "Yeah, I'm good for her."

Tag nodded as though agreeing. "Then man up and top her. She needs it. She's in a corner and she doesn't know how to get out."

"I don't know that I like the idea of her being involved in all that letter stuff," Ten said, eyeing Jesse warily.

But she needed that letter stuff. It was only when he stopped topping her the night before that everything had gone to hell. He shouldn't have slunk away. He should have been her Dom. BDSM could be anything they needed it to be. There was only one thing that was true for every couple who practiced. They had to communicate, to be honest. Yes, he hadn't done that with her.

Jesse took a deep breath. It was right there—the need to punish himself for a mistake, to count himself as something less. Maybe he and Phoebe would have to learn together.

It was time for him to stand up, to be the man she needed, and that wasn't a man who let a few mistakes come between them. It was time to be her man, her Dom, and that meant changing. It meant accepting himself.

It meant forgiving himself for something that hadn't fucking been his fault in the first place.

It struck him forcibly. It hadn't been his fault. He hadn't set the

IED or made the choice to be selected as the Caliph's whipping boy. He hadn't killed his friends. He'd survived and that wasn't something to be ashamed of. He'd survived and he could have a life if he was brave enough to take it.

Jesse stood up. If they were going to have a shot, one of them had to let go of the past, and it looked like it was going to have to be him. He turned to Ten Smith. "This is between me and your sister. I'll take care of her. I'll love her and I'll make sure she's safe. I'm going to try my damnedest to make her happy, but I'm going to do it my way. It's her way, too. She just doesn't know it yet. So you are welcome in our lives, but you will stay out of our relationship."

Ten stared at him for a minute and the room was utterly silent. Out of the corner of his eye, Jesse could see Tag grinning.

Finally Ten nodded. "All right, then. But you should know we'll have a problem if you don't treat her right. If you're going to be my brother, you better get used to how I handle things."

"I know. You'll bring an elite team into my house and I'll kick their ass again." An arrogance he'd never felt before bubbled up inside him. It felt good. He knew whatever happened, he could handle it. He had Tag and Si and the rest of his cobbled together family, and if he worked hard, he could have Phoebe, too. "Ten, I promise. I'll take care of her."

Ten held out a hand. "Jamie would have liked you, Murdoch."

That was probably the best compliment Ten could have given him. He shook Ten's hand. "I probably would have liked him, too."

A little cloud passed over Ten's face. "She's got a story she needs to tell you. She thinks you'll leave her when you hear it."

What the hell could Phoebe say that would make him turn away from her? He went through some scenarios and couldn't think of one where he would leave her. He'd already lived through her lying to him. Everything else was easy. "I won't."

Ten nodded. "I know and that's why I'm giving you my blessing. She isn't thinking straight. She's using what she needs to tell you as a way to hold you back. So she doesn't have to take the scary step of actually being with you. I hope when she tells you that you'll forgive me for the last couple of years. I was wrong about you."

Jesse had learned a long time ago that holding grudges didn't help. It was funny that he'd always counted himself as weak for not being able to stay angry, for offering forgiveness so quickly. But he'd seen real evil. There was no forgiveness for that. Everything else was negotiable. "You're forgiven."

"Just like that?" Ten asked.

"Why not? I've got better things to do than hate you, man. I would rather love her." He'd wasted enough time brooding.

"Then go get her." Ten slapped him on the shoulder.

"I agree with Ten," Taggart said right before his left fist came out and he punched Ten right in the nose.

"Damn it. I just fixed my nose, asshole." Ten put a hand to his face. He grabbed a napkin to wipe up the blood.

Tag smiled and went back to unpacking the food. "This is really the greatest thing that ever happened to me. Well, besides the whole wife-coming-back-from-the-dead and having a baby and shit, but other than that, getting to punch Ten at random is really the best."

"See, anger issues," Kai said with a nod. "Hey, is that lemon?"

"Touch that tart and my anger issues will get shoved right up your ass, Ferguson."

They were still arguing as he left the conference room. Jesse walked out with a smile on his face. It was time to get his girl.

* * * *

Phoebe stood on the rooftop. She probably shouldn't be up here, but she needed fresh air. She took a deep breath and leaned on the wall that surrounded the roof. Someone obviously spent time up here. There were a couple of lounge chairs and a wrought iron table with four seats around it. A long bench was covered in shiny, healthy looking green plants.

At least now she knew why the shrink's assistant came up here every day.

She liked Dallas. She hadn't at first, but then it always took her a while to see the beauty in things. Unlike Jamie. Jamie had a never-ending zest for life. The first time they'd gone to Tokyo together she'd been put off by the lights, the foreignness of it all,

192

but Jamie had been utterly fascinated. After a while, she'd learned to see life through his eyes.

Jamie tried to make even the worst events into something fun. God, when she really thought about it, he was so much like Jesse it hurt. Jesse tried to see the good in everything.

Like the night she and Jesse had gone to some fancy place where they'd been given a tiny plate of food that wouldn't have fed a bird. Most people would have been angry or embarrassed, but he'd laughed and taken her hand. He'd run to the nearest food truck, and they'd sat in their nice clothes in a park and eaten hot dogs and turned something bad into a great memory.

He wouldn't be able to do that with the night before.

She shouldn't have tried. Actually, he'd kind of tricked her. He'd done all that alpha male Dom stuff and she'd been confused. That was it. Most of the time Jesse was sweet and he allowed her to run things. He was devastating when he was sweet, but she could hold him off. When he was sweet and alpha male, it was a combination guaranteed to ruin her common sense.

Once she was back in Virginia, she would find her footing again. Ten was bluffing about quitting the Agency. It was his life in a way it never had been hers or Jamie's. She couldn't imagine a world where Ten didn't follow in their dad's footsteps. Hell, he'd been given full reign over his own team, running and directing some of the most top secret missions the US conducted. He would never leave that.

She glanced down at the parking lot below. She caught sight of Tag's massive SUV and a Jeep she didn't recognize. It was kind of beat up, but it was clean. It must be the shrink's. She'd been told to expect him to join their little band of merry guessers. That's what they were doing at this point. They were guessing and they were gambling with Jesse's life. She couldn't stand it. She wanted facts. She wanted to know exactly where to point and who to shoot at.

Across the street, she saw a truck parked at an angle that would make surveillance easy. She wondered who was on duty and if they were bored out of their minds. Most likely they were calling to tell on her, and someone would be up here to drag her back into the building any minute.

She watched as a van drove slowly by. What would it be like to be normal and happy and able to drive down the damn street without worrying about someone sniping the man you…liked…cared about…? She played around with the words in her head, careful to avoid the one word she couldn't use with him.

She heard the door creak open and turned around.

Jesse stepped out into the sunlight. He was wearing jeans and a black T-shirt that showed off how lean and cut he was. God, he was delicious. His golden hair caught the light and he smiled her way, making her forget about the sun. She was lucky she didn't drool. "Hey, your brother will murder me if you get killed up here."

She turned back to the street, unable to watch him anymore. It hurt too much. "My brother hasn't been trapped inside for a week."

She heard him walking up behind her. "It hasn't been so bad."

Yep, Jesse was already trying to rewrite history, to take something horrible and make it better. She just couldn't do it. "You're kidding, right? Tell me you're not going insane."

"Nah. I kind of like the company."

She had to force herself to breathe when she felt his hands on her waist and he stepped forward, pressing her lightly against the wall. "Jesse? What are you doing?"

He didn't miss a beat. "A couple of things. First of all, I need to apologize. I lied to you. You pissed me off and I was mean and such a liar. Last night was the best sex of my life, and it was the best because it was with you. I loved fucking you, baby. I loved playing with you. I loved being inside you."

God, this was so much worse. Every word that came out of his mouth seemed to race along her skin, like he could physically touch her with his words. "Jesse, please don't."

"Don't what? Don't tell you the truth?" The words were whispered against her ear, his heat warming her up. "Don't tell you how good you felt?"

"Yes, don't say those things." She couldn't say them back, even though she meant them. She couldn't tell him she'd never come so hard in her life, that only he had ever made her scream and beg for more.

"All right. I won't say those things. How about I apologize for not doing what I should have done last night. It was my fault. I was an idiot and I can promise you that it won't happen again."

194

Now he was saying the right things, but his hands were moving up on her body. Those big, calloused, gorgeous hands slowly inched up toward her breasts, and she could feel him behind her. "Jesse, what are you doing?"

"I'm apologizing. I made a mistake. I should never have walked out on you."

Alarm bells started going off in her head, but she was too focused on his hands to properly think about them. "Walked out? You didn't walk out on me. I needed to be alone."

"No. You needed me and I let my own insecurities drive me away. It won't happen again. Phoebe, you should know that if you put a door between us, I'll get it open one way or another. I'll break it down if I have to, but I won't ever leave you alone to cry again. If you're going to cry, you're going to do it with my arms around you. Do you understand?"

No. She didn't understand a damn thing about what was happening. She'd pushed him away. Why was he back here and offering her everything she couldn't have? "You have to let me go."

"You don't get to tell me what to do." His hand was dangerously close to her breast.

"That's only when we're playing." And they weren't supposed to do that anymore.

"No, that's only when we're intimate. Those were the old rules, and those rules got tossed out the minute you locked a door to keep me out. Here are the new rules. I'm in charge."

He was so arrogant. Why did that do something for her? "You can't just decide you're in charge."

He chuckled, the sound rumbling against her skin. "Sure I can. Now, I am going to give you choices. I'm not completely unfair. You can walk downstairs with me and we can have a nice lunch with your brother and discuss the op, but there's a twist to that. Or you can walk down to our bed and take off your clothes, and I'll make a meal of you."

The minute he used that dark voice on her, her whole body softened. She didn't even want to think about her traitorous vagina, which was all for door number two. Hell, her vagina didn't even want to go downstairs. But her brain was in charge. Mostly.

"What's the twist?"

"You'll spend the entire meeting sitting on my lap and I'll feed you."

She rolled her eyes because that was so not happening. "My brother is down there, Jesse. Don't be ridiculous. That's stupid."

"And that's ten," he growled in her ear. "Do you want them over my lap now or do you want to wait until tonight and I'll make the punishment public?"

"Punishment?"

"Punishment. I gave you a choice and you were rude to me. No more being rude to me. I'm not rude to you. If I am, you can spank me, but I assure you I won't be. I'm a Western male and you're my lady. I'll treat you with respect."

"I'm not your lady." She meant that to come out with a strong, resounding command. Instead, it came out with a little whimper because his hand ran over her breast and squeezed slightly, just enough to make her soften and moan.

Fire threatened to spread through her as he took her right earlobe between his teeth and gently bit down. "That's another ten because you're lying."

"Jesse, this can't work." She tried to focus on anything but how good it felt to be held against his body. She looked down at the street. The same van she'd seen before was slowly making its way around again. Must be lost. She was rapidly getting lost, too.

"And that's another ten. I think I'll spank the pessimism out of you." He licked along the shell of her ear while he cupped her breasts. "You're my girl. I simply haven't shown you what that means yet. I meant what I said. I don't care what happens, I won't leave you alone again. You gave yourself to me last night. I won't let you take it back because you got a little afraid."

She gave in. She was so weak when it came to Jesse. It was wrong, but she couldn't fight while his arms were around her, his hands on her breasts. But she had to make one thing clear. "You can't expect me to sit in your lap in front of my brother."

His fingers found her nipples. They were already hard and wanting, and he gave them a nasty twist that seemed to go straight to her pussy. "You will sit in my lap. You'll do it because it pleases me to have you close. I've already had a talk with your brother about keeping his nose out of our relationship. If it helps, I have his blessing."

She tried to turn around. "You talked to my brother about this?"

He tightened his hold. "I talked to your brother about the fact that I'm taking control of our relationship."

"You can't do that. You can't walk in and tell me what to do."

"Tell me you don't want me."

"I can't. You'll spank me for lying."

"See. It's already working. And you like spanking." His hands gentled again, but one of them disappeared under her shirt and found her warm flesh.

She couldn't help but sigh and lean back against him. Somehow when he talked to her like this, it was easier to let go, to give over to what he wanted—to what she wanted. "I know I shouldn't. What if I cry again? I probably will. I can't help it. I'm still in love with him. I don't want to hurt you. If it doesn't work, I'll hurt you again."

"I'm willing to take that chance, and I told you what would happen if you cry. I'll hold you and then I'll make love to you all over again. I'm going to prove to you we can work." He pressed her against the concrete wall. It came to her waist, leaving her torso in full view of all of Dallas. "Do you know what I didn't tell your brother?"

"So many things, I hope." She didn't like to think about what that conversation had been like. Probably very masculine chest thumping and much discussion about how Ten would kill Jesse if he hurt Phoebe and how Jesse would kill Ten if he didn't stay out of their business.

"I didn't tell him how dirty you are, baby. How gorgeously filthy you like it. I didn't tell him that you like being watched." His erection pressed against her backside. "I didn't tell him I haven't played with your ass yet, and that I'm going to. I'm going to get my cock in that tight little ass of yours and I'm never going to want to leave. You're going to be so tight. That little asshole of yours is going to fight me at first, but I'll win it over. When I'm done, you'll beg me to fuck your ass hard and long. You'll want me to do it on a stage in front of everyone. They'll know who you belong to.

They'll watch you writhe on my dick."

"Thank you for not telling him that, Jesse. Really. I'm so glad you didn't." A shaky laugh bubbled up. Ten wouldn't understand the lifestyle. Ten didn't play. Hell, from what she could tell, he didn't date much. He slept with women, but she couldn't see him ever giving anyone the type of intimacy Jesse was offering her.

"I didn't tell Ten, but I think Jake knows." He pulled up her shirt and ran one hand up to her breast, cupping it over the satin of her bra. His other hand dipped past the waistband of her slacks, inching ever closer to her pussy.

Oh, god. Jake Dean was in that truck. He was the one watching. He would have a set of binoculars and he would notice everything going on. He could be watching her right that minute. She had no designs on Jake Dean. None. She couldn't handle the man she did have, much less have any interest in someone else's, but the thought of him watching her, watching what Jesse could do to her got her all hot and bothered again.

When had she become such a pervert? She'd always been so staid.

"You like that he could be watching," Jesse whispered as his fingers found her clit. His other hand tugged gently on her nipple. It wasn't hard to pretend it was his mouth there. "Make a deal with me, Phoebe."

She couldn't think, much less bargain. Her body was completely his to command, and lust made her thinking hazy. Still, the words came as if he was a magician who could call them out. "What kind of deal?"

"Play with me. Be with me. No more running away. Give me until the end of this operation to show you that we can work." He kissed the back of her neck as he started to work her clit. The man knew exactly where to touch her. Though he stood behind her, she couldn't help but feel surrounded by him. It was like there wasn't an inch of her flesh that wasn't aware of him.

"I don't know if I can."

"Just for these weeks. I'm not asking for anything beyond that. Give me this time. Be my submissive. Let me take care of you and all I'll ask in return is that you be my sweet little fuck toy. Your body will belong to me. Mine to fuck and love and worship how I like."

His words were a drug in her veins, racing through and clouding her better judgment. How nice would it be to forget for a while? She would have to go back to reality, but for these days she could be Jesse's. She could revel in his affection and give him hers in return because she wasn't really this girl. She was someone else, but she could sink into the role and for a few days she wouldn't have to grieve. She could live again.

"Yes."

His fingers picked up the pace. "Be still. Let me start out right. You read up about the lifestyle. You know that right now, I'm in charge and you obey me. I won't demand it most of the time, but when it comes to this, know that I require complete obedience. You can stop me if you're scared or if you don't like something, but we'll talk about it. No more running away and putting walls between us. I won't stand for it."

She could barely stand at all. His hands were doing magical things to her flesh.

"Open your eyes," he commanded. "Open your eyes while I make you come and think about how many people could be watching you. There are all those windows. How many people are stopping what they're doing because they can see you? They can see that my hand is down your slacks. They know I'm playing with your pussy. They might want to be the man getting to touch all this sweet flesh, but I'm the only one."

She forced her eyes open. Her pussy didn't give a damn that this was contrary to proper societal displays of affection. Her pussy was not only a traitor but a blatant exhibitionist.

"How does it feel? Talk to me," Jesse ordered. He gave her nipple a nasty twist that made her shiver in his arms.

"So good. Just a little more," she practically begged. She looked down. She knew she should be embarrassed but she couldn't help it.

Jesse's cock ground against her backside, pressing her against his fingers. She was deliciously squeezed by him and it didn't take long before she called out his name and gave in to the pure pleasure he offered her.

She sagged in his arms, staring down at the street below.

"I'm going to take you over to that lounge chair and fuck you in the sunshine," Jesse vowed as he pulled his hands back.

She dragged air into her lungs and braced herself against the wall when Jesse let her go.

That was when she saw it. The van. The same van that had been driving by every couple of minutes was slowing in front of the building.

It was wrong. There was no work to be done here. Taggart wouldn't have anyone in the building he hadn't thoroughly vetted, and he wouldn't have anyone at all who didn't have to be here. Even Kori, Ferguson's assistant, was escorted in and out of the building every day while she gathered messages and files and watered the plants.

Something was wrong with that van.

"Jesse?"

The van stopped in front of the locked gate. Maybe it was turning around. Across the street, she could see the door to Jake Dean's vehicle open and he stepped out, already talking on his cell.

"Who the hell is that?" The sexy growl was gone from Jesse's voice, though there was still a hard edge there.

"Maybe he's turning around."

A SIG appeared in Jesse's hand and he started to pull her away. "We're going inside."

A loud rev split the air and then a crash as the gate gave way to the big van. It smashed its way through, tore through the parking lot and then stopped right in front of the building. She saw another car, this one a massive truck, race toward the building from the street.

Even Jesse watched as the driver's side door to the van opened and then closed. A man in a ski mask stepped out, leveled his gun, and started firing toward Dean.

But it wasn't the gun that terrified Phoebe. It was the fact that he had a small black box in his hand. She heard tires squealing as the truck rammed into the van, but her eyes were on that little box in the tall man's hand.

"Shit, he's got a bomb." Jesse started pulling her away from the side as the world exploded around them.

CHAPTER TWELVE

Jesse felt the heat and tackled Phoebe just as the first blast hit them. It forced him forward, but he was fairly certain he'd taken the majority of the explosion. Pain flared in his shoulder, but it didn't matter because he was far more worried about getting her off this damn building than he was any piece of shrapnel he might have lodged in his body.

The ground beneath him quaked and he felt the fucking building move and shake.

The sound of gunfire split the air again. Someone was having a firefight. He had to think it was Dean and the traitor, though the last thing he'd seen was another vehicle joining the apparent fray. He'd heard a crash and now the sound of gunfire made him think there were more than two people in that firefight. He heard the sound of several weapons firing. Was there more than one damn traitor? It was a scenario they hadn't paid attention to.

"We have to get out of here." he said, rolling off her. He prayed the damn roof held. "Are you all right? I didn't mean to hit you quite so hard. I panicked a little."

She turned over and got to her knees, blood on her palms and her clothes twisted and torn. Still, when he reached his hand out, she slid hers in and allowed herself to be pulled up. "You panicked when the crazy person tried to blow up the building we're currently standing on. That's totally unreasonable, Murdoch."

At least she was staying calm. He ran his hands over her. "You sure you're all right? I didn't break anything?"

She stopped him, forcing him to look into her eyes. "I'm fine, Jesse. I'm good. A little scraped, but alive. Get your gun. We're going to need it."

He nodded. Now that he was sure she was good, he could calm down. Freaking out wouldn't get them anywhere. There would be plenty of time for panic later. For now he let his training take over. He picked up the SIG and checked it out, flicking the safety off. "We have to get to the ground."

"How bad is it?" She looked back toward the edge of the roof.

"You are not going over there to look." He caught her hand again. It was too dangerous. He had no idea what kind of structural damage had been done.

"Ten and Ian were in the conference room. Oh, god, it's toward the front of the building." Her breath caught. "What happened to my brother?"

"He's alive." There was no other acceptable outcome. Before the bomb had gone off, he'd seen Dean on his phone. Dean was as smart and instinctive as an operative could be. He'd known something was up the minute that van moved in, and Tag would have hustled everyone to safety. He was fairly certain the front of Sanctum was blown all to hell, but he had to believe that Tag and Ten and Kai were safe. He couldn't think anything less. Still, when he turned, the wall he'd just been standing at was gone, and about three feet that was formerly Sanctum now was a hole that led down to the street.

Their bedroom had to be gone. He could see rebar and smoldering ruins where their roof used to be.

He tugged her close, wrapping his arms around her. He could have lost her. They'd been standing right there. He'd been holding her and talking to her, trying to seduce her, and then someone was trying to kill him and about to take out her while they did it.

"We have to move." The SIG was a happy weight in his free

hand. It was going to be used for what it was meant for this afternoon. He would defend them with it and he would take down anyone who got in his way. "Stay close to me. You're not carrying, are you?"

Her mouth turned down and her hand squeezed his. "No. I left my piece downstairs, damn it. I wasn't thinking."

She'd been emotional. He understood that now. "It's all right. We're going out the back, but we have to get downstairs first."

"We have to find Ten."

"No. This is one of those times that you obey me, Phoebe. This is one of those times that I'm in charge. I get you to safety and then I'll go back and find Ten. It's what I want. It's what he wants—you safe. Come with me."

She didn't argue further as the gunfire increased. He led her toward the stairs. They were in the center of the building. They should still be somewhat solid. He hoped. Jesse opened the door and started down tentatively.

The door closed behind them and they were in the dark. The power had been knocked out by the blast.

Phoebe's hand tensed in his. She was scared.

"Stay close. Baby, keep close to me. If we fall, I'll go first and I'll cushion you."

"How about we don't fall at all?" Her voice was solid in the gloom. That squeeze of her hand was suddenly reassuring.

They were a team. She would follow his lead and watch his back. He wasn't dumb. She wouldn't go quietly when the time came to leave her safely behind, but he liked that, too. She was fierce, his woman.

"Who the hell is out there? That's more than two people firing," she whispered as they started down the stairs. He could feel her fumbling with something and then there was a bright light illuminating the stairwell. "Flashlight app. I did have my phone."

Jesse stopped, allowing his eyes to adjust as he took in the space. "Text Grace. A simple 911 will do. It will bring everyone here. I don't think there's any way the cops aren't already on their way. Derek is going to have some work to do. And that's definitely more than two guns. Someone was using an AK-47 and the rest sounded like semiautomatics. Apparently our traitor has some friends."

"The text is sent," Phoebe said. "But I don't think they were friendlies. It doesn't make sense. I can buy one person can get past me and Ten, but not several. Besides, they didn't have outside connections. I think Ten's men are smart and highly suspicious. They wouldn't leave the investigation to McKay-Taggart. They started looking at their own team. I would bet anything someone was tailing the same people we were. I think Case drives a truck like that."

"Why would he drive into the van?"

"If he suspected there was a bomb in the van and that it would take out the whole building, the best play he had was to force the van as far away as possible. Maybe that's why it took out the right side of the building and not the center. It makes more sense to blow up the center and hope the thing falls in on itself. But it looked like the east side got hit the worst."

Fuck. He hoped Case hadn't been in that truck when it blew. He wasn't sure Ian could handle losing a brother even if he didn't really know the man. He worried that if Case had been in that truck, Theo had probably been sitting beside him.

"Can you shine that down?" The stairs seemed solid beneath him. They were close to the center of the building so if they were solid this far up, the stairs should hold up enough for he and Phoebe to get down. Unfortunately, with the exception of the rooms upstairs and the front doors, there were no windows in Sanctum. Given the nature of what the space was used for, Tag had found an industrial building that hid the inside from view of any curious passersby. It also meant that they would be totally in the dark and the flashlight would give away their position once he opened the door and entered the first level.

They took the stairs cautiously, Jesse listening to the continuing gunfire. It sounded closer now. They were in the building.

"Stay behind me. Hold on to my belt and don't let go. We're going to have to turn that off once we're on the club floor."

He felt her hand grip his belt at his back. "Yes. It'll be a beacon. Hey, please shoot us."

Her voice was calm, but she had to be terrified. She was an

operative, but she'd mostly had desk jobs. The idea of losing Ten had to send her into a tailspin, but she was quiet and following instructions. They reached the door that would lead them past the privacy rooms and on to the club floor.

Jesse closed his eyes and tried to see the layout. The locker rooms were toward the east wall and they were likely in complete ruins. There was a storage room behind the main stage in the dungeon that led to the basketball court. Since he couldn't take her out front, it was his best bet. She could scale the fence and be out of harm's way. They were coming after him. Whoever it was would let Phoebe run because he would be far too busy hunting down one Jesse Murdoch.

Adrenaline pumped through his system. As soon as Phoebe was safe, he was ready for this fight. He wanted his damn life back and that meant figuring out who the traitor was and confirming his own theory.

He turned when they reached the door. "Hey, it's going to be okay."

She nodded. "Yes. You're not going to let that fucker kill you so it's going to be okay."

He leaned over and kissed her. He meant to do it swiftly, just a little affection before going into self-defense mode, but Phoebe's arms came around his neck and she opened her mouth under his. When he felt her tongue swipe across his lower lip, his passion took over and he devoured her. It was only a few seconds, but he needed them. He needed to remind himself about what mattered. His anger didn't matter. She did. Tag and Ten and Kai did.

What was waiting for him was not a traitor but a man who had died a long time ago. Now he was simply a predator to be put down. Anger had no place here. Cool precision would win the day. His opponent was desperate. Jesse had to be the opposite.

"Turn off the light and follow me. Whatever happens, don't let go."

The light went out and he opened the door. Pure darkness surrounded them as he took his first tentative step out into the hallway. This was the hall with the privacy rooms. There were three of them. Two on his left. One on his right. He put his left hand out and felt for the wall before moving forward. One door brushed under his fingers. He walked forward slowly but steadily. Door number two. His heart rate calmed. His breathing got back to normal. He could feel the adrenaline, but it wasn't affecting him the way it used to.

He stopped where the hallway ended and listened. Up ahead he could finally see some light. It was where the doors had blown open and the afternoon was now shining through. Once they left the hallway, anyone waiting would be able to see them.

There was a crash ahead, a piece of the ceiling dropping, and he saw something that terrified him.

Smoke. He took a deep breath and could smell it. Some part of Sanctum was burning. He had to get her outside.

"Murdoch!"

Phoebe tried to pull him back, but he stood his ground.

"I'll kill everyone to get to you. I already took out Dean. I don't feel bad about any of it. They're all perverts of the worst kind. Infidels. But you're worse because you've seen the truth and you still turn from it."

"I think that's Ace," Phoebe whispered in his ear.

He took a step back. The door they needed was across the dungeon, where they would be completely exposed. But he could stash her in one of the rooms. If Ace was telling him the truth, this was between the two of them and he would leave Phoebe out of it. He just had to convince Phoebe. He found the first privacy room and thanked god it was unlocked. As quietly as he could, he opened it and drew her inside. "Stay here."

"No," her voice came back as a whisper but there was no way to miss the outrage there. "I'm not leaving you."

"It's me he wants. I can't deal with him and you at the same time. He says Jake is dead, but I can't believe it. If he's bleeding somewhere though we have to get to him, and that means going through that fuckwad out there. Please, Phoebe. Stay here and I'll come for you."

Arms went around his middle. "Work fast, Murdoch. I won't stay here for long."

He did believe that. She might be able to follow orders for a few minutes, but after that she would go looking for her brother and then he would have to worry about her.

So he needed to get this done and quickly. He turned and quietly went out the door.

"Come on, Murdoch. Your friends are dying." Ace's voice echoed through the space.

Jesse concentrated, trying to figure out where the fucker was. His eyes were useless so he focused on the sounds. He could hear the *thwack* of falling metal. Something was moving to his left. The conference room was that way. From the sound of it, his friends were trying to dig out. Every instinct told him to rush to help them, but then he would be a target. Of course, they would be targets, too. The minute they made their way out, Ace would start picking them off.

"How could you see the truth and turn from it?" Ace's voice was different. In previous meetings, he'd had that laid-back, easy Western drawl it seemed to Jesse that most pilots had. Now there was a harshness to his tone, a certainty that he couldn't mistake. This was the real man who existed in Ace's body. "I'm happy to kill you myself. I'm happy to perform this duty for my master."

Jesse felt for the wall and crept out. Ace had to have come through the blown out eastern section. As he moved into the club, light began streaming in. He let his eyes adjust. In the distance, he heard the sound of sirens. They wouldn't move Ace. The DPD could swarm in and Ace would hold his position. He would shoot the cops and not have a single regret as long as he got his target.

Jesse couldn't let those cops walk into a trap. He had to bring Ace out into the open.

He clung to the wall, his eyes adjusting to the new light. Sanctum was in ruins. All around him the usually neat club was utterly destroyed. One of the big sofas from the bar area was on its side in the middle of the dungeon floor.

"Once I'm finished with you, I will return to our master in glory and he will cover me with Allah's blessing."

Crazy motherfucker. Jesse took cover behind the sofa. That voice was to his right. Behind him, he could hear something heavy moving. Any minute now Tag was going to find a way out and then all hell would break loose.

"You're going to die. He sent you in here to die," Jesse called out.

207

A shot rang out, but it went wide. Ace didn't know his exact location and there were more than enough places to hide since the dungeon was strewn with tables and big pieces of the locker room for him to take refuge behind. Ace would have to come out to look for him.

"I will die a hero's death. I will gain my place in heaven."

Yeah, yeah, Jesse had been fed the seventy-two virgins line, too. He could remember looking up at the Caliph and explaining that he never really had a thing for virgins. He preferred dirty girls. Now if he could promise him seventy-two fully experienced women with a taste for the nasty, they still wouldn't talk because having all those women to please sounded a little more like hell than heaven.

He'd been beaten thoroughly for that quip. Apparently Ace liked them inexperienced and in mass quantities.

The sirens were right outside. Any second the first responders would race in, likely firefighters because smoke was starting to fill the place now.

Seconds. He had seconds before Ace started taking out the first responders.

"Give it the fuck up, asshole," a familiar voice yelled out.

Jesse breathed a big sigh of relief. "He said you were dead, Dean."

"I'm not letting some fucked up radical kill me," Dean said as Ace unleashed another volley. He dove for the sofa and rolled beside Jesse. "I do have a nice-sized hole in my gut though. If Case hadn't shown up with his truck, this whole place would have gone up."

"Is he alive?" Jesse whispered as he started to peek around the sofa.

"Think so. He and Theo jumped out of the truck before it hit. Pretty sure Case broke something. He better have with all his cussing." Dean's T-shirt was covered in blood. "We have to make a move or he'll take hostages. Shit. Shouldn't you have locked her up somewhere?"

Phoebe was creeping out of the hallway. Well, she'd told him to work fast. They were going to have a long talk about the definition of the word fast. His hand would be talking to her ass before the day was through.

Ace stood, firing toward their hiding spot. That was when Jesse realized Phoebe didn't intend to simply come out of hiding. She was going to help. Shit. She had a thick cane in her hand and she brought it down on Ace's head. He heard it hit, but Ace didn't go down. He turned on her.

"Drop!" he screamed as he stood and fired.

Ace's body froze, suspended for a moment, and then he fell forward.

Jesse ran, praying he hadn't hit her. He knelt down next to her. "Phoebe?"

She reached for him. "You took too long."

Thank god. "We'll have a talk about that. Go out to the front, hands up. The cops are here. Explain what's going on and that we have injured. We need at least one bus. Jake took fire and he's going to need surgery."

"Where's my brother?" Phoebe asked, her eyes wide.

"I'll get him out. I promise. Go." He helped her up and she strode to the entrance, her hands up.

Jesse felt something snake around his ankle. He looked down and Ace was barely alive, his eyes staring up. Sympathy crept into Jesse's gut. This man hadn't asked to be tortured and turned. He knelt down. Ace's gun was well out of range and it was easy to see he wasn't long for the world. "It wasn't your fault."

"Was," he managed. "Should have found you sooner. Should have killed you. But there are more of us, brother. My master will send more. He will never stop."

Ace's eyes went blank.

"Is he dead?" Dean asked, staggering over. "Because I would really like to kill that motherfucker again."

A loud crash rattled what was left of Sanctum as Tag pushed through the rubble. He was bloody and battered, but alive...and pissed off.

"You're paying for this Ten," he bitched as he pulled the other man through. "The US government can write me a big fat fucking check. Do you see what he did to my club?"

"Where's my sister?" Ten ignored him, his eyes finding Jesse. "Where's Phoebe?"

"I sent her out to make sure the police don't come in guns blazing. She's fine, though she's in serious trouble."

"He dead?" Tag nodded to the body on the ground.

"Yeah." Jesse took no pleasure in Ace's death. There was no triumph, just a weary truth.

This wasn't over and it wouldn't be until he took the Caliph down. He had to face his demons. There was no more hiding. He had to end this.

"Kai? Do you have it?" Tag started to pull Kai free.

"I have it, you freak." He passed Tag a package and dusted himself off. "My home just blew the fuck up and do you know what Big Tag was concerned about?"

"His dessert." Jesse knew the man well.

"One good thing is going to come out of this," Tag swore. "Dean, you look half dead. Let's get you to the hospital."

Dean swayed on his feet. "Don't tell Serena. It's not that bad."

Jesse caught him just as he passed out. He eased Dean down to the floor. His pulse was strong, but they weren't going to be able to hide a couple days worth of hospital stay from Serena. "Get the EMTs in here. The quicker we get him to the hospital, the better."

Ten started toward the door, and Tag looked down at Jesse.

"I'm taking you out the back. Ten is going to smooth things over, but you understand what has to happen, right?"

He did. "I died here. The Caliph needs to believe Ace did his job. And then I need to do mine."

In Dubai. Where he would finally end this.

CHAPTER THIRTEEN

Phoebe felt numb as she stepped inside the large suite. Three days had passed since almost losing Jesse, but they'd flown by in a blur of preparation and travel. Even as Ten had driven through the streets of Dubai, she still couldn't quite believe she was here. Now she was led into the king of Loa Mali's suite at the Burj Al Arab Jumeirah, one of the world's top luxury hotels. Everywhere she looked there was something sumptuous and beautiful, and all she could think about was hearing that gunfire and knowing that she would find Jesse bleeding and dying.

She couldn't do it again. She just couldn't.

"You okay?" Ten looked down at her. He still had cuts on his face and hands where the explosion had gotten him, but he swore he was fine.

Jesse was dead. Oh, he was standing at the big bay window with Simon, looking out over the spectacular view of the Persian Gulf. He smiled that crazy-sexy smile that made her catch her breath and he pointed to something in the distance. She'd watched the news report his death and now his golden hair was a muted brown and he wore aviators when they were in public. She didn't like it.

"I'm fine." She watched him, but her mind kept going back to those newscasts. Jesse Murdoch, former soldier, killed in an accidental explosion at the club he worked at. It had dredged up all the former nasty allegations, and some of the news agencies were even speculating that Murdoch had been the bomber.

They would have a mess to deal with after this, but Ten swore he would make it right. It was one more crappy thing she'd brought into Jesse's life.

Taggart had worked quickly, covering up everything with the full cooperation of the Agency and the DPD. No one it seemed wanted to publically acknowledge the war that was happening right in the streets of the US.

Ace Monroe had been killed in the explosion as well. He was scheduled to be buried with full honors at Arlington National Cemetery later that week. "He should have been exposed."

Ten sighed. "You know Jesse was the one who wanted it this way. If we'd opened up that can of worms, we might have sent the Caliph back underground. It was a necessary evil."

But Jesse hadn't seen it as evil at all. He'd explained that he didn't want Ace's parents to know what had become of their son. Ace Monroe, Jesse had explained, died in Iraq. His body had simply survived his soul. Everything that made up the soldier had been destroyed by the Caliph, and it did no one a lick of good to ruin a dead man's reputation.

He was too good for her. Just looking at him made her heart ache.

She couldn't do it again. No way. She was going to leave when this op was over.

Jesse strode up to her and took her hand. "Come over here. You've got to see this view."

He pulled her over to the window, his hands winding around her waist and his head settling next to hers. They'd been separated for days. Jesse had been in hiding and Phoebe had been working with Ten to prep for their trip. It had almost been a relief to be apart from him. She'd dived into work, studying all the power players and writing up reports on each. She'd found a proper distance.

Now her body heated up and she could feel her willpower

draining away. The minute his hands were on her, she was reminded that he was alive and she couldn't resist him. It was dangerous.

"Do you know what I'm going to do to you tonight?" Jesse whispered in her ear. "I owe you some discipline. Don't think I've forgotten how you disobeyed my very direct orders back at Sanctum."

"I'm tired," she managed.

"Won't save you. Besides, you managed to sleep on the plane."

Only because he'd dragged her into his lap the minute it was safe to do so. He'd pulled her out of her chair and petted her over and over while he and Simon and Ten talked. At first she'd been uncomfortable with her brother there, but Jesse had been patient. In the end, she'd been draped across his body, sleeping in his arms.

Tonight she would do more than sleep in his arms. Tonight she would let him spank her, make love to her. She would fall more helplessly in love with a man she couldn't have. Shouldn't even want.

"God, you two get a room," Erin said irritably as she walked in followed by Theo Taggart.

Jesse just grinned. "We're working on it. Any word on where our contact is?"

"He's on his way. Apparently he has a massive entourage, so we're going to try to blend in," Theo explained. "I also just talked to Case. He's deeply enjoying his bonding time with big brother."

Case had broken his femur when he jumped from the moving truck. Just being reminded of it made Phoebe a little queasy. If Case hadn't been tailing Ace and the bomb had gone off where it should have, they would all have been gone. Her brother, Taggart…Jesse. She'd dreamed about it the night before. She'd dreamed she was the sole survivor walking through their bodies.

"What did he really say?" Ten asked.

"He told me that Ian's a fucking maniac and I better come back to the States and get him out of there. He wants to know why he couldn't have gone out to the Circle M, or pretty much anywhere else."

Ten shrugged. "I owe Tag. Also, Charlotte was very insistent. I do not argue with pregnant women, especially not one as good with firearms as Charlotte is."

"I'm thrilled he's getting to spend a little time with the old guy." Theo frowned. "Could we forget I called him the old guy?"

"I'm texting him now," Erin replied, her phone in hand.

Simon stepped away from the window. "How about you two stop bickering and we get to the reason for our very long flight. Did you read through the files on the plane or just insult each other?"

"She's the one who's in the perpetual bad mood," Theo shot back.

"That's because my real partner got replaced with a little boy," Erin complained. She had not been thrilled when Tag had pulled Li from the op. With Dean in the hospital and Alex on paternity leave, Li had stayed behind to do much of the day-to-day operations. Ten had stepped up to lead because Ian wouldn't leave Charlotte, and Theo had replaced Liam on their team.

Theo towered over Erin. "I'll show you just how much of a man I can be, sweetheart."

"Stop it both of you," Simon ordered. It was obvious Simon was the senior McKay-Taggart operative.

Erin turned to face Simon, her body at attention. You could take the woman out of the Army, but in Erin's case, it looked like the Army wasn't out of the woman. "Yes, sir. I did read the files. I think it could be any one of those pompous assholes. I'd just shoot them all to be completely sure. But that's just my opinion, sir. Isn't Murdoch supposed to know him by sight?"

"I was pretty much either high or brutally beaten most of the time I actually spent with him," Jesse explained. "I've got three suspects. Until I'm in the same room, it's hard to tell. Those men are the right age and they're close to what I remember."

"Two of those men are members of the al Fareed family," Simon said grimly.

Phoebe whistled because that was not good news. Every man here was powerful and wealthy and had more clout than anyone else on the planet, but now they were talking about almost royalty. "Damn. If that's true, we've got real trouble. They're one of the wealthiest families in Saudi. And they're moderates."

"They say they are," Ten murmured.

"Just because one member is a radical doesn't mean the whole family is in on it," Simon replied.

"But if they know what he's doing and they've given him any aid, it could seriously damage US/Saudi relations." She didn't even want to think about what it could do to the price of oil or the destabilizing effect it could have on the world economy.

The doors opened and a gorgeous man burst through. Six foot four, with dark hair that brushed his shoulders and sun-kissed caramel skin, the king of Loa Mali had been blessed with more than money and power. Even Erin's eyes widened as he strode in with a charming smile on his face. "My friends."

About a dozen people followed him, men in suits, and one or two carrying laptops. Three women immediately found the luxurious couches or chairs and dropped into them, posing artfully, as though the king required fashion models around him at all times.

Ten stepped up and shook Kash Kamdar's hand. "Thank you so much for the work, Your Highness. McKay-Taggart considers you a valued client and you should know we're here to help with your every security need."

It had been agreed on that the rest of Kamdar's team wouldn't know the Agency was involved, so Ten was playing the corporate lead.

"I'm always happy to have my friends with me. Please tell Mr. Taggart I missed seeing him and his lovely wife. Such a smart woman. I owe her a yacht, you know. My beautiful boat was almost blown up, but the lovely Charlotte saved it." His head turned and Phoebe was almost blinded by his smile. "Although you seem to have brought me another beauty. Hello, pretty girl. What's your job? I think you should be my personal guard. You can take good care of me."

Simon stepped up. "Your Highness, do you remember when I told you about my friend? I explained that he sometimes loses a bit of control when he's angry?"

"Yes, you describe this man like the Hulk. He smashes things. I like the Hulk."

"You're touching his girl," Simon said with a smooth smile. "He also bites, from what I understand."

Kamdar slowly backed away. "I was only looking. Did I touch? This was a misunderstanding, my friend."

Ten shook his head, but Jesse moved in, threading their fingers together.

"I don't blame you for looking, Your Highness. She's a gorgeous woman. She's also quite good at her job, so I think I'll let her handle you." Jesse winked down at her. He'd taken off the sunglasses and she could see the amusement in his eyes.

Without losing a beat, Kamdar turned to Erin. "And you. Hello, lovely lady."

Erin went a little red and stared for a moment like she'd never seen a man before. "Hi."

"She's working," Theo said, stepping in front of her. "You can stop drooling now."

Erin slapped him across the shoulder. "You are not the boss of me. And I wasn't drooling."

They continued bickering, but Kamdar turned back to his team. He waved his hand. "You may go. Chapal, please stay so we may talk to our friends. The rest of you, find your rooms and try to stay out of trouble." He pointed to the three women who sullenly got up. "Except for you three. I expect much trouble from you. Go out and flirt and bring me back information I can use. A new wardrobe to the girl who brings me the best dirt."

That seemed to make them move a little faster. Their stilettos picked up and clattered as they moved across the marbled floors. Finally, the doors closed.

Kamdar frowned. "Are we being listened to?"

Ten shook his head. "Theo did an early walk-through. We're clean for now, but we'll do a check twice a day from here on out."

Kamdar stepped up and held out a massive hand toward Jesse. "You, my friend, are a very brave man. It is my honor to aid you in this operation."

Jesse nodded and shook the royal's hand. "I thank you for making this possible. It would have been hard for us to get into this place without an insider taking us with him. I know this was supposed to be a security detail. We'll make sure you're protected, but I appreciate the chance to get this job done."

"The United States government thanks you as well," Ten said.

Kamdar bowed his head as humbly as a man who owned a country could. "Excellent. I put through the changes as you requested. No one will question my detail. Your security badges and conference packages are in your bedrooms. I decided to bring Mr. Murdoch and Ms. Grant in as my marketing and finance leads. I fear if I left them on the security team, they would be on the sidelines for many of these meetings."

"We thought it was a perfect idea," Simon replied. "Ms. Grant has a business degree and Jesse and I have gone over enough that he should be able to make it work. He's going to be the shy, quiet type."

"Damn straight," Jesse added. He groaned a little. "Wait. Does this mean I have to wear a suit?"

Simon slapped him on the shoulders. "I picked it out myself."

"Damn it."

"My cousin has some questions. His name is Chapal Kamdar." Kamdar gestured the thin young man with the laptop forward. "He is the suspicious type. Always questioning things. I would fire him, but his mother and my mother talk, and dear god, the hell I would get if he has to work for a living."

Dark eyes rolled. "As if you could go two days without my help, you overgrown bag of hormones. Who managed to get your last sex tape off the Internet?"

Kamdar shrugged. "I performed beautifully on that tape and with three women. All of them were well serviced. I didn't see the issue."

"One of them was married to a member of a European royal family, you walking penis. You could have started a war."

"She was a lovely girl and so very polite." Kamdar sighed. "Anyway, apparently there is a Washington politician who is a last-minute entry to our little conference."

Little conference? It was only a place where the world's wealthiest men met to collude and set the prices of the energy the rest of the world ran on. Just a little conference, though.

"Who is it?" Ten asked with a frown. "I should have been apprised of any VIPs going to this thing. The Agency likes to know where our country's politicians are."

"He's not on the list. I wouldn't have known about him attending if I hadn't picked up some chatter about the conference. I like to keep my ear to the ground, so to speak," Chapal explained.

"He is a senator from Texas. Hank McDonald."

"The head of the subcommittee on Energy. I guess that makes sense, though if he were here in an official capacity I would think I should have been informed." Ten pulled out his cell. "I'll make some calls, but he really is in charge of a committee that oversees energy and new forms of energy in the US."

"He also travels to the Middle East often," Chapal said.

"Again, he would likely do so for his job, but I'll put my people on it," Ten promised.

Chapal shrugged. "I will continue to look into it myself. I have a radar for these things. Something is off about this. If I find anything, I will share with you."

"I appreciate that." Ten started for the door. "I'm going to find my room and make some calls. We have the opening dinner tonight. Everyone get some rest so we'll be ready this evening."

Kamdar pointed around the room. "There are three suites off this living area. I have the whole floor, but this is your wing. If you go to the suite down the hall, I have a bar staff on call twenty-four hours a day."

Chapal shook his head as he followed his cousin back out into the hallway. "Perhaps I will go and work for intelligence in the US. Then where will you be, cousin?"

"You have to have some intelligence to work for them. Besides, Auntie will barely allow you to leave the country. You should kiss my feet. Without me, you would spend your life playing silly games and having online relationships with women who turn out to be hairy American men."

"There was only the one. Why do you always have to bring that up?"

Thankfully, the door closed behind them.

"We've got three hours. Phoebe and Jesse, take the private suite to the left. Ten is taking a room in the center closer to Kamdar. He'll share with Hutch when he gets here. Theo and I will share the larger of the two rooms left, and Erin can have a private room," Simon explained. "The luggage has already been delivered so you should have everything you need. Since Hutch is still in the air, I need to call my wife and get her started on a profile of the senator. I'll have Adam look into him, too. I don't care what Ten says. US senators don't routinely travel to the Middle East."

"Come on," Jesse said with a slow smile. "We have time for a shower."

"I don't think Erin should be left alone," Theo complained. "That dude was looking at her."

"And what's wrong with that?" Erin's eyes narrowed. "Are you saying it's so weird that a man as hot as Kamdar might find me attractive?"

"No, I'm saying he's a king…" Theo began.

"And I can't possibly be a queen? You know Grace Kelly wasn't royal to begin with."

Theo turned a nice shade of red. "I wasn't saying that. I was just trying to watch out for you."

"Watch this, asshole." She turned and stalked off to her room.

Theo watched her, his eyes right on her ass. "I really would feel better if she wasn't alone here. Phoebe?"

It would be the perfect excuse. If she was bunking with Erin, Jesse would have less of a chance to get her in bed.

"No," Jesse said in that tone that let her know he wouldn't be swayed. "You watch out for your chick and I'll do the same for mine."

"She's not…damn it." Theo disappeared, following Erin into the west wing of the massive suite.

And she was left alone with Jesse.

Days. She only had days left with him. It would be the right thing to break it off now. She wasn't even sure she should hold his hand, but she couldn't seem to stop.

"Come here." He pulled her close and his head dipped down, covering her mouth with slow, drugging kisses. "Let me take care of you. Come on. I'll show you how I treat my queen."

So sweet. He was so perfect and she'd caused him nothing but pain. Still, when he pulled her along, she didn't stop, but went willingly with him.

Just a few days of paradise. That was all she had left.

* * * *

Jesse checked the temperature of the shower. Perfect. It was nice and steamy. Just what he wanted. He grabbed the items he'd prepped for this private scene and placed them on the handy shower ledge. It was time to start preparing his princess for what he wanted.

Which would run completely counter to what she thought she wanted. He stepped back out into the lavish suite they would share while they were here. He wasn't a complete idiot. He knew what was going on in her head. She thought she would be free to walk away as soon as this operation was over, but he intended to make that impossible.

He stopped. She was sitting on the edge of the bed, her hands in her lap, her eyes on the wall in front of her, obviously lost in thought. He took a second to study her. She really was an interesting mix of the woman he'd first met and the contemplative, distant woman she'd become. The real Phoebe was under all that guilt and he intended to bring her out. She was a sensual, affectionate, passionate thing who loved with her whole heart.

He was going to make her love him. He wanted it more than he'd ever wanted anything, more than he'd even wanted out of the prison he'd been in. That had been about surviving. It was a primitive thing, an instinct any animal had. Loving Phoebe was about living, and he was sure at this point that he was the only man walking the face of the earth who could properly love her. Only Jesse.

He knew damn well there was only Phoebe for him.

"Come here, baby."

She turned, looking over at him. "Jesse, maybe we should get some sleep."

Coward. Luckily, he'd figured out how to work her. "Take your clothes off and come here, Phoebe. We're going to get this over with and then we'll take a nice nap. I promise to have you ready for work, but this is my time."

She stood and her hands went to the buttons on her blouse. "This wouldn't work all the time, you know."

But it was working now. She shed her blouse and pants as she followed him into the bathroom.

"Why can't it work?" It felt so right to be alone with her. All the faking-his-own-death shit had kept them apart for days. He'd been worried the time would push her further from him, but he'd brazened through and before she'd known what was happening, he'd had her on his lap.

The key, he'd discovered, was simply overwhelming her with what she needed so desperately—love and affection.

And no small amount of dominance.

She frowned even as she worked her bra free. "Because real life would come into play and you can't just order me around all day."

Her breasts were really lovely. She was beautiful and feminine, and damn but he was already hard. "I don't intend on ordering you around every day. I intend on being your partner. You're smart. I'll listen to everything you have to say and when you know more than I do, I'll happily follow your lead. Off with those panties. They offend me."

"They're perfectly nice panties." She shoved them off her hips. "They match the bra and everything."

"But your pussy matches your breasts even better. God, you're beautiful, Phoebe." He shoved out of his jeans and boxers. He wanted to spend as much time naked with her as he could. A certain peace fell over him the minute he touched her, as though something fell blissfully into place and he was finally complete.

Her eyes went right to his cock. Even though he knew she wanted to deny him, she wasn't going to. There was something deep inside Phoebe that couldn't refuse his claim. "You're a pervert."

She could try to fight it all she liked, but she belonged to him now. "I'm your pervert. Come here."

She hesitated for a moment but walked into his arms.

He guided her into the shower. "Relax and let me take care of you."

She leaned back against him, letting the water caress her breasts while he picked up the soap and made long, slow circles with his hands. He soaped her breasts slowly, not wanting to miss an inch. His thumbs flicked over her hard nipples. She couldn't hide her response to him.

But they had things to talk about. "I know you're scared."

She was silent, only the slight tension in her shoulders proof

221

that his words bothered her.

He wasn't going to shy away. She didn't need him to respect some distance that served neither one of them. She needed his strength. "What happened at Sanctum scared you."

"I'm fine, Jesse," she murmured. "I'm a fully trained operative. I've been in bad situations before."

She was going to fight him every inch of the way. "You weren't scared for yourself. You were scared for me, baby."

The tension in her body was no longer slight. She went totally stiff and started to move away from him. "I don't want to talk about this."

"Then just listen." He knew she wasn't ready to admit anything and that was all right. "I didn't die. I'm not going to. I'm here and alive, and I'm going to take care of you. I know you don't believe me, but I'll prove it."

She shook her head. "When this is over, I'm leaving. I have a life to get back to."

"Your life is with me now. If you still want to walk away in a week, then I'll accept it." He was pretty sure that was a lie, but it was one she needed right now. "But for now, I won't pretend I'm not planning a life with you at the center of it. You're the sun in my sky."

"I can't be."

"You already are. There's nothing for you to do." He pushed her hair to the side and let his lips find the soft skin of her neck. This was where he'd wanted to be for days. He'd needed to be here with her, even if she was crying and afraid. She would be that without him. She would be that way for the rest of her life if he didn't fight for her. He couldn't stand the thought of her being alone.

Oddly, he could be alone because he would think of her. He would allow himself to dream about her, to share her with the man she'd loved. But if he didn't break through, she would utterly pine away.

"Reach over and lean on the bench in front of you." She only cried the once and then during discipline. She needed to cry and he could give that to her.

Her immediate obedience was proof to him that he was doing

the right thing. It was the first move she'd made that was eager. Her ass was in the air almost before he finished the command. She wanted this. Needed this.

"You disobeyed me in a dangerous situation."

"I also helped you." Her ass wiggled a little, an invitation to play.

He thought about how fast Ace had moved, his gun in hand. He'd turned toward her, ready to shoot, and Jesse had known he could lose her.

Maybe she wasn't the only one who had bad dreams about that day. "He could have killed you. My number one job in life is protecting you. You made me fail and I demand satisfaction. It's a count of thirty."

She groaned and he watched as she straightened her spine, preparing for his hand.

He gave her a moment, a moment where warm water caressed her and the possibility of what was to come hung over her. One moment where she held her breath to see if he could handle her. A Dom's job wasn't simply about punishment. It was about making that punishment a moment of bliss.

His hand arced, making contact with her soft flesh and crashing through the shower with an audible smack.

Her whole body shook, but she held her position. He gave her four more slaps in rapid-fire succession. "That's five. You stay still or it will be more."

"I thought I had thirty," she complained.

He smacked her again, loving how she groaned. "You'll get them all, but when and how I say. Now stay still."

He grabbed the lube and was deeply grateful they weren't doing this in his tiny shower. He'd never spent much money on his place. It was small, clean, and in a good part of town, but Phoebe would need more. She would need a house and a yard and a place to call a home.

A real home. One where he belonged, where he was wanted. One where she was.

And it would have to have a nice-sized shower because he liked how her skin turned a pretty pink between the hot water and the smacks. He definitely liked how her ass looked.

Her legs were spread perfectly, her back flat so he could see her asshole. It was a pretty pink, too. He dribbled lube right on it, watching as a shiver went up her spine. "What are you doing, Jesse?"

"What I've wanted to do for a really long time. I told you I would get inside you any way I could." He rimmed her petite hole, already thinking about just how tight and hot she would be when he finally shoved his cock up her ass.

She clenched the minute his fingers touched her there.

He wasn't about to have that. Five more quick smacks. "That's what I'm saving them for. Don't try to keep me out. It belongs to me."

"Couldn't you pick another part of my body to own?"

"Oh, I own the whole damn thing. Every sweet pink part and ripe little morsel is mine. I claim every inch of you, Phoebe."

"When we're playing." She said the words in a hesitant whisper, as though she was just trying to remind herself of her version of the truth.

"If that makes you feel better, you can say it." He wasn't going to push her into forever. He couldn't or he might lose her. "But for now, there's no question that this belongs to me."

She groaned as he pressed his fingers to her asshole. He didn't need to ask the question if she'd done this before. It was obvious. She'd had one lover and they'd been very young. They'd thought sex was sacred and it was, but they obviously hadn't learned that it could be dirty and nasty and fun, too. Phoebe needed to see that.

Play. He bet there hadn't been much of it in Phoebe's life. She was so serious and always in control. He was going to strip that control away from her and show her it was safe to play with him.

He slowly worked his finger inside, rolling over and over her flesh, teasing and playing until he finally slipped inside.

And that was when he used his free hand to continue the punishment.

SMACK. SMACK. SMACK. SMACK. SMACK.

She squealed beautifully and her asshole clenched hard around his finger. "Oh my, god."

"Tell me how it feels." If she hated it, he would stop. He didn't need to take her there if she couldn't enjoy it.

224

She whimpered a little and then seemed to relax. "Pressure. There's pressure, but it doesn't hurt. I don't know how I feel."

He rimmed her and her pelvis moved, not to get away, but to keep him inside.

At least her body knew what she wanted. He rimmed her again, opening her wider before giving her another five smacks that cracked through the shower.

She shivered. "Is that all you have, Sir?"

Oh, she was so getting more. He grabbed the prepped plug and replaced his finger with something much closer to his own size. She whimpered and wriggled as he lubed her again and then pressed the plastic against her flesh. She moved her hips, aiding in the insertion. The tip slipped inside, and Jesse watched the way she moved against it. He fucked her gently with the plug, giving her more and more with every pass. Every time he fucked, she opened a little more, accepting another inch until she was finally moving against the toy actively.

Jesse's cock was fully erect and damn straight jealous of that stupid plug.

He pressed the plug in, seating it. He stepped away and grabbed the condom he'd placed on the bench before he'd escorted her to the shower. He watched her as he rolled the condom on. He adored every curve of her and the way her hair hung around her, making her look like the sweetest, sexiest drenched kitty he'd ever seen. And a naughty one since she hadn't fulfilled her punishment yet. His cock would have to wait.

"Hold on to that plug. If you don't keep it, I'll make you wear it to dinner, and you won't like the way I lube it up. You'll squirm all night because your little asshole burns."

Her breath hitched. "Burns?"

"Because I'll put ginger lube on the plug and then make you wear it all night. And when it starts to feel all right again, I'll find a private place and I'll switch the plugs so you won't have a minute's relief. You'll be squirming all night and everyone will be watching you. They won't know why, but they'll see the way your skin flushes and how you can't quite sit still and they'll know. They'll know you need something, but they won't be able to give it to you. Who can give you relief?"

225

"Only you. I'll be good. I'll keep it."

He loved how husky her voice got when she was really aroused. He washed his hands off before paying attention to her backside again. He spanked her with purpose, ready to move on. He kept the count, speaking each number aloud before bringing his hand down again. He spread out the discipline, giving every inch of her ass attention until it was finally through and he was able to run his fingers over her pussy, to feel just how wet she'd gotten.

Perfection. Her pussy was pure perfection. It was wet and soft and waiting for a cock. "Tell me you want me."

"I want you."

"Say my name, Phoebe." He had to know she was thinking about him. He could share her in a lot of ways. He wouldn't demand that she pretend her husband hadn't existed or that she'd never cared about anyone but Jesse, but he had a sudden need to know she was thinking of him when he fucked her. "Say my name."

"Jesse."

He cupped the curves of her hips from behind, his cock touching her pussy. "Tell me you want me, you want this."

There was only a tiny moment's hesitation. "I do want this. I want you, Jesse."

That was all he needed. He lined his cock up and sank in, his vision shrinking down to only her. She was all he could see or feel or think of. His world focused in on how soft she was, the way she moaned and how she clenched around his dick.

He forced his cock in as far as he could, holding himself hard against her. "I want you, too, Phoebe. I've never wanted anything the way I want you."

He let his right hand move around her waist, skimming down to find the pearl of her clit. He wasn't going to last. He had to make it good for her. She was too tight, too hot and wet, and he could feel that plug dragging on his cock with every hard thrust.

"Oh, Jesse, it feels so good." She moved back against him. She fought to keep his cock and then slammed against him when he thrust back in. They found a perfect rhythm, his cock thrusting hard and his finger pressing down in time.

She shuddered and her pussy clamped down around him. She

called out his name as he rode the mini wave of her orgasm. He kept up the pace until he couldn't do it one second more because his cock exploded inside her, giving her everything he had and lighting his body up like a firecracker splitting the night air.

He ground against her, milking every second he could before he caught her in his arms and brought her up against his body.

He wouldn't make the mistake of leaving her alone for a second. Though his body was humming with satisfaction, his hands roamed all over her skin. He held her close, his front to her back. He kissed her neck and cupped her breasts and let her sag into him.

"Are you all right?" He had zero intentions of ignoring what had happened the time before. He was going to face it, get her through it.

Her head fell back against his shoulder. "I think so. I don't know."

It was better than listening to her cry through a closed door. He would have to thank Kai and Tag for giving him the kick in the ass he needed.

He turned her toward the showerhead and grabbed the soap. She was quiet, but he wasn't going to force her to talk. She just needed to know that she could and that he wouldn't leave her alone. They were silent as he started to soap her body and finally washed her hair, his fingers moving over her scalp.

He turned her around to help wash the shampoo from her hair and saw the tears in her eyes. Damn, but they kicked him in the gut.

"It's not about him," she said quietly.

He wasn't sure she was being honest, but he simply brushed them away and kissed her softly. "It doesn't matter, Phoebe. I don't want to push him out. I just want a place in your life."

"You won't."

"Because of this horrible thing you have to tell me?"

"Because sometimes we make mistakes in the past that cost us our futures," she explained.

He kissed her nose. "All right, princess. Well, if I'm going to be so deeply disturbed, we should enjoy the time we have."

"Jesse, this isn't a joke."

"I'm not treating it like one. I just know something you don't."

"No, you don't and that's the problem."

"I wasn't talking about your little secret." He moved her under the water, gently tilting her head back. She seemed determined to be dramatic so he had to be the sensible one. He was all right with the role. "I was talking about the fact that I happen to know there's nothing you can say that will make me turn away from you."

"You're wrong." Her head was back, the water sliding down her body. When she opened her eyes, her hands came up, cupping his face. "Promise me you won't hate me. I can't live with you hating me."

"Never." He found it hard to hate anyone. He couldn't imagine hating the woman he loved.

"I'll hold you to those words, Murdoch." She went on her toes and kissed him before hugging her body to his. Her head went to his chest and he could have sworn she was listening to his heartbeat. He let his hands find her head and held her there, warmth surrounding him.

They stayed that way for the longest time.

CHAPTER FOURTEEN

He was going to make her crazy. Phoebe watched Jesse as he moved through the ballroom. He was dressed in a tux and looked so predatory she almost didn't recognize him. She'd only seen him in the building when they were working before. This was Jesse in the field, and he was a gorgeous beast.

"Ms. Graham, is it?" A man in an expensive tux approached her, his silver hair slicked back. He was at least six foot two and lean, obviously a man who cared about his appearance.

She glanced at his nametag. Dale Albertson, assistant to US Senator McDonald. Now she was intrigued. She put on her game face. In this place, she wasn't a woman trying to figure out how to let go of the best man she'd ever met. God, she included Jamie in that list. Jesse Murdoch was the best person she'd met. But here she wasn't Jesse's or Jamie's. She belonged to the Agency, to the United States of America, and she was deeply interested in why a senator was here without the backing of the Agency.

She smiled at Mr. Dale Albertson and gave him her best British accent. She'd traveled on a British passport, and according to all of her security paperwork was a marketing consultant from London specializing in the energy industry. "Yes. Phoebe Graham. It's so nice to meet you."

Her British accent was perfect, of course.

Dale held out a hand and she took it, fighting to hide her distaste when he moved past professional. He covered her hand with both of his, holding it just a moment too long to be anything but a come-on. "You're with the crazy king, aren't you? I have to say, we're all curious about Kamdar."

Which meant her cover was holding and her brother had been the paranoid son of a bitch she loved him for being. She was proud to be his sister, but for now she was another woman entirely. "The king is a brilliant man. He's put his whole country to work with his initiatives. If he's correct about his potential output, he could fundamentally change the way people use energy in his part of the world."

"If he's correct. I seem to remember he claimed he was close once and then there was that terrible explosion. I guess that kind of thing is really better left to the First World."

She studied him for a moment. His lips had curled up slightly as though he knew something he thought she didn't. "I'm not concerned about a repeat of that particular incident. The king learned a lot from it. It hasn't taken him long at all to get his lab working again."

The explosion in Loa Mali hadn't been about worker error. It had been an act of corporate sabotage perpetrated by an ex-CIA operative. Eli Nelson had been turned years before by the shadowy group known as The Collective. They were the elite of the elite, the wealthiest men in the world, and they hadn't taken kindly to the king of Loa Mali potentially killing their oil revenues.

Eli Nelson was dead thanks to the Taggarts, but someone would quickly take his place.

The thing they'd been missing was the government tie. Phoebe had been able to tie The Collective to various criminal organizations and foreign countries, but she knew they would also have a group of US politicians under their sway. She had to wonder if she wasn't looking at one. Well, at his assistant anyway.

"We'll see about that. Why is a man who is determined to change the world over to solar and wind power here at an oil conference?" He leaned in, just a little flirty. "Can I get you a drink?"

"Sure." A little flirtation might help. She wanted information, too. "I'd love some champagne."

He held up a hand and immediately a tuxedoed waiter turned to bring them glasses of champagne. She took hers and held it to her chest. She wore a designer black dress that Jesse had claimed should be illegal, but then he was the gorgeous pervert who had promised to fig her if she didn't behave. Yes, she knew what that was. She read. A lot, lately. And every damn hero turned into a blond hottie with a Western accent. She pretended she was looking at Dale and let her chest thrust out. Jesse watched her from across the room, and the minute she turned his way, his eyes flared. Because Jesse liked her boobs. A lot. "This is an energy conference, Mr. Albertson. The king has every right to be here."

"Energy in this part of the world means oil."

"It doesn't have to. Not if my boss has his way."

He tipped back his champagne, swallowing the whole glass in quick order and grabbing another before the waiter could move away. "There are a few people who think he shouldn't be here."

There had been more than a subtle hint of threat in those words. "Really? Do you think he's in danger?"

Albertson glanced around the room, his eyes shifting until they found Kamdar. The king was holding court, his bevy of gorgeous ladies surrounding him and laughing at his very horrible jokes. She was a little surprised to see Erin was hovering around the king. "I think Kamdar needs to play ball if he wants to keep his position."

"His position is hereditary and they don't play ball there. Cricket is really more popular in Loa Mali." She was starting to feel the slightest bit uncomfortable. He was more inebriated than she'd counted on, and she couldn't take him out with a quick uppercut. She was supposed to be a marketing consultant, and women in this part of the world weren't exactly smiled on for kicking ass.

Albertson nodded. "Funny girl. What do you say we go back to my room? I would do just about anything to get out of this hotel, but apparently it's the only place where we can get a damn drink in this country."

She was tempted to lead him out into the city anyway. Even slight inebriation in public could get a citizen arrested in Dubai. It

231

might be fun to watch this dipshit rot in a Middle Eastern prison for a while.

Unfortunately, she wasn't dressed for the streets of Dubai since a woman could get arrested for showing her knees, so that little pleasure would have to wait. "I'm afraid I'm supposed to stay here at the conference. My boss was very insistent we all stay and do our jobs."

"Which is what?" He was openly looking at her breasts now and Jesse had noticed.

He started across the ballroom, but luckily Simon was there to stop him from doing something stupid. She breathed a sigh of relief as the big Brit put a hand on Jesse's shoulder and started talking to him.

"Phoebe, that's the senior assistant to Senator McDonald you've ensnared with your far too on-display bosom." Ten's voice came over the tiny communications device in her ear. Ten and Hutch were watching from the suite, having cut into the security feeds. She could hear them, but she couldn't directly respond since she wasn't alone. The small bug planted in the broach on her left side allowed them to hear everything going on. She simply looked to her left, acknowledging the camera there to let him know she'd heard.

"I'm here to help the king with packaging and marketing his product to the outside world. As an alternative energy source, I've got to convince the big oil boys that we're not really a threat. After all, they control the world when you think about it. We just want a tiny part of the market."

"To begin with," Albertson shot back. "You know Kamdar isn't the first person to try this. His crap will go the same way the electric car went. He's a dreamer if he thinks the cartels will allow him to have any kind of a foothold."

"Well, it's a good thing that they don't get to have a say in it. And I don't know if you've noticed but hybrid vehicles are very popular these days."

"Because we allowed it," he said, his voice taking on a nasty edge.

"Oh, I like that 'we.' That's a very interesting statement," Ten said.

"I always love the personal pronouns, too, boss." Hutch put in his two cents.

She needed to bring the testosterone level down a bit. She smiled up at the senator's aide. "I wouldn't know anything about that. I did work on a few of the hybrid marketing plans in Europe. We did spectacularly well with women in Southern Europe. I've found the key is to give them a choice of pretty colors and have a proper celebrity endorsement. You have to get Clooney for Italy. He could sell anything there. They love him."

The man stared at her for a second and then laughed, that menace in him gone and the drunken playboy back. "It's good to know American star power is still at work."

"Get him talking about the senator, sister," Ten said into her ear.

She really wished she could flip him off. She knew how to do her damn job. "So you work for a real senator?"

He leaned in, giving her what he probably thought were sexy eyes, but they mostly made him look sleepy. "As real as they come. I don't know how closely you Brits follow American politics, but my boss is going to make a real run at the White House in a few years. Senator McDonald from the great state of Texas."

That was what all the news stations believed. Hank McDonald was eyeing the presidency. He was an older man with all the charm of Clinton and the backing and power base of a Bush. "What is the US government doing here?"

"We're not here in a strictly professional capacity. We're just looking out for US interests. That's kind of my job."

"Is it?"

He looked left and then right and leaned in closer. "I watch out for my country, if you know what I mean."

She heard Ten snort. "I do believe he's going to try to convince you to sleep with him because he's a spy."

"Well, you know that's the only reason I joined up," Hutch replied. "I was promised an enormous amount of tail."

Out of the corner of her eye, she caught sight of the ballroom door opening and a group of men in traditional Arab robes and keffiyehs covering their heads entering the room. She turned to get a good look at the new guys. "I thought you were an assistant to

Senator McDonald."

"That's just my cover. I really work a much more important job. Ah, the Saudis are here. I'll have to set up a meeting. The al Fareeds are old friends."

"Really?" That was interesting. They were represented by Ibrahim and Hani. From the reports she'd compiled, she knew they were brothers, both in their forties, and they had taken over many of their family's business operations recently. Like many wealthy Saudi sons, they'd been educated in the west. They'd both attended Oxford. Ibrahim had graduated with a master's in world politics. Hani had a degree in business administration. The brothers had been back in Saudi for the better part of two decades and seemed uninterested in anything but business. On the surface, they were perfect family men who eschewed all the decadence their wealth could afford them.

"Yes, good men. Reasonable men, unlike your boss. I think you should really think about changing jobs." He winked at her. "I can talk to the senator about finding you a place that will really offer you job growth. I think you'll find Loa Mali is a dead end. Trust me. I know things other people don't know."

She didn't like how certain he seemed. "I'm always on the lookout for a better opportunity. Any smart girl is. Perhaps you could introduce me to your friends."

She didn't want Jesse anywhere near the man who tortured him.

And killed her husband. She might be standing in the same room as the man who killed her husband and the only thing she could think about was protecting Jesse from him. She should be ready for vengeance, but all she could think about was what she could lose.

Didn't Jamie deserve more?

He frowned. "Oh, I don't think that's such a good idea. You know how your boss loves women and surrounds himself with them at all times? The al Fareed brothers are pretty much the opposite. They have wives, but they don't speak, if you know what I mean. They stay in the home and those men don't party."

"But they're friends with the senator?"

"More like business associates."

"The senator is actually in the business? I thought he was on some committee."

"He is, but hey, there's always money to be made. Everyone knows that." His fingers ran up her arm. "Let's head back to my room and we'll talk about it some more."

"Let's let Murdoch go insane on his ass," Hutch chuckled in her ear. "It's been a while since I saw some blood sport."

"Phoebe, you are not to leave that damn room. Am I understood?" Ten's voice held no humor.

Like she would docilely walk away with her would-be rapist. Not likely. Still, she would love to put a bug in his room. She wanted to know what kind of money the senator thought he was going to make while here. No. She would just have to make sure the poor man couldn't possibly perform. "How about one more drink? I'll get it this time. I think I want something stronger than champagne."

He glanced back down at her breasts and she knew she had him. "Of course, gorgeous. A whiskey on the rocks for me."

She winked his way and started toward the open bar. "I know what I'm doing, Ten."

She heard him curse but then came a grudging, "Do you have everything you need? Erin? Can you back her up?"

"Already there." Erin strode up to the bar. She looked more sophisticated than normal. Erin was a boots and jeans kind of girl, but Phoebe could admit that she cleaned up quite nicely. She wore a green gown that was fairly modest, but there was no way to truly cover Erin's curves. The emerald color complemented her skin. "I've got everything we need to have a fun time."

Phoebe ordered the drinks and almost didn't see the moment Erin tipped her hand over the whiskey glass and poured the roofie in. "Want to have a threesome?"

Erin grinned. "Oh, and I thought I was going to get through this entire conference without a single ménage à trois with a douchebag I would rather punch in the face than look at. Thanks, friend."

They picked up the drinks and started to make their way back.

"Phoebe, you get in, you plant a bug and you get out," Ten's voice commanded. "Right now Jesse's working with Simon on

235

something, but the minute he gets back he's going to look for you. I swear to god this is the last time I take a couple with me on assignment, especially where the male is a possessive caveman. Make it quick."

Albertson turned and his eyes went wide. "Hey, who's your friend?"

Erin's lips curled up in a surprisingly seductive grin. Apparently there was a reason Tag had hired her that had nothing to do with her ability to kick ass. "Phoebe and I both work for Kash, but he's busy." She looked back to where Kamdar was holding court. "He's got enough female attention, don't you think?"

He licked his lips right before downing the entire glass of whiskey. "I think he's got more than enough. Come on, girls. Let's go party like real Americans."

She caught Theo watching them as they began to walk out of the ballroom. He was practically staring a hole through Erin, but he held his ground. His face flushed slightly, and she wondered what her brother was saying into Theo's ear. Poor Ten. He was used to his band of merry men who had each other's backs, and the biggest drama they had was where to buy beer. There was a reason he never worked with couples. No matter how professional, they couldn't stay cool and collected when the one they loved was in danger. Theo and Erin weren't a couple, but it was obvious Theo was interested and not in sharing her with some politician.

"I've got some good Scotch in my room. Nothing but the best," Albertson said, starting to slur his words.

"What floor are you on?" Phoebe asked as they walked into the elevator. She needed to get him as close to his room as possible before he couldn't walk on his own anymore. Even in the hotel, there could be issues with anything considered lewd behavior, including men and women touching in the halls.

"Five. Jeez, you've got nice tits, babe." He stumbled into the elevator and hit the button. Luckily, they were alone. He threw an arm around Phoebe's shoulders and another around Erin's. "You two are hot. Are you going to kiss?"

Erin nodded. "I'm so much more likely to kiss her than you."

He just sighed. "Show me your tits."

Oh, he was a charmer. "As soon as we make it to your room. I need to relax a little. You can help me with that, right?"

His eyes were starting to close. "Yeah. I can help. You just stick with a winner. I'm a winner."

His head fell forward and Phoebe groaned under his weight. For a slender dude, he was solid.

"I'm going to need a room number," Erin said quietly, keeping her head down. "What's his name?"

"Albertson. He's going to be listed with the senator's party," Phoebe said, doing the same. There were cameras in the elevators.

"Chill, sweetheart," Hutch said, his voice smooth over the comm. "I believe you will find that the cameras in this elevator and on the fifth floor are going to have a little trouble. You have five minutes and then I can't stop them from coming back on. You get in and out fast, you understand, Thelma and Louise?"

Ten took over. "He's in 5105. It's four doors down from the elevator you're in. Take a left and move it. I don't want anyone to remember you tomorrow. That roofie should erase the last thirty minutes or so. If anyone remembers you walking out with him, you were helping him to his room."

"Understood." The doors opened and she and Erin started down the hall.

"I think by calling us Thelma and Louise, Hutch was giving me permission to shoot this guy in the balls."

Erin was way too eager to shoot dudes in the balls. It seemed to be a viable pastime for her. "I think he was trying to tell us to not go over the Grand Canyon in a Thunderbird. Damn he's heavy. Can you get the key card?"

"I knew you'd make me do the nasty stuff." They made it to the room Ten had told them to go to. The halls were quiet and they weren't going to have a better shot at getting through this than now. Erin reached into the completely deadweight asshole's pants pocket and came back with the key card. She swiped the card and they stumbled through, Phoebe turning and locking the door behind him.

Erin let Albertson drop right to the floor.

Phoebe sighed. "We have to get him to the bed."

"Why?" Erin was already moving through the room, checking the closets and the bathroom. "He looks so peaceful there."

She stepped over Albertson's body and prayed Erin hadn't

actually killed him. She wouldn't put it past Erin to overdose the bastard. She reached into her small bag and pulled out two tiny bugs. "You see anything?"

Erin stepped out of the bathroom, holding a brown pill jar. "He takes the little blue pill. So much for our big stud."

"That doesn't matter." And it wasn't totally surprising. She moved into the living area of the suite. It looked like Albertson was bunking by himself, which likely meant he really was high up in the senator's organization. She glanced around, looking for the best place to plant the bugs. There was a small sitting area and a desk with a laptop. "Check and see if that's password protected."

She slipped the tiny listening device under the coffee table, placing the sticky piece to the inside. It would capture any conversations that occurred in this part of the suite.

"Sorry," Erin said, closing the laptop again. "It's locked up tight. I'm sure Hutch could break it, but I'm not exactly Suzy Hacker. I could smash it if you like. It's fun to break things."

Phoebe shook her head as she walked through to the bedroom. She flicked on the light and strode across to the bed. She ran a hand inside the headboard, looking for the best place to situate the device. "You planning on breaking Theo?"

She couldn't help it. She knew she shouldn't pick on the redhead, but it was so easy to do.

Erin showed up in the doorway and entered the bedroom, going straight for Albertson's briefcase that was placed on the bedroom desk. She rifled through it. "I will if he gives me more trouble."

Phoebe placed the bug and held it to make sure it stuck. "He's not a bad-looking kid."

That was an understatement. He was a young Ian Taggart, so Theo looked a little like a Viking god.

"Kid is the vital word in that sentence." Erin sifted through a stack of papers. "He's twenty-nothing for god's sake."

"He just turned twenty-three. You're not that much older." She glanced around the space. They had roughly two and a half minutes before they needed to be gone.

"I'm thirty-four, and I've seen more in my lifetime than that little boy has ever imagined. He's got mommy issues. I don't need a kid." There was something hollow about the way she said it, but then she shook her head. "Now, that pretty king on the other hand is definitely on the table."

Phoebe hoped Ten enjoyed listening to Dale Albertson and the inevitable bevy of hookers he brought to the suite. She checked one last time to make sure it was secure. "Really? He doesn't make you think of a walking venereal disease? Don't get me wrong. He's hot, but he also travels with a harem."

Erin didn't seem fazed. "I'm just trying to scratch an itch. I shove a condom on his probably lovely penis and we're good to go. He looks like a man who knows what he's doing and he doesn't look sticky, if you know what I mean."

"I don't." She groaned a little when she realized they couldn't leave Albertson on the floor. If they were going to keep up the story that they'd been helping a drunk dude get to bed, they should probably actually get him there. "We need to get him on the bed."

Erin shoved the papers back in. "I'll get him. So I was talking about sticky dudes and how Kamdar is really the perfect guy for me to play around with. Your boy is a perfect example of sticky."

"He is not." Jesse was scrupulously clean. And he kept her clean. She could still feel his hands soaping her body and washing her hair. His fingers had run all along her scalp, relaxing her. He'd even dried her off and made sure she was warm.

Erin stalked out and it only took a second before she walked back in, hauling him by one arm. Phoebe had to give it to her. Erin was a strong woman. "He is stuck to you like glue. When you walk into a room, bam, he sticks."

He did kind of make sure he always had a hand on her when they were together. It was nice. It made her feel safe. Protected. Loved. She didn't want to lose it. Didn't want to lose him. "There's nothing wrong with that. It just means he cares."

She huffed a little as she leaned down and then hefted Albertson up on the bed. "I don't want anyone to care. I've done the married thing before. I won't again. So pretty boy Theo can find some other idiot to play his games with."

"I don't think he's trying to play a game."

"It's always a game, Phoebe. Haven't you figured that out yet?"

A minute and a half. She would have to figure out Erin's damage another time. "Time to head out. We need to get back to the party. The cameras come on soon."

Erin nodded and pulled the covers over him. "Let's do it." She turned and then stopped. "Shit."

Phoebe turned and saw what Erin was looking at. Right there on the dresser was a newspaper. *The Dallas Morning News*. She recognized the issue. It had a picture of the husk that was Sanctum after the bombing and a shot of Jesse Murdoch in all his blond glory.

Phoebe stepped up and looked down. The article was marked, certain information circled, and even worse, there was a notepad beside it with two names written on it. Ian Taggart and Tennessee G. Smith.

She heard the sound of Erin's phone as it took one and then two pictures, and then she felt a tug on her arm. "Time to go."

She let Erin lead her out of the room, her heart racing.

Someone was on to them.

* * * *

"I'm not a complete moron," Jesse said as he pushed through the doors into the suite.

Simon closed the doors behind them. "Funny, because you do seem to be acting that way. Were you or were you not about to accost your girlfriend in the middle of the ballroom?"

"I wasn't going to accost Phoebe. I don't really know what that means. But I was going to castrate that son of a bitch." He knew how to do it, too. He'd castrated a couple of bulls in his time. The trick was to do it quick, before the damn thing knew what was happening. He wouldn't be cruel when he did it. He would be as humane as possible, but that little pecker wouldn't be rubbing against Jesse Murdoch's girl again.

"Yes, cutting that man's balls off would absolutely have helped our mission," Simon replied drolly.

"He was looking at her breasts." Those were his breasts. He took care of those breasts. He loved them and rubbed them and sucked them, and they were fucking his.

240

"I believe that was the point of putting them on display. She was trying to get attention so you and I could look around and attempt to uncover your former torturer. And her dress is quite modest by Western standards."

"Well, by my standards, he was looking at her breasts." He knew he was being stubborn, but the idea of that man getting his hands on Phoebe made him sick. She was precious. She shouldn't have to get pawed by some man who didn't love her.

He was the only one who got to paw her, damn it.

"I doubt he's looking at her breasts now," Simon replied.

Jesse sent his partner a nasty look and forced his way into the control room. "Where is she?"

Hutch had a Red Vine licorice sticking out of his mouth like a cigarette. His setup was neat, but it was obvious the man had a sweet tooth. Besides the pack of Red Vines, there was a dish of Tootsie Rolls and another of peppermints. He reached up and pulled the licorice out as he frowned, pointing at the bank of laptops he had going. "She's fine. Well, I'm pretty sure she's fine. I had to work a little magic and get those cameras to go wonky. The guys in security are probably flipping out by now."

Ten stepped in, a bottle of water in his hand. "Their time's up. Bring the cameras back online. Security can buy that the system has a glitch for only so long. They'll be on their way to fix it if we don't get them back online."

Phoebe was out there and the only thing protecting her was the camera blackout. "No. Wait until she calls back."

Hutch ignored him, hitting the button that brought the cameras back up.

Phoebe and Erin were in the elevator, speaking animatedly. Hutch hit a button that put their comms on speaker.

"How much had that guy had to drink?" Erin asked.

Phoebe shook her head. "Enough that he was disgusting. Someone should talk to the senator about him. That was embarrassing."

Jesse breathed a sigh of relief. Their heads were turned up as though they couldn't care less if a camera caught them. Just two women who had been hit on by a jerk. They'd still done the right thing by making sure he got to his room.

241

Ten put a hand on his shoulder. "She's a pro. You have to let her do her job. You can't pull the caveman act on her. She's smart and quick and she can take care of herself. I did you a solid by having Weston get you out of there." He leaned over and touched a button on Hutch's system. "You two come on up. We're good for the evening. We'll let Murdoch sift through some of the footage and see if we've got a lead on anything."

Over the elevator feed he heard Erin say, "I'm tired. Let's tell the boss we're done for the night."

Phoebe nodded. "After dealing with that wanker, I just want to go up to the suite and forget men exist at all. I can't believe I left London for this."

He wasn't about to let her forget. He intended to make sure she knew he existed. He sighed and stepped back. He'd damn near fucked up everything. "I'm sorry."

Ten's green eyes were icy cold as he looked him over. "Next time you'll be out. I'll ship you back to Taggart and you'll do this job from several thousand miles away."

He deserved that. "Yes, sir."

Ten softened marginally. "I didn't like the way he looked at her either, but I've had years to get used to the idea that my sister has a job. You don't, so you better hurry up and get with the program. And we men stick together on my team. No one's going to mention that Murdoch here has a possessive caveman side and a dick with zero IQ."

Hutch grinned around a licorice stick. "It's forever our secret."

Jesse nodded to let Ten know he was grateful. "Let me know when you're ready for me to look through the footage."

Hours and hours of his life would be spent sifting through the surveillance footage they'd gathered from both the security cameras and the personal equipment they'd been wearing. He'd learned that espionage was a lot like soldiering—hours of tedious, careful work, and then some shit exploded.

He stepped away and looked out over the balcony. The moon hung low, illuminating the beauty of the Persian Gulf. He felt someone step up, and there was no question who it would be. "How do you deal with it, Si?"

"Having my wife in harm's way from time to time?"

"Yeah."

"Mostly she's behind a computer, but when she's out in the field, I have to trust her. I'm almost always out in the field. She's got to deal with that every day. Chelsea is smart and she won't take chances she doesn't have to. You've got another problem entirely."

He knew what his real problem was. "She's already lost one husband."

"Exactly. I wouldn't spend my time railing at her for scaring you. She's doing her job. Praise her for it."

"He touched her."

"And she handled it." Simon seemed determined to be the voice of reason. "She wasn't alone. She had Erin to back her up, and for all of Erin's foibles, she's a damn fine agent. She wouldn't leave a teammate in the field to save her own life. They can handle things."

It would be easier if Phoebe was behind a desk like Chelsea, or so pregnant she couldn't work like Charlotte. Maybe Ian had the right idea. Just keep her pregnant so he could keep her safe. Except pregnancy wasn't exactly totally safe, and then there were kids. Kids weren't safe. Kids were small, crazed maniacs who thought playing in traffic and eating shit they shouldn't was fun. Then he would spend his every waking hour terrified he would lose not only Phoebe but his kids, too.

Nope. Tag was an idiot.

"Are you all right?" Simon asked.

"I was just thinking about family."

"And it made you turn slightly green?" Simon laughed, slapping him on the shoulder. "Don't think about it. Just do it. There are no guarantees in life except that if you waste it, you'll regret it. Take it all—the good, the bad, the risky. This is yours and it's all you have. Having a family is the most frightening thing in the world if you really let yourself think about it. All that pain waiting out there if you lose one of them. And still, it's meaningless if you don't have them. We find our families, Jesse. Some of us are lucky to find them when we're born, but a lot of us have to look. So be grateful and welcome every single person who becomes family to you. Hold them close and yes, mourn them when they're gone, so at the end of all of this you know you had a life."

He took a long breath, forcing his emotions deep because he was going to do everything he could to have those troublesome, frightening children with Phoebe. Neither one of them had good parents, but it didn't matter because he did have a family to rely on. When he had questions, he could ask Simon or Jake or Alex. His children wouldn't be alone like he'd been. They would be surrounded by cousins who would occasionally have to help fend off office attacks if their Uncle Ten and Uncle Tag couldn't get along.

He just had to convince Phoebe it was worth the risk.

"It doesn't look like our night is over." Hutch pointed to his computer screen as Jesse turned back around. "Who is that, boss?"

Ten stepped up behind them. "Can't tell. Do we have a better camera angle?"

Hutch hit a couple of buttons, grimacing. "Nah. I don't have anything that picks up his face. Phoebe and Erin were moving toward the elevators when he stopped them."

Jesse moved to his side, trying to get a good view of the feed. At least she was back in the ballroom. There was less chance of something bad happening to her with the entire conference crowd surrounding them.

On the camera feed, Phoebe was talking to a man in a thawb, the traditional Arab robe. It was long and covered every part of the man's body with the exception of his hands. His head was covered in a keffiyeh. He was standing right in front of Phoebe, but Jesse couldn't see his face. Phoebe's was clear on the camera and there wasn't a hint of distress. She seemed calm and pleasant.

"Can you get audio?" Ten asked.

Hutch nodded and Phoebe's voice came over the line. "Thank you so much for asking. I am well. There was a moment's distress, but it's all been handled."

"I saw you leave with the American. He was not in his right head." The voice was dark, rich. It sent a shiver down Jesse's spine. It made his stomach curl.

"He was drunk." Erin stood beside Phoebe. "It was embarrassing. We couldn't find his friends so we got him upstairs."

"Did you?" That deep voice asked. "Clever girls, but you should be careful here. Next time, ask a man to help you. You shouldn't be required to see that part of the world. It could also give the rest of the attendees the wrong impression of your character. They might not understand that you were trying to help. They would only see two women alone with a man who is not their husband."

Jesse forced himself to stay standing. It was right there, the impulse to hide, to make himself as small as possible so no one noticed him. He could hide from that voice. It didn't have to find him.

"Thank you, Mr. al Fareed." Phoebe gave the man a polite smile and elbowed Erin, who looked like she wanted to say something.

Don't say anything. Don't talk. Don't argue. Just survive.

The man's head bent slightly, as though acknowledging her gratitude. "You are with the Loa Mali contingent?"

"Yes, sir." Phoebe's accent was crisp, and he liked the fact that it was one more bit of armor she could put between her and the man in front of her. "My friend and I are in public relations and marketing for the king."

"He's an interesting man." Al Fareed bowed slightly. "And he has interesting friends. Be careful. It would be a shame for nice women like yourselves to get caught in a war."

"A war?"

"Business is always war and war is always a matter of business. Don't ever forget that. And stay away from the Americans. They drink too much. Men, I've found, are nothing but dogs to be trained. That one needs a tighter leash. Good evening."

He stepped out of the frame, his face never turning to the camera.

"Jesse? Are you all right?" He heard Simon talking, but it sounded far away.

Before he really knew what he was doing, he found himself running. There were shouts behind him, but he paid them no mind. He wasn't going to listen to that voice in his head. That voice led him nowhere. There was a new voice that shouted for him to take action.

He ran out of the suite and headed for the stairs. They would be so much quicker than the elevators. His team might catch him waiting for the elevators. They wouldn't understand. The devil had to be caught. The devil wouldn't be caught with cameras. He could manipulate those. He could only be caught by someone who knew him.

His mind raced as he flew down the stairs. One flight and then two and three and four. He lost track of how many. All that mattered was getting to the ballroom and unmasking the devil, showing him for the true evil he was.

His eyes caught on the door that led to the ballroom and he burst through it.

Sound and lights hit him. He was suddenly surrounded and in a sea of white.

His breath shuddered, but he forced some calm to slip over him. There were a few business suits, but mostly the entire room consisted of men in thawbs and keffiyehs. What color had the headdress been?

Red. It had been red, right?

Did every fucker in the room have to be wearing some damn form of red on his head?

His heart rate ticked up. He was here. The Caliph was here and he was wearing a mask. How the fuck was he supposed to find him when they all were wearing the same masks?

And there it was. That was the same keffiyeh he'd seen in the video feed. Red and black. He'd found him.

Jesse reached for the Caliph's elbow, pulling him around, ready to stare into the face of his own nightmare.

"Can I help you?" an elderly man asked, his brown eyes softening with concern. "Are you all right?"

Not the Caliph. Not even close. Jesse stepped back. "Sorry."

His heart sank and he stumbled a bit. He wanted to shout. Thought about it for a half a second. He could shout out and finally be done with this.

"Jesse?"

He stopped in the middle of the room. Phoebe. His hands were shaking. His heart racing. He wanted to walk away from her so she didn't have to see him, didn't have to know how this affected him and made him turn into a reactionary moron who hadn't even thought about the consequences of running in here like a madman.

He looked up and hundreds of eyes were watching him. He was supposed to be a ghost, someone who clung to the sidelines and no one noticed, but he'd just made himself a massive target. He'd placed them all in danger because he couldn't control himself.

He turned, knowing he had to get them out of here. She would be furious. He plastered a smile on his face that utterly belied his need to scream and roar and berate himself. "Hey, I was looking for you." Yeah, they would believe that. "Heard you had some trouble."

Erin was standing beside Phoebe with a frown on her face. "We took care of it. Looks like you're having some trouble, too."

"Back off," Phoebe said under her breath. "We'll deal with this upstairs."

He turned and suddenly was taken back to that moment he'd been placed on an airplane to go from Ramstein AFB back to the States after he'd been found. He'd been in the hospital for weeks, and then they'd come for him. Five MPs. They'd been there for his "protection" his CO had claimed, but that hadn't been how it felt.

He'd felt like a prisoner, like a man no one trusted.

As Simon and then Theo took up places on either side of him, he knew what it felt like again.

He walked forward toward the elevators, his gut in a nasty twist. He'd fucked up and it was going to cost him everything.

They got into the elevators and the silence was damn near devastating.

Phoebe's head went down, avoiding the cameras this time. "I know. Ten, I will handle it. I don't care. Yes, I'll let him know."

"Jesse," Simon began.

Phoebe turned, her eyes flashing. "You will wait until we get upstairs and then you will wait until I've had my talk with him. Is that understood?"

So Phoebe was going to deliver the dressing down. Yeah, that was the icing on the cake. That was the final fucking blow. He was going to lose his job and her in the same moment.

"You don't have to say anything," he began.

"Be quiet," she ordered.

The doors opened again and they marched out toward the suite. Ten was standing there waiting when they walked in.

"Do you have any idea what you just did? Every security team here is trying to figure out who you are. You have put every single one of us in danger," Ten said, his voice as cold as ice.

Phoebe got right in her brother's space. "I told you to stand down."

"You don't run this team," Ten shot back.

"I don't care. He's mine and I will take care of him. You and everyone else will back the fuck off. I'm going to do this in private. We'll deal with fallout later and that is my final say. Unless you want to fire me, you will let me deal with this my way."

Ten scrubbed a hand through his head and stalked off.

Phoebe's hand found his. It seemed a little cruel of her, but he was numb. He allowed himself to be led off. She walked right to the bedroom they'd shared. She wouldn't be sharing with him anymore. She led him inside and then turned and locked the door.

Jesse stared ahead, not wanting to look back at her. "I know I fucked up."

She moved around to stand in front of him, and there were tears in her eyes when she reached for him, her hands cupping his face as she stared up. "I will not let him hurt you. Do you understand me?" She wrapped her arms around him and suddenly he was held tight. "I won't ever let him hurt you. God, Jesse, he's here. I talked to him, didn't I? That's what Ten said. It was the only reason you would do that. I won't let him get near you. I promise. You're safe, Jesse. You're safe."

It took him a moment to take in her words, to understand that he wasn't being rejected. He was being pulled close. Her feminine body offering protection and comfort to his masculine one. He'd fucked up and she was promising to take care of him.

She was crying for him.

He let go, not of her, never of her. He let go of the idea that it was wrong to cry. He wouldn't do it in public or with his friends. But he could with her. She was safety and affection and acceptance.

A shudder went through his body and he let himself cry because he'd thought the nightmare was over, because it had never really gone away until this moment when she began to take some of the burden from him.

He laid his head on her shoulders, finally safe in her arms.

CHAPTER FIFTEEN

Phoebe sighed as she stepped out of the room the next morning. Ten was on her immediately, as though he'd waited all night for the chance. He might have. He might have paced outside her bedroom door all night long, waiting for the shot at taking a hunk out of her flesh. He'd probably listened, trying to hear if they were fighting or fucking.

They'd done neither. She'd held him and then they'd gone to bed, his head on her breast, his arms wound around her.

He'd needed intimacy the night before. He'd needed to know she was there with him.

"Good morning." The best way to deal with Ten was to brazen through. If she gave him a moment's weakness, he would pounce like the predator he was. She nodded in his direction and then walked straight toward the coffee, letting her nose lead the way.

Ten followed, hard on her heels. "Good morning? Are you fucking kidding me?"

"Nope. I'm being an optimist this morning." It wasn't true. She was sick to her stomach because she knew the op was almost over and so was her time with Jesse.

Unless he meant what he'd said and he really could forgive her. She wasn't sure she could risk it. It might be better to know he still cared about her than to risk everything and lose it all. Maybe they could still see each other. She would have her work and he would have his and they could spend their free time together.

Because a week or two a year was better than nothing, right? Until he found the woman who wasn't too damaged and he got married and had kids. Yeah, it would be great.

"Damn it, Phoebe. Do you understand what happened last night?" Ten followed her into the living area of the suite where a long table had been set with a buffet overflowing with fruit and yogurt and eggs, small pastries, and even a row of perfectly made crepes with whipped cream.

She just poured a cup of coffee. She didn't really have much of an appetite. "I understand that Jesse had to face something most of us can't even conceive."

"He completely lost it."

"Maybe, but I think in this case, it's understandable. He heard that voice again. It was the voice that did it." They hadn't talked about it, just held on to each other, but it was the only thing that made sense. Phoebe had been well aware of where the camera was, but any subtle attempts to turn them had been rebuffed by the very elegant Mr. al Fareed.

Even when she hadn't realized who he was, he'd scared her. Not in a run and hide sense, but she'd known he was a predator. Her instincts had flared the minute he stepped in her way.

It was in his face. He was actually an attractive man when she considered his features on a separate basis. He had everything it took to be quite handsome. Until she got to the eyes. His eyes were flat. Obsidian and flat, like a reptile's. She'd seen those eyes in a crocodile or a shark. They held no hint of humanity or compassion. No humor.

Ten sighed and sank down into one of the chairs. It was easy to see the toll the last few days had taken on him. "Yeah. At least I think so. One minute I was watching you and the next he was taking off. Tell me it wasn't as bad as it looked on the monitors."

She wished she could. "The good news is it was contained to the back of the ballroom. He didn't get very far in, but at least a third of the people there were well aware something odd was happening."

"Then everyone knows."

The gossip would spread very quickly. "Probably." There was an upside to this particular clusterfuck. "It's all right, Ten. Jesse needs to stay up here now. We should keep him out of the line of sight. We know who our target is. Now the rest of us gather intel on the al Fareed brothers."

"Which one was it?"

Oh, he was so not going to love her answer. "I don't know. His badge simply said Mr. al Fareed. Do you have pictures?"

"They're practically twins," Ten said with a grimace as he reached for his tablet. He slid his finger across the screen and passed it to her.

Two men stared back. The two brothers looked very much alike. Both handsome and lean. In the pictures they had, both men sported dark beards, but the man she'd met the night before had cropped his close. "I think it's this one. Ibrahim. But I'll be honest, it wasn't until he started talking about war and business that I really looked at him. I was trying to play down my aggressive American side, so I tried not to look him in the eyes."

"Probably a good play given what part of the world we're in. I know it's hard on female operatives, but we have to be sure here. I need you to take another look," Ten said as though he found the request distasteful.

"I'll make sure this afternoon. I'm going to sit in with Kamdar on a couple of the sessions. The al Fareeds are expected to attend. I'll get you what you need and then we can build a case against him." A case that would hopefully forever get the stain off Jesse Murdoch's reputation. It might be the only gift she could give him.

"All right. I hate sending you back in. I take it everyone saw you walking out with him?"

It was a problem, but she wasn't willing to scrap the mission because of it. "I'll be fine. I'll take someone with me. Hey, if he flees the conference, we know we've got him on the run. Once we're sure of the name, we don't need to stay here. We set up long-term observation and we get Chelsea digging into his past. We'll find something."

"You are not to go anywhere in this hotel without a bodyguard. I know you can handle yourself, but I'm not taking any chances." He sighed and sat back. "When the hell did I lose control of everything?"

She'd wondered when they were going to have this talk. There hadn't been time before they'd had to come to Dubai. She sat down across from him. Ten could hold things in for a very long time, but it seemed he'd always been willing to open up eventually with her or Jamie. "Ace wasn't your fault, Tennessee."

"Hell yes, he was." He looked straight on, his eyes stubborn.

She simply moved to where he was staring so he had to look at her. "You couldn't have known. You did everything you could with the information you had. He came highly recommended. He passed every single test the Agency gave him. This isn't your fault."

"I've trained all my life to see things that aren't there. From the time I was a kid, I knew I would do this job, and that fucker got past me."

"He got past everyone." She knew she was talking to a brick wall at this point, but she couldn't help but speak the truth. Eventually it would get to him. "What happened at Sanctum wasn't your fault and last night wasn't really Jesse's. He saw a threat, and not only that, he saw me standing next to the man who killed his entire team."

"Yeah, I didn't think about it that way. Jesus, Phoebe, now that I do think about it, I kind of want to run around until I find the fucker, too." He leaned forward. "That man killed my brother. He tortured and killed my brother and I was thinking about the fucking op."

"Which is what you were trained to do," she pointed out gently. "It does Jamie no good for you to blow everyone's cover. You have to be rational about this because Jesse can't be."

"How about you?" Ten asked, his voice softening. A somber smile slightly curled up his mouth. "You were standing right next to the man who killed Jamie and what were you thinking about?"

She set the coffee down and guilt swamped her as she admitted the truth. "I was thinking about Jesse." She'd thought about Jesse all night long. How could she do that? "Ten, I'm so sorry. I thought about Jesse."

Ten sat up, his hands on the table between them. "As you damn well should have. I wasn't blaming you. I was pointing something out. You're a fool if you think you can leave that boy behind."

It took her a moment because she'd been so wrapped up in the drama with Jesse that she hadn't given Jamie more than a passing thought. It had been right and good to offer Jesse comfort. It had felt like her right to hold him. "But I stood right in front of the man who killed my husband and all I could think about afterward was protecting my boyfriend from him."

"Because Jamie's gone, honey, and life is for the living. Hell, I won't kick the boy's ass for that fact alone." He sat back, crossing his legs. "I knew Jamie better than you did."

"I was his wife." She was the one looking away now, but Ten wouldn't allow her that comfort any more than she'd allowed him. He caught her eye.

"Yeah, well, you didn't grow up with him and you weren't his best friend. I think if he'd lived, you would have been, but you were both so young you never got past the mad in love stage. You didn't have to really live together the way couples with mortgages and kids and crappy jobs have to. He put you on a pedestal and you're doing the same with him. He wanted that mission. Do you know why he wanted that mission?"

"No." And maybe she didn't want to know.

"Because he wanted to best me. He wanted to head a team of his own."

Phoebe shook her head. It went against everything they'd talked about. "No. We were getting out. We agreed that if we were going to have kids, we couldn't put ourselves on the line like that."

Ten reached for her hand, covering it with his own. "I know that's what he told you and he definitely wanted you out, but it was in his blood. He tried to convince the director that he could run a black ops team better than me. He wanted my job or one just like it, and he decided taking on the truly dangerous operations were exactly what he needed to do to prove it."

She wanted to pull away, but she couldn't. All she could do was protest even though something in Ten's words rang true. "No. Jamie loved you."

"Hell, yeah, he loved me. We were brothers. You think

brothers aren't competitive as hell? You think it doesn't burn the big brother's ass when little brother becomes his boss? I'm not maligning Jamie. I'm just saying that you take all this guilt on yourself when you didn't force him to go."

Jamie wasn't the only one she felt guilty about. Even if she accepted that she hadn't forced Jamie into anything, she couldn't wish away her other problem. "And Jesse? They were looking for Jamie. I'm the one who came up with the plan to send Jamie in. I'm the one who led the Caliph right to Jesse."

"And a fucking butterfly flapped its wings halfway across the world and it rains in DC," Ten argued back. "The butterfly had as much intent as you had. The asshole in DC who forgot his umbrella doesn't blame the bug."

He was throwing chaos theory at her? "That is a stupid argument."

"And it's true. You had zero idea it would turn out this way. You never intended to cause him harm and wouldn't have proceeded had you known the outcome."

Not even if Jamie had survived. She would never have placed a unit in that harm's way. She hadn't known the Caliph even existed. "No, I wouldn't have."

"Jesse won't blame you. He might be surprised, but he won't blame you and he won't let you walk away from him. That's the only hope I have now that Jamie might rest in peace knowing he got what he wanted."

"What's that?"

"You happy. I was the best man at your wedding. I took Jamie out for a bachelor party of two because the last thing he wanted was a bunch of strippers when he had you. I say I took him out, but all we really did was pick up a bucket of wings and go back to his place."

She laughed, the memories coming back and somehow whisking away the bad ones. "Mine wasn't much better. I went to a club with some of the girls from work and spent all night texting Jamie."

Ten smiled, real tenderness in his expression. "Still better than his. I bought a case of beer and we watched football and talked about you. After the game was over, he flipped through channels and found a freaking marathon of those wizard movies. He made me watch one. Couldn't you two have found something more masculine to bond over?"

Even though the thought brought tears to her eyes, they were sweeter now. They weren't sad. They reminded her of how nice it had been and not simply of what she'd lost. When had that changed? When had thinking of Jamie become something wistful and not an ache in her soul? "Nope. Those are our books. He kissed me for the first time while we were reading on the patio. At first I thought he only read them because I liked them, but Harry won him over in the end."

She'd started reading them when a librarian had suggested the first book. She'd been at an inner-city school, one of the rougher foster homes. She'd read that first book so many times the librarian swore she wore it out. When Franklin Grant asked her what she wanted for her birthday, she'd asked for her own copies. Jamie had started reading them even though Ten had teased them that they were for kids. Jamie hadn't cared. He'd wanted to have something to talk to her about and they'd spent hours reading and talking and watching the movies. They argued over whether Hermione should end up with Harry or Ron. Silly things, but it had brought them closer.

"Do you know what I asked him that night?" Ten's question brought her back to the present. "I asked him why he was getting married. I wasn't being rude. I just didn't understand it. He said he wanted to make you happy. He said if he wanted one thing in the world it was that you would never be alone again, never be unhappy again. This tragedy goes past him dying. He would hate the fact that you can't move on, that you can't find a way to live. You think you honor him by being miserable, but it's not true."

She was saved by the door to the far suite opening and Erin walking in. Phoebe turned quickly and tried to shove the unwanted emotion deep because Ten was starting to get through to her. He was starting to make sense, and that meant she would have to choose between a life with Jamie's memory or one with Jesse. She wasn't ready.

Except maybe she was. It had been right to hold Jesse. It had been right and good and she couldn't work up the will to fight it.

Something deep inside wondered why she would even try.

What if she got a second chance? Should she turn it away because she didn't trust it? Would she take back loving Jamie so she didn't have to lose him?

Was she that much of a coward?

"Back off, minor Taggart," Erin said as she strode into the room. She wore slacks, a white button down, and a smart-looking blazer this morning. Her hair was in a neat bun. She was ready to play the role of the hard-nosed businesswoman with the singular exception of her shoes. She had fuzzy bunny slippers on, but they were ruined by the nasty edge to her voice. "I don't need your advice."

Theo was right behind her. He looked like he'd gotten as much sleep as Ten. "I'm just saying you have to watch out around that guy. He's a playboy."

Erin's eyes rolled. "Funny, you sound just like that douchebag who told me I was dressed like a slut."

"I never said that." Theo looked over at Ten like Ten could help him out. "When did I say that? What does that even mean?"

Ten held up his hands. "I got nothing except to tell you that hookers don't give a shit what you say. And I know a couple of very flexible ones."

Her brother was a giver.

"Hey, did you blow Murdoch? Because he looked like he could use it." And Erin was pure lady. She grabbed a plate and started filling it up.

"Oooo, someone got a little something?" Hutch asked as he walked out and immediately grabbed a Danish. "I thought we weren't supposed to get laid here. I got a very strict 'no touching the locals' lecture and Erin threatened my balls if I looked at her the wrong way. What's your problem with a man's balls, woman? They're sacred."

"They're delicate so that's where I strike. Are you made of sugar, dude? How do you stay so thin?" She didn't wait for Hutch to reply, simply shook her head and turned back to Phoebe. "So did you fuck Murdoch so hard he forgot all about his troubled past?"

Phoebe couldn't help but laugh, but Theo frowned.

"Don't make fun of her. Just because Phoebe's got a

compassionate heart doesn't mean you should tease her."

Simon stepped up to the buffet, pouring himself a cup of coffee. "You weren't angry with him? I was a little worried that you rushed him off for a private dressing down. I stayed up in case he needed me."

"Why would I be mad at Jesse? Now the rest of you are idiots and we should talk about that." She warmed to her subject because it was so much easier than the last one. "You treated him like he was the bad guy. Yes, he shouldn't have taken off like that, but he was trying to do his job. He was supposed to identify the Caliph. He couldn't see his face on the tape. Why didn't anyone try to follow him on camera? He had to have walked past a camera."

"I totally tried after I stopped watching Murdoch take the stairs three at a time," Hutch said around his third Danish. The boy really could eat and he seemed to prefer sweets.

"Hutch did try, but al Fareed kept his face down until he got back to his room," Ten admitted.

"So he knew we were watching. Did anyone think to follow him on foot? Hutch could have given you directions." She didn't wait because she knew the answer. "No. You didn't because you were all too busy making Jesse feel like shit."

"Baby, it's all right." Jesse stepped from their suite, his hair still wet from a shower. He was in jeans and a T-shirt and no shoes, and she wanted nothing more than to jump all over him and forget everything that was happening. When he kissed her, she couldn't think about anything except him. "I knew why they were doing it. Now they know I'm here. He knows I'm here. Even if he didn't see me himself, he heard about the crazy American who seemed to be looking for someone. He'll have brought up the tapes and despite the hair color, he'll remember me. A master doesn't forget his unfinished work."

The thought chilled her. She couldn't stand the fact that the Caliph very likely knew Jesse was here. She got up and poured him a cup of coffee, one cream and two sugars. The least she could do was help him get ready for the day. He needed her support. "Come and sit down."

"I think that's my line." He walked to the seat anyway.

"Not today. It's mine today." He could Dom her all he liked, but she was going to take care of him today. She handed him the coffee and then made a major decision on the spur of the moment. If she was in, she was going to be all in, even if it was only for a few more days. She sat down on his lap, nestling against his chest and letting her head find the crook of his neck.

She felt him sigh, a long, pleasurable sound, and then he relaxed around her.

"Ten, what's my damage?" This time when he spoke, any hint of timidity was banished. "How can I fix it?"

Ten shook his head and then plowed forward. "It will help if you don't show your face today. Stay in here and review the tapes. Phoebe's right. He's got to have screwed up at some point. We'll catch him and you'll identify him and then we'll go from there."

Phoebe winced a little as she hadn't exactly given them all the information she'd acquired either. "We might have a bigger problem."

Erin's eyes widened. "Shitballs. We didn't mention what we found. Damn. I'm blaming even littler Tag for that. He distracted me with his obnoxiousness. I've been getting the same lecture for twelve hours."

"Well, that's because you won't listen," Theo said.

"Erin, what have you found?" Simon asked with a sigh.

Erin exchanged a look and nodded, giving Phoebe the floor.

She sat up as properly as she could while she was still on Jesse's lap. It was odd, but it seemed to give him comfort so she was going with it. "The little prick who's working for the senator had the newspaper article from the Sanctum explosion on his desk. He seemed very interested in Jesse's death and he had two names written down." This was the really bad part. "Ian Taggart was the first one. Ian was listed in the article so I suppose he might have gotten it from there."

Ten had gone utterly still, as though he knew there was a rattlesnake in the room and it was about to bite him. "Who was the other name, Phoebe?"

"Tennessee G. Smith."

"Shit." Ten rose to his feet and immediately got on the phone. "Damn it. I'm sorry. I know it's late Charlotte, but I have to talk to him."

Her brother walked into his room and the door slammed shut.

"I find it interesting that he called Big Tag and not his director," Erin mused.

"He's worried there's a mole," Jesse said. "That's it, right?"

"The name Tennessee Smith doesn't appear in records," Phoebe replied. "Only the Agency is supposed to know his name, and even then only men with the proper security clearance. When he works with anyone outside his circle, he goes by the tried and true."

"Mr. Black," Simon supplied. "Yes, I've met a few of those in my time."

"After the problems Taggart had, he took to calling himself Mr. White, but it's all the same. It's there so you don't ever really know the name of who you're working with. I know you won't believe me, but it's as much for your protection as his."

"Sure it is." Erin set her plate on the table. "So someone figured out his name. Big whoop."

"Ace knew his name." Jesse's hand smoothed up and down her back. "We have to assume he gave the Caliph all the intelligence he had on the team. We know he was in contact with him."

She let his heat sink in even as she pointed out the problem. "I can assure you that my brother has never revealed his middle name to anyone on his team."

Theo shook his head. "I don't know it. I'm closer to Ten than most."

"Does the G stand for George?" Hutch asked.

Jesse huffed. "Obviously it stands for Grant. He considered the man his father. Why didn't he change it legally?"

And they teased him for being dumb. "He didn't want a big paper trail connecting him to me and Jamie. He's paranoid. Until he flipped out when he thought Tag was going to murder me, none of his team knew he had a sister. I was just a fellow employee."

"So we have bigger problems," Simon mused.

"Yeah, we've got another damn mole and one who's close to a senator." Hutch reached for a pastry. "So now we need to figure out why that drunk boy knows Ten's super secret middle name. He really looked more like a George, you know."

"So you'll look into Albertson?" She shot Hutch a pointed

look. "Like now?"

Hutch grabbed another plate. "Fine. You know other people on this team get time off." When no one replied, he just shook his head. "Fine. I'll go wake up Chelsea and she's going to be irritable."

"Send her my love," Simon said with a wave. He looked back at Phoebe and Jesse. "And you two get ready. Phoebe has a session soon and you need to look through the footage."

"Simon?" Jesse started.

"I'll go with her. I won't let her out of my sight," Simon promised.

"Thank you, brother," Jesse said with obvious relief.

So Simon was the only one he really trusted. She should have picked someone from her own team, but that didn't mean anything now. Jesse was her team and he would feel better with Simon watching over her. She wasn't going to question him.

She turned her head up when Simon left to clean up and Erin and Theo continued bickering over breakfast. She and Jesse were left to themselves. "Are you okay?"

His hand came up, smoothing back her hair. "I'm as good as I can be, thanks to you. Your brother should have fired me."

"Not if he knows what's good for him."

"Phoebe, I screwed up last night. I put us all in harm's way."

"You had a bad moment."

"And that one moment could get us all killed. I don't want you to go out there today. I want you to come with me and we'll go to the airport and we won't even go back to Dallas. We'll go somewhere no one knows who we are. We can just hide."

"Jesse," she started.

His hand came up and he put a finger to her lips. "I said that's what I want to do. What I'm going to do is tell you to be careful because you're precious to me."

How was she supposed to resist him? The universe was cruel and oh so kind. She leaned forward and kissed him. "I promise."

He wrapped his arms around her and they sat that way until it was time to go.

* * * *

Six hours later, Phoebe stood beside Simon as the session on new ecological laws in First World countries came to a close. It was the third session she'd sat through and the final one of the first day of the conference. Frustration threatened to bubble over. "I didn't see the al Fareed party at all."

Simon nodded shortly and leaned over to speak to her in a quiet tone. "I didn't either. I think we have to believe they might have left. There's a private meeting this evening, but Kamdar isn't invited to it. It's only oil companies."

She looked around, but found not a single familiar face beyond Theo standing guard in the background.

They were running out of time and their prey was proving to be elusive. The conference itself was only four days. If she couldn't identify the man by then, she feared they would lose him. He knew what was happening. It would be easy for him to simply disappear into his country and start his work all over again.

Business is always war and war is always a matter of business. The words had played through her head. What else had al Fareed said? She reached up and tugged on Simon's suit coat, stopping his forward progress. "He was interested in Kamdar."

Simon turned to her. "That's not terribly surprising. He's rather making himself a massive target. I hear he was talking about putting them all out of business last night. He's an interesting fellow, but I'm afraid these very conservative men are going to find him arrogant and obnoxious."

"That's what al Fareed said. Interesting. He said the king was an interesting man with interesting friends."

"I don't think anyone would argue with that." Simon looked at his watch. "Tea's about to be served. We should walk through before we give up for the evening. We'll make sure we've got surveillance on his suite and that boardroom, but we can't simply stand around and hope to catch sight of him. It's more important than ever that we keep our cover."

He didn't understand. "I think he was talking about Jesse. It was in the way he said it. I think when he was talking about Kamdar's interesting friends, he was talking about Jesse and possibly Ten."

"But Jesse hadn't blown up when you met al Fareed."

"That's my point exactly. 'Business is always war.' He said that and that I shouldn't get caught in the middle. He was specifically talking about the king of Loa Mali at that point. We never figured out who paid Eli Nelson to blow up Kamdar's first experiments with green energy. That explosion should have set him back years."

"You think it could have been al Fareed."

"I think it's bigger than that." The lines were starting to be drawn in her head, faint at first, but getting stronger. "I need to think about it for a while."

She needed to think about al Fareed and The Collective.

How had he known where Jesse's unit was going? It hadn't been a random IED that took them out. There had been nothing random about any of it.

That unit was headed back in from a mission. She needed to talk to Jesse. He was the only one left who could tell her anything.

The thought made her sick, but she had to tell Jesse the truth. He needed to know.

"Are you all right?" Simon looked down at her. "You went pale."

She shook her head. "I'm good. Let's do a quick turn through the tea and then head up for the night. The al Fareed brothers will be in the oil meeting hatching all sorts of nefarious plots. They won't be at the dinner for the poor people."

By poor people she still meant seriously rich, but the men who would be in the private meeting were the world's wealthiest oilmen.

Was it also a meeting of The Collective?

She followed Simon out, her thoughts running amok. It was like this when she was considering a puzzle. Chaotic at first. It was hard because there was so much information and she had to sift through, to sort it into something that made sense.

How had the senator's aide known Ten's middle initial?

How had al Fareed known about Kamdar's "friends" before Jesse had outed himself? Now that she thought about it, he'd used words that would have a direct impact on Jesse. He'd talked about dogs and leashes, his voice becoming sharper, as though to highlight what he was saying. As though he'd known Jesse was somewhere listening to him.

And Ace. She couldn't forget Ace. He was the link. He'd been placed, but by whom? Yes, it seemed to be al Fareed on the surface, and certainly he'd been there to do the Caliph's bidding, but no Middle Eastern oilman could have that much influence on the Agency.

Not without help from the inside.

She was grateful for Simon because she likely would have gotten lost without him. She didn't really see where she was going. She saw the puzzle in front of her.

"Have a seat." Simon held out the chair for her. "I'll get us some tea. We'll put in an appearance and then we'll leave. Don't move."

He walked toward the elegant buffet.

"Well, well, if it isn't the whore from last night," a low voice said.

She looked up and there was her old friend Albertson. He was dressed in a perfectly cut suit, his hair slicked back, and a ten thousand dollar watch around his wrist. Still, his eyes told the tale. They were bloodshot and tired. She started to stand because there was zero point in arguing over his opinion of her. "I'll excuse myself since you can't seem to be a gentleman."

He reached out, catching her elbow. "I might have been a gentleman if you and your friend hadn't drugged me. Did you think I wouldn't catch that, bitch?"

"Since I did nothing of the sort, no, I didn't think you would. Let go of my arm." She glared back at him. "As drunk as you were last night, I'm surprised you remember me at all."

His lips curled in a sneer. "You were counting on that, weren't you? Too bad you were working with a pro. I've had far more to drink and still managed to fuck some dumb bitch and maintain my memory of the encounter. I'm not stupid. You tried to roll me last night. Since my wallet was in place, I have to think you're looking for something else."

"Hey, take your hands off her. Now." Theo moved in, his big shoulders encased in a suit. Despite the well-tailored look, there was no way to mistake him for anything but muscle.

Albertson let go of her arm and stared for a moment. "Shit. For a minute I thought you were…" His face went red and he held his hands up as though giving in. "Hey, the lady and I were just talking. No big deal. She needs to understand that when she plays with fire, she's going to get burned. But then you should know all about that."

Theo stared at him. "Why would I know about that?"

"You're old enough to know that a man can lose the things he loves the most, the places he feels most comfortable in if he doesn't know when to back off or who to be friends with," Albertson said pointedly.

Theo's eyes narrowed. "Is that right? You want me to deliver a message to my brother? Because that's sure what it fucking sounds like."

"I don't even know who you're talking about," he replied with a smile that belied his words. He was enjoying playing with them.

"It's okay," Theo promised, taking her by the elbow and gently bringing her to his side. "You might not know who he is, but I promise you, he knows who you are. Tell the senator hello from a lowly bodyguard. And if you come near her again, I'll cut your balls off and make a toy out of them for my cat. I don't actually own a cat, but if I have your balls dangling on a piece of string, I'll get one just for the pleasure of watching it bat your boys around. Am I understood?"

Albertson took a step back, but he didn't take his eyes off her. She could feel him watching her as Theo walked toward Simon.

"I suppose I can order us tea for the suite." Simon sighed and put the cups down before walking toward the elevators.

"You sound a lot like your brother," Phoebe told Theo as the doors closed.

"I guess the ability to threaten a man runs in the family," Theo replied. "He was an asshole and he was lying. He thought I was Ian. I talked to Ian last night. He says he doesn't know who this guy is."

"I don't think he's our problem. I am interested in his boss, though." The doors opened again and she heard Ten shouting.

She picked up the pace, shoving through the door that led to their rooms.

"Listen to me." Ten was red in the face, his boots ringing on the marbled floors. "You don't understand what I'm doing here."

His head turned down and a low growl came out of his mouth. "You can't...yes. I understand. Yes, sir. By morning. Good-bye."

"What was that about?" Jesse looked up from his seat next to Hutch.

Ten locked eyes with Phoebe and she could see the beast that was always just under his surface. She watched as he subdued it and shoved it back down. When he spoke he was calm again, though his words were clipped, his annoyance plain. "We've been recalled to DC. Hutch, shut her down. We've got to be packed and ready to go. They're sending a plane to pick us up early tomorrow morning." He turned back to Simon. "Agency only, man. I'm so fucking sorry."

"What?" Phoebe shook her head, trying to wrap her mind around the words. "Why would they call us in? Who called us in?"

"The executive director. He's revoked my privileges. All operations under my command now have to be approved. I've been demoted and if I don't show up in DC tomorrow, I'll be fired."

It was so much worse than being fired. "They threatened to disavow you?"

He nodded sharply. "You know what that means."

It meant that Tennessee Smith would cease to exist. He would have no name, no passport, no home or bank accounts in the United States. He would be a ghost.

Ten turned to Jesse. "I swear to you, I'm going to figure out what's going on and we'll handle the Caliph. If I have to have the fucker assassinated, I will. But I have to find out what's going on first."

"I think it's the senator," Phoebe said. "I think somehow he's working with al Fareed."

"Proof?" Ten asked.

She shook her head. "I have a whole lot of conjecture, but I need to know who recommended Ace. I was right about that. He couldn't have made it on an Agency black ops team without some serious recommendations. Who was it?"

Hutch turned to his keyboard and his hands flew across it. He sat back and then tried again. "What the fuck? Boss, I don't have access to those records. What the hell? I've got the security clearance. Why am I blocked?"

She exchanged worried glances with Ten. They weren't just being called back. Ten's job was on the line and he was about to have his life picked apart by bureaucrats because he'd stepped into something none of them understood yet. Phoebe made her own command decision. "Simon, get your wife on the phone or better yet, get Adam. They could be watching Chelsea. Her job is on the line, too."

Simon snorted, an oddly elegant sound. "She doesn't particularly care one way or another. If the Agency fires her, she'll just go to work for Tag. I'll call Adam as well. We'll have an answer soon."

Jesse stood up. "I'll start looking for flights for me and Si and Erin."

There was something about the way he said it that made her wary. Already, they were splitting up. Hutch and Theo were moving toward each other, talking in low tones. Simon walked out of the room. Erin and Jesse exchanged a glance.

"You're not going to leave, are you?" Phoebe asked.

Jesse's jaw went stubborn. "I don't have to answer to the Agency. I answer to Ian Taggart. We'll see what he says. I suppose you'll be on that plane."

What did he expect her to do? "I would think you of all people would understand the chain of command, Jesse. I was ordered by my superior officer to return to base."

He stared for a moment as though he could imprint his will on her. "You can choose. You don't have to work for them. This isn't Ten telling you what to do. This is someone with an obvious agenda. They are working against our mission."

"Those people you're talking about run the CIA."

"Oh, and there's never been corruption there. Now who's being naïve, Phoebe? You want to be on that plane, I don't think I can stop you. Erin, go talk to Kamdar. Explain what's going on. We still need his cooperation in order to continue."

Erin nodded and like the good little soldier she was, trotted off to do his bidding.

"They can't stay," Theo said, his eyes widening when he realized what was going on. "They don't have any backup. They don't have anyone who can help them out if they get into trouble. If they get arrested, the government won't do a damn thing about it. She can't stay here."

Phoebe kept her eyes on Jesse. "He has a point."

Jesse shrugged. "I never expected the government to help me out anyway. What I do have is Ian Taggart, and I assure you he won't leave my ass in a prison for months and months. We're not the Agency. We don't take our time or wait for the right political situation. We don't leave our men behind."

His words hit her squarely in the gut.

He'd been left behind. In essence, she'd left them both there, Jamie to die and Jesse to be tortured.

"We looked. Do you think we didn't look for you?" The question came out on a shaky breath as every one of her insecurities bubbled to the surface. All the guilt she'd started to toss out settled over her again.

Jesse took a step toward her. "I'm talking about the present, Phoebe. Not the past. You are so damn caught up in the past, I should have known what you would think."

She turned and walked away. She couldn't have this argument with him. Not when she was leaving and he seemed determined to destroy himself. It struck her quite forcibly that she could lose another man she loved to that animal because Jesse couldn't think straight about this. He couldn't control himself. Last night had proven it. He needed to step back and let Ten handle it.

Did she just think that word? Did she put that word into her head? Love? She couldn't love him. She couldn't save him. Hell, she hadn't saved Jamie. She didn't even deserve a chance with Jesse. She just didn't.

"Hey, Phoebe. Stop." Jesse followed her into the hallway.

She couldn't face him. Her carefully constructed walls were rotting at her feet. She was the reason Jesse was here now. If she'd been better at her job, he would likely be back in Dallas, going on with his life.

She killed the men she loved.

Her chest was far too tight as she opened and closed the door to the bedroom. She needed time. The lock clicked into place and she looked down at the way her hands were shaking. She was caught. Trapped, just like when she'd been a kid and she knew something was wrong but she couldn't do anything. No one wanted to hear her cry. It made things worse. She needed to cry, but it was stuck inside. Everything was ending. She was losing Jesse and maybe her job, and she might cost Ten his. She wanted to wail and punch and fight and all she could do was try to drag a breath in.

"Phoebe?"

She couldn't right now. She stayed silent. He would get the hint. Maybe in an hour or so she would be able to face him with some hint of dignity.

How could she walk away from him? How could she fucking not?

"Baby, I need you to step back," Jesse said. "Do it. Now."

The door came crashing open and there he was, rebalancing himself after kicking the damn door in. His shoulders were squared and his jaw formed a hard line as he stepped inside.

"What did you do?"

A stern look lit his face as he walked in and shut the door as best he could. "I told you. No more doors between us."

"There's going to be a couple thousand miles between us by tomorrow. You planning on kicking their asses, too?" He wanted to be the tough guy? She could do that, too. She'd practically written the book on how to bury what she was feeling deep.

So why was her every emotion simmering right under the surface?

"Stay with me."

She couldn't do that. She couldn't watch him put himself in the Caliph's orbit again. "Come with me."

His eyes held a steely will as he towered over her. "Marry me and I will."

"What?"

He stepped forward, getting into her space. "I meant what I said. Marry me and I'll follow you. Marry me and I'll quit if that's what you want. I'll find another job. Hell, I'll try college or something."

She stared up at him, not quite sure she'd heard him correctly. "You love your job."

His hand came out, his fingers brushing across her cheek. "I love you more, Phoebe. So give me a reason to walk out of here with you. I'll pack us up and we can sleep at the airport. I'll be the first one on the plane."

He couldn't do that. He couldn't leave McKay-Taggart. She couldn't ask him to do that. "You love your team."

"I do. I love you more." He said it so simply, as though the words didn't threaten to change the course of her life.

She started to turn away. "I can't."

He gripped her elbow, hauling her back. He pulled her close, not giving her an inch of space. "Then I'll take what time I have. Until you step on to that plane and out of my life, you belong to me. You're fucking mine. Nothing comes between us. Not your brother. Not the Agency. Not that ghost you keep holding on to. Tonight, you're mine and you're going to obey every command I give you, and the first one is take those damn clothes off and get on your knees."

Her breath hitched. "I can't."

His head dipped, his lips hovering above hers. "You can. You think I don't know what you need? You think this is all for me? It's not. You're on the edge. You need an excuse to cry, to let go, and I'm going to give you one. I would do this for the rest of our lives. I would take care of you, but you won't let me so I have one last night to love you. My way."

"I can't love you, Jesse. Not like you deserve, but you should know that I will miss you every second of every day."

"Every second of every day I want you to remember this." He pressed his erection against her, moving until his hard cock rode right against her clit. "Remember every second that you could have had a man who worshipped you with his body and soul. You could have had a man who thought of you all the time, who put you first."

"I don't deserve that."

He breathed a sigh and his eyes softened a bit. "And there is the real problem. I'll show you that you're wrong about that, too. On your knees."

Hands shaking, she dropped to her knees, ready to give him everything she had.

CHAPTER SIXTEEN

Jesse watched her drop to her knees, knowing the fight wasn't over. Not even close. She thought she could have one more night with him, thought she could take what she needed and still walk away.

He planned to make it impossible for her.

He needed to figure out what all this guilt was about and banish it from their lives forever because he had no intention of living without her. He placed a hand on her head, for the first time in his life feeling like a real Dom. It had all been play before, light and teasing. There was nothing playful about this. Phoebe needed him. She needed a Dom, but mostly what she needed was a husband. It was all just different words for the same thing. Love. Dedication. Commitment. He was committed to her and she was about to discover what that truly meant.

"Tell me your secret, Phoebe."

Her breath caught and she shook her head. "No."

"Does it have something to do with leaving a man behind?" She'd shut down when he'd made the crack about the Agency leaving agents. "Was that what happened to your husband?"

She went utterly still. "Don't talk about him."

That hurt, but it wasn't unexpected. He'd known when he

started this that it would be a long night. It was the only night they had if he didn't break down her walls. He was out of time. He needed to get her mind off all the crap that was happening and on the present. "Undo the fly of my jeans."

A look of relief crossed her features and her hands immediately came up, working the button on his jeans and bringing the zipper down. His cock sprang free. He'd been erect from the moment she'd walked into the room. Even during their argument, his cock had been slamming against his jeans, desperate to get close to her. She stared at him, his dick pulsing. "You're so pretty."

He'd never once been called pretty before, but he would take any compliment she gave him. "I think you're the pretty one. Kiss me, Phoebe. Show me you want me."

She leaned over and those gorgeous lips of hers opened and her tongue came out, swiping at the head of his already weeping dick. His eyes nearly rolled into the back of his head when she sucked his cockhead behind her lips.

"I do want you. I want you so much." Her words rumbled along his cock, trembling against his flesh and making his balls draw up.

"Take more." He had no intentions to come. He wouldn't do that until he was buried deep inside her ass, but he so wanted her mouth on him. They both needed the connection.

She looked up as she ran her tongue down his cock, whirling it around and around. She sucked the pre-come off him and drank it down. Her hand came up, circling his stalk and drawing him in deeper.

So good. She felt so good. His Phoebe didn't half ass anything, so when she sucked him, she meant it. She worked her mouth around him, drawing him deeper and deeper inside. Her hands went down to cup his balls, nails scraping lightly. His hand sank into the softness of her hair and he tilted his pelvis, forcing her to take more. Her breasts bounced as she ate his dick. He hissed when he felt the sharp scrape of her teeth, but it was just one more sensation to be had. Her tongue soothed the little ache and before he knew it, he felt his balls pulsing, getting ready to explode.

With pure willpower, he pulled her off. "Not yet. You're not getting off that easy, baby. Take off your clothes, go to the bed, and

271

kneel on it. Ass in the air, face on the mattress."

Her gorgeous mouth was perfectly puffy as she dragged her tongue across her lower lip. "Why am I being punished?"

"You're not. You need this. Tell me you don't need this and I'll just make love to you. I'll make love to you all night, but it won't mean a damn thing if you can't relax. Do you want to enjoy our last night?" Manipulative, but necessary. He didn't feel a moment's guilt over it. Though he certainly didn't intend for it to be their last night, the rest was true. She needed the discipline in order to let go and relax. He kicked off his shoes and quickly undressed. He needed to be with her, nothing between them.

"I don't know why, but I do need it. Jesse, I'm sorry I can't give you what you need. Why would you take care of me when I can't do the same for you?"

That was easy. "Because I love you and that's meaningful to me. Even if you never love me back, I'm glad I love you. I'm a better person, stronger, happier for loving you. And I'll explain to you why you need it, but not until you do as I ask."

She got up with grace and then quickly began taking off her clothes. There was no teasing in it, no playful lover. She was a woman who needed. His question was did she even understand what it was that drove her as she climbed onto the bed and placed her body in a position of complete vulnerability?

His dick tightened as he stared at her perfect form. She hadn't been trained in any formal way, but she'd learned from the few times they'd played. He reached out and let his hand touch the curve of her ass. She sighed, relaxing the moment he caressed her.

"You need permission to connect, baby. You don't. Not really, but somewhere in your mind you've got the idea that it's wrong to feel pleasure, connection, joy, just about anything but pain." He drew his hand back and gave her the smack she needed. He didn't hold back. He slapped her ass with a sure show of his strength.

She cried out but didn't move, didn't do anything that would stop him from spanking her again. "Please."

"That is all in the world I want to do," Jesse whispered. "Please you. Love you. Be with you." He spanked her again, five times in rapid succession. Her skin went a nice pink and she let out a long cry.

"Jesse," she started, but whatever words were there remained trapped.

Like his Phoebe was trapped. She would stay that way if he didn't free her.

"I love you. You walking away from me won't change that." He kept up the hard whacks, being careful with her. She needed enough to feel it, not enough to harm her. Oh, he had no doubt she would harm herself if she could, but he was in charge. He was the Dom. "I will go to my grave loving you, woman."

The first real sob came from her throat. He looked down and tears poured from her eyes. They slid down her cheeks and onto the bed. Even as she wept, her body relaxed and he knew she was there.

He smacked her backside one last time, holding his hand to her flesh as if he could keep the heat in.

She was crying, allowing the pain and stress of the day to leach from her system, but he wasn't about to let up. If he gave her an inch, she'd be right back in her head, worrying and creating guilt. There was no place for that in their lives tonight.

"Don't move." He went to the bathroom. He'd already planned a nice scene for the evening, so all the tools were clean and laid out. He grabbed the large plug and some lube and wrapped the rest of his torture implements in a towel to bring along. He had plans for his pretty princess and they included a few decorations.

She was still crying when he returned. He immediately went to work, dribbling lube all over that gorgeous asshole he intended to make his this night.

She squirmed a little.

"Do I need to tie you up?" He'd considered it. It would likely make her feel secure, give her one more reason to give in.

"No. I'll be good. It feels good, Jesse. Why does it feel so good? Shouldn't it be wrong?"

He lined the plug up and started a slow massage of her asshole, letting it sink in inch by inch. "I thought it was wrong at first. When I met Alex and Eve, I tried to save her from him. I thought he was abusing her because I didn't understand that there was more than one way to love someone."

She gasped, her hips moving ever so slightly, trying to

accommodate the plug as he started to move it in and out. "Do you think it's possible to love two people?"

At least she was asking the question. "I think what I've figured out is that we don't have a limited amount of love. It doesn't get all used up and then there's nothing left. We choose. We choose who we love and how we love, and there is nothing between two consenting adults that brings them connection and pleasure and joy that's wrong. This is ours, Phoebe. No one else gets a say in it. This is our relationship, our partnership. If you let it, it will be our marriage and there's only room for you and me. We make the decisions and the rest of the world can go to hell."

She let out a deep breath and the plug sank home. Gently, he turned her over. She looked up at him with wide eyes. "I want to believe you."

Fuck, she was beautiful. "Then believe me. The outside world doesn't matter. All that matters is what happens between you and me. We can take care of all the rest of it together. Now tell me your secret."

She shook her head. "Please. Just touch me. Let me touch you."

He could order her, but he would rather earn it. If he forced it out of her, she would resent him no matter what the outcome was. "Don't lose that plug. I want to play dress-up."

"What does that mean?" Phoebe reached and wiped her tears, relief obvious in the relaxation of her body. She'd purged the emotions that held her back, but he intended to get her all tense again.

"It means I'm going to torture you for a while." Another word he'd hated for the longest time. Like all words, it had many meanings at its heart and his torture would be the sweetest kind. His torture would lead to their bonding, their bliss. "I want you to close your eyes."

After a second's hesitation, her eyes drifted closed. "All right, Sir."

"Listen to my voice. We can't do this here. It's far too dangerous, but I'm going to tell you what's going to happen when we get home." He let his hand play along her neck, gently encasing it with his palm. Dirty talk got her going. Luckily for her, he thought very dirty thoughts when she was around. "First, I'm going to do what I didn't do before. When Tag sends that plane for us, I'm not going to let you sleep on my lap again."

Her eyes came open. "Jesse…"

There was a very pretty nipple just waiting to be tweaked. He twisted her right nipple between his thumb and forefinger, gratified by the little shriek that came from her mouth just before her eyes dilated with arousal. "Hush. This is my fantasy. Close your eyes and listen. I'll tell you when you need to talk."

This was the only place he was ever really going to be in charge. He wasn't about to let her take over here, too. Her eyes drifted closed again and he rewarded her with a long stroke of his hand, from her collarbone all the way down to just above the junction of her thighs. "Now, I was talking about the plane. We were very well behaved last time. That's not going to be the case on the way home."

He moved back to her breasts. That was a good place to start. Her nipples were big and needed a good tweak to get really sensitive. It was why he'd brought along the nipple sticks. They were a simple toy, nothing more than two pieces of polished wood held together by screws at either end. He'd made this set himself. Jake Dean had taken up woodworking and had a shop in his backyard. Jesse found it soothing to work with his hands. While Jake had worked on Tristan's cradle, Jesse had made paddles and spanking benches and nipple sticks.

It was a good hobby.

He eased the sticks apart and decided to sensitize her before the torture began.

"On the way home, all those stuffy Agency boys will be gone and it's just going to be you and me and Si and Erin. They won't care so I will lay down the rules, and rule number one is you don't wear clothes while we're in the air. I want you naked and ready to take my cock at any moment. That plane is my pleasure palace, and I won't let you forget that I'm the king."

"I don't think Erin is going to like that," she said and winced even before he could pinch her nipple.

After that nasty pinch, she probably needed a little love. He leaned over and trailed kisses across her breasts. "Erin is even more submissive than you."

"Are you serious?"

This time he nipped her, taking her nipple between his teeth and gently biting down until she squirmed under him. "Yes, I'm serious. She's been playing with Kai since she got here. There's nothing between them, but Erin needs submission the same way you do. She can't relax or let herself be without it. You have a lot in common with her." Her face tightened and he gave in. "One sarcastic remark is allowed here."

"Erin is the female version of Conan the Barbarian. I can't believe Kai is willing to play with her. He's obviously less sane than I thought."

He was so going to enjoy the next few minutes. He adjusted the nipple sticks so both of those sweet pink things were in between. "Kai is the most sane person I know. He's also got a nice streak of sadist in him. Now be quiet. I'm putting your nipples in the stocks."

Her eyes flew open, but it was too late. He was already tightening the screws, squeezing her nipples between the lovingly made boards.

"Oh my god." She whimpered as the boards pressed down and her nipples bulged beautifully.

"There." She looked gorgeous with her breasts upthrust and her nipples a deep pink. He ran a finger over one and she bucked underneath him. "Perfect. Now they're more sensitive. Now I can play with them."

"You're killing me, Murdoch."

"And you forget my name when we're alone together. I could make one of these for your clit."

"Sir. Sir. Please don't, Sir. I'll be good."

He loved how breathless she got. It was like she utterly forgot to be self-conscious when they were playing. She gave in to her role and became the sweet little sub who only wished to please her Master. Outside this room, she would aggressively fight anyone who tried to control her, but here she proved she trusted him.

Here she took his plug and gave her nipples over to him, and she would take his cock any way he wanted her to. He flicked a nipple, his dick hardening when she squealed. Maybe Kai wasn't the only one with a streak of sadism.

He leaned over and licked the nub. "I'll tie you up on the plane and force you to take my cock in your mouth. Si and I will sit and go over the debrief while you take care of me. That's your only job during that trip—taking care of my needs. Sucking my cock and offering me all of your pretty parts to lick and suck and torture."

"I'll do it. Simon will be shocked."

He chuckled. She had only seen the team on their best behavior. "Where do you think I got the idea? The last time we were all on a plane together, Chelsea served him his tea and she wasn't wearing a stitch of clothing. And we knew which parts of the plane to stay out of if we didn't want a show. You're my woman. When we agree to play, I'll take you whenever, wherever I want. I'll indulge your every fantasy. If you want me to fuck you on the conference table in the middle of a meeting, I will make it happen."

He slid his hand down her body. He was perfectly comfortable that she wasn't thinking about anything but him now. The minute he felt all that slick arousal coating her pussy, he leaned over and gave her nipples another lick.

Phoebe's whole body tightened. She was close. He hadn't had to do more than spank her, clamp her, and talk dirty to her.

"You like that, Phoebe. You want them all to know. Tell me what they'll know on that plane." He wanted to hear her talk dirty, too.

"That I'm yours." She moaned when he toyed with those tortured nipples. Their color had deepened and he was going to have to release her soon.

He found her clit, starting to rub circles. "Not just mine. You're my little fuck toy. Say it."

"I'm your little fuck toy. I'm yours. I'm here for your pleasure, Sir. I want to take you any way that pleases you."

"Your pleasure is my pleasure." It was the truth. Her pleasure meant everything to him. He could play with words, but she was the sun in his sky. It was why the words got her so hot. They were play. She wasn't a fuck toy. She was everything. He rubbed her clit faster, feeling her breath pick up, her hips start to move against his hand. "Come for me. You come for me now."

She shivered and shook, her whole body tightening and then releasing. She cried out and then relaxed. Her arousal coated his fingers.

He sucked them inside, reveling in her tangy sweet taste. "Now comes the fun part. Now you're going to give me everything I want."

* * * *

Her whole body ached but in the sweetest way possible. Despite the orgasm that was still thrumming through her system, she was deeply aware that he hadn't come. While the feeling was sweet, there was a disconnect. She wanted to come with him inside her, giving as much as she got.

"Don't scream." His blue eyes stared down at her, the slightest amusement on his face. "This is going to hurt a little."

He unscrewed the nipple sticks and her breasts came free.

Pain flared, whipping through her tortured flesh, and it was all she could do to hold in the shout that threatened.

Bastard. Sadist. Asshole.

He chuckled and then he was kissing her right where it hurt. His tongue came out to soothe her. His lips and his tongue eased the ragged edge of pain. His hands caressed her and she could feel his leg against hers. Not to mention the plug he'd worked into her ass. She could feel that, too.

The images he'd put in her head were just as hot. She couldn't help it. She really did get turned on by dirty talk and by thinking about people watching her. The idea of Jesse watching her with another man did nothing for her. She didn't want anyone but Jesse, but she couldn't get the performance fantasy out of her head. When he talked about showing her off, she felt confident and sexy in a way she never had before.

It was counter to everything she'd thought about sex, but somehow Jesse made the dirtiest things seem intimate and loving. Maybe he was right and there was no wrong way to love. Maybe there was simply their way. Hers and Jesse's.

"I love the way you squirm." He moved to the other nipple, lavishing it with affection as his hand moved between her legs.

"You love making me squirm and whine and beg." Though when she really thought about it, it wasn't so much he made her as he allowed her a safe place to do all the things she'd never even known she wanted to do. He gave her a place to explore and discover sides of her sexuality that would have stayed hidden forever had she not met this man.

"I do. I'm going to make you do it again." He rubbed his face between her breasts, breathing in her scent before he started to kiss his way down her body. "I'm going to make you beg me to shove my cock in your ass. Do you want your Master's cock in your ass?"

"Sure." She said it in a way that was utterly unsure.

He chuckled. "I see I have some work to do. Let me put it to you this way. That little starter orgasm is all you're going to get until you beg me." He worked his way down until his face was right at her pussy. He looked up her body, his eyes catching hers. "How long do you think you can hold out on me?"

She was kind of afraid of the whole anal thing. "Maybe longer than you think."

He turned his face back down, staring right at her pussy. Again, it should have made her deeply uncomfortable since she'd never really thought of a pussy as being something a person would want to stare at, but somehow Jesse made it hot. His fingers traced her from the top of her clitoris all around. Just a light touch. It was enough to remind her just how good it could feel. "I think you want it deep down."

"I think you're bigger than that plug and you won't just sit there." She let her head fall back, the heat of his breath warming her up all over again. Now that she thought about it, it really had been a starter orgasm. A little quake when he could give her a 9.9 on the Richter scale. She clenched around the plug, feeling the fullness there and wondering what that would feel like when it was Jesse's flesh sliding in and out.

He licked her clit, a slow stroke of his tongue. "No, I won't. I'll fuck you. I'll fuck you long and hard. I'll try to make it last, but your ass is going to be so tight." A single finger slipped into her pussy, rotating and tantalizing. "You'll grip my dick until I can't see straight. I'll have to fight not to come the minute I feel you all around me."

His words were as hot as his tongue. Phoebe had to force herself not to roll over and just offer herself up. "What if I don't like it?"

"You have your safe word, but you won't use it." That finger started to move in a slow groove. In and out, curling up to stroke her sweet spot. Not enough. Never enough. He punctuated each stroke with a lick and a sweet suckling of her clit. "You'll like it. You'll love how deep I'll go and how close we are. You'll love the fact that you're sore tomorrow because you'll still feel me there. I'll still be with you every time you feel that delicious ache or when your breasts brush against your blouse and your nipples get a tweak of soreness. You'll remember that I had you and that I'll have you again."

Or she would remember what she'd given up. She would remember what she could have had. She likely wouldn't be on that plane with Jesse. She would be with her brother, going back to DC to face a fight they didn't even understand.

Yes. She wanted that ache in her body because it would match the one in her soul. Any remembrance of him was worthwhile, would fuel the long years ahead when she would mourn two men.

"Take me, Jesse."

"Not enough." He kissed her clit and then drew the little nub between his teeth. He gave her the finest edge, that remarkable spot between pain and pleasure when the world fell away and all that mattered was what happened between them. It was the place where she could cry, where she could submit, where she could feel pleasure without guilt.

The sensation built, starting low in her pelvis and threatening to become a wildfire across her skin. Just as the orgasm threatened, he pulled back.

Frustration welled as he petted her sweetly, but not anywhere close to what she needed. "You're a horrible man."

He moved up the bed, sliding his body along hers. His fingers came out to play with her nipples again, but this time she welcomed the ache. "I am a kind Master. You have no idea the lengths I can go to."

"With who? With the club subs?" Jealousy was another kind of ache. She hated the thought but she knew once she was gone, there would be any number of beautiful, sexy, younger women to take her place. They wouldn't give him half the trouble she had. He wouldn't have a problem finding a new submissive. They would likely form a line when they knew she wasn't coming back.

"You're jealous." He touched her nose with his. "There's no need to be. I wasn't talking about my past. I was talking about all the dirty, nasty things I want to do to you. I've never had a submissive of my own. I serviced them when they needed a partner, but I never played with my own sub. I want to play for hours, Phoebe. I want you tied up and at my mercy. I want to hear you scream out my name because you can't take a single second more of life without my cock inside you."

He was touching her pussy again, starting the slow tease of her senses. He'd sensitized her, gotten her hot and wanting. Now he could take her right back to the edge with a stroke of his fingers. She felt the warm flush of arousal, felt him sink two fingers in and then draw them back out. He stared right at her as he licked her essence off.

"You taste better than any meal, any sweet, any liquor. You're the best drug I ever had."

How the hell was she supposed to fight that? Every good intention fell away. Every bit of reason she had melted under his warmth, his affection. He was the perfect blend of sweetness and dominance, guaranteed to break her down. "I'll marry you."

The light that hit his eyes was like the sun coming from behind years and years of clouds. "I love you, Phoebe. You won't regret it."

"You might. Take me. I'm begging you. Please, Jesse. I need you."

He smiled, but there was that sweetly sadistic light in his eyes when he twisted her nipple. "Where do you want me, wife?"

Everywhere. In her life. In every second of every moment she had left. But that wasn't what he wanted. He was playing and he wanted her dirty. She could give that to him. She wanted nothing more than to be his dirty, nasty, beloved girl. "In my ass. I want you in my ass. Only you."

She'd given Jamie her virginity, but she could give this to Jesse. Her second love. Her second chance. She would only have two lovers her whole life, and she wanted to share this with him and him alone. It would be sacred between them, a bond she hoped the past couldn't break.

"Only me." He kissed her, his mouth fusing to hers in a way that felt a little like wonder, like she was young again and the world was opening up. Like she'd never been kissed before and could discover what love had to offer her all over again.

He moved between her legs, letting his body cover hers. He didn't hold back his weight and she didn't want him to. She loved how he pinned her to the bed, sinking in. Her nipples ached where he touched them, but it was just one more part of the puzzle. His tongue rubbed against hers and she moved her legs, wrapping her body around his. The plug slipped out and for a second she missed the feeling, but it wouldn't last long. He would fill her up.

He got to his knees after one last kiss and reached to the bedside table, grabbing the lube.

She watched as he picked up what now really seemed like too small a plug by the base and put it away.

"Bring your legs up." He grabbed a pillow from beside her. "Let me get this under you."

"Shouldn't I turn over?"

"No. I want to watch you. I want to see your face. I told you I wouldn't hurt you. I'll make sure of it." He moved between her legs, easing the pillow under her hips and shifting her into the place he wanted her.

She let him. She was willing to give him anything.

She trusted him with her body, her soul.

Could she trust him with her secrets?

Vulnerable. With her legs draped over his thighs and her pelvis tilted to him, she felt so vulnerable. She was opened wide for him, her body lay out like the offering it was. She felt him touch her. So intimate. There was the momentary chill of the lube and then the heat of his left hand, massaging her. He took his time, rubbing it in, his eyes steady on hers. Finally, he spread the lube on his cock, his hand moving over his flesh. She watched him stroke himself, preparing to take her. He was truly lovely, his cock reaching almost up to his navel, the head rounded, and below his balls were tight and heavy. She could still taste him, still feel the way he filled her mouth.

"I'll go slow, give you time to adjust." He was right there, the broad head of his cock settling against her.

She hadn't expected it to be so intimate. She'd thought he would turn her over and go at it, but not her Jesse. No. He had to turn it into something she couldn't hide from, to make her watch as he pressed against her. It would have been easy to let it happen, but he'd found a way to draw her in. To bring them closer.

Pressure bit through her, but she couldn't concentrate on it. All she could see was his face and how their bodies connected like puzzle pieces nestling together. Alone they were separate, functional, but incomplete. Together their bodies seemed to become something more, something beautiful.

His jaw tightened and she gasped the moment his cockhead breached her. A slow shudder went through him and he flushed, sweat breaking out on his brow. "Are you all right?"

She was surprised to find she was. He was distracting her with how gorgeous he was, but now she focused on the sensation of having him moving inside her. Little thrusts at first, as though his hips just couldn't stay still a second longer. There was pressure, a feeling of fullness that wasn't entirely comfortable. It wasn't painful either. She shifted to adjust and loved the way his eyes widened as she took another inch.

"Baby, you feel so good." He gripped her hips. "I need you to take all of me. Take me, Phoebe."

In a smooth glide, he entered her. His cock slid in until there was no space between them, nothing left for her to take. He filled her, heating her up and making her so aware of his every movement. She would have sworn she could feel him breathing, could time her every breath to the movements of his chest.

She was so full, but it was good. She wanted the moment to freeze, to last. If they could just hold right here, she would stay forever. She would be connected to him for as long as she could.

"All right, here we go." He gave a shaky laugh, his face so tender it made her want to cry. He might have chosen the position so he could watch her, but it forced her to see him, too. This wasn't mere sex for pleasure for him. It was more. It was so much more.

She brought her hands up to cup his face, loving the way the little bristles of his beard felt under her fingers. He would shave in the morning and be smooth again, but it never failed. By nightfall, there was proof of just how masculine he was. "I love you, Jesse."

He should know. He should hear it every day from some worthy woman, but she was the only one who was here.

"I love you, too. And I'm going to love you for the rest of my life. I promise. Now hold on to me. Don't let me go." With a careful breath, he began to drag his cock back out.

Jagged pleasure caused her eyes to widen, her breath to stop for a moment as it overwhelmed her. She shook as he went slow, allowing her to experience every second of sensation.

"That's what I wanted." The sexiest grin lit his face as he pushed back inside her body. "Now I can do my worst. You're going to come for me."

He forced her back on his cock, but she was eager for it now. She knew what it brought and couldn't wait for the downstroke to bring its crazy pleasure. She tried to hold him, wanted him inside her all the time. He let go, fucking her hard.

Time seemed to slow, giving her what she wanted. More time with him. More connection. She held on to him, her nails sinking in, but he didn't seem to mind. He groaned a little then ground into her with a low growl. Over and over he thrust and retreated, pressure and pleasure becoming one.

"Knew I wouldn't last," he said on a panting breath. His thumb covered her clit and he pressed down. "Come for me, Phoebe."

He rotated her clit and then his cock hit just the right space. Her whole body shook under the force of her orgasm and it seemed to send him straight into his own.

Jesse held himself tight against her and she felt the heat of his release. When he fell forward, she wrapped her arms around him, blood pumping through her body in a pleasant rhythm. She held him, arms and legs tangled, stroking his hair because for the first time he was really hers.

And she was about to lose him.

His head came up and he kissed her, a light touch of the lips. His eyes were serious as he stared down at her. "Tell me your secret."

She nodded because it was time.

CHAPTER SEVENTEEN

Jesse watched as she came out of the bathroom. He knew alarm bells should have been going off. She'd dressed, putting on jeans and a long-sleeved blouse, though she'd left off her normal makeup. Her hair was in a conservative bun.

It looked like she'd pulled all her armor around her, ready for his inevitable harsh rejection.

Yep, all the alarms should have been going off, but she'd really only tripped his drama-llama alarm. He had to give it to her. His future wife was very dramatic.

He sat on the bed as she paced and wondered if he should look more worried. He'd never been a great actor, but he could probably pull off more concern. Maybe he should try to rage a little at whatever the hell she was about to tell him.

Wait. He'd just thought of something that might give him pause. "Did you start life as a man? It's not a deal breaker because they did a fabulous job on that pussy. I'm serious. If that's man-made, then bravo medicine."

Her jaw dropped. It was good to know he could still surprise her. "This is serious, Jesse."

"So not a dude?"

"No, asshole. I'm not a dude."

"Carry on then." He waited. It looked like he was going to do a lot of that since she was right back to pacing.

"I'm trying to figure out how to say this."

"Words are good." Although if she wanted to draw it out, he would let her. He wasn't great at Pictionary though.

There were tears in her eyes when she looked back at him. "Will you please stop joking?"

Damn it. He hadn't meant to make this harder on her. He got up and closed the distance between them. "I'm sorry. I'll be serious."

She didn't push him away when he reached for her. "It's bad."

"Okay. Then you should just tell me. You should just get it out."

"I have to set it up first." After a second, she stepped back.

He took it as his cue to move back into "audience" mode. She seemed to need to play out this scene, and he was going to let her. Afterward, he would take control again and he would let her know that whatever deep dark secret she held wasn't going to come between them ever again. "All right. I'm listening."

"My husband's name was James, Jamie. He was probably the first real friend I ever made. There were some in a couple of the foster homes, but mostly I tried to keep to myself. My mom OD'd when I was a kid. I spent most of our time together taking care of her, hiding stuff from the authorities when a teacher got suspicious. After she died, I really shut down. It wasn't all bad, but none of the good stuff stuck with me until I met my dad and Jamie and Ten."

He was curious about her background. No file could really tell him what it was like for her. Despite the fact that he'd had a home, he'd been as lonely as she was. "Your dad wanted to recruit you?"

"Yes, but it wasn't as cold as it sounds. I don't know. It's the same with any family. I can tell you what it was like, but only Jamie, Ten, and I really understood. Dad wasn't a bad man. He believed in his country and he thought he was doing good. I think if he hadn't taken me and Ten off the streets, we would be dead or in jail by now. I don't know about Jamie, but then I'm not exactly unbiased when I talk about him. Ten thinks I put him on a pedestal."

"You were in love with him. You should have." He knew deep down that he should be jealous of this guy. Jamie Grant still had a hold on Phoebe's heart even after all these years. And yet he was able to summon up nothing more than sympathy for a man who'd died. He'd died serving his country. He didn't want Phoebe to think less of James even if it would help his case. "I told you. I know you're always going to love him. I just ask that you love me, too."

She stopped, her eyes closing, and she took a deep breath before she opened them again. "I do love you, Jesse Murdoch. I didn't think I could ever love anyone again, but I can't deny it."

"Then know that everything is going to be all right."

Her eyes slid away from his as she continued. "After college, we went into training and then we started working under my father's direction. I spent some time in Asia and Jamie and Ten went straight to the Middle East. Jamie and I got married. And then my dad died and Ten took over some of his responsibilities. Of all of us, Ten was the truly brilliant operative. A couple of years back, he started hearing rumors about US corporations and politicians working with hostiles in Iraq. They were after resources and business interests, of course. It wasn't unusual, but I started to think that one of their payoffs was handing over troop movements and US Army intelligence."

That was a kick in the gut. He knew there were always people willing to sell out soldiers for cash, but the thought of elected politicians being involved made him pause. They had influence. They could potentially not simply hand over Army intelligence, but actively influence Army strategy. "Did you find the evidence?"

"We needed to move around with impunity. There were people we needed to interview, but Iraq was a massive war zone at the time. I came up with the idea of embedding an operative in an Army unit."

"What?"

She nodded, resuming her pacing. "You heard me. I thought people would talk more freely to a soldier than an operative. Some of the people we needed to interview were soldiers themselves."

"We didn't like to talk to spooks." He had an inkling of where she was going. When had her husband died? What year? What time?

"See. I knew that. That's exactly what I was trying to avoid by embedding our own. And it worked. The operative hadn't served more than a few weeks when he came up with something."

"Don't call him the operative. I'm dumb, but I'm not stupid." The words came out harsher than he'd intended, but now that he was here, he found himself getting emotional.

If he was right…oh, god, if he was fucking right, so much made sense. And he had a story of his own for her.

She paled and then nodded, her movements almost robotic. "Jamie. It was Jamie. I picked a unit that was close to the action and that routinely patrolled some of the areas where the informants were."

"Phoebe, was it my unit?"

"Yes."

Jamie. Jimmy. The kid who'd joined them three weeks before it had all gone to hell. He'd actually gone on a couple of those interviews with him. Such a dumbass. He'd believed the story that Jimmy's stepmother was Iraqi and that was how he'd spoken such fluent Farsi. He'd been thrilled at the time because they'd lost their translator. So very stupid to believe. It made sense now. "Private James Greene. He didn't call himself Jamie though. Jimmy."

"It's always good to come close to the truth," she said in a monotone. "That's why I used my real first name and a close last name when I came to McKay-Taggart. If you looked me up, you wouldn't find the real Phoebe Grant along with my construct and I can remember it easily."

"He was a good soldier." He'd been brave during the one firefight they'd gotten into. He'd held his line and hadn't panicked. He'd had Jesse's back.

"He wasn't a soldier."

"For those few weeks, he was. He did his job and he did it well." How the hell was he going to tell her what he needed to say? Now it all made sense. At the time, it had been the mutterings of a dying man. "He didn't endanger us. Is that what you're worried I'll think?"

Her hands became fists at her sides. "I endangered you, Jesse. It was my plan and it backfired. Somehow it got out that an operative was coming in with information. Jamie was due to come home and he was bringing his intelligence with him."

"And that's when we were captured." The truth hit him. He'd been captured because the Agency had been playing spy games. Phoebe had come up with the plan. She'd pulled the trigger and he and his unit had paid the price. "He was trying to turn the CIA agent." Jesse couldn't help but laugh. It was a bitter sound. "The idiot thought it was me."

"Yes. Maybe it was because your names were similar. You look a little alike. Jamie always looked younger than his years, so maybe that was the problem. You probably looked more like the age of the operative than him. But yes, I believe the Caliph mistook you for Jamie and that was why he tortured you."

And she'd taken all that guilt and pain on herself. Or was there another reason she was pulling away from him? It hurt. It was a real physical pain to even think it. "Were you mad? Were you angry that I survived and he didn't?"

Her eyes slid away, focusing on the floor. "At first. At first I believed everything they said about you."

"You thought I turned. You didn't realize they thought I was Jamie."

"I thought maybe you had sold him out."

"I didn't."

"I know that now."

And it wasn't fair to ask her if she was happy now that he'd survived. She couldn't be. She could never be happy that her husband had died, but he had to make her see that somehow, someway Jesse had survived for her. "You didn't sell him out either. And you didn't sell me out. You had a problem and you came up with a solution that made sense."

"I came up with a solution that got everyone killed."

"That's what happens in war. Your husband and I both knew the risks. We both understood going in what could happen and we made the choice. We chose to serve, and that means we chose to die if the sacrifice must be made. I was ready to die for my country."

"It wasn't your country you were going to die for. It was some fucking businessman who wanted to make a profit."

Finally she made some sense. "Yes. Yes, it was. So stop

blaming yourself and let's look to finding him. Our first step is to find the Caliph. He'll lead us to whoever this man is. After we're married, that is. And I think it would be easier to do it with my team. The Agency seems to have some problems right now."

She stared at him for a moment. "Have you heard a word I've said?"

"Yes. Is that all?"

"Isn't it enough? Jesse, I'm the reason you were tortured."

He managed to stifle a sigh. "No. The Caliph is the reason I was tortured. You merely did your job. Am I surprised? Yes, and for reasons you'll understand in a moment, but I told you. It doesn't matter. I love you. I'm standing by you."

"Why?"

"Because he gave you to me. Because I've searched and searched for one good thing to come out of this, for the fucking universe to give me a goddamn break, and I found it. It was always you, Phoebe. I went through hell but it led me to my family and it led me to my wife. I would do it all over again."

"I don't understand."

"It's my turn to talk and I'm going to tell you something I haven't told another soul."

She shook her head. "Jesse, I can't."

"You can because I have a message for you. One man who loved you, he gave a message to another man—a man who would come to love you."

"Jamie? Jamie talked to you? I don't know if I want to know. Did he hate me for sending him there?"

"Oh, he loved you. He was in the cell next to mine and he talked about his wife and brother. He never told me your name. Always just called you his wife or his love. He wasn't angry at the end, Phoebe. He tried to keep my spirits up. He told me his brother would find us. I thought he was a little crazy at that point. Now I know he was talking about Ten."

"We tried."

"Hush, he knew. He knew you and Ten were out there. He knew you wouldn't give up. Phoebe, the night he died he gave me a message. He was out of it. Broken, but he said one thing. God, I wish I'd thought about it for two seconds. You showed me those movies and now I understand. Those books, they were your shorthand, right?"

"What?"

"He told me to find you for him and give you one message. Be the girl who lived. He said it over and over, like a mantra. Be the girl who lived. Harry Potter was the boy who lived, right?"

"Yes. He lived because his mother loved him so much she protected him from real evil."

"He loved you and he might not have known it at the time, but he sent me to love you, too. I know that because the last words that man said to me were take care of my girl. I thought he meant to find you, make sure you were safe, and maybe that was all he meant, but that wasn't what happened." He stepped up to her, knowing in his heart what Jamie Grant wanted for his wife. He knew because he loved her, too, and if he'd been the other man, he would have wanted the same thing. "He wants you to live, Phoebe, and not in some half-assed, waiting to see him again way. He wants you to live every moment with passion. He wants you to have a beautiful life and when it's over, if there's any way for him to see you again, he will. He will wait for you and he won't ask you to choose between us. If there's some magical afterlife, get ready for a ménage because we both love you."

"Are you sure?"

"I know one thing. I know what it means to love Phoebe Grant, to want to protect and adore her. So I know what Jamie would want. Marry me, Phoebe. Take the chance again because it's worth it. Because we're worth it."

Tears flowed down her cheeks and a sob was wrenched from her chest. He'd seen her cry, but not quite like this. He held her tight because this was a storm and he would never leave her alone. He held on while she wept and couldn't help but cry a little with her. For her and Jamie. For himself.

"I love you, Phoebe. I love you." He told her over and over again because she'd been deprived of hearing it. If he said it enough, maybe she would believe it.

Finally, she began to quiet and her arms wrapped around him. He kissed her and then slowly undressed her. He was certain she'd dressed for a quick retreat, but now those little bits of armor were no longer needed. He smoothed the clothes off her, worshipping her body with his lips, murmuring "I love you" as though he could breathe it through her flesh and into her soul.

He eased them both back, settling on the bed. The world had long since turned to night and a sweet weariness settled over him, like he'd done a good day's work and it was time to rest.

She settled her head on his chest. "I love you, Jesse."

He brought the covers over them. "Will you marry me? You said yes before but that was easy because you thought I would walk away. Now you know I won't ever leave you, not if it's in my control. But I could die. I want whatever time I have on this earth to be spent loving you, Phoebe. So I'm going to ask you again. Will you marry me?"

"Yes. And I'll stay with you. I'll stay here with you and we'll finish this together."

Together. It was everything he wanted.

He held her close and slept.

* * * *

Phoebe stepped out into the hallway, closing her robe around her. The sun wasn't up yet, though it wouldn't be long. Phoebe had slept for the longest time, missing dinner and whatever discussions had happened among the team. She'd woken and showered and couldn't quite slip back into bed without trying to talk to Ten first. There was very little time before they were all supposed to be at the airfield. She'd made her decision and she prayed he understood.

"Hey." Ten sat in the suite's shared living area, staring down at his computer. "I was wondering if I was going to have to wake you up. My flight's in two hours."

"I have to talk to you about that."

His face came up, an affectionate smile belying the weariness she saw there. "I said my flight, sis. I know you're not going to be on it. I knew it the minute he kicked in that door. Well, and when the screams started. You could spare me those. Please."

She felt herself blush. "Sorry."

He gave her a wan grin. "You tell that boy he better take care of you or he'll answer to me."

Relief washed over her. At least she didn't have to convince Ten. "I love him."

Ten closed his laptop and stood up. "I'm so glad. I'm glad you found your way out." He closed the space between them and enveloped her in one of his big, all-encompassing hugs. "I'm going to miss working with you, but I expect to be invited to all your very normal holiday celebrations. Well, normal if Taggart doesn't show up."

She held on to the man who'd been her brother for half her life now. When she thought about it, he'd always been her brother. They just had to find their way to each other. Family was like that sometimes. "You have to promise you'll come and visit us often."

He squeezed her tight. "I promise I'll try. Hell, darlin', I might be sleeping on your couch soon."

Because he wasn't certain of his job. She was scared about that too. "I think we could find you a spare bedroom."

He kissed the top of her head and then moved away, sitting back down and crossing one leg over the other. He hadn't changed clothes. He was still in his usual uniform. Black T-shirt, jeans, and boots. "I'm sure Murdoch would love having a roommate. I'm putting him on a clock, by the way. He's got a year to ask you to marry him."

"He already did."

"Damn. That boy works fast. You say yes?"

She nodded. "I did. I know it's quick and…"

He held out a hand. "No need to explain. Life is short, baby girl. You take every little piece of happiness you can get. I'm happy for you. Jamie would have liked Jesse."

"He did." She bit back tears again. Now that she'd opened the floodgates, they didn't seem to want to stop, but they felt different now. They were somehow sweeter, almost a reminder that she'd been loved and was loved again. As if grief itself was a way to remember the sweetness of life, to magnify and celebrate it. "Apparently they became friends in jail. You do understand what happened, right?"

"Yeah. I've thought about it for a long time. The Caliph was looking to turn an operative. He got Jesse instead. Jamie couldn't have known."

"Even if he had, he couldn't risk it. Jesse knows that, too." Her almost husband was a remarkable man. His ability to love and find some way to move forward had taught her so much. "Jamie asked him to give me a message. Be the girl who lived. It's silly because it's from a book, but it means something to me, a little more than what I told Jesse. I think Jamie meant it for you, too, Tennessee."

"I didn't read that stuff you did."

"It doesn't matter. It's the same message. Love can save you if you let it. It can put up a wall that protects you, but you still have to face it. The truth is bad shit is going to happen and there's nothing we can do about it. How we deal with it, that's the measure of our lives. Do we roll into a ball and hide like I did? Or do we open ourselves, even knowing how much it could hurt if we lose it? I'm going to open myself. I'm going to love that man with everything I have, and if something goes wrong, at least I'll have had that love. I am grateful for every second I had with Jamie. Every moment was precious, and now I'm going to honor him by living. I want to have babies, Ten."

She could have sworn her brother's eyes got misty. "I want that for you more than anything."

"I want you to have a family, too."

"I always knew that wasn't the way it was going to go."

"Why?"

"I wouldn't even know how to be a father. I'm not built like that."

"You are. We all are." She backed off a little. Her brother would be a long-term project. "How about you try dating? I bet Charlotte Taggart could find someone to set you up with."

His eyes widened. "That is the meanest thing you've ever said to me. Don't put that woman on me. She doesn't give up."

Sweet laughter bubbled up at the thought of Charlotte playing matchmaker. "I promise nothing."

He sobered, leaning back and running a hand over his head. "I'll smooth things over with the Agency for you. You have to know though that I don't have the pull I used to have. We've opened a mighty big can of worms here. You and Murdoch need to watch your backs."

"We're not leaving. We have to figure this thing out or we'll be looking behind us for the rest of our lives. I don't imagine this guy is going to give up. There's more at stake here than simply his identity."

"There's the identity of whoever he's working with," Ten agreed. "I'm waiting on Chelsea to get back to me with Ace's files and the name of who recommended him. It's going to take some patience. Apparently they wiped his files when he died. She swears nothing is ever really gone. I have to hope she and Adam can figure it out."

"I'm worried about you going to DC." She wasn't sure what waited there for him.

He shrugged. "What are they going to do to me? At least they're bringing me home if they're burning me."

Disavowed. Alone. She hated to think about it. The Agency had been Ten's family for a very long time. But being burned wasn't what scared her. "And if they're bringing you home to do more than fire you? Ten, we don't know what we've stepped into."

"Assassination? Nah. It's easier to discredit me. I have too many people who would give a shit if I died." He stopped for a moment, a huff coming out of his mouth before he laughed. "Holy shit. That's what he was doing. That old son of a bitch. I always wondered."

"What?"

"Dad. I always wondered why. He wasn't tasked by the Agency to find young recruits. He did it on his own. He grew up without a family. His parents died when he was in high school and he didn't have siblings. It was precisely why he was recruited. Smart, excellent deductive reasoning skills, and no ties. It's why we were told not to talk much about considering each other family. He didn't want them to know we had too many ties. He took three kids who had no one and nothing and gave them the only world he understood. But he didn't put us in there alone. He gave us each other."

"The Agency would have written Jamie off."

"I couldn't because he's my brother. And they won't kill me because you would never let it lie."

Because her love would protect him. "I'm not the only one. Taggart, for all his flaws, would take on the Agency for you.

You're the only one who ever thought you were alone. You had a whole family standing around you and you're right. Dad gave us that. He's still protecting us even after he's gone." She reached out and took Ten's hand. "So don't tell me you don't know how to be a dad. You learned from the very best."

"We'll get through this, Phoebe. I'm going to make sure this goes away one way or another," Ten promised.

There was the sound of a crack and Phoebe whipped her head around.

Ten stood. "That was a semi." Ten reached behind his back and came up with a SIG Sauer in his hand. Her brother was never unarmed. "Stay here."

There was another volley of gunfire and then the sound of a woman screaming. Ten opened the door to the hallway and disappeared, his lean body moving against the wall.

"What the fuck?" Hutch had his boxers on and seemed to have only stopped long enough to grab his weapon. And he'd been having a nice dream, so it seemed. Or the sound of gunfire in the middle of the night got him hard. It could be either with him.

Theo was right behind him, though he'd managed to put on a pair of sweats. "It's coming from Kamdar's room. We need to move. You have a piece?"

She hadn't brought her gun out when she'd come to talk to Ten. She'd thought she was safe in this ridiculously expensive hotel, but naturally she was proven wrong. "No."

"Take my backup." Because Theo apparently slept with two guns. He handed her a semi and then he and Hutch started for the door. She followed, grateful that Jesse was a heavy sleeper. No matter what she said, she hated the idea of him being in danger. She wouldn't ask him to quit. It was a part of who he was, but she would definitely use any excuse she could to let him sleep so he didn't have a chance to get shot.

The outer room was complete chaos. There was smoke and suddenly the detector went off.

"Everyone calm down!" Ten yelled.

Erin was in the middle of it, waving her hand to disperse the smoke. "Some asshole set off a smoke bomb outside the king's room."

Theo's gun came down at his side as he stared at Erin. "What were you doing in his room?"

Kamdar stood in the middle of it all, his big chest on display. He wore nothing but a towel wrapped around his lean hips. "She was protecting me from harm. This is all a ridiculous prank. Everyone get back into their beds. It's too early to deal with protesters."

"I heard gunfire." Simon joined the group. He'd pulled on a pair of slacks and his dress shirt was open. Like everyone else, he was carrying a gun. It was likely the best-armed floor of the hotel.

"I heard it, too. What happened? Did someone take a shot?" Ten was down on one knee, inspecting the box someone had left outside Kamdar's door.

"One of Kamdar's bodyguards got a little freaked out. I think he thought it was a real bomb or something biological," Erin replied. "And I wasn't sleeping with Kamdar. Not that it's any of your business, Taggart."

"She is right. There was no sleeping involved," Kamdar said with a solemn look on his face.

"And this was definitely biological." Ten grimaced as he stood back up. "It's shit in a bag someone lit on fire. What the hell is going on?"

Kamdar shook his head. "The oilmen, they do not like me. I'm too handsome, far too smart. They think they can scare me off with their shittings, but they are wrong. I will simply take their biological waste and use it to power my vehicles. That will show them. Come along, beautiful. Let's celebrate our victory over their waste."

Erin's face went as red as her hair and she started in on the king. "Listen here. I don't care how royal your ass is…"

Something was wrong. It didn't make a lick of sense.

"I'm going to review the tapes, but this looks like some sort of practical joke." Ten looked up at the fire detectors. They blared through the space. "Can we get these turned off? I can't think."

Simon moved beside her. "Where's Jesse?"

"He's asleep."

Why would anyone risk a practical joke in a building where everyone was armed to the teeth?

Simon looked back at their suite of rooms. "In your room? The one that's farthest from the lifts?"

She nodded. It was the farthest from the elevators and everything. "Why?"

But she'd already started to answer her own question. If it wasn't a joke, then what was it? A distraction. Everyone should have been in bed. She and Jesse had the room farthest from the king's. She doubted Jesse would even have heard the gunfire if he'd been awake, but the outer bedrooms would have heard it easily.

Phoebe turned back and started to run. Her heart pounded in her chest. It wasn't true. It couldn't be because they would have to have gone through the hallway. She would have noticed someone dragging a body down the hallway. No one had gone past her so it was all right.

"Phoebe?" Ten was behind her.

"Jesse. This was about Jesse." Simon kept up with them.

She just ran. She ran past the living area and back to the room where she and Jesse had become man and wife. Maybe not in the eyes of the law, but they'd bonded in their hearts. Her husband was sleeping and she was going to laugh because she was so damn paranoid.

Except she wasn't. She flung open the door and the bed was empty. There was a huge hole cut in the window and she could see the ropes that had allowed the team to lower the scaffold down.

She watched in horror as a helicopter flew past and then moved quickly into the distance.

Jesse was gone.

CHAPTER EIGHTEEN

He was stuck again. Damn. He knew this dream. It started with the world going hazy. His eyes wouldn't focus. He could shake his head, but somehow the world remained fuzzy. His stomach twisted and that was when he realized that whatever he'd eaten was about to come back up.

He was on his back. That wasn't good. Even with the world spinning around him, he knew he couldn't stay on his back. With sheer force of will, he turned just before the bile got to be too much.

So fucking weak. He needed to make it to the bathroom, but his gut wouldn't wait. He got to his knees and then let it go. He shuddered and shook, but when it was done, he finally felt the tiniest bit better.

He moved away from the mess he'd made and tried to focus. This time it was a little easier.

"Phoebe?" He seemed to have some sort of flu. Or he'd eaten something he shouldn't have. He couldn't remember. Why couldn't he remember? The last thing he could recall was Phoebe in his arms. She'd cried herself to sleep, but it had been a good thing. It had been healing.

Where was she?

Why was the ground under him so hard? Their room had plush carpet. Everything about it was luxurious, so why had his knees banged against what felt like concrete? He forced himself to really still. His eyesight finally stabilized and he could see the ground beneath him. Definitely concrete and not the pretty, stained kind. This was the color of dull steel.

He wasn't in his room.

His back was to something. His hands were free so he reached around. A wall and then to his left was metal. Through the haze he recognized a cot. He'd been laid on the cot in a room he didn't recognize.

"Hello, Mr. Murdoch. It's a pleasure to see you."

He was going to be sick again. That voice. Yes, this was a nightmare and he needed to wake up because he was going to scare Phoebe. He could get violent when he dreamed, but since he'd started sleeping with her, he hadn't had the dream. Not even once.

His hands shook. Fine trembles that were as much about fear as they were the shaky state of his body. He was afraid. He'd always hated that, didn't want people to see it. After he'd come home the first time and started seeing Eve and then Kai, he'd told them he wasn't afraid. It was a lie meant to save face. And then Ian had sat him down with a beer one night and told him that only a fucking idiot wasn't afraid and that fear was a gift to help the intelligent creatures of the world not get their asses blown away.

So he was willing to admit just how scared he was and somehow in accepting it, he was able to control it.

"I see you're not as used to our cocktails as once you were. I'll have them dial down the dosage for next time. I don't want you to be sick. I need you good and healthy for our training sessions." The voice had a deep, almost hypnotic quality to it. Just the sound of it sent him back years to that horrible place where he wasn't Jesse Murdoch anymore, to where he was someone's dog to be beaten and abused.

His vision started to fade again. That was when he realized this might not be a dream. In his dreams, he always stayed in control and fought. He was a better version of himself in his dreams. In real life, he retreated and let some fucking beast take over. Or he gave in to the drugs and pretended nothing was wrong.

"You're wondering if you're dreaming," the voice mused. His shoes rang against the concrete as he moved closer. "Aren't you? Let me ask you this. What would be worse? Learning that this is the only reality? That the last few years were only a dream brought on by the narcotics I gave you? In that scenario you've really lost nothing, but you gained nothing as well. Your woman was simply a dream. Or is it worse if she's reality and you've lost her?"

This was what the fucker did. He loved to put scenarios out there. He could talk all day.

He could talk all day.

If the Caliph was talking, then time was passing, precious time Jesse needed.

"I don't know. I think she was real. It felt real." Phoebe was real. She was the realest thing in the world. He looked around, trying to take stock. He was weak now, but there might come a time when he could try to get out of here. "Is she here?"

He fought back the urge to dive deep. He had to stay in control. He had to figure out what had happened. Where was Phoebe? How had he gotten here?

A small room. There was a door, but he could see it was sturdy, likely reinforced. He glanced around. One window, but it was barred. There was nothing in the room at all except a cot, a bucket, and shackles attached to the far wall. He could only imagine what that was for.

Hani al Fareed looked down at him. Yes, it was the younger of the two brothers. Now that Jesse was close, he could match the man to his file. He focused on the man, really seeing him for the first time he could remember. The Caliph was in his forties, with a handsome face and cold eyes. He'd taken off his white robe and was dressed more casually in loose white cotton pants and a tunic. "Would you be frightened if she was here?"

Sometimes honesty was best with the Caliph. He tended to see through the lies, and there was punishment until he got the answer he wanted. Jesse nodded. "Yes."

There was no way to hide the fact that he loved Phoebe. The last thing he remembered he'd been in bed with her, so they'd either killed her or left her behind.

If Phoebe was dead, he would let that beast out. It wouldn't matter anymore. Nothing would matter if Phoebe was gone because she was the one. Kai had said something about his love saving him, but it was his love for Phoebe and only Phoebe. If she was gone, he wasn't sure what would happen, but it would be nasty and bloody and wouldn't end well.

"You like the female? Perhaps that's a good place to start. You know I have no formal training in psychology, but it's been an obsession of mine since childhood. I would watch my father train dogs. People are like dogs, though they often require more pain to learn a lesson. You know if you properly train a dog, you can give them as much pain as they can take and they will still defend you."

"Like Ace."

"Yes, much like your brother." The Caliph stared at him for a moment. "You're an interesting subject. I wasn't able to modify your behavior before. I believe I simply didn't have enough time, though some of my colleagues claim you're simply too stupid to change. Maybe I didn't have the proper motivation. If I bring out your female sexual partner, would that change? Would you do my bidding if it meant she was safe from pain? From rape? Rape is always a good way to control a female, but oftentimes it can only be used once to control a male partner. At least in my world, that's true. Women lose their value when they're tarnished. How many times could I fuck her before you would see her as a whore?"

That was an easy answer. "I don't know a number big enough."

He chuckled. "I don't understand Western men. You don't see the true and only value of a woman. You marry non-virgins and then expect them to be faithful. You're all fools. And no, I do not have her. She was not in bed with you when we took you, so she escaped, though now I think that was a mistake on my part. Do you think she was cheating on you? It's what women of your culture do."

Jesse didn't give a flying fuck what that asshole thought about his culture. He valued Phoebe for more than her sex, more than his singular possession of her body. He loved her soul and the Caliph couldn't touch that, so no matter what happened to her, he would still love her, still want her.

And she would want him.

The truth settled over him. The Caliph could do his worst. He could beat him, batter him, get him hooked on drugs again, but as long as he held on to his soul, Phoebe would love him. Phoebe would stay with him. She would be there when he came out of this.

The deep need to regress, to give over to the darkness, faded. It always seemed to be there, something he had to fight back, but now that place was filled with something else. Her. He didn't need the darkness if he had her.

She was alive. The Caliph rarely lied. His truths tended to be the things of nightmares, and he'd once told Jesse that the master didn't bother to lie to his dog. Phoebe was alive and that meant Ten would protect her.

And Simon would look for him. His partner would do everything in his power to find him. That Brit wouldn't stop. The only question was could he keep Phoebe from getting in trouble because Jesse doubted she would stop either.

"No. She wasn't cheating on me." She'd likely gotten up to talk to her brother, to explain why she wasn't going back to DC.

He needed to give them time. He wasn't sure how much time had passed, but they were likely still in the UAE. Simon would have his best shot if he could find Jesse before they took him to Saudi or some other country. Jesse had to find a way to give his partner that time.

The Caliph liked to talk. The Caliph didn't bother to lie. Why not buy a little time with some conversation? He had a few questions for the man.

"Why bother with me? Why come and get me at all? Was it about concealing your identity? You know I can talk all I like. No one will believe me." He had a unique opportunity for information gathering.

"Why did you fake your own death? What was the purpose of that?"

"I thought you would send someone else after me. And I thought you might avoid the conference if you knew I would be there. If I was dead, I couldn't be there. That is why you sent Ace to kill me, right?"

His lips curled up slightly. "I didn't want to kill you. I'm sure that surprises you, but the choice to kill you was not my own, but my business partner's. When I learned that you would be here in Dubai, I was excited again. It's been years since I had such a challenge. No. I didn't want to kill you. I wanted to collect what was mine and finish the job. However, I agreed to send your brother after you to appease my partner."

His brother. God, al Fareed didn't even understand the meaning of the word. "Your business partner was afraid I would recognize you?"

One shoulder shrugged as though it was not of great matter to him. "Again, I didn't believe it would truly harm me, but apparently you have some powerful friends now. Don't worry. My partner is busy discrediting them. Once their reputations are in threads, no one will listen anymore."

"You're behind the Agency recalling Ten."

"No. I have nothing to do with the CIA. I find them to be distasteful. I leave that to my partner. Note, I do not call him my friend. He is distasteful as well, but compromises must be made. Once I have all I need, I'll cut ties with him in the most profound way possible. I will enjoy it. Now, soon we will be traveling. I think it's time for you to come to my home. I can take my time there, properly assist you in understanding your true place in the world."

His place was with Phoebe and his family. Again, the need rose to fight, to argue, to scream. None of that would help him. That kind of rage was for men with nothing to hope for. For men with no faith.

Faith was what he lacked the first time. He could see it now. He'd been an animal fighting for his life purely out of instinct. Now his fight was defined and deeply emotional. His fight was to survive to get home to her.

His faith versus the Caliph's.

He bowed his head. "I would love to hear what you say, Caliph."

His eyes narrowed. "Really? Is this a new tactic? Your prior tactics were always so physical."

"That didn't work. Nothing really worked. I've been back in

304

the real world for a while now. They don't see any value in what I have to offer. You read the papers I'm sure. Even my new boss only sees me as a body to put in front of the employees he does care about." The Caliph might not care to lie, but Jesse had discovered a little lie could go a long way. "I cared about the girl. I did, but she's Agency. She'll leave me behind in a heartbeat. You're the only one who ever gave a damn about what happened to me."

There was a moment of silence, a tension Jesse could feel despite the languor of the drugs still weighing him down.

"I will think on this," the Caliph said. He stood abruptly. "In the meantime, I believe you should be punished for killing your brother. Was it you who pulled the trigger?"

"He was trying to kill me at the time."

"It matters not. It merely shows me that you forget who your master is. I decide if you live or die. I am your god. Let this be a reminder."

The door opened and Jesse watched as two of the Caliph's guards entered, one carrying a four-foot bullwhip. Jesse was fairly certain the asswipe wasn't as good with it as he'd become. He could wield that whip with delicacy, never opening up a sub's skin. That wouldn't be the case today because that whip was like anything else—a tool. Jesse would use it for pleasure and this man would torment him with pain.

"See if you can get him to break. I don't like this calm in him. He's different," the Caliph said in Farsi. "I need the dog back."

He didn't fight as they tied him to the wall. There was no point. He would need his strength.

When the first blow struck, he closed his eyes and thought of her.

* * * *

Phoebe tried not to panic as she washed her hands, but all of her training was going right out the door. She was supposed to stay cool and collected, but she could feel the tears streaming down her face.

He was gone.

She looked at the clock. Morning had broken and now he'd been missing for an hour and thirty-nine minutes.

She looked into the bathroom mirror and saw the face staring back. Pale. Haunted. She'd seen it before. After Jamie had gone missing, this face had stared right back at her. Widow. It didn't matter that she and Jesse hadn't technically been married. She would be his widow.

A sharp knock broke the silence. "Hey, princess. You through in there?"

Erin. God, she'd hidden in the bathroom to get away from everyone. The minute they'd realized Jesse was missing, Ten and Simon had jumped into action. They'd had Hutch, Chelsea, and Adam attempting to track the helicopter. They'd managed to find a security feed that showed a man being taken to the rooftop helipad and the chopper flying off.

His face had been down, his head covered in a keffiyeh. The helicopter was owned by al Fareed Oil. According to all the reports, it had been cleared to land at the hotel to take a very sick party member to the hospital.

There was no record of it arriving at any hospital in the UAE.

How far could they have gotten?

She couldn't stand listening to them as they discovered absolutely nothing. Every trail seemed to come up cold.

"Or have you just gone ahead and hanged yourself?" Erin's voice once again separated her from her thoughts. "Be sure to use something sturdy. Too many people try shower curtain rods. They never hold up."

Erin's sarcasm was exactly what she needed to make the morning complete. Phoebe slammed the door open. "What is your problem?"

Erin looked her over. "Good to see you still have a little fight left."

Phoebe started to move past her. If Erin wanted the bathroom, she could have the fucking bathroom. Phoebe could find another place to wait.

Wait for the news. Wait to find out if Jesse was gone forever. How long would she wait this time? At least she'd been able to surround herself with Jamie's things the last time. She'd been able to sleep in their bed, find refuge in their home.

She and Jesse had just started out. The first place they'd made love was smoldering ruins now. How much more was going to be taken from her?

"Or not. You going to hide in the closet this time?" Erin followed her into the bedroom.

"Fuck off."

Erin stopped, shaking her head as she looked Phoebe over. "You know, I think I will go and do something else. You're useless. I have a friend to find. I don't need to babysit a whiny little bitch."

"Whiny little bitch?" Shooting Erin would make her feel better. Infinitely better.

"If the offensively titled shoe fits, I think you should wear it."

"My fiancé is out there in the hands of the same man who nearly killed him and you're calling me names?"

"Well, you're running away from the problem and I'm not known for my sensitivity. I skipped that class in school. All those dudes out there will pat you on the head and tell you to go cry and try to protect you, but I'm going to tell you the truth."

What arrogance. "And what's your version of the truth, Erin?"

"Not a version. This part is black and white with no gray. Your brother is out there putting his job on the line for Jesse. Me and Si, we'll put our lives on the line for him. Theo and Hutch, they missed that plane, too. The Agency isn't going to give a shit that they did it for a good reason. They'll lose a lot because they're willing to sacrifice for a teammate. And what are you doing? You're crying in the bathroom like an eighth grade girl at a dance."

Anger started to thrum through her system. She had to admit that it was better, more invigorating than the utter despair she'd been feeling. "You think I wouldn't sacrifice for him? You think I wouldn't do anything to take his place?"

"I think you're fantasizing because that's not going to happen. I think if you keep moping around, you're going to hate yourself a couple of days from now. You Agency fucks don't have the balls for the real game. You spent too much time behind a computer and not enough in the real world or you would be in there helping."

There wasn't anything to do. They didn't even have permission from command to still be in this country. They had no real backup. No resources. "You wouldn't understand."

Erin had her hair pulled back, making her look even more stark than usual. "Oh, I understand. I understand entirely too well. I understand that in your mind, he's already dead because it's easier to just face it than it is to fight knowing that the outcome will likely be the same. I understand that you already lost one husband and you feel like you're cursed. I totally get that he's out there and we got nothing. No clues. No leads. We've got no map and not a single direction."

That summed up the devastating situation they found themselves in perfectly. "So what do you want me to do?"

Erin got in her face. "I want you to suck it the fuck up, sister, because it's go time and there's no crying in the bathroom until we have a body on our hands. Until I have visual confirmation that Murdoch is dead, he's alive, and that means we have a chance to find him. I do not give up and I will not allow you to. It makes us look like pussies, and we both know pussies get a bad rap. So suck it up because I think they're on the wrong track."

Phoebe refused to back down. "And what track is it you think they should be on?"

Erin groaned and took a step back. "Fuck if I know. I'm the muscle here. You're supposed to be the one with all the damn brains. I like to shoot people, not outthink them. Take two seconds to breathe and then clear your mind. If this were just a mission, what would you do?"

For the first time since she realized Jesse was gone, she took a deep breath and tried to banish her fear. Erin was getting to her, reminding her that there really was a job to do and that job wasn't to worry. It was time to take action. "I would take stock of my resources."

"Okay. What are our resources?"

"A couple of guns no one will resupply, four Agency trained operatives, two otherwise trained operatives. A little cash."

"Don't forget the nerd squad. I assume they can wire us cash if we need it. And Hutch has like fifteen pounds of candy, so we won't starve. That dude is like made of sugar. And I've got enough bullets for Bertha to take out a good portion of this country. I also brought a sniper rifle, some C-4, and a dozen flashbangs." Erin shrugged. "A girl likes to be prepared. So we can totally start a war if we want to."

If Phoebe was running an Agency team, she would hire Erin in a heartbeat. "We have to figure out where to look. We can't just start blind. What do we know about al Fareed?"

"One brother is still here. He's at the conference according to Kamdar's guys. It's the older brother, Ibrahim. No sign of Hani."

"That tells us nothing except they're trying to keep up appearances." Phoebe started to pace, her mind revving up. "Although if they're smart, Hani will make an appearance, too."

"He's set to give a speech this evening. It would be news if he missed it."

This was good. "He won't. He's too smart to skip that meeting. It gives him an alibi. So they're potentially holding Jesse somewhere in Dubai. They're set to go back to Saudi tomorrow afternoon. They need everything to go according to plan. They won't take Jesse on that plane. They have to expect we'll look for him."

"I think they expect we're all going home. At least the Agency types are going home. Do you think the Agency knows about me and Si?"

"Probably. I don't know. Ten wouldn't have told them. So how did they know?"

"Unless they have an operative here themselves."

"Ten would have known."

Erin stared at her, disbelief plain in her eyes. "I don't think Tennessee is in the Agency loop anymore. You ask me, they're going to take him down."

"He still has friends there. He would have known if there was another team working this conference." But there were other options. "He might not know if someone inside the Agency is feeding a civilian party information."

"Another mole?"

Phoebe didn't think so. "Al Fareed had to have had a contact. If he wasn't Agency, then he's likely someone connected politically."

"I hate the spy shit. Give me someone to shoot any day of the week." Erin sighed as she looked around the bedroom. "You and Murdoch do it on the couch?"

"No. Why is that any of your business?"

She sank down and spread out. "Because I do my best thinking sitting down, but I don't want to get gross stuff all over me."

Finally she could get the tiniest bit of revenge. "Oh, in that case, I totally lied to spare myself the embarrassment of admitting we did it everywhere. Bed, bathroom, shower, against the window that now has a gaping hole in it. And definitely on that couch."

Erin popped back up and flipped her the finger. "You suck, Grant."

"Yes," she agreed. "I did that, too." There wouldn't be an inch of that hotel she wouldn't associate with Jesse.

Not an inch. Or a room. She would remember the ballroom where she'd had to save him. It was the first time she'd really realized that she had something to give him past a few nights in bed. He'd needed her. If only she'd been a little quicker in getting rid of that douchebag...

The douchebag who claimed he was a spy. The best lies always had a grain of truth.

"Where's the senator? More importantly, where's his aide?"

"You talking about the asshat we tagged the other night?"

She'd forgotten about him in her haste to find al Fareed. "There's a connection I'm not making here and it runs back further than we thought. We've always known The Collective had politicians in their pockets."

Erin strode to the bathroom, turning on the water and scrubbing her hands. "I think I need to change clothes."

"Are you OCD?"

She shrugged. "A little. I don't like germs. They're like predators waiting to take us down. The flu is like a battle in your own body and god, I hate mucus."

"Pay attention, soldier. Eli Nelson worked for The Collective, more specifically, he worked against anything that might have disrupted big oil interests." The pattern was suddenly right there. Oh, it was circumstantial, but she'd learned that the rules tended to apply to most mysteries, no matter what Hollywood's twisty-turny movies would say. The easiest path between two points was a direct line.

She could draw that line. She just needed one little piece of information to make it all click.

Without another word to Erin, she walked out of the bedroom. The living area was a hum of activity. Simon and Hutch were both at laptops. Theo was moving luggage into the hallway, and Ten was on his cell.

"We have a situation. I explained that to you, you little piece of shit bureaucrat. Get me to the director. I don't care what time it is." Ten grimaced and brought the phone back down. "They won't put me through."

Theo stacked their equipment. "That's not a good sign."

Ten turned and his face softened when he saw her. "Hey. Why don't you go lie down for a while, sweetheart? I'll tell you if we find anything."

Erin was right. She hated when Erin was right. Ten was going to treat her like she was made of glass. She wasn't and she had to pull it together because she was not losing another man she loved. She wasn't going to lose Jesse. Not without one hell of a fight.

She'd asked herself how long she would have to wait. She knew the answer. She wouldn't wait at all. This time she was stronger. This time she would be the one searching. If she'd done anything wrong when Jamie died, it was leaving the fight to Ten. She was stronger than that, strong enough to search and never stop. If she was an old woman with a fucking cane, she would still look for her husband because Jesse would endure. He would trust her and find a way to survive.

Faith. She had to suck it the fuck up, as Erin so lovingly put it, and have a little faith.

"I'm not going back to bed. I need to see Ace's file. I don't care how the hell we get it. I'll pay the nastiest hacker in the world to figure out who wrote his recommendation."

"I am the nastiest hacker in the world, thank you very much," a voice from her left said. "Turn me around, babe. I believe Hermione is impugning my reputation."

Simon turned his laptop and Chelsea Weston glared out at her from the screen.

"You know calling me Hermione isn't an insult," Phoebe

explained. "She was kind of badass."

"Yeah, well, she was also in a kid's book, so there's that."

She wasn't ever going to win with Chelsea. "What do you have on Ace?"

Even through the screen, she could see the way Chelsea flushed. "They've purged his records. I need something else. I need somewhere to look. The Internet's a big fucking place."

"Politicians keep records." She was taking a big step that would likely blow up in her face, but she had to do it. "I need you to hack into Senator Hank McDonald's files."

"Phoebe!" Ten put his phone down, staring at her in obvious shock. "You're talking about a United States senator."

And why wouldn't he be shocked? She'd been the perfect little Agency soldier. She'd done everything she was told, with the singular exception of ignoring the kill order on Jesse Murdoch. She played everything by the book because that's the way her father taught her. But this wasn't her father's Agency anymore and she wasn't going to let a man she loved die because she couldn't take a chance.

"On It." Chelsea's eyes lit up and her hands flew across the keys.

Simon shook his head and took a long breath as though he was used to worrying about the NSA showing up at his house.

"Phoebe, do you know what they'll do to you?" Ten asked quietly.

"I don't care. He's involved, Ten. I can feel it. He's the connection. He's the line between Eli Nelson and Hani al Fareed and The Collective."

"He's also a goddamn United States senator with the kind of pull you can't even imagine." Ten put his hands on her shoulders. "This is the kind of thing that gets an operative killed."

"Then what are we fucking fighting for, Ten? He doesn't get to use us. He doesn't get to dishonor his vows and sell out his country. And as far as I can tell, we're the only ones who can even try to stop him. If I'm right, he's already cost me one husband. I won't let him take another. I'll take him down even if I have to go down with him."

"Bingo. Son of a bitch has a file of recommendations," Chelsea said. "Mostly it's kids getting into military academies, but Ace Monroe is here. There's no recommendation for the CIA job, but Ace's father worked on McDonald's campaign for Congress way back when. He wrote the recommendation that got Ace into the Air Force Academy. There's your connection." Chelsea winced. "He also has some e-mails to al Fareed. They date back years. He asks how al Fareed's experiments are going. He knew what the fucker was doing. Phoebe, I think you're right. There's nothing here that would hold up in a court of law, but when you put it together, there's only one logical conclusion."

Ten had gone a little pale, but he wasn't arguing.

Hutch stood up. "Sir, I request permission to leave."

Ten frowned. "Of course. The next plane home will be here in an hour."

Theo moved in beside Hutch. "Me, too, sir. But Hutch isn't talking about leaving the team or the operation."

"No, sir," Hutch agreed. "I'm not going anywhere but downstairs to where that motherfucker is probably eating breakfast. I intend to lop off his dick and shove it down his throat."

Theo nodded in agreement. "He sold out Ace. He sold out Murdoch. I don't know why, and I don't give a shit. He needs to be brought to justice. One way or another."

Ten looked at his men. "Do you understand what this means? What you're giving up? They won't let this go lightly. We'll be disavowed if we go after this man. He's probably the very one who's influencing the director to call us back. You don't understand how bad this could get."

"I'm in. So's Case and so's Mike and Boomer," Theo said.

Hutch nodded. "I'm in and we've got Bear and Deke, too. They're waiting to come over if we need them. Screw the Agency, Ten. We're your team. We follow you. And hell, if it worked for the damn A-Team, I figure it's good enough for me. Disavow me."

They weren't alone. Ten wasn't alone.

He stepped forward and put his hand out, reaching for Theo, who grasped it. Theo shook Ten's hand and then Ten hauled him in for a hug. They did the manly back beating thing and then Ten turned and brought Hutch in for the same.

He took a deep breath when he stepped back and he looked

over at Phoebe. "All right, sister. He's your man. This is your op. What do you want to do?"

"Erin, I need you to sweet talk Kamdar into lending us one of his men. There's no way we get close to the senator, but I think Albertson knows everything he does. We need to get him up here and we need to find out what he knows." She steeled herself. "By any means necessary."

"Thank god." Erin started for the door. "I'll have that fucker up here before you know. Please let me do irreparable harm to his man parts. It's been a long time."

Theo practically stumbled, trying to run after her. "I'll just go and make sure she doesn't need backup."

Ten stared after him. "That is the single dumbest boy I've ever met. Did he not hear her talk about man parts?"

Hutch sank back into his chair. "The course of true love never did run smooth, boss. I've got a list of properties in the UAE owned by al Fareed Oil and its many, many subsidiaries. Adam's trying to pull them up on CCTV, but there's a lot of blind spots."

She looked over Hutch's shoulder. It was a long list. "Dismiss the large buildings. I need something small and possibly deserted. He works in private." And she was going to have to work the same way. "Simon, could you please set up a room where we can meet with the senator's aide?"

Simon stood up and adjusted his tie. "Of course. We'll use the back bedroom. Have Kamdar's guards keep the cleaning staff out." He started to walk away and then turned. "Give me your list of questions, Phoebe. Write it down. You won't be involved in this."

"I will."

Ten shook his head. "No. Simon and I will take care of it." He stepped up and put his hands on her shoulders. "You don't understand how this can affect you. Murdoch does and he would be the first person to beg one of us to save you from this."

"Phoebe, I can't allow it," Simon explained. "I know what my partner would want and I know what he would do for me. This isn't some game. This is torture and pain, and if there was any other way, I would take it because it's not what humans should do to one another."

"He's right. This is a sacrifice you don't have to make." Ten's face turned grave. "I took these sins on my soul a long time ago. I'm not going to let you do it. Hell, I wouldn't let Murdoch do it and Simon, you can be in the room, but I'll handle the actual questioning."

"Ten..." Simon began.

Ten shook his head. "You haven't done this before. You have to be able to go home to your wife and sleep at night, brother. Hell, I don't sleep at all anyway."

She could see this was a losing battle. "I'll listen in and feed you questions if you really think I can't handle it."

Ten frowned. "I know you can, but I don't want you to see me like that. Can you understand?"

She hugged her brother and wondered how much he'd sacrificed over the years. He was giving up his career, possibly his freedom, for her and Jesse. "I do. I love you, Tennessee."

He nodded and he and Simon went back to set up the room.

Phoebe sat and did the one thing she didn't want to do. She waited.

CHAPTER NINETEEN

Phoebe stared at the clock. Four hours twenty-two minutes. How much had he been forced to endure already? What had he been through in the hours she'd been sitting in this hotel room?

"Stop thinking about it." Erin's head fell back with a groan. She was sitting on the couch, the same place she'd sunk into an hour and a half before.

Theo stopped his pacing. "How is she supposed to stop thinking about it? I'm not in love with the dude and I'm thinking about it."

Kamdar crossed one leg over another and sat back. "I am thinking of this as well. Mr. Murdoch did me great service once. I don't like the idea that he's being tormented in a non-sexual fashion."

"Yeah, well you would know all about the other," Theo muttered under his breath.

Erin brought her head up and sent Theo a glare that could freeze water. "Give the dude a break. He's now bankrolling this whole enterprise and he put his butt on the line, too."

Kamdar looked as innocent as a decadent royal could look.

"My buttocks are strong and completely at your disposal, Miss Argent."

Erin sighed before turning to Phoebe. "Think about nice things. Get your head out of whatever horror show is playing through it and picture something nice."

"I'm not going to be able to think about puppies and babies right now."

Erin's face screwed up in distaste. "Eww. Both of those things poop. I was thinking about what's going on behind that door. I bet they've ripped off his fingernails by now. Maybe waterboarded the fucker. I don't care what the Agency says. That shit is awful. And beautiful in its own way."

Theo shook his head, a look of horror on his face. "What is wrong with you? Were you deprived of love as a child? Did someone drop you on your head and destroy the center of your brain that controls your humanity?"

If Erin was offended, she didn't show it. "Nah. I grew up with three brothers and a four-star general father. Ma left when I was two. Hooked up with some academic type. I was the youngest and I was raised by a barbarian horde. Hit the military when I was eighteen and haven't looked back. Look, some chicks dig rom coms and quilting. I study torture techniques, and that's why it's so fucking unfair that I get left out here at the kiddie table."

Kamdar leaned toward her. "When we return to my island, I will bring you many men to torture. I will begin with my cousin. He annoys me greatly."

"I'm right here, asshole." Chapal had taken up the cause as well, joining Hutch at the computers.

"Ignore him. I do. Tell me more about the things you would do to a very, very bad man," Kamdar said, his voice low. "Go into detail."

Theo smiled. "Yeah, Erin. Kamdar there wants you to do bad things to him. From what I hear, he kind of likes a little bite of pain."

Well, at least Theo was happy. According to Jesse, Erin was the sub and she was pretty hard-core. The only torture she was into inflicting was on the real bad guys. Otherwise, she wanted to be on the receiving end. Apparently Theo knew it, too.

"Miss Grant?" Chapal looked up from his system. "I think we have something."

Finally. She walked over to where Hutch and Chapal had lined up a bank of laptops. "What is it?"

Hutch pointed to his screen. "We found four locations that would work. Two small, unoccupied office buildings and two residences. One of the residences is pretty big though. It's on the outer edges of the city by the beach."

"Could they land a helicopter there?"

Chapal nodded. "But there is also a helipad at the two office spaces. We have to consider the fact that they sent him on. It's possible they've already smuggled him out of the country and into Saudi. They could drive, though it's a long way to Riyadh, where they live."

The door opened and Ten stepped out. There was no way to miss the blood on his hands and shirt. He was wiping his forearms off as he looked to Phoebe. "I think he's ready to talk if you want to have a word."

She nodded, her heart in her throat. She was trained for this, too.

She followed Ten into the room and tried not to think about how Albertson's shirt had been white at one time.

"Bitch," he managed between swollen lips. "Do you know what my boss is going to do to you?"

"Nothing if he wants to continue in his current role." Phoebe kept her voice calm and even. "I can connect the senator to a group known as The Collective. I can also prove that he sold information about our troops to a man who calls himself the Caliph. If you cooperate, I'll ensure you're not prosecuted for high treason. Do you understand what the United States does to traitors? Especially traitors during times of war."

It was all a big bluff, but she meant to make that case. Chelsea was pulling documents together, going through payments and looking into the senator's accounts.

Albertson's eyes got wide and she knew she had him. "I didn't have anything to do with that."

"But you know something."

He finally nodded.

Whatever Ten had done had softened him up. "Right now, what I need to know is where the Caliph is."

"You're talking about Hani al Fareed. He's a crazy motherfucker. He's insane and he broke our deal. If what Smith says is true, you have to know we didn't know that fucker was going to take Murdoch. Murdoch was supposed to be dead. When we figured out he wasn't, he was supposed to go home. The senator pulled some strings and the Agency was supposed to call you fuckers home. It's your fault. You didn't follow orders."

She ignored all the problems with his argument because only one thing mattered. "Where would al Fareed go?"

"He's got a place on the beach, but it's heavily fortified. I've been there. It's got armed guards all around. I can't go to jail." His eyes were glassy when he looked up.

"What's he on?"

Ten's face was a complete blank. "A little something the boys in R&D cooked up. First I gave him a shit ton of pain and then I gave him something to take it away because we're friends, right? Aren't we friends, Dale?"

The man in the chair nodded. "Good friends. Don't want to go to jail. If I tell the lady everything, I won't die here."

Ten turned back. "The drugs have the added effect of wiping his short-term memory. He's going to wake up outside the hotel with zero memory of how he got there. Hutch took care of the cameras so our asses are covered."

Her stomach turned and she understood why Ten wouldn't let her be involved past the actual questioning. This was psychological torture, the very thing that had been done to Jesse. The thing he might be going through now. It was necessary, but it was ugly and she wondered if her brother dreamed about it. A dream where he was the monster.

"What do you know about al Fareed's travel plans?" Phoebe asked.

"He flies. He's like a bird. Private jet."

Simon stood and walked to the door. "I'll have Hutch look into it."

Albertson's head drooped as though he couldn't hold it up a moment longer. "You were supposed to go away. Go home. Go home."

She stepped away and spoke to her brother in a low voice. "We don't have the firepower to take on a compound."

"We just have to make it seem like we do. In this case, illusion is more important than reality. We need to do what they did. Distract. We need some chaos. I'm more worried about the authorities being called in. We're not on firm ground here," Ten said. "We have to move fast and get him out of there and then we have to split up. We can't go through the airport. They'll look for us there. We need quick transport out of this country."

They would be on the run and because the CIA wouldn't acknowledge their presence in the country, they would be on their own. They would split up, and she was a little worried she might not see her brother again.

"Jesse would want you to be safe. Maybe you should go to Loa Mali with Kamdar's people and wait for us there."

The king had already agreed to give them sanctuary. Of course, he'd actually clapped his hands and pronounced the whole thing a party, but it was really sanctuary. But Ten wasn't getting rid of her until they absolutely had to break up the team. "Jesse can't always get what he wants. I'm not leaving this country without him. So we better get ready."

"Hey, Hutch has something and I was talking to Kamdar about the exit plan. We've got everything ready, but he thinks we need to move soon. I agree. The Agency knows where we are. They'll send someone soon," Erin said from the doorway. Her eyes lit up. "Oh, he's so fucked up. Did you break his nose? Can I break some of his fingers?"

Albertson moaned and started crying.

"How did you get past Eve?" Ten asked with a shake of his head.

"Didn't have to," Erin replied. "Got past Kai. He likes a little psycho in his chicks, if you know what I mean. And I'm serious. Hutch caught the chopper on a couple of cameras. He's almost certain it was headed for the beach."

Then that was where they were going.

* * * *

Jesse let his head fall forward as they took him out of the shackles and began to drag him across the floor. Blood soaked his back. He wasn't sure how long they'd gone on. Twenty lashes? Fifty? He'd lost count, lost all sense of time. He was fairly certain they'd left him hanging by the shackles for a while.

He thought they would drop him onto the cot, but they kept going. He forced his head up, his heart threatening to pound through his rib cage. Where were they taking him?

He was certain they hadn't left Dubai. He could still hear the ocean and he'd heard someone talking about the conference. They were still close, and if they were close then Phoebe and Si would be looking for him. They would have a chance, but if he got moved to another country… It had taken them months to find him before, and the Caliph would be smarter this time.

No. Al Fareed. His name was Hani al Fareed and Jesse wasn't going to give him that power anymore. Like fucking Voldemort.

Phoebe would be proud of him.

Power. There was power in knowledge, in intelligence. He was supposed to do that. Gather intelligence. He'd forgotten it the first time. He'd given in to pain and despair, but he was more than just a grunt. He looked down at the floor. Polished marble. Expensive. He was in a residence. There were closed doors to his left and a half wall to his right. Upstairs. At least two floors. He would have to look out that window to figure out how far up he was.

They walked past a guard who stood by the stairwell, an AK-47 over his shoulder. He was lazy, leaning against the wall and not paying a lick of attention to anything but his phone. Jesse's bodyguards muttered about it under their breaths, complaining that the guards here in Dubai were slacking.

He could use that.

"You need to get this one cleaned up and ready for transport. The boss will be in here soon. We're leaving for the airport after his speech at the conference, so you need to keep this shit calm for the next few hours," the larger of the two men said, this time in English.

He was dragged into a much bigger room, this one painted white. Antiseptic hit his nostrils and he had another shitty moment.

There had been a doctor. How could he have forgotten? There

321

was always a trip to the "clinic" after the sessions. Couldn't have the dog dying, now could they? The Cal...al Fareed would join him and the fucker would talk.

So much damn talking. Jesse was pretty sure he preferred the whip to having to listen to that fucker talk about how screwed up Western society was.

"Ah, Mr. Murdoch. Lovely to see you again." The doctor was a skinny fellow with a receding hairline. He spoke English with a British accent, but Jesse thought he remembered hearing the man was from Pakistan. "It's been a while since I had a subject. Our Caliph has been playing by the rules since he lost you. Put him on the bed. Facedown. I need to clean those wounds."

Jesse groaned as they shoved him onto the medical bed. It was taller than a normal cot and twice as uncomfortable. His body ached, but he knew what was coming would be so much worse.

Could he do it? Could he run if he had the chance? He wouldn't let them kill him. He had far too much to live for. This wasn't some insane suicide mission. He would take the pain if he had to, endure the humiliation, but if he had a shot, he would take that, too.

The doctor seemed to be preparing some sort of tray, likely filled with shit that would make him howl. "I was surprised you would even place yourself on the same continent as the Caliph. You seemed a bit smarter of a lad."

Jesse groaned and pretended to try to move his head. He let it fall back down, a conscious show of weakness. Let them think he couldn't move, but already he felt adrenaline starting to pump through his system. He'd heard the door close, but not the snick of a lock. He was alone with the doctor.

"And you've lost some of your will." The doctor clucked like a sad mother hen as he brought the tray over. Jesse could see it sitting almost within grasp of his left hand. There were a few bottles on it, some bandages, and what looked like tape. He caught the gleam of something metal. Scissors for the tape. And naturally there was a hypodermic needle. Narcotics. They loved their narcotics. He couldn't let them inject him. He would be helpless when they came, unable to signal to his team.

"No," he said without lifting his head. "The will is still there.

It's the body that's weak. I'm out of practice being beaten half to death."

"I suspect our leader will get you right back into practice. You were always his favorite, you know. He's risked a lot to get you back."

Awesome. The one place he was teacher's pet. "Where is he going to take me?"

"He has a home in Riyadh. I suspect we'll go there in order to keep up appearances." He slipped a blood pressure cuff around Jesse's limp arm and went through the motions. "His business partners will be a tad upset if they discover what he's done, so he'll try to keep it under wraps. He'll go through with his speech and behave as though nothing has happened. Once we're certain the heat has died down, as you Americans say, then we will move you to our training compound."

"So he's training terrorists now?" The cuff slipped off his arm.

The doctor made a note on the chart. "Soldiers. They are soldiers in our war, and yes, we are building our army. You'll be our little mascot, I think. You Westerners love mascots."

He would be the Caliph's grand experiment. He would be tortured and brainwashed until one day he forgot who he was and where he came from and became nothing but a weapon for them to use. "I think I'll have to get away before that happens."

The doctor picked up a bottle. "I doubt that. This is going to hurt quite a bit."

Pure hellfire rained on his back and Jesse let out a shout. Alcohol. The bastard poured alcohol on his open wounds. The pain nearly made him faint. He saw the edges of his peripheral vision begin to fade.

That was it. *Play possum. Look weak.*

He let his whole body go limp and knew the next few moments would be some of the worst of his life, but he would get through them. When the second assault came, he somehow managed to stay still.

He heard the door open, heard that horrible voice again. "He is well?"

The doctor sighed. "He passed out. I suppose the pain was too much."

It was hell to keep his eyes closed. It went against every instinct he possessed. He needed to see, needed to fight. But he remained still.

Patience. Breathe in. Breathe out. Wait for the moment.

He heard Big Tag's voice and then Simon's.

Have faith. Wait for your team. We won't let you down.

But mostly he heard her voice.

I love you.

He beat the panic back by concentrating on those voices. Slowly, the fire across his skin settled to a low but manageable ache.

"Your brother can't be happy with you," the doctor said. "I'm going to need to stitch a couple of these."

"Do what you need to do. I want him healthy." Jesse felt the man move, place his hand on Jesse's ankle. It made his skin crawl. "When I break him, he will be my masterpiece, my proof that righteous will bends all to the truth."

Now he was going to vomit. Asshole. His greatest enemy was right there. He could kill the Caliph, but would probably die in the process. At one point in time, he would have done it. It would have been worth it. He would have traded his life for even one shot at revenge, but that time had passed. He would trade all the revenge in the world for one shot at a life with Phoebe.

"As for my brother, I believe his usefulness is coming to an end. He's too close to the truth, and he would undo everything I've done. I caught him in my office. I think he suspects I'm working with the senator."

That was interesting. He needed to hold on to that little tidbit.

"You should dose him before you continue," al Fareed said. "I wouldn't want him to damage himself. That's my job."

The doctor sighed. "Fine, but I have my own experiments. I want a couple of my own subjects. Are you sure you can't capture his friends? I saw the red-haired woman. I would love to spend some time taking the arrogance out of her."

Erin. He was a bastard because he was relieved they weren't talking about Phoebe, but he would be damned if he would let them take Erin either. He couldn't watch another team member die.

He heard the door open. "They're gone. Their plane took off a few hours ago. The Agency themselves verified it. He's alone. I have no doubt that Smith fellow will look, but this time I'll be ready for him. I'll send him back to the States in pieces. Perhaps I'll send parts of him to newspapers. That would create some chaos. I think I'll start with the *New York Times*." He laughed, a truly nasty sound. "It's going to be a new world. With Ibrahim gone, I won't need to hide any longer. Get him ready to go. I want to leave as soon as possible."

The door closed and once again he did not hear a lock.

They were getting complacent.

"So your friends have all abandoned you. Poor boy. And you don't need painkillers. He's being too indulgent with you."

Pain flared as the doctor started to sew the places where the whip had opened his flesh. This time Jesse welcomed it. He even gave the fucker a good groan.

He opened his eyes. The scissors were there, waiting to be used. They weren't terrifically sharp, but they would do.

He heard the sound of something rattling floors below.

The doctor stopped and turned to the door.

Jesse moved, forcing his body to work. He ignored the pain, ignored the fear. He focused. The scissors were in his hand and in one smooth move, he planted them in the doctor's neck. He never gave the man a chance to scream. With aching arms, he held the doctor tight until the scissors had done their job and he went limp.

Think. Think. Adrenaline rushed through him, making it easier to focus. The doctor had a gun. Jesse pulled it from the holster on his waist. He couldn't make too much noise, but he would use it if he had to.

The hypodermic needle was much quieter, though it could only be used once.

He glanced out the window. Too far up. He couldn't jump and there wasn't enough roof to land on. But he could see the ocean. If he was on the ocean, he couldn't be far from others. Al Fareed had said he was going to the conference. That meant they were still in Dubai, and it was a well-populated city. He had a shot.

First, he had to get out. He had to find a way to communicate with his team.

There was another bang and the floor seemed to shake. Jesse

flattened against the wall, holding back a groan as his back hit. The door flew open and the guard strode in. His eyes immediately went to the doctor's body, and that gave Jesse the shot he needed. Two steps and he plunged the needle into the man's neck. The guard turned, but his movements were already slowing. He hit his knees and then his body fell beside the doctor's.

And Jesse had another gun. It looked like he would be making some noise on his way out, but he wasn't the only one.

He opened the door as quietly as he could. Gunfire. No way to mistake the sound. It peppered the air around him in short volleys and then he could hear someone shouting.

Chaos. It was a soldier's enemy but an operative's friend.

He took a deep breath and stepped out. He looked back at the stairs. They were his best bet. He flicked the safety off both guns and made his way.

Pain flared as he felt a bullet hit his left shoulder. He went down on one knee, pivoted, and took his own shot. The second guard. He was approaching, but stopped suddenly and looked down at the hole forming in his chest. He shouted out, but Jesse was already on the move again.

He stopped at the top of the stairs and surveyed the battle that was going on below. The front doors had been blasted through and hung limply on their sides. Two men lay on the marble below, though they twitched and moved. Smoke was beginning to dissipate, but it looked like someone had chucked a grenade or two through the door.

Or C-4. Erin. She liked to play with explosives and she wouldn't hesitate to try to rescue him.

"Are you coming or not?"

Jesse looked down and Simon strode through the wrecked door, his gaze on the stairs. Though he was wearing all black, including a black cap covering his hair, Jesse would know Si anywhere. Theo was behind him, watching Si's back. The sweetest sense of relief pierced him. Months he'd lain in a cell, every day a pure torture, losing piece after piece of himself and he hadn't even dreamed of rescue.

He hadn't doubted it for a moment this time.

He wouldn't dream about it again. The Caliph had utterly lost his power over Jesse Murdoch.

Jesse took the steps two at a time. "Where's Phoebe?"

"She's with Ten. They came in the back," Simon explained. "Erin is causing as much chaos as she can, and Hutch took over the security system. He's relaying everything he can to us."

Jesse heard the sound of a window breaking and then the house shook again. Yes, Erin was likely enjoying her work.

Simon stopped, obviously listening to something Jesse couldn't hear. "We've got incoming."

Three men rounded the corner of the big house.

Jesse dropped to one knee and took aim, popping off three quick shots. Theo took out the one on the left.

"I have no idea how you're standing much less firing a weapon." Simon reached out a hand, helping him up before touching his ear. "We have the package. Fall back." Simon nodded toward the open doors. "I think it's safe to go out the front. Erin's watching and we took out the guards at the gates. Do you know where he is?"

He didn't need Si to say anything more. "No. He left me about ten minutes ago. He was heading to the conference."

Simon frowned. "Then he likely took the helicopter. Damn it."

"Don't. It's fine. We know who he is and I know who he's working with. We'll have to be happy with that." Jesse followed them outside.

"I won't be happy until he's dead, Jesse. What the hell did he do to your back?" Simon kept moving.

Theo took Jesse's six. "Whipped him good, and not the way big brother does it. Damn."

"It's fine. We need to get out of here." He needed to get Phoebe out of here. "Where is the extraction point?"

Simon touched his earpiece again as he looked back before moving on. He frowned fiercely. "What do you mean? How the hell did that happen?"

They turned the corner and Jesse realized how wrong he'd been. The Caliph had plenty of power over him.

The Caliph stood next to his helicopter, the blades just beginning to rotate. Jesse nearly stopped breathing when he realized that Phoebe was beside him, a gun pointed at her head.

CHAPTER TWENTY

Phoebe fell in beside her brother as the first explosion occurred. She tried not to think about the two bodies she and Ten had taken out in the guard station. It had been necessary. They'd been ready to shoot, but still, it had been a long time since she'd been forced to kill a man.

"We're going around back to make sure the dock is secure," Ten said into his comm.

"I should be with them," she whispered as they moved around the massive main house. She watched their back, making sure no one came around.

"You're clear as far as I can see. Erin, good work on that door. You've got two coming in at three o'clock." Hutch's voice was a low buzz in her ear. He'd been left in the guardhouse monitoring the security systems. The compound had a complex set of cameras that seemed to cover every inch of the grounds.

Someone was a paranoid freak, and that totally worked in their favor.

She heard a volley of gunfire and then Erin spoke. "Got 'em. Do you have eyes on Murdoch? I don't want to blow him up. Tag would send me to the doghouse. Seriously he bought one and he's threatening to use it. I think that violates labor laws, right?"

"I got him. You're clear to blow up anything but the center of the main house. He's on the move and he's being feisty," Hutch said.

"Is he okay?" She couldn't help but ask.

"He's already taken out two. Simon, if you go through the hole Erin blew, you'll see him going across the top of the stairs."

"On it." Simon came through loud and clear.

She breathed a sigh of relief. They weren't out of the woods yet, but she felt better knowing Simon was about to have Jesse's back.

They rounded the corner. The dock was up ahead.

Ten touched his earpiece. "Kash, you can bring the boat in. We're a go."

The boat Kash had bought was a small speedboat that would take them to a large yacht anchored in the gulf and waiting to haul it as fast as they could to Loa Mali and safety.

To her left, Phoebe watched as a door opened and five men started out. They surrounded a sixth.

She realized what would happen in a moment. The helipad was between them and the dock. If they saw the boat coming, they could easily shoot it out of the water. If they took off, it would be simple to gain the high ground and potentially take them all out.

But more than anything, if they turned soon, they would have her and Ten outnumbered. Even if they survived, that was al Fareed they were protecting and he was about to get away. Jesse wouldn't be safe until the Caliph was dead. He would be out there lurking in the shadows and manipulating their lives.

It was time to gamble. They obviously knew she was with Jesse. Al Fareed's intelligence was too good to not know that she was spending her time in the same room with Jesse. She would make an awfully good hostage in exchange for Jesse's good behavior. She had to think they wouldn't kill her.

She touched her earpiece. "Ten, find a sniper position. We have to take him out. Forgive me."

She took off, screaming. "Jesse! Jesse!"

"Phoebe? What the hell?" Ten's voice became a low growl in

her ear. "I'm going to tell Murdoch to beat your ass for this. Don't you fucking die. Not until I get the chance to murder you myself."

She dropped her gun when they turned and gave her best impression of shrinking away in fear.

"Don't shoot her. Bring her to me and then go and find the prisoner. I'm not leaving without him." He spoke in Arabic to one of the men around him and he turned and ran to the chopper.

One of the guards grabbed her and dragged her back to al Fareed, who immediately brought her close, putting a gun to her head and using her to shield his own body. "You're my dog's little bitch, aren't you?"

"I just came for Jesse. Please tell me where he is." She wasn't going to argue with the man. Certainly not when he pressed that gun so close to her temple. It hurt where he held her, too. So tight, as though he wouldn't ever let go.

"How many did you bring with you?"

"It's just me and a couple of his friends," she replied, her voice shaking. How long would Ten need?

"A couple of friends destroyed my house?"

There was a volley of gunfire as his guards rounded the corner to get back to the front of the house. She prayed Hutch, the all-seeing, had warned Simon and Jesse.

"When they bring him to me after killing your friends, I think I'll kill you in front of him. Or perhaps I'll take you with me and you can serve as another method of control. That would be an interesting experiment." He was dressed for the conference and his keffiyeh covered her shoulder. He spoke into her left ear and hadn't seemed to notice that her right ear had a comm buried in it. She could still hear the team speaking.

"We have the package. Fall back," Simon's voice said in her ear.

They had Jesse. Jesse was safe. Now all she needed was for Ten to take his shot. He could give her cover after al Fareed was dead. He would have the high ground. She would run.

She was going to run all the way to Jesse and they would get away and they would be safe.

She believed. She would will it to happen. No more hiding.

"Get him to the damn boat." Ten's accent always thickened

when he was pissed, and it was like molasses now. "I've got to deal with another issue. Al Fareed has Phoebe. She got it in her head she could stop him from leaving and then I would shoot the fucker. Keep Jesse away from the west side of the compound. I don't need *Romeo and Juliet* playing out in front of me."

She hoped Ten was getting into position.

And then she saw him. Simon rounded the corner and then seemed to hear Ten and paused, his hand coming up and making a fist. It was a clear signal to stop.

Jesse still came around the corner and she watched in utter horror as he caught sight of her. He was shirtless and she could see blood on his chest and arms. He moved without his usual grace.

What had he been through?

"Yes. Now you'll come in handy." Al Fareed pressed the gun to her temple. He walked across the grass, putting distance between them and the helicopter.

Phoebe struggled to stay upright. The ground around her was soft and her feet seemed to sink in.

"I'm almost in place. Almost there. I'll take al Fareed first, but we still have to deal with the guard," Ten's voice purred in her ear. She'd watched her brother work before and invariably he calmed as he got close to doing the actual job. He would slow down and even his voice would slip into his deep, Southern accent when he focused. "Drop when I tell you and don't give him a chance. I'll take him before he knows what's happening."

She had to buy him some time because now they were in a standoff. The guard next to her had his weapon up, pointing at the same side of the house the other guards had disappeared behind.

Jesse walked out, dropping his gun to the ground and holding his hands up.

"That was inevitable," Ten said and she could almost see him shaking his head. "Darlin', I've got a shot lined up, but unfortunately your head is in the way. When I tell you to, you need to move about two centimeters to your left."

This was going to get so icky. And then there was the problem of the gun to her head. It was pressing her to the right. And the problem of Jesse, who moved toward them with the singular purpose of a man who was going to save his woman no matter what the cost.

God, she loved him. She had a gun to her head and all hell was breaking loose around her and she thanked the universe for Jesse. And Jamie. And Ten. For the love she'd been given.

"Don't cry, baby," Jesse said. "I'm going to get you out of this."

Simon and Theo stalked behind Jesse, their guns trained on al Fareed.

"Hand over the girl and we'll let you get on that helicopter," Simon explained. It was easier to hear now that they were away from the chopper.

She felt al Fareed's head shake against hers. "I think you would simply blow up my helicopter. No, I'll take one of you with me. I wanted to take them both, but I fear two would be too much."

"Me." Jesse stopped a dozen feet away. "You'll take me. I'm the one you want. Let go of the girl and I'll go willingly with you. Anything you say."

"And if I want to put a collar around your neck and walk you through my training camp to show my soldiers how we should treat Americans?"

Her stomach churned because it was everything Jesse feared. And yet he simply nodded.

"Yes. Anything. Just let her go."

Her captor started to back away, dragging her with him. "No. I no longer believe you. I think she's the only thing that will keep you in check. You surprise me. I think I failed with you. I think I would always have failed with you."

"No." Panic was plainly stamped on his face and he started toward them.

One wrong move and al Fareed would shoot one or both of them. The guard moved with his boss.

"Si, you got a bead on the guard?" Ten asked. "Nod to verify."

"Jesse, stay back." Everything would go to hell if that guard got his hands on Jesse. She saw Simon nod.

"I can't let him take you." Jesse moved toward her.

"Three," Ten's voice said.

If he came closer, Ten wouldn't be able to take his shot. "He won't. Have faith in me. Don't take another step."

"Two."

Jesse stopped. "I do."

"Such a little fool," al Fareed said in her ear. "Perhaps I will break you instead. Let's go."

"Now." Ten's voice was as calm as a man reading the news.

She went completely limp in al Fareed's arms, ducking her head and trusting her life in Ten's shot. She heard the ping and then she was falling. Before she could hit the grass, Jesse was there. He lifted her into his arms and then fell to his knees, but not before he pulled her free of al Fareed's body. The guard dropped beside them. He'd never had a chance once Simon had him in his sights.

"Erin's with the boat and I'm coming in," Hutch said cheerfully as if he hadn't just witnessed a bloody battle. "Simon, I'm going to need that chopper. Could you hurry? He's going to try to take off."

Simon moved in and there was the sound of another shot.

She looked in horror at Jesse's back as she scrambled to her knees. It was a mass of welts and cuts. He was bleeding from his shoulder. "Oh, baby."

He stared at al Fareed's body, but the minute she spoke, he turned and reached for her. "It's over now. Phoebe, we can go home."

As gently as she could, she wrapped her arms around him. "My home is wherever you are."

He held her tight. "Good, because the minute I can, I'm putting you over my knee."

Suddenly Ten stood above them. "Murdoch, you all right?"

Jesse took the hand Ten held out, letting his future brother-in-law help him up before doing the same for Phoebe. "I've never been better. You gave up a lot to come after me."

"I owed you, brother. I'm sorry I had to kill him. That was your right."

Jesse shook his head. "No. I didn't need to kill him. I already beat him. I beat him when I survived and I beat him again when I thrived." His hand found hers and he threaded their fingers together. "And now we'll move on and have a family. I wouldn't have Phoebe without him. I won't say I'm grateful to him, but I would go through it all over again to find my wife."

She squeezed his hand. "Let's get out of here."

He nodded and started for the docks. Theo and Erin were already at the boat and she could see Kamdar hadn't pawned the job off. He'd told her he would get off on the adrenaline. Simon waved at Hutch, who stepped over the pilot's body as he got into the cab of the chopper. Hutch was taking the helicopter?

She looked back and her brother wasn't behind her. Ten stood by the chopper as Hutch fired it up.

He looked so alone standing there. He nodded her way and held up a hand. His mouth moved, but she couldn't hear him over the helicopter blades. She could see what he said.

I love you.

He hopped in, gave Hutch the thumbs-up, and the chopper lifted into the air.

"It's okay," Jesse said. "We'll meet up in Loa Mali."

He tugged on her hand and she followed, but she knew the truth. Her brother was gone. He was in the wind, disavowed and alone.

And very likely looking for revenge.

Still, even as she prayed for Ten, she followed Jesse because he was her future, her gift.

Two Months Later
Dallas, TX

"Are you sure you want to do this?" Big Tag asked the question in an exaggerated whisper. "Because we can still get you out of here. I've got an extraction team standing by."

It took all Jesse had not to roll his eyes. Even in a situation like this, his boss was sarcastic. "I think the extraction team is all here."

"That's what I meant. We can get you out in a heartbeat. This is insane. No one does this willingly."

"Oh and Charlotte had to drag you down the aisle?" After all, Tag was trying to save him from his wedding.

The big guy shrugged in his tux. "We eloped so it was all sex and a British Elvis impersonator. None of this fancy shit. That's the way to go. I got married in a T-shirt and jeans."

Alex McKay shook his head and passed Jesse a drink. Rum and Coke. He couldn't stand that Scotch stuff. "Don't believe him. I've seen the pictures. He was wearing a nice pair of slacks and she even got him into a tie. And Ian, I heard Charlotte tell Eve that she thinks you two should have a recommitment ceremony after the babies are born."

Ian went a little pale. It was good to know one little sonogram could shake his boss. Charlotte Taggart was pregnant with twins. Big Tag didn't half ass anything. "She's high if she thinks she's getting me in a monkey suit."

Sean looked up from his phone. "Dude, you're in a monkey suit now."

"Yeah, but Murdoch here's paying me."

"No, I'm not." He was enjoying the camaraderie of his brothers. Just the night before they'd arranged a bachelor party for him. Poker and piña coladas. It had been perfect.

"See, that's what you think, but there's always a price," Tag replied.

The door opened and Simon walked in. Naturally his tux was perfect and custom made. No rentals for the Brit. "Theo and Case are here. They send their regards from the rest of the team."

Ten's team had reported to Langley, even Hutch, who had showed up a day late and claimed to have absolutely no knowledge of where their former boss was. Hutch claimed Ten had ditched him in Oman. Theo had told him and Phoebe that Ten wanted them to remain at the Agency. He hadn't wanted a single one to sacrifice for him.

They were all on another team now. Only Ten had been disavowed. What Ten didn't know was that every single one of them were still his men. They would fight for him when the time was right.

Where the hell was Tennessee Smith? He knew Phoebe was hoping he'd somehow hear about their wedding and show up, but that was a miracle that likely wasn't going to happen.

Simon put a hand on his shoulder. "It's time."

Tag sighed and turned to Jesse as the rest of the men filed out. "You know Phoebe tries to kick my ass every time I call you a dumbass."

His almost-wife was a little protective. "I'll talk to her about it."

Tag nodded. "Good because I'm not changing my management style just because my accountant is a delicate princess. I like her, you know. And I'm proud of you, Murdoch. I made the right call."

Tag walked out to join the rest of the groomsmen, leaving him alone with his best man.

He'd grown up alone. His childhood had consisted of trying to placate a nasty old man. Alone had been his state of being, but now he was surrounded by family. Everywhere he looked there was someone he cared about, some kid he was going to get to watch grow up. The world had become a precious place.

"Are you ready?" Simon asked.

"I was born ready for this."

He followed Simon out and took his place, surrounded by brothers but with the knowledge that two were missing. Ten and the brother he'd known so briefly, the only other man who knew what it meant to love Phoebe. He wasn't here, but Jesse could feel his presence. Jamie Grant's memory would always have a place in their home.

The music began and there she was. She wore a white dress and carried a bouquet of flowers, but all he could really see was her beautiful face.

"Hi," she said with a glorious smile when she reached him.

"Hello, baby." He took her hand.

They turned to the pastor and there among their family, Jesse and Phoebe began their forever.

Later that night…

Ian Taggart reached out and placed his hands on his wife's belly. Smooth and round and one of the little fuckers kicked him firmly. "Charlie, that's not a foot. It's a horn. We're having a demon. I know it."

He couldn't help it. He loved to tease her. It was his greatest joy in life.

She rolled her pretty eyes and sighed. "They're your girls so they're probably slightly demonic. Are you all right?"

He took a deep breath. He'd faced down a lot of shit in his time and nothing scared him quite as much as the feel of that baby kicking against his hand. The problem was there wasn't just one set of feet in there. "I think the doctor was high and it's just a really big boy."

"With four legs?"

"Maybe that's just his boy parts. Maybe he has two."

"You're insane, but I love you."

He tugged on her hand, bringing her onto his lap. This was his favorite part of the day. He would pull her on his lap and just sit and watch the night while he cuddled his wife. Now he cuddled his children, too. It wouldn't be long before they were squirmy little things, so he relished the peace of holding them all in his arms for the moment. His girls.

"It was a beautiful wedding." Charlie leaned into him, nuzzling his neck.

"There was a Harry Potter cake, Charlie. And mai tais. Those two were made for each other."

"I just wish Ten could have been there."

He stilled because there were still some secrets he couldn't tell his wife. Not yet. "If the bastard had shown up, I would have slapped him with the bill for Sanctum."

She sat up and grinned. "I know that having the club blow up was horrible, but the new Sanctum is going to be so beautiful."

He agree with her on that point because this time around, he'd built his personal heaven with one person in mind—her. Every piece of furniture and equipment had been chosen with her comfort and pleasure in mind. Every tiny detail selected to delight her. She was his queen and she would have her personal castle. A perverted castle, complete with a human hamster wheel. "It's fuck all expensive."

He noticed something out of the corner of his eye and realized the time had come. Someone was on his land and they'd managed to get around his security system. There was only person he knew who could manage that. He needed to get Charlie to safety until he figured out what was going on with his guest.

She helped him out by sitting up and stretching. "I'm going to take a shower and get out of this dress. You want to join me?"

More than anything. There was nothing he wanted more than to get in a shower and worship his reason for living. He stood and crowded her as much as he could with her big belly between them. He leaned over and brushed his lips against hers. "In a little while. I need to call Sean about something. I'll meet you in bed and rub your feet and go over all the ways I'm going to torture your sweet ass when you're able to play again."

Her hands came up, sinking into his hair. His Charlie never shrank from a challenge. "You better come up with something good, Taggart."

She walked away, the sway of her hips calling to him.

He stepped inside, grabbed the Scotch and two glasses, and then walked back out. He heard the shower turn on and settled down into one of the Adirondack chairs that sat on his big porch. He looked out into the trees that surrounded his house. "You can come out now. We're alone. Did you enjoy the wedding?"

"It was beautiful. I wish I could have come to the reception." Tennessee Smith came out of the woods like a wraith melting away from the camouflage and finding his form. He was dressed in black with a ball cap on his head and a backpack over one shoulder. And his face had exploded.

"Dude, you look homeless, and what's all that shit on your face?"

Ten stopped and stared for a moment. "You know, I'm gone for months in a hostile place with everyone in the Agency looking to drag my ass in and your first words are about my beard?"

"Is that what that's supposed to be? Because it looks like a fucking poodle died on your face." He poured the man a Scotch because he really looked like he'd been through hell.

Ten shook his head and then laughed. "Fuck you, Tag." He dropped the backpack and then stepped up, taking the glass Ian offered. "Damn but it's good to see you."

"It's good to see you, too. You could have written. Maybe a call letting us know you're all right."

Ten shook his head and settled into the other chair. "Too

dangerous. It's why I forced Hutch to come home. I was in Saudi and then Iraq."

"And now you're home."

"I am. Has there been any blowback from killing al Fareed?"

Tag shook his head. "No. The asshole you questioned couldn't remember a thing and the whole incident was written up as a street crime. Albertson was fired from the senator's team. What the hell did you do to cover up the op at al Fareed's compound?"

"I talked to his brother," Ten said. "Ibrahim al Fareed is as far from Hani as a person can get. He's why Hutch and I didn't get caught. He'd been suspicious of his brother for a long time. He was happy to cover it up. He doesn't want the stain on the family name. He's an ally."

It was good Ten had found someone to help him. And definitely good to know the senator wasn't coming after them anytime soon. It had been a peaceful couple of months. Tag was ready to kick a little ass. "Tell me you're here for a reason, brother."

Ten nodded, his mouth a grim line. "I've found it. I've found a way to get to Hank McDonald."

The man who had used his influence to burn Ten. The man who had sold Jamie Grant out. McDonald was the reason Jesse's unit had been murdered and he'd been tortured for months on end. Yeah, he wanted a piece of that. That pie was going to be filled with all kinds of revengey goodness. "Tell me."

"According to my intel, he keeps all his records and files on a private system offshore. The bastard owns a compound in the Grand Caymans, and my sources say that's where all the evidence will be."

Ian was fairly certain he didn't want to know how Ten had gotten that information. Ten looked older and infinitely harder, as though the last few months had taken all the party boy out of him and left nothing but the predator. "All right. How do you get on the island?"

Ten's eyes gleamed in the moonlight. "He has a daughter. Once a year he throws her a no-holds-barred party there. I'm going to get an invitation to that party."

"Nice. How are you going to do that?" His brain was already

working. They would need to plant a few operatives in that house, maybe around the island, too. He wasn't going to allow Ten to go in alone.

"By seducing her and becoming her boyfriend. There's one problem with that."

Tag saw the obvious problem. "Yes, that shit on your face. Unless she's into Grizzly Adams, you're going to shave."

Ten's green eyes rolled. "Not that, asshole. She's in the lifestyle."

Now it was Ian's turn to grin. Oh, this was going to be so much fun. He slapped Ten on the shoulder. "Then it's time to Dom you up, buddy. And I know just the place to do it."

But the man had to shave. After all, Sanctum had its standards.

* * * *

Tennessee Smith and the rest of the McKay-Taggart crew will return in *Master No* coming August 4th, 2015.

AUTHOR'S NOTE

I'm often asked by generous readers how they can help get the word out about a book they enjoyed. There are so many ways to help an author you like. Leave a review. If your e-reader allows you to lend a book to a friend, please share it. Go to Goodreads and connect with others. Recommend the books you love because stories are meant to be shared. Thank you so much for reading this book and for supporting all the authors you love!

Sign up for Lexi Blake's newsletter
and be entered to win a $25 gift certificate
to the bookseller of your choice.

Join us for news, fun, and exclusive content
including free short stories.

There's a new contest every month!

Go to www.LexiBlake.net to subscribe.

ADORED
A MASTERS AND MERCENARIES NOVELLA
Masters and Mercenaries 8.5
By Lexi Blake
Coming May 12, 2015

A man who gave up on love

Mitch Bradford is an intimidating man. In his professional life, he has a reputation for demolishing his opponents in the courtroom. At the exclusive BDSM club Sanctum, he prefers disciplining pretty submissives with no strings attached. In his line of work, there's no time for a healthy relationship. After a few failed attempts, he knows he's not good for any woman—especially not his best friend's sister.

A woman who always gets what she wants

Laurel Daley knows what she wants, and her sights are set on Mitch. He's smart and sexy, and it doesn't matter that he's a few years older and has a couple of bitter ex-wives. Watching him in action at work and at play, she knows he just needs a little polish to make some woman the perfect lover. She intends to be that woman, but first she has to show him how good it could be.

A killer lurking in the shadows

Assigned to work together on an important case, Mitch and Laurel are confronted with the perfect opportunity to explore their mutual desire. Night after night of being close breaks down Mitch's defenses. The more he sees of Laurel, the more he knows he wants her. Unfortunately, someone else has their eyes on Laurel and they have murder in mind.

MASTER NO
Masters and Mercenaries 9
By Lexi Blake
Coming August 4, 2015

Disavowed by those he swore to protect...

Tennessee Smith is a wanted man. Betrayed by his government and hunted by his former employer, he's been stripped of everything he holds dear. If the CIA finds him, they're sure to take his life as well. His only shot at getting it all back is taking down the man who burned him. He knows just how to get to Senator Hank McDonald and that's through his daughter, Faith. In order to seduce her, he must become something he never thought he'd be— a Dom.

Overcome by isolation and duty...

All her life, Dr. Faith "Mac" McDonald has felt alone, even among her family. Dedicating herself to helping others and making a difference in the world has brought her some peace, but a year spent fighting the Ebola virus in West Africa has taken a toll. She's come home for two months of relaxation before she goes back into the field. After holding so many lives in her hands, nothing restores her like the act of submission. Returning to her favorite club, Mac is drawn to the mysterious new Dom all the subs are talking about, Master No. In the safety of his arms, she finds herself falling head over heels in love.

Forced to choose between love and revenge...

On an exclusive Caribbean island, Ten and Mac explore their mutual attraction, but her father's plots run deeper than Ten could possibly have imagined. With McKay-Taggart by his side, Ten searches for a way to stop the senator, even as his feelings for Mac become too strong to deny. In the end, he must choose between love and revenge—a choice that will change his life forever.

THEIR VIRGIN MISTRESS
Masters of Menage 7
By Shayla Black and Lexi Blake
Coming April 14, 2015

One wild night leads to heartache…

Tori Glen loves her new job as an image consultant for Thurston-Hughes Inc. The trouble is, she's also in love with the three brothers who own it, Oliver, Rory, and Callum. They're handsome, successful, aristocratic, and way out of this small-town Texas girl's league. So she remains a loyal professional—until the night she finds a heartbroken Oliver desperate for someone to love. Tori knows she should resist…but it's so tempting to give in.

And a desperate plan…

Callum and Rory have denied their desire for Tori, hoping she'll heal their older brother, who was so brutalized by his late wife's betrayal. But when Oliver cruelly turns Tori away in the harsh light of day, she tenders her resignation. Rory and Callum realize that to save their brother, they must embrace the unconventional sort of family they've always wanted—with Tori at its center. And it all starts with seducing her…

That could lead to happily ever after—or murder.

Isolated with the brothers at an elegant English country manor, they begin awakening Tori to the most sensual of pleasures. But consumed with regret, Oliver won't be denied the chance to embrace the only woman worth the risk of loving again. What begins as a rivalry veers toward the future they've only dared to dream of. But a stranger is watching and waiting for a chance at revenge. Can the brothers come together to embrace the woman they love and defeat a killer?

SCANDAL NEVER SLEEPS
The Perfect Gentlemen, Book 1
By Shayla Black and Lexi Blake
Coming July 7, 2015

They are the Perfect Gentlemen of Creighton Academy: privileged, wealthy, powerful friends with a wild side. But a deadly scandal is about to tear down their seemingly ideal lives...

Maddox Crawford's sudden death sends Gabriel Bond reeling. Not only is he burying his best friend, he's cleaning up Mad's messes, including his troubled company. Grieving and restless, Gabe escapes his worries in the arms of a beautiful stranger. But his mind-blowing one-night stand is about to come back to haunt him...

Mad groomed Everly Parker to be a rising star in the executive world. Now that he's gone, she's sure her job will be the next thing she mourns, especially after she ends up accidentally sleeping with her new boss. If only their night together hadn't been so incendiary—or Gabe like a fantasy come true...

As Gabe and Everly struggle to control the heated tension between them, they discover evidence that Mad's death was no accident. Now they must bank their smoldering passions to hunt down a murderer—because Mad had secrets that someone was willing to kill for, and Gabe or Everly could be the next target...

* * * *

"I want to see you."

Even in the low light, he noticed her breath hitch. "You want me to turn on the lights?"

"That's not what I meant." He never took his burning gaze from her. "I want to see you naked. Take off your dress. Show me your breasts."

"I'll close the curtains." She started to turn to the windows.

He caught her elbow, gently restraining her. "Don't. We're high up. No one can see in. Take off your dress. Let me see you in the moonlight."

Her gaze tangled with his, and he could see a hint of her trepidation. A gentleman might have backed down. But he knew what he wanted. She must want him too or she wouldn't have agreed to spend the night with him. He wasn't giving Eve the easy way out.

Finally, she turned her back to him and lifted her arms, struggling to reach the metal tab. "There's a zipper down the back."

He moved closer. "Let me."

Gabe ran his hands up her spine before finding the zipper. She lifted her curls out of his way, exposing the graceful column of her neck. Her skin looked pale, almost incandescent in the low light. He couldn't help himself. He leaned over and kissed her nape, feeling her shiver under his touch.

Slowly, he eased the zipper down, his fingertips brushing her spine. Once he passed her neck, she let her hair fall free, the strawberry-blond mass tumbling well past her shoulders, gliding over her skin. Her tresses were soft, too. Not severely flat-ironed. Different, like the woman herself. Fuck, he could lose himself in Eve.

She shrugged, allowing the straps of her dress to fall past her shoulders and drop to her waist.

Her bra looked plain and white. He was used to delicate garments meant to entice a man, so he had no idea why the site of her utilitarian bra made his cock jerk. She hadn't been seeking a man this evening, much less intending to seduce a lover. When she'd dressed, it had been for comfort. But now, she was here with him, slowly peeling away her clothes.

With practiced ease, he unhooked her bra with a twist of his hand and slid his fingers under the straps to strip them off. He closed his eyes and allowed his hands to roam across the wealth of smooth skin he'd just exposed. He drew her back against his chest and grazed his way up her abdomen until he found her breasts. Full and real, he loved the weight of them in his palms. He drew his thumbs over the nubs of her nipples and Eve rewarded him with a long intake of breath.

"That feels so good." As she leaned back against him for support, she shuddered and thrust her breasts up like twin offerings.

He would absolutely take everything she had to give.

Gabe filled his hands with her flesh, cupping and rubbing and discovering every inch of her breasts before he grew impatient to have her totally bare and pushed the dress over the curve of her hips. It pooled on the floor at her feet.

Her underwear matched her bra. If she were his, he would buy her La Perla. He would dress her like a goddess in silk and lace and know that she wore the most come-hither lingerie for his eyes only. She could wear her ladylike dresses and cover herself with all appropriate modesty if she wanted—but only until they were alone.

As he stripped off her panties, a wild possessiveness blazed through his system. Gabe turned her to face him, well aware that he needed to slow down but utterly incapable of doing so. He took in the sight of her breasts. They looked every bit as perfect as they'd felt.

"You're beautiful."

"I don't feel that way." She tilted her face up to his, drinking him in with her stare. There was nothing coy about her expression. She looked at him with naked yearning. "Not most of the time. But you make me feel sexy."

"You are. I want to be very clear about how beautiful I think you are." He kissed her again, lifting her up and out of her dress, heading back to the bedroom while his mouth ate hungrily at hers.

She didn't fight him, didn't fidget to make him set her back on the ground. She simply wrapped her arms around his neck and let him carry her. Her fingers sank into his hair and she held tight while her tongue danced against his.

Luckily, he knew Plaza suites like the back of his hand. He maneuvered her toward the bed, his cock throbbing insistently.

He wouldn't last long. God, he couldn't believe he was even thinking that. Usually, he could go for hours, but Gabe knew the minute he got inside Eve, he was going to lose control. He needed to make it good for her now because he'd barely touched her and already he wanted to throw her against the wall and shove his way inside her.

As he approached the mattress, he stopped and eased her onto the luxurious comforter. She lay back on the elegant duvet, her hair fanned out and her legs spread. Wanton and yet so innocent. He pulled at his shirt, hearing a button or two pop off, but at the moment he didn't give a shit. The need to be skin to skin with her drove him to haste. He unbuckled his belt and shoved his pants down.

"Foreplay." Freaking hell. He was so ready to go, he'd forgotten about that. Women liked foreplay. It tended to be necessary for them.

She shook her head. "The kissing was foreplay. We're totally good."

Shit. He had to slow down. He wasn't exactly a small guy. She needed to be ready to take all of him.

Gabe took a deep breath. "Need you aroused. It's okay. Just give me a minute."

"Gabriel, I am as aroused as I have ever been in my life. I'm a little worried about what kind of stain I'm going to leave for the staff on this duvet. So really, can we get this train moving?"

He gripped her ankles and slid her down the bed, spreading her legs wider in the process. His cock twitched when he saw that she was right. Her pussy was wet. Juicy. He could see its slick gloss from above, even in the shadows. A little kissing, some groping, and she was ready to go. He'd never had a woman respond to him so readily. "Tell me again."

"I'm ready," she vowed. "I am *really* ready."

"No, tell me this isn't normal for you," he corrected. It was stupid. She was right there, able and willing to give him the pleasure he sought—but he craved more. He needed to know that tonight was special for her. "Tell me you want me and not just sex."

She gave him a sheepish smile. "This isn't at all normal. I guess I've gone a little crazy tonight, but I don't do one-night stands. I can count the men I've had sex with on one hand and I wouldn't need all my fingers. And I've never, never wanted anyone as much as I want you right now. Gabriel, I don't need foreplay, just you."

THIEVES
A new urban fantasy series by Lexi Blake

Read the first book, Steal the Light, for free at all retailers!

"Author Lexi Blake has created a supernatural world filled with surprises and a book that I couldn't put down once I started reading it."
Maven, The Talent Cave Reviews

"I truly love that Lexi took vampires and made them her own."
KC Lu, Guilty Pleasures Book Reviews

Stealing mystical and arcane artifacts is a dangerous business, especially for a human, but Zoey Wharton is an exceptional thief. The trick to staying alive is having friends in all the wrong places. With a vampire, a werewolf, and a witch on the payroll, Zoey takes the sorts of jobs no one else can perform—tracking down ancient artifacts filled with unthinkable magic power, while trying to stay one step ahead of monsters, demons, angels, and a Vampire Council with her in their crosshairs.

If only her love life could be as simple. Zoey and Daniel Donovan were childhood sweethearts until a violent car crash took his life. When Daniel returned from the grave as a vampire, his only interest in Zoey was in keeping her safely apart from the secrets of his dark world. Five years later, Zoey encounters Devinshea Quinn, an earthbound Faery prince who sweeps her off her feet. He could show her everything the supernatural world has to offer, but Daniel is still in her heart.

As their adventures in acquisition continue, Zoey will have to find a way to bring together the two men she loves or else none of them may survive the forces that have aligned against her.

Steal the Light
Steal the Day
Steal the Moon
Steal the Sun
Steal the Night
Ripper
Addict—Coming Soon!

ABOUT LEXI BLAKE

Lexi Blake lives in North Texas with her husband, three kids, and the laziest rescue dog in the world. She began writing at a young age, concentrating on plays and journalism. It wasn't until she started writing romance that she found success. She likes to find humor in the strangest places. Lexi believes in happy endings no matter how odd the couple, threesome or foursome may seem. She also writes contemporary Western ménage as Sophie Oak.

Connect with Lexi online:
Facebook: www.facebook.com/lexi.blake.39
Twitter: twitter.com/authorlexiblake
Website: www.LexiBlake.net

Sign up for Lexi's free newsletter at www.LexiBlake.net.

CPSIA information can be obtained
at www.ICGtesting.com
Printed in the USA
FSOW01n2145231017
40267FS